Life in Three Acts

Shirley van der Bank

To Derek my long time "other half" and "soul mate" who without his faith and help the book would never have been finished.

ACT ONE:
Betrayal

ACKNOWLEDGEMENTS

I would like to acknowledge the support given by all my family members. I would also like to thank Helen Cooper and the project team at McArthur Publishing for all their help and guidance.

Life in Three Acts

CHAPTER 1

She had thought it might be an important phone number on the small piece of paper tucked securely in the back pocket of the jeans. In the dark recesses of her brain, she half wished she hadn't found it. Checking pockets had been a routine over the years, but she still wished she hadn't found it. Now, she would *have* to face it. A fear she had suppressed for years pierced her brain like a shaft of bright light; it was painful, so painful. She had been scared that this would happen one day. But not with this person.

Her eyes blinked and focussed down on the piece of paper. Smoothed it gently, almost reverently. Elizabeth…. The scrawled handwriting was so familiar. The pain in her head stabbed across her forehead, forcing her to close her eyes against its intensity. She lifted her coffee cup and it rattled against her teeth, slopping the coffee into her lap. She brushed absentmindedly at it and then clasped her hands tightly together.

When had Drew last worn jeans?

The kitchen clock ticked in the silence. Friday—it had been Friday at the barbeque. It had been such a lovely early spring day. An impromptu evening barbeque had seemed like such a good idea.

"Longing to touch you. Can't wait till we are together again."

Again. She had written again. How many times did again mean?

The pain now reached her stomach and hit her with a vengeance. She doubled over, her head on the table, a taste of vomit in her throat. Her mind started drifting back to things she would rather not remember, and she prodded at them like a painful tooth.

Drew with his toned body. His long legs encased in fitted and expensive, washed-out jeans and his laser blue eyes, which he used to devastating effect. He also carried just the right amount of muscle for his six-foot frame. Little wonder the other women couldn't seem to keep their hands off him. Or, for that matter, his off them. She had got used to over the years turning a blind eye to all his little indiscretions. For the most part, they never seemed to last long, and then he would be home early bearing flowers, booking cinema tickets and tables in restaurants. Gazing into her eyes.

All the years the children had been growing up, she had enjoyed the easy lifestyle in a beautiful home, driving the latest cars, with hours spent in the garden and in the local health club. After all, a successful man running a powerful ad agency was expected to have a smart wife.

Her clothes and jewellery were expensive but understated and classic. Her hair was long, light brown, and worn up, as Drew liked it. This morning, however, it hung down, tangled and uncombed. Her eyes were drawn again to the familiar writing on the letter. How many times had she seen the carelessly scrawled signature before Elizabeth, her next-door neighbour and friend. The auntie to the children, the recipient of years of shared confidences over cups of tea and coffee. Elizabeth…. The betrayer and her husband's mistress.

Her stomach contracted in pain, almost like giving birth. She crossed her hands across her middle and bent forward with the force of the sensation. She finally straightened up when the pain passed and sat still, her thoughts churning around without making any sense. "Longing to feel your hands on my body."

They had been neighbours for years. *How long had Elizabeth and Drew been lovers? And why hadn't she seen it? Was she blind?* She wracked her brain to try and drag up something that should have alerted her and found nothing. How clever they must have been and how they must have laughed at her. The pain hit again. This time, she didn't give in to it and stood up. With a sudden moment of clarity, she knew that whatever happened, she couldn't bear to be here when Drew came home. She hadn't got the strength to face him with it or to carry on the charade any more. With her son Marty in the New York branch of the agency and her daughter Caro running a small boutique in London and well established in a flat shared with two very good friends, their lives wouldn't be disrupted.

With a strange numb feeling, she removed her clothes and stepped into the shower. Thirty minutes later, she was dressed in black trousers and a white vest top, with a long draped jacket in black thrown across the bed. The suitcases still had the airline tags attached to them from the last holiday. She tore them off and threw them on the bedside table. It had been a shitty holiday anyway, with Drew constantly carping over everything from the hotel to the prices in the local shops. Still with the same numb feeling she applied light makeup and swept her hair up in its usual style. Underwear and nightclothes, makeup, toiletries, and jewellery were packed with no problem, but she sat heavily on the dressing table stool with her mind completely bank. What the hell did you pack if you didn't even know where you were going?

Trying to think rationally was too hard, so she started at one end of the long mirrored wardrobe and inspected hanger by hanger, taking out familiar, comfortable clothes and outfits that would mix and match. The haute couture and stiff dressy suits she left hanging.

She finally felt she had all she needed apart from a couple of coats that she zipped up in Drew's plastic suit bags. She tossed the suits carelessly in a heap on the unmade bed. She dragged the suitcase downstairs and out to the car, then back to the house for the keys and coats, and suddenly, the enormity of the whole situation hit her.

Where would she go…? What would she do? She hadn't worked for years. *Think, think. First, load the car, then find a hotel until the brain starts working again.* The commuter belt around Hertfordshire had many hotels, but they were too close to home. Google was the place to start. She picked a hotel in Bedfordshire that she thought was far enough in the opposite direction to be safe and phoned in a reservation from her mobile.

Next thing was cash. If she used her credit cards Drew might be able to find her before she was ready to be found. She would have to go into the bank and risk running into someone she knew after all. No matter, they would all know sooner or later anyway. She took the creased letter and clipped it to a blank piece of paper on which she wrote, "I hope you'll both be very happy."

Parking in town was a bit of a problem, but finally, she made it to the bank. All their accounts were in joint names, as Drew didn't want to be bothered with mundane household bills. It seemed more sensible to draw from the savings account that was put aside for holidays, etc., than to draw attention to a large withdrawal from the current account.

The bank manager greeted her warmly by name and came out from behind his desk to shake her hand. He asked after Caroline and Martyn and said how lovely it was that she and Andrew were taking a holiday so early in the year. The savings account stood at £18,000 and she arranged for £7,000 in cash. After assuring the bank manager that she would be quite safe carrying such a large amount of money, she was out of the bank and back in her car in forty-five minutes. Suddenly, her numbness seemed to disappear; it was replaced by a feeling of freedom and an overwhelming cold rage.

CHAPTER 2

Drew sat easily in the big swivel chair in the boardroom and watched the slick and faintly erotic images projected onto the big screen at the end of the room. This advertising package had taken him months, and this was the day of reckoning. Adam, his friend and fellow director, was not so at ease as he watched the representatives of the large multinational company viewing the new concept of their product for the first time. Their faces were expressionless, and they sat very still, something that Adam found almost impossible to do. If this was accepted, it would mean millions for the company, but if it was rejected, the money already spent would mean a very substantial loss.

The final scene was of a saucy and suggestive wink from a beautiful eye, belonging to a beautiful and nubile girl, with the muted sound of the company's well-known jingle in the background. The image faded and Drew flicked a button; the machinery stopped. There was a rustle of papers and a shifting of positions from the group of representatives, but still the silence.

Drew uncoiled himself from the chair and moved over to the coffee machine. An expensively dressed and handsome grey-haired man was the first to speak.

"The girl…is she prepared to sign an exclusive contract with us?"

"Yes," said Drew without turning around.

"No catwalk work or association with any other product."

"Yes," said Drew, raising the cup to his lips and turning at the same time.

"Then you've got yourself a deal. Our lawyers will be in touch with all the necessary documentation."

Just like that, just a cold acceptance, not even a hint of praise. Drew exerted every ounce of restraint to prevent himself from leaping and yelling like a kid, and instead walked slowly across the room to shake the hand of the grey-haired man who so obviously held all the authority in his dry, papery hand. The other men gathered up their files and followed him silently out of the room.

The door closed behind them, and for a long moment, the two directors just stood there completely immobile. Then, as if on cue, they grasped each other around the waist and danced an insane jig all around the room.

"We did it, Adam. Christ, we bloody did it."

"God, Drew, did you see their faces? I thought we'd blown it. What a hard-faced bastard Sullivan is. We pulled it off. I can't believe it."

Adam sunk heavily into a chair with an idiotic grin on his face. Almost immediately, the phone started to ring. The office grapevine was in full swing and congratulations were coming in from all over the building. Thirty minutes later, the New York office had also been informed; emails and phone calls started pouring in. What a day. Drew had never felt so high.

Sometime later, when things had calmed down a bit, he phoned home. He let the phone ring for quite some time in case Jess was in the garden. The absence of the answerphone clicking in meant she hadn't gone out, but the phone still rang. It seemed strange but Drew's mind was so full of other things he didn't dwell on it too long. Elizabeth was at home, though. She answered, sounding out of breath. He remembered it was her morning for an early swim and a workout. He must have just caught her coming in the door. She was ecstatic for him and cooed down the phone to him, stroking his already inflated ego, while he preened and glowed with her praise at the other end. He asked if Jessica was in the garden as she was not answering the phone. Elizabeth looked out through the patio doors into the next garden.

"No sign of Jessie and her car is gone."

"Funny," said Drew, "she never forgets the answerphone when going out."

Elizabeth's mood abruptly changed when Drew broke off their date for that evening. There was a celebration dinner in a Mayfair hotel for the directors and the department heads, and he had to get hold of Jessica to make the arrangements. Even though he promised Elizabeth a lunch in bed followed by a passionate afternoon in their favourite motel the following day, she was not pacified, and slammed the phone down hard at the end of the conversation.

Damn Drew! Always calling the tune and expecting me to dance. One of these days, I would not be available. This was a scenario that had been played in her mind many times, but no matter how firm her resolve, when Drew turned on the charm, she always gave in. No women's liberation organisation in the world would have invited her to join with her mental attitude. *Anyway,* she thought, *I actually like getting wolf whistles.*

Funny about Jessie, though. Elizabeth went around to the front of the house and rang the doorbell. The house felt empty, but she peered through the lounge window anyway. *Nobody there but mice,* she thought and went back into her house.

CHAPTER 3

After taking a couple of wrong turns, she found the hotel without too much trouble. She booked in with her maiden name, just in case. The receptionist asked if she required lunch. LUNCH…was it only that time. It felt like hundreds of hours ago that she had found the letter. She looked at her watch; it was only 1.45 pm. She suddenly realised that she was, in fact, very hungry, but still didn't trust her stomach to behave. She played safe and ordered a cheese omelette and some apple pie, which tasted delicious and stayed down.

Her room was like hotel rooms all over the world, comfortable and impersonal. She sat in the armchair by the window and felt the feeling of freedom starting to evaporate. Her shoulders slumped, and a sense of gloom made all her muscles feel tired and lethargic. She glanced out of the window onto the lush grass and gardens and knew she must not brood, or she would lose her nerve and go back.

Straightening her back, she stood up, opened her suitcase, and pulled out a baggy tracksuit and her trainers. Get out…walk…breathe fresh air, anything but stay in this impersonal room, and maybe she would stay strong.

The air outside was crisp and clean, with just a hint of warmth. A rare and beautiful spring day. The grass was soft and springy under her feet, and for a brief moment, she was transported back to holidays spent with Polly, her old school friend, at an old farmhouse in Dorset. That was when the children were small and Drew was still working his way up through the ranks. Money was tight and holidays abroad were still only a pipe dream. Polly had married a farmer who was ten years older than her and considered himself to be a confirmed bachelor until Polly had decided he was going to be hers and set about wearing down all his resistance. Once he had accepted the inevitable, his reluctance turned into an all-encompassing adoration of his small, round wife, and they made up for lost time with the birth of three lusty sons in fairly quick succession.

The children of both families were much about the same age, and holidays on the farm consisted mostly of lazy days surrounded by horses, chickens, and all sizes of dogs and cats. Gargantuan meals of good, wholesome food and jugs of cider got hauled to the beach, and hours were spent sitting around the huge kitchen table after the kids were asleep, discussing everything imaginable.

Polly, of course, Polly. Why hadn't she thought of her before? Polly would know what to do. She had a way of creating order out of the worst chaos imaginable. Even though they hadn't seen each other for a couple of years, they had still kept in touch, albeit not very regularly.

The room that she had so hurriedly left, she now returned to even quicker. She just hoped that the number in her phone was still valid. It was.

"Hi, Polly, it's me," she said.

"Well, well, as I live and breathe, if it's not Jessica Cameron herself. It's been so long, I was beginning to wonder if you had departed this mortal coil and left the rest of us to struggle on without you."

"Polly, can I come down tomorrow, please?"

Something in the tone of her voice must have alerted Polly as there was a brief pause before she said, "Yes, of course, it will be really lovely to see you. What time will you get here?"

"Better expect me when you see me, Poll. I'm in Bedfordshire at the moment, and I don't know what the traffic will be like. Hopefully it will be before lunch sometime."

Polly cleared her throat and said, "Is Drew with you or is it girl talk time?"

"Oh, Polly, I really need to talk to you. I have to get away. It's all so complicated and awful. I can't get things straight in my head and I really don't know what to do."

Her usual modulated voice turned into a babble bordering on hysteria until Polly interrupted her. "Jessica, Jessica, listen to me. Whatever it is, we'll get it sorted. I'm always here for you. Please, just concentrate on getting here. Don't think about anything. Just stay calm. You've got to stay calm. You are going to worry me to death if you are going to be driving in this state. Get a train and I'll pick you up from the station."

"I can't; I'm in a hotel. I drove this far before I could decide where to go." She took a deep breath. "Sorry, Poll, I didn't mean to scare you. I'm OK now; I really need to be with a friend. I'll get away early tomorrow and phone you on the way."

"Jessica, please take care, and if you need to speak to me again before you leave, I'll stay by the phone. I presume if Drew calls, I'm to act dumb."

"Oh, please, Poll, I need some time to sort things out without Drew anywhere near me."

"I figured that was the case," Polly said. After she said goodbye and hung up, it suddenly struck her that Polly had not asked what the trouble was. Or that she seemed all that much surprised.

Wise understanding Polly, the typical earth mother with a sensitive streak a mile wide. *During all those halcyon days of the past when Drew's every word enchanted her, did Polly see through him? Did she keep silent rather than hurt her friend?* Thinking back, Polly never appeared to seek out Drew's company like most of her other friends. In fact, the only time she seemed to engage him into any kind of conversation was when they were all together. *Oh, Polly, you knew all these years and you knew about him.*

The tears came from nowhere. They bubbled up from the bottom of her soul and burst from her eyes, her nose, and her mouth in great fountains of painful, gut-wrenching grief. Her face twisted into an ugly mask with the sheer force of it. Her throat constricted and emitted a tortured, inhuman animal howl. Her body convulsed, her knees were drawn up to her belly, and still the tears came. Years of humiliation were long buried. Dozens of nights trying not to imagine his long, lean body naked and fused with someone else's. The faint traces of perfume on his shirts, she pretended not to notice, and still the tears came. *Elizabeth!* Her eyes swelled to slits and her face was sore from the body fluids gushing over her skin. *Drew, Drew, I loved you so.... You were my life, did I mean so little to you?* The copious tears slowed to be replaced by painful, gasping, dry sobs that hurt her stomach and her chest, and finally, exhausted from the huge outpouring of her inner strength, she slept.

CHAPTER 4

Drew sat in the barber's chair and made grunting sounds at regular intervals in yet another long diatribe of Tony's about the government, taxes, crime, and sport. The grunts could have meant either a yes or no but seemed to satisfy Tony who never listened to any reply anyway. The talk flowed over him as he reflected yet again on the number of calls he had so far made to his home number and Jessica's mobile without any reply. He had intended to stay in town and meet up with her later for dinner, but now he was going to have to go home and hurry her up. The whole evening was going to be a hell of a rush.

Tony stood behind him with a hand mirror for Drew to view the always impeccable handiwork. His hair was thick and dark and flecked with grey now. He kept it very regularly trimmed, so there was never a drastic change in the style. He wore it slightly longer than the shaved fashion that was so popular now. The longer style suited him and gave him a slightly rakish look that should have been at odds with the severely tailored business suits but wasn't. His laser blue eyes were direct and clear. He was totally aware of the devastation they caused to the female nervous system, and he used them frequently.

As Tony brushed him off, Drew glanced at his watch and mentally totted up the time it would take him to drive home, organise Jessica, and get back into town again. If he left now, he would get out of London before the traffic started to build up and maybe get a clear run all the way back. That would give him enough time at home to phone a good hotel and book a room for the night, shower and change, and get back on time.

The traffic out of London was heavy but moving at a reasonable speed, and once on the A1M, the powerful Mercedes engine made light of the remaining miles. He remembered to fill up with petrol to save time later and swung into the drive, pleased at having made such good time.

Jessica's car was not there, and his good mood soured as he realised that he was going to have to track her down, which was going to take even more time. The party was mainly in his honour, and the last thing he wanted was to be late. As the heavy front door swung open, he started shouting her name; his voice had a hard edge to it. He glanced into the lounge, threw his keys on the hall table, and headed for the downstairs toilet. Jessica had forgotten to replace the hand towel, and he walked through to the kitchen, flapping his hands and heading for the handrail by the back door.

There was a pile of clothes in front of the washing machine, which he puzzled at, and an acrid smell of burnt coffee. *Christ, she'd left the filter coffee machine on; the jug was dry and was red hot. Whatever was the woman playing at?* It was a wonder it hadn't exploded. He switched it off at the plug and turned the kettle on. *Maybe her car had broken down.* He went through to the hall to check the answerphone before remembering it hadn't been switched on all day. He went back into the kitchen, made a mug of coffee, took the cordless phone off the wall, and sat down at the kitchen table. He reached into his inside pocket for his address book at the same time as idly picking up the two pieces of paper in the middle of the table anchored down on one corner by a dirty coffee cup. He read the words on the top piece of paper without them making any sense. It was only when he flipped over the sheet to the one underneath that the jolt hit his stomach. He read the two pieces of paper several times as if he couldn't quite believe his eyes.

He had always been so careful with notes and always made sure he had never put anything in writing himself. *Jesus, when had Elizabeth given it to me? Think. How long had Jessica been holding on to it? Think.* Yes, he remembered, last Friday at the garden barbecue. He had furtively read it, sought Elizabeth out with a long, deep moment of eye contact, and been amazed at the speed and force of the hard-on he got. He remembered her eyes briefly flickering downwards and a secret smile curving her mouth when she saw what had happened. He had folded the note very small and tucked it into the back pocket of his jeans to be put on the fire when no one was around. However, after all the beers, the whiskeys, and the jugs of Sangrias, he had forgotten about the note. *Why was Jessica so methodical? Most women would have washed the damned jeans without even finding such a small piece of paper.* His anger turned towards Jessica as if she were the guilty party and not him. Trust her to spoil his big night. Well, he would go without her and tell everyone that she had a migraine. He would probably have a better time anyway. Maybe the new head of the accounts department would fancy going night-clubbing later. She had caught his eye on several occasions, and was tall, elegant, and educated. Be good to see what she looked like with her feathers ruffled, plus she was married, always the safest sort. Yes, he'd go and have a good time. *Jessie would be sure to be here by the time he got home tomorrow.*

He was actually whistling as he ran up the stairs. The whistle, however, died on his lips when he entered the bedroom. The unmade bed, his crumpled suits, the half-empty dressing table and wardrobes, and the carelessly discarded airline labels gave every indication that this was not going to be a token disappearance.

He sat on the corner of the bed and put his head in his hands. For the first time since he arrived home, he considered the implications and arrived at the conclusion that this time, it had really hit the fan. It was going to take a lot more than charm to get off the hook this time.

CHAPTER 5

She looked in the mirror and hardly recognised the face that stared back. Her dark brown eyes were red and bloodshot, her skin looked blotchy and dry, and her hair was unbelievably tangled and knotted. She couldn't believe she had slept so long. Completely disorientated and still fully clothed, she had woken up at 5.30 am with a raging headache. She removed what was left of her makeup and washed her hair. The hotel hairdryer blew her hair into a crackling mass of electricity, but at least it was tangle-free and clean. Worn loose, it fell softly to her shoulders and softened her whole face, but she clubbed it in a thick bundle at the back of her neck with a silver slide.

Her body ached all over and as it was still very early, she ran a hot bath instead of her usual quick morning shower. The hotel sachet of bath salts smelt pleasantly fragrant, and some of the stiffness in her body disappeared after a long soak in the warm water. Nothing much she could do about the bloodshot eyes, so she applied a light shading of brown shadow and some mascara and tried to hide the worst with her sunglasses.

The baggy tracksuit looked even baggier now. It was discarded for a pair of jeans and a sweatshirt, and the old faithful trainers. She wondered what time breakfast started and dug in around the bedside drawer for the hotel brochure. *7.30 am, good.* 7.05 am now, just time to pack the few bits she had taken out of her suitcase and get down to the dining room early.

As soon as the dining room door opened, the smell of breakfast bacon was all around her, and she realised from the grumbling in her middle that she had missed dinner and hadn't eaten for hours. A full English breakfast, toast, marmalade, and a whole pot of coffee later she felt almost human again. She stopped by the reception desk, paid her bill, and arranged for a porter to bring down her luggage.

The spider's web on the bush outside the hotel doors was covered in dew and looked like it was made out of spun glass. In passing, the porter brushed her suitcase against the bush and the beauty disappeared to be replaced by the unblemished web that was there all the time. Jessica felt a pang of sadness that something so lovely could be lost so quickly.

The journey was uneventful. Most of the traffic was going towards London and not away from it. She took the country roads rather than the motorways. Across Salisbury Plain, the weird configuration of Stonehenge stood tall and proud. *What a pity it had all been fenced off now. What was it that made the present generation want to destroy and disfigure things that had been there for generations, and would probably stand for generations to come if given some respect.* The countryside looked almost lime green this early in the year. The green seemed to deepen as the seasons passed, until in the late summer, the green was deep, dark emerald, and the sun's rays changed from pale primrose to mustard. She had always loved the West Country. Whilst her batteries seem to get recharged in the country, after a while Drew's attitude always got restless and fidgety with inactivity.

She detoured to drive along the coast road from Abbotsbury towards Bridport, stopping high up on the road to look at the sea before turning inland towards the farm and Polly.

The double gates at the entrance to the farm were open and she drove straight up to the house. Polly must have been watching for her and was out of the house before Jessica even had the car door opened. As Jessica straightened up, she was enveloped in a tight bear hug and immediately breathed in the scent she always associated with Polly. A clean-scented soap kind of smell she had never smelt on anyone else.

With their arms around each other, they leant back to look at one another, and Jessica got the shock of her life. The little round dumpling she had always known had disappeared, and she was now looking at a slim, petite woman with a fashionable bobbed hairstyle, whose round cheeks were now smooth and pale tan with shaded brown eyes shining at her. Jessica's jaw dropped, and Polly's face split with a huge grin.

"God, Jessie, it's so good to see you. I was so worried last night, but now you're here I can stop pacing backwards and forwards. I must have put at least ten year's extra wear on the carpet. The kettles on, let's go and have a cuppa. John can get your bags later."

Jessica, still totally speechless, just looked at her friend and couldn't believe how incredibly pretty she was. "Polly, what have you done? You're so beautiful and so trim."

"Well," Polly said, "when the boys grew up and went off to agricultural college, and then off out with their friends and girlfriends, they never seemed to have time, or even want, huge great meals anymore, so there didn't seem to be much point in cooking all those pies and cakes and stuff. As you know, John has never been one for all the sweet things, more a meat and two veg man really, so when I stopped cooking it, I stopped eating all the wrong things as well. Suddenly, the weight seemed to fall off me, and I liked what I saw. John did too and became a recycled, raunchy man, and I loved it. Suddenly, I found that I had hip bones and cheekbones, so I started going to aerobics and walking a lot. This is the new edition Polly, and I feel wonderful. When the boys bring home their friends, I get compliments from them about sexy older women." Polly smiled a broad smile. "It knocks years off me. Anyway, you didn't come all this way to talk about me. Judging by the pink eyes and white face, plenty of tears have already been shed. Do you want to tell me about it? Or shall I just provide a healing silence?"

"Oh, Polly, I need to talk. I seem to have spent years papering over the cracks in the hope that everything would be hidden, but now

I know the only one I was hiding it from was me."

So, the talking began and flowed in an unstoppable deluge that had been building up for years. The deluge choked to a halt on the name Elizabeth and then the tears started again. Polly did not put her arms around her friend or comfort her in any way, knowing that this would have turned the trickle of tears into a river. Instead, she lit a cigarette and waited.

Three soggy tissues later, the tears had calmed down to a sniffle. Polly poured Jessica another cup of tea and pushed it towards her. The silence deepened as Jessica's mind returned to some point in the past.

Suddenly, she said, "You knew about him, didn't you?"

Polly made a show of grinding out her cigarette and avoided looking up while she contemplated whether to be totally honest with her old friend or continue being kind. She decided that enough cover-ups had been provided on Drew's behalf, and it was time for some truth at last.

"This is a small place," she said. "People talk."

Jessica's eyes flew wide open. "He had affairs down here." She gasped.

"Oh, Jessie, Drew was constantly on an ego trip. He had to be worshipped and adored wherever he was. Your love he was always sure of, so there was no challenge. To him, all the fun was in the seduction. Once the women started to love him, he had won, and discarded them as soon as it started to become complicated and demanding. He then went out to find another heart to conquer. The more uninterested and unapproachable, the better."

"Why didn't I see this," Jessica said. "I can't believe I didn't suspect anything."

Polly walked across the large kitchen and filled the kettle again. After switching it on, she turned and leant against the worktop. "You were busy bringing up the children and putting a home together. At some point along the line, you started treating Drew more as the father of your children than a lover. This is only natural in most families, but with Drew's insecurities and huge ego, he couldn't handle it. He wanted the security of you and the children at home, but he craved the extra buzz of feeling like a stud."

Jessica stood up and started pacing. "You certainly go for the throat when you start, don't you?" she said.

"Isn't that what friends are for," Polly said with a smile.

Jessica stopped pacing and, crossing her arms, turned to face Polly. "Why did he need to be a stud? I never refused him, you know. Our sex life was always good."

"Yes, but you were too familiar. He knew what turned you on; there was no need to extend his sexual knowledge with you. You adored him already. He could have grown warts and sprouted hair from his teeth and you would have still adored him. He always knew where you were every minute of the day, so there was no mystery left at all."

"So, you're saying it's all my fault. He has all these affairs for years while I stay faithful and give him all the support he needs, and suddenly, it's my fault for not being a raving nymphomaniac twenty-four hours a day." Jessica's voice became shrill and angry, and she could feel the tears bubbling again to the surface. Now, her friend did hold her in her arms, stroking her and smoothing her.

"No, Jessie, it's not all your fault, of course it isn't. You were everything a man could need in a wife. Drew should have paid you much more attention than he did. He didn't realise what he had, and he probably won't until he's been without you for a while, but somewhere along the line, you forgot his needs. After the children grew up, you could have gone with him on many of his business trips. He used to ask you in the beginning. You could have spent some quality time together. Explored new places and learnt to know each other again without the demands of the children. But you always chose to stay at home, giving Drew the opportunity to find something or someone to fill the hours alone."

They stood silently still with their arms about each other. Jessica finally spoke, her voice muffled in Polly's shoulder. "What must I do, Polly?"

"I can't tell you that," Polly said. "All I know is, you are going to stay with me until you feel strong and able to make the right decisions, whatever they may be. You can relax with me at yoga, get muscle burn at aerobics, and help me with the chickens and goats. I taught you years ago how to milk them; I just hope you haven't forgotten. But first, I think you must write to the children, and although you might not want to, send a short note to Drew. You just need to tell them that you want time to yourself, that you are alright, and you will keep in touch. Otherwise, they might involve the police."

For the first time in what seemed like years, Jessica smiled. The skin on her face stretched painfully as though, in some way, it had shrunk, but when she looked at Polly, her friend smiled back, and Jessica could feel the knots in her stomach starting to ease.

"Let's walk over and see John. He's usually home by now, but he would have seen your car coming up the back road and figured we needed a bit of time. But I bet he's starving. We'll take some sandwiches and a flask over and then come back. I'll prepare us a delicious low-calorie and healthy lunch. Then we'll go out; I've got something I want to show you."

Jessica poured herself another cup of tea while Polly was making the sandwiches. She picked up the cup with one hand and noticed her hands had stopped trembling.

CHAPTER 6

The journey back into town was uneventful, and Drew spent most of the time ruminating on his plan of action regarding Jessica. On entering the dining room, he got a round of applause, followed by a lot of backslapping and congratulations. He apologised for Jessica's absence and received many condolences on her behalf. Jessica was well-liked by everyone, and it had been whispered on more than one occasion that she was too good for Drew.

The dinner got going and was then followed by endless speeches by numerous wits. Usually, Drew would have entered into the spirit of it all and laughed falsely and loudly like the rest, but tonight, he couldn't seem to centre his mind and was finding the whole thing overlong and boring.

The elegant lady from accounts had turned up in a slinky black number with a thigh-high split and minus her husband. He felt her eyes on him on many occasions but studiously avoided any eye contact with her. She gave it up as a bad job in the end and latched on to another department head who was there without his wife. He seemed to become totally transfixed by the split in her skirt that crept even higher up her thigh every time she shifted in her chair.

Drew stood it as long as he could and, using Jessica as an excuse, started to take his leave. Adam's wife, Cassie, stopped him on his way to the door. "Is Jessica OK, Drew? I've been trying to phone her all day with the good news, but there's been no reply. Are you sure she's alright? I've never known Jessica to ever suffer from migraine headaches."

"She's had one or two lately," lied Drew. "She unplugged the phone today to get some peace."

"Shall I come over tomorrow and find out if there is anything she needs?" Cassie asked. "It's not like her to miss your big night."

"No, no, Cassie, she'll be fine."

"Well, get her to phone me for a chat tomorrow, will you?"

Drew felt like he was being grilled, and with Cassie's hand on his arm, he was finding it very difficult to disengage himself from her. Cassie's direct stare made Drew feel that she could see right through his lies and it was making him feel uncomfortable. He was saved by the waiter with a tray of drinks, and he quickly made his escape.

The underground carpark was quiet and dimly lit. He sat in the car with his hands on the steering wheel and his forehead resting on the backs of his hands. The muscles in his face ached from all the unnatural smiling and his stomach felt bloated and unsettled. The journey home seemed to be an impossible feat, and he contemplated staying in town, but almost immediately, it was dismissed. For some unfathomable reason, he knew he had to go home.

He hardly remembered the journey home. He drove in an almost dreamlike state. On turning the corner at the bottom of the road, he glanced immediately at the house and felt a sinking feeling when the house was shrouded in darkness. When he arrived in the driveway, he was reluctant to go in. Somewhere in the recesses of his mind, he had hoped that the lights would be on. He wearily climbed out of the car, locked it, and let himself into the dark, unwelcoming house. For years, when the children were young, they had pestered him for a dog. He had always refused them, despite all the many tantrums, but this was one time when he would have welcomed a warm, uncomplicated living thing just to be there.

He plodded slowly up the stairs, carelessly pushed his suits off the bed and onto the floor, undressed, and climbed into the unmade bed. It was too late to phone any of Jessica's friends, but tomorrow, he would track her down and mend some fences. She had never been able to stay mad at him for long, and if he could find her, he knew he could woo her back. With that thought, he fell into a fitful sleep.

By lunchtime the next day, after dozens of phone calls, Drew was getting very weary. He had not wanted to ask directly if Jessica was there, so spent useless time chatting, knowing all the time from the tone of their voices that they hadn't seen her. Caro sounded surprised when he phoned. Usually, Jessica spent hours chatting with their daughter and passing all the chit-chat on to him, most of which he didn't even listen to.

"When are you rich people coming up to take us poor people out for an expensive slap-up nosh with a doggy bag to take home?" Caro said. That used to be a regular thing when Caro first moved out. Her two mates were super funny, and Drew and Jessica spent many hours in various restaurants in side splitting mirth at all their antics. It had been so long since the last time, and Drew felt a sudden pang of loss.

"Well, Dad, it's really great to hear from you. Love and kisses to Mum. Got to go, the shop is full and I'm getting some black looks. Bye, Dad, love you." The connection was broken with a loud click, and Drew put the phone down on the kitchen table.

No good ringing Marty. Her passport was still upstairs; he'd checked that earlier on, so she was not winging her way to America. Elizabeth! In all this time, he hadn't even thought of her. She must be already in the motel waiting for him. She must have seen his car in the drive. She probably thought that Jessica and him had come home last night after all instead of staying in town as planned. Elizabeth wouldn't have come around this morning in case Jessica invited her somewhere and she had to think up an excuse for not going.

He dragged out all the slips of paper in the pocket of his wallet and dialled the motel number. The motel people knew them after all the times they had been there, but apart from a few knowing looks, they had always been discreet. Elizabeth answered on the second ring. "Hi, it's Drew."

"Where the fuck are you, you bastard."

"Oh, Christ, Elizabeth, are we in trouble. Jessie found the note that you gave me at the barbeque, and when I got home last night, she'd packed up and left...."

"Oh my God, you are such a stupid prat. Why did you keep the bloody thing? What the hell are we going to do now? Do you think she'll tell William?"

"How the bloody hell should I know. I don't even know where she is. I've phoned everyone I can think of. If she was going to confront your husband with the evidence, then she's made a balls up of it because she left the bloody note behind."

"I'll come straight back, and we'll find her."

"No, don't come here. If she comes back and finds you here, it'll be the last straw. Best stay away and plead ignorance. I'll keep you in the picture. If you come around make sure it's with Will until the heat dies down."

Drew put the phone down and sat gazing into space. Jessica was such a soft soul; sad books and movies made her cry, even happy stories made her cry. Many times, he had shouted at her and she had stood like a child with her eyes wide and frightened, and her lips pressed tightly together. In the beginning, she had shouted right back at him, but over the years, she stopped retaliating. When he would calm her down and take her in his arms, she was always trembling. Her face would burrow in his shoulder to hide her eyes.

For the first time, he stopped thinking about himself and thought about her. His throat constricted when he thought of the pain she must be feeling and the damage he had done.

CHAPTER 7

Two fields and dozens of cowpats later, Jessica was glad she was wearing her old trainers. She had borrowed one of the many waxed jackets hanging in the back porch and was now grateful she had. The sun was warm, but there was still a keen edge to the wind that was making her ears hurt. She had the flask tucked under her arm and her hands in her pockets.

Polly trudging along beside her seemed super fit now, as she kept up a non-stop conversation without even sounding breathless. Jessica was put in the picture about her three sons and all their friends, the other farms and their problems, the girls at the gym and yoga class, and everything else pertaining to rural life in general. Jessica was content to conserve her breath and listened to her friend all the time marvelling that she could cram in so much activity as well as all the things that a farmer's wife had to take on. She learnt that Steve, the eldest son, was at an agricultural college and was excelling all their expectations. Ben was also there and doing well; Jack was due for his A-level exams at the private boarding school where the other two had gone. Polly missed her sons and had taken up most of the other activities to fill the empty spaces in her life.

As they came over the crest of the hill, they saw John unloading bales of fodder for the cows off the back of a trailer. Polly shouted and waved with a returning wave from John. As they got closer, Jessica saw John unload the last of the bales, turn, and, with a grin going from ear to ear, hold out his arms wide. Jessica ran into them and was gripped in a bear hug that threatened to crack her ribs.

"Jessie, my girl, it's been too long between visits. We've missed you."

"Oh, John, I've missed you too. I didn't realise quite how much till now," Jessica said.

John released the vice-like grip and turned to his wife. His eyes were soft as he looked at her and bent his head to kiss her mouth. "Christ woman. I thought you had forgotten you had a husband. I work my fingers to the bone, and I don't even get a crust to keep me going."

"Rubbish," Polly said. "You're getting such a paunch on you. If I didn't feed you for a week, you could still survive on your hump like a camel."

"See what abuse I have to take," John said. "I don't know how I put up with her."

"'Cause you love me," Polly said, sitting down on a bale.

"Can't argue with that," John said, rummaging about in the basket for food.

Jessica looked at John and thought for the millionth time how little like a farmer he looked. Granted, he was burly with a craggy, weather-beaten face, but he had an elegance about him. His brown hair had two distinguished wings of grey either side, and his moustache was thick and soft with hardly any grey in it. His brown eyes were clear and had lines running out from either side of them that had always been there and never seemed to get any deeper. He had an easy way with him, not slow, but unflustered and dependable. Polly and John had characters that were poles apart but had an almost impossible-to-break bond.

Jessica felt a savage pang of envy, tinged around the edges with jealousy, and immediately felt ashamed. *Why the hell should she begrudge someone else's happiness just because she was miserable?*

"What do you think of this skinny woman now, Jessie?" John said. "I used to have something to grab hold of. Now it's all skin and bone."

"And don't you just love it?" Polly retorted. "Most of the time, you're just like a randy old goat, disgusting at your age."

"Don't hear you complaining much," John said, his mouth full of ham sandwich. Polly just laughed and punched him on the arm.

They sat and chatted while John ate. The reason for Jessica being there was not spoken of, but Jessica had the feeling he knew. He and Polly would have talked, and besides, there would be ample opportunity to go into it at a more convenient time. John kissed both Polly and Jessica and then told them to push off to let the working class get on with some of it. They both laughed and started back to the farmhouse in companionable silence.

Back at the farmhouse, they lunched on toasted tuna sandwiches and salad, followed by cheese, biscuits, and an apple. Jessica took a quick shower and changed into the black slacks she had worn when she left her house the day before, and a cream fluffy jersey. Polly had changed into a soft brown corduroy dress with a long skirt and tan suede boots and was driving the Range Rover around to the front of the house as Jessica came down the stairs.

"Where are we going?" Jessica said as Polly was locking up.

"I'll tell you on the way," Polly replied, getting back in the driver's seat. She opened the window and lit a cigarette before they drove off. "Even with all the healthy living, I still can't give these things up," Polly said, blowing smoke from her nostrils. "I've cut them right back, though. Don't smoke half as many as I used to. Maybe I'll try those patches or start vaping."

They were travelling along a back road that led to one of the higher parts of the farm, but it wasn't as Jessica remembered it. There used to be just fields as far as the eye could see, now there were buildings and caravans.

"What on earth has happened here?" Jessica said.

Polly grinned and stopped the Range Rover. "This is our new leisure complex. When the boys went away, the farm got too big for John to cope with, so he sold off part of it to a company that was in the holiday business. We invested part of the money back into the scheme, some for ourselves and some for the boys, too. So, we have a vested interest as it were. We also insisted on an agreement that we would have some say in the final layout. We wanted to make it acceptable to the local people and prevent the countryside from being abused too much.

"The main part of the complex was kept low and in an L shape. One branch of the L has a mini market, launderette, coffee house and snack bar, and a really good restaurant. The other branch has all the leisure facilities. The gym is fully equipped with a solarium and a sauna. There are also badminton and squash courts. There's a good hairdresser, and our latest addition is a small ten-pin bowling alley. This has proved extremely popular; you always need to book a lane in advance, or you can wait hours. As well as the chalets, there are also mobile homes. Some belong to the complex and some are privately owned. All the electricity, gas, and water are laid on, and there is already a waiting list for people who wish to park their homes here all year. Those buildings at the side are the ablution blocks and kitchens for the touring caravans and tents. The complex is open for visitors and locals for a small fee. Most of the local people who regularly use the complex, take out a membership; it works out cheaper that way."

Polly's voice had taken on a note of pride as she was talking, and Jessica realised that John and Polly were proud that the land they had sold had proved to be such a benefit to the community. Polly also told her that apart from the management, all the jobs available had gone to the local people, helping in job creation where before there had been very few. Polly started up the Range Rover and they drove on through the main gate to the carpark outside the reception area.

"John's birthday is coming up soon," Polly said, switching off the motor. "So, while we're here, I might as well book the restaurant for a bit of a knees up. They allow it to be used for private functions during the week. They lose too much money if it's closed to the public on weekends."

The double glass swing doors led into a quiet and well laid out reception area. The carpet was a swirly pattern in blue, and the circular reception desk was in light pine with a blue marble top. Comfortable chairs were placed around low pine tables, and a profusion of plants of all sizes were scattered around in white pots. The whole impression was of a cool and efficient welcome.

The only ripple on the pond was the grim face of the woman behind the reception desk. There was no greeting smile. In fact, when she finally looked up, her eyes were cold and unblinking, like a lizard, Jessica thought. She had straight greying hair and had what her mother would have called a pudding basin haircut. Her half-eye specs accentuated the bags beneath the eyes, and her clothes looked as if they had been picked out haphazardly with no thought for colour or style.

"Hello, Mrs. Sheldon," she said. *Even her voice was colourless and monotone*, Jessica thought. "What can I help you with?"

"Hi, Mrs. Creed. I'm here to show my friend Jessica around. She's staying with us for a while and hasn't yet seen our pride and joy. I also want to book the restaurant in for John's birthday."

The lizard, Mrs. Creed, made no reply other than to open one of the stacks of books by the telephone. "I hope you are aware of the rules governing the licensing hours and the general conduct rules for hiring the function room," she said.

"I would think so, Mrs. Creed. My husband and I drew up most of them."

"That's all right then," the lizard said without even a hint of a change of tone.

Polly completed the booking and strode back to the swing door, her heels coming down hard on the soft carpet. "That woman," she said, "why in the hell they ever hired her, I'll never know. If I got here after a long journey and was greeted by that po-faced old crow, I'd be tempted to turn around and go home."

Jessica giggled, "She is a bit daunting, isn't she."

"Daunting!" Polly exclaimed. "That's not what I would have called her. If you ask me, I think she's a dried-up old prune who wants a good man to make her even half human. She calls herself Mrs., but nobody's ever seen or heard of any husband in the last twenty-five years. She probably looked at him, turned him to stone, and he's now standing in the garden of some stately home."

Now Jessica did burst out laughing, and Polly soon followed her. Smiling, they started the grand tour. They quickly walked along and passed the mini-market and launderette to the coffee shop. The carpet was a beautiful lime green in the seating areas, with white wickerwork screens dividing the tables. Lots of greenery everywhere, as there was in the reception room, but the feature that made the whole room so light and airy was the fact that the ceiling was a huge glass dome, making it feel like you were sitting outside. The waitresses were all in crisp green uniforms, and the whole place was spotless.

Jessica was very impressed. They ordered coffee and sat under the dome. Most of the clientele were young and dressed in jeans. The girls all had long, straight hair, and most of the boys wore their hair short and gelled. They nearly all wore t-shirts with logos on the front or back, almost as though it was a kind of uniform. *Maybe in our youth, we all wore the same sort of clothes without being aware of it,* Jessica thought.

A beautiful, casually dressed woman approached the table smiling. "Polly, I thought it was you."

"Viv, you're back," Polly said.

The woman sat down at the table. Jessica thought what a

gorgeous-looking woman she was with her mane of dark, shaggy, streaked hair and large African-type earrings. Her long skirt and tunic top had a look of linen about them, and the creamy colour set off her chocolate brown skin which was smooth and velvety. Her bright pink lipstick framed her beautiful white teeth as she gave them a wide smile.

"I'd like to introduce you to my very best and longest friend Jessica, who is staying with me at the moment," Polly said. "This is Viv. She takes all the aerobics classes and helps out with the yoga ones. She has been away for a couple of weeks on an advanced course in therapeutic massage so she can get rid of all the kinks she creates in the first place."

The three women talked for a while, and Polly promised to bring Jessica to the next day's aerobics class.

The restaurant was a revelation. Jessica had never seen such a plush place outside London. It was dimly lit and when she wondered why, she saw it had no windows. It was an evening restaurant that served only dinner. The décor was deep dark red with dark mahogany wood. The tables all had starched white tablecloths and were all illuminated with coloured flower-like lamps made from opaque shells. The wall lights were made of the same type of shells. There was a small dance floor at one end, with a raised platform behind it. The whole place was expensive and elegant.

The head chef, Barney, came bustling out from the back. "We aren't op…. Oh, Mrs. Sheldon, it's you. I thought it was another lot of new arrivals wanting burgers and chips. We get them wandering in here all the time until they realise it's a cordon bleu restaurant and not a hamburger joint."

"Barney's very proud of his reputation around here. He would never lower himself to cook a burger," Polly said. "You have to book a table days in advance to eat here, and if you arrive without a booking, you'll probably still be here when hell freezes over."

Barney seemed almost to plump his chest out like a pigeon at Polly's praise, and a grin split his chubby cheeks. "What a flatter you are Mrs. S," he said. "But there must be a reason for this daytime visit."

Polly told him about John's birthday. After a brief discussion, they booked a date and decided on the menu. Barney left them to return to his kitchen and both spent the next forty-five minutes going around the sports complex and bowling alley.

Jessica stared longer than was strictly proper at the client in the hair shop, having her long locks all cut off. Hanks of hair fell to the floor in a glistening mass, and she looked near to tears. Jessica was itching to ask her what prompted her decision to be shorn after all the years it must have taken to grow it, but Polly was impatient to get home to start supper. "We'll be back tomorrow," she said, and they started the short drive home.

CHAPTER 8

The next few days passed in a blur for Jessica. Polly was determined she was going to leave her no time to brood and filled Jessica's days with chickens, goats, ducks, cooking at the house, aerobics, yoga, and swimming at the complex. The only time they talked in depth was at supper around the large kitchen table or in the comfortable and well-used lounge later on. Even though Polly kept her busy during the day, there were still nights to get through. Jessica's thoughts kept returning to Drew, and for too many nights, there were still tears on her face when she finally fell asleep.

She had sent a short note to Drew, telling him she had many things to think about and needed time to herself. She told him she was OK and would contact him when she felt ready to talk. She also wrote to Marty and Caro and was surprised to find those letters more difficult to write than the one to Drew. She explained to them that Dad and she were having some problems and needed some time apart to get back on track again. What Drew would tell them if they contacted him, which they were bound to, she didn't know. A sales rep who was passing through promised to post them further up country so the postmark would not give her away.

In her quieter moments, she could feel her shoulders drooping and a black depression creeping over her. In her mind, the decision she knew she was going to have to make soon was still more than her brain could cope with. Her money was not going to last forever. She didn't want to keep sponging off Polly and John. They had been so good to her already, but on the other hand, there was no way she could bring herself to ask Drew for anything. If she was going to continue on her own, she had to prove to him and herself that she could make it on her own. She needed this to give her back some self-respect.

After all these years, she wasn't qualified to do anything very much unless being a housewife and mother are counted as a trade. The vacancies in the paper seemed to need all sorts of qualifications, most of which she'd never even heard of. It may not be too late to learn some skills, but that thought was dismissed straight away. *What would she live on in the meantime?* Besides she was a bit too long in the tooth to be a student. The thought of her with all those young, fresh people and coming out of school made her smile. At times, she felt a bit like Scarlet O'Hara in *Gone With The Wind.* Her answer to problems was always, 'I can't think about that today, I'll think about it tomorrow.'

She could sell her car if push came to shove. Drew had always made sure she had a new, reliable, and sometimes boring car. He knew nothing about car mechanics and changed her car every two years. She had always fancied something small and fast but always got over-ruled. So, after a while, she got used to going along with his choice without any argument.

Her VW was comfortable, quick, and in excellent condition, being only ten months old. If she got an older car, it would give her some spare cash if she needed it, but she would leave that until it was absolutely necessary. She really did need to think rationally about the future. *I suppose I could pick the phone up and tell Drew I'm coming back.*

Then she thought about meeting Elizabeth again. She knew there was no way she could go back yet. Maybe if Drew sold up the house. So…it looked like it would be a fair bit of time till her return, which left her no choice. She had to get a job and find somewhere to stay so Polly and John could have their lives back.

It was the twice-weekly aerobics class day. Plus, Polly wanted to speak to someone at the complex to try to hire some musicians for John's party evening. Jessica changed into sports bra and leggings and dragged out her old faithful trainers. The new keep-fit gear she'd bought from the shop at the gym, but in her new state of independence, she decided the trainers on sale there were a bit too expensive for her reduced circumstances and made do with her old ones.

The reception area that was usually so tranquil was today in an uproar. They called there first to find out about the musician for the party and walked into a knockdown fight between Mrs. Creed and Stacey, the office manager.

"How dare you be so rude and insulting to an important customer," Stacey was shouting. "It's not the first time we've had complaints about your attitude to the people booking in, but this time you've gone too far."

Stacey looked around when she realised that there were people standing in the doorway, but as Polly was a shareholder and one of the founder members and not a visitor, she turned and continued her tirade.

"That gentleman and his wife, who you were so rude to, happen to own four mobile homes parked permanently with us, bringing in a great deal of annual rent. Now, because of your insulting and malicious tongue, they want to remove all their homes from this site, losing us a great deal of money. When Michael Standing and the rest of the directors hear about this, I hope they fire you. Also, while we're on the subject, the booking deposits and the cash that's been banked have not been balanced for weeks. Maybe they'd be interested in the reasons for that, too."

Mrs. Creed's face was red and blotchy, and her eyes looked even colder. "Well, at least I'm doing my job and not running around with a different male visitor every week like a strumpet," she ground out between clenched teeth.

"Why, you mealy-mouthed old bat. You're a good one to talk when you've been pretending to be married all these years and everyone here knows you've never had a man in your life."

At this, Polly stepped forward, feeling that the whole thing had gone far enough. "Come on, ladies, this is no place for all this. You should be having this all out in private."

Mrs. Creed's head disappeared below the counter and she came up clutching her handbag. Her head was up so high her neck seemed to stretch by several inches. "You won't have to beg the management to fire me," she said, "I would not stay here if it were the last job in the world."

With that, she strode purposefully towards the door on flat brown brogues. Stacey couldn't resist one parting shot, and Mrs. Creed closed the door on Stacey's voice, saying, "As far as you're concerned, it probably will be the last job in the world."

The three women stood there for a few seconds in uncomfortable silence. Stacey was the first one to speak. Her voice sounded shaky; her temper had gone. "God, now I've done it. My dad always said my mouth was going to be the death of me. When they find out about this, the muck's really going to hit the fan. I know nobody liked her, and there have been numerous complaints, but why did it have to be me that opened my big mouth?"

Polly sat down in one of the chairs. "Surely, if the management finds out how unpopular she was, it won't be too bad for you, will it?"

"You don't understand, Polly. We haven't got anyone else to cover the desk, and we're coming up to the busiest time."

"I could do it," said Jessica quietly.

Both women turned and looked at her. Polly with her mouth open. Stacey came round to the front of the desk and sat down. She looked at Jessica for a few minutes in silence...then she smiled. "I reckon you could too," she said. "I'll see what I can do."

Up till then, Jessica had not realised she'd been holding her breath. Suddenly, she knew she wanted the job. She wanted it and could do it. Now, all she had to do was wait.

CHAPTER 9

The body lying beside him was dark and firm. The breasts were small but good, and she had a delicious round, ample bottom. His index finger traced lazy circles around her breasts, over her midriff, and down to the triangle of dark hair. He followed his fingers with his mouth and heard her moan. She bent her left knee and rolled over towards him. Her body needing to touch him.

"God, Drew, don't tease me anymore. I want you inside me. I'm going to die if you don't make love to me."

Their mouths fused and their tongues licked and sucked. She could feel his erection all along her belly and tried to pull him over on top of her. Drew took his time, then slowly turned her over on her back and came up on his knees. Her legs opened to welcome him. And when he entered her, she was moist, smooth, and silky. He thrust slowly, then his mouth left hers, his eyes opened, and a look of panic crossed his face.

Just as smoothly, he slid out of her, no longer erect but soft and limp. He rolled onto his back with a groan and covered his eyes with his arm. Her legs closed and straightened.

"Oh Christ, Alex, I'm sorry. I don't know what's wrong with me."

"Don't worry, it happens," Alex said, trying to slow her breathing and keep the frustration out of her voice.

"Not to me, it doesn't," Drew answered, his arm still across his face.

He felt like his body was betraying him. This was the fourth time this had happened, and he was powerless to prevent it. He climbed slowly from the bed without touching her and headed for the bathroom.

Elizabeth had been the first to witness his failure. They had kept apart for as long as Drew could fend her off, but in the end had met her in the usual place. When his hard-on had disappeared and defied all her ministrations to revive it, her remarks had been spiteful and scathing.

He had always called the tune. Whenever she got fed up with all the run around he gave her and distanced herself from him, he had always been able to bring his considerable charm to bear, to bring her back to him shuddering and moaning. Now, for once, she held the cards, and the opportunity to berate him brought forth all the times he had treated her like his plaything.

Drew let the cold shower run over him; it was all Elizabeth's fault. If it had not been for her stupid note, things would have carried on as normal. He thought the gorgeous Alex would have been able to stimulate him into his old vigorous lovemaking, but even she had failed him. He dressed in silence all the time, avoiding her eyes. If he could just get out of here, he would regain some of his self-esteem. "Sorry, Alex," he said again.

"So am I," she replied.

As he let himself out of her house, he vowed to give the local department store a wide berth for a while. The affair was dead before it had ever got started. He headed for the squash courts, needing some violent action to get rid of his damaged ego. That was also a disaster. He got a game with one of the younger and more inexperienced players and got beaten! The young man left the court with a Cheshire cat smile, and again, Drew tasted failure.

He had stopped calling friends after he got the note. He had fended off Marty and Caro with vague explanations about a woman's mid-life crisis. The letter had been postmarked Birmingham, but they didn't know anyone in Birmingham. He couldn't think why she had gone there, but he knew he would never be able to find her till she wanted to be found.

He had taken some leave. After the advertising coup he had pulled off, all the hard work had been done, and Adam could cover anything else that came up. Due to the long hours he had been putting in, the company was not surprised at his request for leave, and all wished him a good holiday.

The only one who got on his back was Cassie. She kept tackling him about Jessica not contacting her. In the end, he told her she had gone to stay with friends. Cassie didn't seem to be mollified and pestered him for more details until Adam intervened and told her to stop nagging. Drew got the impression that Cassie was not going to let it rest there and hoped to have some more details about Jessica's whereabouts by the next time he saw her.

He had put aside the whole afternoon for Alex. But now, even after the squash game, he was still left with time on his hands. After rejecting the cinema and a meal, both of which were no fun alone, he decided to go home. The house was now a bit of a tip. Drew had never been expected to help in the house, not by his mother or Jessica, and he didn't have a clue how things were done. He had managed to change the bed linen. Putting the new cover on the duvet had nearly driven him crazy. After wrestling with the thing for what seemed like hours, he had lost his temper, swirled it around his head and slung it across the room, breaking a bottle of aftershave on the dressing table and stinking the house out. He mopped it up and threw away the glass but saw later that it had taken all the stain out of the wood and left a horrible great patch.

The garden looked like a jungle. The grass was about a foot high and weeds were in glorious profusion all along the patio. If this situation continued, he would have to look for a cleaner and a gardener. *Yes,* Drew thought. *That's what I'll do this afternoon. I'll get my life in order. Prove to Jessie when she comes back that she's not indispensable and everything's ticked along without her.* None of their local friends employed cleaners or gardeners that he knew of, but he finally hit pay dirt from the small ads section in the local paper.

After several phone calls, he had arranged for three gardening firms and two domestic agencies to call the next day. He allowed himself a small smile of satisfaction as he rinsed out a coffee cup from the pile in the sink and made himself a cup of instant.

Now what can I do, he thought. *I'll wash the car. I can manage that, and lord knows it needs it.* He had just rolled out the hose after changing into old tracksuit bottoms and a t-shirt when Will, Elizabeth's husband, pulled into the drive next door.

"Hi, Drew, no work today?"

"Took some time off now that big contract under my belt," Drew replied, trying to look too busy to chat.

"Jessica back from her friends yet?"

"Not yet. Sometime soon," Drew said, walking over to the tap.

"From the look of the garden, it looks like you miss her," Will chortled.

"Got that all sorted now. Getting it all done this week. Wouldn't do for Jessie to come home and rake me in for all the donkey work, would it?"

The grin on Drew's face felt like rigour mortis, and he wished the loud, brash fart would clear off. He'd never liked him, and now even less. Will must have finally got the point when Drew turned on the hose and went around to the other side of the car. He watched for a few moments, then started walking towards his front door.

"See you soon, mate," he shouted.

Not if I see you first, MATE, Drew thought. "Yeh, see you," he replied tightly.

Sometime later Adam phoned and pressured Drew into going to a stag night at the golf club. "Come on, Drew, we've always had a good time. Do you good to lay one on."

"Oh, Adam, I don't know. I've got things I really need to sort."

"Bloody hell, never thought I'd see the day when I had to beg you to go out and get drunk and drool over some stripper's pussy."

"OK, if you insist." Drew tried to force a smile into his voice.

"Good man. Get a taxi and I'll meet you there at eight."

Adam rung off, and Drew wondered if he could plead a headache and not go. *Even I couldn't get away with that,* he thought with a wry grin.

CHAPTER 10

Later, Drew wished he had eaten something before leaving the house. The whiskey was churning around in his stomach and threatened to erupt any minute. He staggered to the men's room and splashed his face with cold water.

The comedian had been very blue, and most of his remarks had been aimed in a very derisive fashion at women's private parts in general. Usually, he laughed, but when the comedian started on about a poor bastard who couldn't get it up, Drew went some way to understanding why women fought so hard against the demeaning and insulting attitude of a lot of the male population.

Perhaps the women who had tiny breasts, buck teeth, or any other defects died a little at being the butt of someone's jokes, even if unintentionally, as he had a moment ago when his problem was laughed at. *Christ, whatever was eating him? The last of the male chauvinists and he was starting to develop a conscience in his forties. Time to do something about it.*

He went back to the party. The first of the strippers was on. She had a mane of white-blond hair and was wearing a black basque, stockings, and suspenders. Most of the men were howling and whooping already. The stripper seductively unhooked the basque with a little help from the guy in the front row, who was already pissed as a fart. She peeled off the basque slowly, a bit at a time, and swung it around her head in an arc, throwing it behind her. The mini panties were also black, and her breasts were well-formed but fairly small.

"Bloody hell," the bloke next to Drew said, spraying him with spittle at the same time. "If my old lady had tits that size, I'd send her back to her mother and ask for my money back."

Drew forced a laugh and looked at the speaker. He had thinning mouse-coloured hair, baggy eyes, and a gut hanging over the waistband of his trousers. His shirt had a top button undone, exposing a few straggly chest hairs, and he stank of sweat. *The great British lover,* Drew thought, his lip curling.

The stripper had rolled down her stockings and peeled them over her feet, throwing them on top of the basque. The suspender belt was unhooked. She passed it between her legs, sliding it backwards and forwards and locking her lips suggestively at the same time. Drew looked again at the bloke beside him. His eyes were almost glazed over, his mouth was slightly open, and he had a flushed look about him.

I'll bet he'll be the first one out of here later. His 'old lady' won't know what's hit her when he gets home tonight. It'll be the only time he'll get it up this month, Drew thought with distaste.

Adam was frantically beckoning him up to the front table, so Drew pushed his way through the baying throng of men.

"Come on, Drew, what the hell is wrong with you tonight? Why are you right at the back?"

Drew had, on many previous occasions, got 'in on the act,' as it were. The do's were always private, and he had enjoyed showing off. He downed his double whiskey in one swallow and moved down to the front table.

"Get in there, Drew," came from all around him, but he waved his hand dismissively and sat down. He downed the whiskey waiting for him amid disappointed remarks from all around him.

The stripper failed to enlist anyone else's help and left the stage, swirling her panties over her head. She was really a brunette, Drew noticed.

As the party continued, so did the supply of drinks. Drew's head was spinning, and he couldn't seem to concentrate on what people were saying. He really didn't feel in the mood for this. He tried to watch the next stripper, but the long feather thing she kept swirling around was making his head pound.

Adam slapped another drink down on the table in front of Drew. "Come on, mate, you're lagging behind the rest of us."

Drew raised the glass, got a smell of the whiskey and his gorge rose. He shoved everyone aside in his dash for the men's room. He almost made it to the bowl before throwing up. The vomit gushed from him in a fountain and forced its way down his nose. When the worst of it was over and the dry retching had subsided, he sat on the floor with his head back against the wall, feeling shaky and shivery. The black feeling of depression descended again. Adam found him there sometime later and put him in a taxi.

CHAPTER 11

Jessica waited four long days before she heard from Stacey. During that time, the weather had changed. It got cold and blustery, and Polly put the heating back on. The Aga in the kitchen made short work of the chill and was the nicest place in the house to be.

The second day, the rain started, and the two women got soaked to the skin, seeing to the goats and chickens and walking the two dogs. Buster the Labrador usually went with John, but he was getting old now, and his old bones didn't like being out in the rain too much. As soon as he realised the Aga was on again, Buster took up his favourite position at the side of it. Polly constantly had to prod him to stop snoring. His only answer was several thumps of his tail before resuming a regular snore. After a while, Polly gave up.

"I think it's a lost cause." She smiled, looking fondly at the faithful old dog. Buster lifted one eyelid as if he knew she was talking about him, thumped his tail again, and went back to sleep.

The other dog was Chad, who was a little terrier, not quite a Jack Russell, but nearly. He was young and full of beans but not a dog to be petted. John had worked him to search out rats or other rodents on the farm, and Chad was one of the best. If he felt like being fussed, he would ask for it by pushing his muzzle into someone's hand or standing up on his hind legs. The rest of the time, everyone had a healthy respect for Chad's personal space or risk getting nipped.

There was a motley assortment of cats around like every farm. A couple of house cats, but the rest roamed around the barns and came to the back door when their bellies were empty. Silver was a beautiful fat grey tabby and was almost part of the furniture. She spent two-thirds of her day snoozing on the window sill but would find a space on someone's lap as soon as they sat down. She never seemed to do much and looked down on the cats in the yard as if she thought they were beneath her.

Charlie was the other house cat and was always busy, constantly moving in and out all day. When out, he would plead to come in. When in, he fussed to go out. Whoever was in the kitchen seemed to spend most of their day opening the back door for Charlie. The highlight of his whole week was when the back door was left open and he could sit on the doorstep, neither in nor out.

John had come home drenched and cold despite his oilskins. Polly ran him a hot bath and fussed around him.

"Do stop fussing, woman," he growled. "Anyone would think I was made out of ice cream."

"I don't want you to get sick, sweetheart."

Polly ladled out a steaming bowl of beef and tomato soup and added croutons.

"You had bronchitis last winter and worried me to death."

"Don't worry, Pol, you sexy piece you, I'm going to live long enough to be a dirty old man and spend my retirement in bed with you all day. What do you think of that then, wife?" He slapped her bottom, and she punched his arm.

John snapped his teeth at Polly's bum as she passed his chair. She shot away sideways from him, and he burst out laughing. Jessica was also grinning. She felt so relaxed with them but knew that she would have to find a place of her own soon. It wasn't fair to wear out her welcome.

Neither of them would take any money from her, so she kept on buying them gifts. A couple of best-sellers for John to read, perfume, bath oil, and a very see-through and lacy nightdress for Polly, which

John couldn't wait to see on and then couldn't wait to get off. The two women laughed about it the next morning, but there was a glow about Polly that told Jessica the gift had been much appreciated.

On the fourth day, Stacey telephoned. "I've spoken to our head office and told them that it's very urgent to have this vacancy filled before the rush," Stacey told her. "The head office is sending down the personnel manager Alan Todd to do the interviewing. I recommended you, but they want to see a few others as well, so the ads going in the local paper this week. Can you come by and fill out one of our job application forms so I've got it by me? I'd really like you for the job, but it's out of my hands now. However, I'm going to have a quiet word with Alan himself when he comes down. He's a nice bloke, and when I started, he was very kind."

"Oh, thanks so much, Stacey. I'd really like this job, and anything you can do to help will be great," Jessica said. "I'll be by later on today for the form, and I'll get it back to you tomorrow."

The rain had finally stopped, and Polly had walked over to help John move the cows to another field, so Jessica showered, changed, and left a note for Polly saying where she'd gone.

Her car spluttered a bit when it started. She hadn't used it much in the last few days; they always seem to use the Range Rover. *I must take it for a run,* Jessica thought as she headed for the complex. The reception desk was unmanned, so she rang the bell. Stacey came out from the office and smiled a welcome.

"That was quick; I didn't really expect you till later. Polly with you?"

"No, she's helping John today, so I popped over on my own."

"Well, you just timed that right. You can keep me company over a cup of coffee. I'll just ask Alice to keep an eye on reception and get my bag."

They strolled around the corner to the coffee shop and found a seat by the window. Stacey sunk into the chair with a sigh.

"The sooner they find someone for reception, the happier I'll be. I'm really getting behind with the office work, having to run backwards and forwards all the time. I really hope you get the job. I feel I know you, and God knows we could do with a friendly face."

"Oh, Stacey, I don't know," Jessica said, stirring her coffee thoughtfully. "It's been so many years since I worked. I haven't got any qualifications. I see all your bookings are done on a computer. Marty and Caro always had them, but I never learnt."

"Can you type?" Stacey said, cutting into her Danish.

"Well, yes, I did most of my husband's correspondence, and he insisted it looked professional."

"Then you should have no trouble with our computer. It's fairly basic and once you know the right buttons to press to bring up the menu and the files to find what you're looking for, it's all pretty straightforward. At the press of a button you can find out who's booked what and for when, and add any new bookings as they come in. All simple stuff. Anyway, we are hardly going to chuck you in at the deep end without any kind of training, and besides, I'm only the other side of the door."

Jessica gazed out of the window at a group of kids kitted out with towels on their way to the pool.

"Do you think I've got a chance? I ran my eyes over this application form while you were getting the coffees, half of it doesn't seem to relate to me at all. Most of it seemed to be about A levels and other exams."

"Don't worry about it," Stacey said with a grin. "We have a lot of staff employed here who have said the same thing, but they still got the jobs. Personality and an aptitude to learn is just as important in this line of work, plus being able to turn your hand to helping out all round, and getting on with the assortment of people you'll meet."

"OK, I'll give it a go. When do you expect the guy from head office?"

"Alan phoned today. He's due to come down for his monthly visit anyway, so he's going to do the inspection at the same time and thinks he'll probably get here sometime tomorrow."

Jessica picked up her bag and keys and stood up. "Well, I'd better get my head down over this, I suppose. It'll take me all of twenty-four hours to remember dates, times, and places of my youth for this form."

Stacey looked down and cleared her throat. "Before you go, Jessica, can I ask you a very personal question? You don't have to answer if you don't want to," she said quickly, looking up at her. Jessica sat down.

"Ask away," Jessica said, knowing what was coming.

"Well you are obviously married, but you obviously don't live locally as you are staying with Polly, but is there a Mr. Cameron, or are you divorced?"

Jessica cupped her chin in her hand and stared unseeingly out of the window. She took a while to answer, and Stacey waited in silence. Jessica straightened up. "Let's just say I'm having marital difficulties, and I need a while to get myself sorted out."

"Do you think you will?" Stacey said, toying with a coffee spoon. "I'm just enquiring really because I wouldn't like to see you get the job and then in a few weeks' time, when we're busy, you decide you're going to go back to wherever."

"No, you were right to ask. It wouldn't be fair for me to do that." Jessica took a deep breath. "I don't think I will be going back."

CHAPTER 12

Jessica kept herself busy over the next two days and tried not to wonder about the job. There was always plenty to do around the farm. After making the decision not to go back, at least for a while, finding a job was the first priority. If she could do that, she would have climbed the first rung of the ladder of independence. That would enable her to find rented accommodation somewhere and go up another rung.

Thoughts of Drew were always with her. She had picked up the phone to call him on numerous occasions, once even dialling the number and hearing it ring. Then, she nearly threw the mobile across the room as a feeling of sick dread made her hands shake. *No, not yet,* she thought. *I'm not strong enough to hear his voice yet.* Since then, she had not been tempted.

Stacey phoned three days later. Jessica could hear the smile in her voice as she said, "Well, my friend, you've got yourself an interview."

Jessica's stomach lurched, and she sucked her breath in. "When?" was all she could get out.

"Tomorrow afternoon at three thirty, if that's OK."

"Oh, Stacey, that's great. Thanks so much for everything. Even if I don't get it, I'm really grateful; you've been so good to me."

"Well, Alan has seen a few and hasn't been impressed by anyone yet. So you've got every chance in the world."

"God, Stacey, what do I wear? I haven't been to an interview in years."

Stacey let out a bark of a laugh. "Gracious me, you always look so good you could wear a sack and get away with it. Just pop on whatever you feel comfortable in."

"Right, I'll be there. All dressed up and ready to go. See you tomorrow, and thanks."

After a fairly sleepless night, the day seemed equally as long.

"Bloody hell, Jessie," Polly growled. "I've been speaking to you for the last five minutes and you haven't heard a damn word I've said. How much longer have I got to talk before your ears unblock? Anyone would think you were waiting for a death sentence."

"Sorry, sorry, sorry," Jessica said, trying to recall one item of Polly's conversation, and failing.

"What did you say? Never mind," Polly said, lighting a cigarette. "I never say anything earth-shattering anyway. I don't suppose you'd take it in if I repeated it."

Jessica had washed her hair, and it hung down her back. "My hair is really getting on my nerves lately. The ends are all split and it's too long. Wonder what I'd look like with a style like yours."

"Great, I should think," Polly said unexpectedly.

Jessica looked at her quickly. "Well, you've changed your tune. Whenever I've mentioned having it cut before, you always talked me out of it. Like that time, I was on holiday here, and we spent hours getting the bits out of it after haymaking. I wanted to cut it then, and you nearly cried."

"That was then, and this is now."

"What's that supposed to mean?" Jessica's voice took on an edge.

"All right, Jessie, don't get into a shit. I just meant that you've had the same style for years, and quite frankly, whether you like it or not, it's beginning to look a bit dated."

"When I'm ready to have it cut, I will, and not before," Jessica said primly.

Polly burst out laughing. "OK, madam, forget that I spoke."

"Sorry, Poll, guess I'm a bit strung out."

At three o'clock, Jessica was ready. She'd tried on and rejected nearly every outfit she'd bought with her. After consultation with Polly, she decided on a simple light jersey dress with a cowl neckline in ivory, with a black handbag and shoes. Her hair had sent her crazy. It wouldn't stay up and didn't feel secure. She was finally ready to go. As the car drove out of the yard, Polly breathed a sigh of relief. *Thank goodness, I'll never have to go through that,* she thought. *I'd have died of a heart attack by now.* She let Charlie out and started to prepare some vegetables. "Better be here when she gets back. I might have to hold the tissue box or open the wine."

"You're nice and early," Stacey said as Jessica walked into reception. "He's got someone with him, but he's running pretty well on time. Which means he hasn't found anyone worth keeping longer than their allotted time. A good sign for you, I'd say."

Jessica sat down feeling very shaky. "God, why do I feel so nervous? I normally behave calmly and controlled. Right now I am feeling like a teenager before her first date," Jessica said in a small voice.

"You'll be fine," Stacey said, coming round to the counter and sitting down in the next chair. "The waiting's always the worst bit of everything."

The door to the office opened and a tall blonde walked out smiling. "Thank you for your time, Mr. Todd," she said over her shoulder. "I'll look forward to hearing from you." She smiled at Stacey and swung out through the door, leaving a heavy waft of expensive perfume behind her.

Stacey stood up and went through to the office. A few minutes later, she opened the door and beckoned Jessica over. "Good luck."

She smiled and winked.

Jessica walked into the room, trying to look assured and confident. Alan Todd had his back to her and was pouring out a cup of coffee from the machine. He was dressed in a charcoal grey suit and had almost black hair that was thick and lustrous.

"Please sit down," he said, still with his back to her. "All this talking has given me a dry throat."

He turned around and a quiff of hair fell over his tanned forehead. He ran his fingers back through his hair, looking at her. Jessica's attention was drawn immediately to his waistcoat. It was a riot of red and blue swirls on a grey background. The outrageous waistcoat overshadowed the conservative suit and tie. She had a fleeting thought that a therapist would have a field day with this one.

Alan Todd sat down and glanced at her application form. When he looked up and smiled, Jessica got another shock. She met the merriest eyes she'd ever seen. The lines at the corners of his eyes crinkled, and she had never believed that eyes could twinkle except in books, but these did. She felt her stomach unclench a bit.

"Well, Mrs. Cameron, what makes you think you're what we're looking for in a receptionist?" He leant back in his chair and sipped his coffee.

Now for it, Jessica thought. She took a deep breath. "I have no official qualifications, but I can deal with people, young or old. I'm organised and methodical and, for the most part, cheerful." She remembered Mrs. Creed. "After a family has travelled a long way, I think they need to be greeted by a friendly face and a bit of help to settle their frayed nerves. I know what it's like to travel a long distance with children, so if their arrival is dealt with smoothly and with the minimum of fuss, it makes the complex seem well run and efficient, as well as starting the holiday off well. Also, if they have any complaints while they are here they need to be listened to and the problem dealt with quickly. I'm not familiar with the computer, but

I can type, and I'm sure it won't take me long to learn."

Alan Todd put his cup down and clasped his hands lightly in front of him. For the next twenty minutes, he fired rapid questions at her. Jessica kept her cool and answered them all honestly and truthfully. He leant back and looked at her. "Would you like a cup of coffee?" he said, smiling.

"Yes, please," Jessica replied.

The next fifteen minutes were spent in general chit-chat about the complex. Alan Todd had been involved with it from the start and had a very soft spot for it. It always gave him pleasure every time he visited, and he agreed with Jessica that the first face the visitors saw should be a happy but professional one. He concurred that hers would suit very nicely and then asked her when she could start.

"I didn't think you would let me know today," Jessica stammered. "Thank you very much."

"It doesn't seem much point beating around the bush. I'm only here for a short time. I'll get Stacey to contact the other applicants, and we'll start you on a three months' trial period. The salary you already know and it will be up for review later on this year."

Alan Todd stood up and shook Jessica's hand. "Congratulations, Mrs. Cameron, I hope we'll get along fine."

Outside, Stacey looked concerned when she saw Jessica's face. "Oh my God, you look at white as a maggot. Was it that bad?"

"I start on Monday," Jessica whispered.

"Whoop, whoop," Stacey shouted.

The office door opened. "Could we have a bit of decorum in front of the new staff, Stacey?" said Alan Todd with a wide grin.

"Yes, sir," said a beaming Stacey.

And Jessica became a working woman.

CHAPTER 13

The light hitting the outside of Drew's eyelids hurt his head. He had a sour taste in his mouth, and when he moved, the crick in his neck from sleeping awkwardly caused him to cry out, which hurt his head some more. He very gingerly sat up and straight away fell back in the bed again. *Christ, I'd really laid one on.* The pounding in his head was like a heartbeat, and he knew it would last for the whole day. He never used to suffer from hangovers. Now, they were positively evil.

After a few minutes, he got up and made his way to the bathroom. His eyes were mere slits against the light. He had fallen into bed without drawing the curtains, and the sunshine streamed in the window and was crucifying him. The bathroom was also bathed in sunshine, and he quickly drew down the blind. *This must be how Dracula felt in the morning,* he thought, scrabbling around in the cabinet for some tablets.

He stood under the shower for a long time, hoping it would revive him. It didn't. He felt slightly better after cleaning his teeth, trying to rinse out his mouth without bending over which made the pounding in his head worse. He dragged out some jeans and walked slowly and carefully downstairs.

He made a pot of filter coffee, but couldn't wait for it to finish filtering, and made a cup of instant while he was waiting. He was sitting at the kitchen table nursing his coffee and feeling very fragile when the doorbell rang. He stood up too quickly and felt the top of his head nearly lift off.

Who the bloody hell is this so early in the morning, he thought and made his way to the door, glancing at his watch. It wasn't early; it was already ten thirty. The woman at the door was fiftyish and a bit plump, and when she spoke, her voice rang through his head. "Mr. Cameron," she screamed.

"Yes, what can I do for you?" he said very quietly, his head held at an angle like a tortoise coming out of its shell.

"More what I do for you," she boomed.

"I'm sorry, I'm a bit slow this morning. Should I know you?"

"I came from a cleaning agency; I told to call on you."

Oh, Christ. He'd forgotten about all this lot arranged for today. "You'd better come in," he said, standing aside.

She bustled in and stood in the hall, waiting for him to close the door. He ushered her into the lounge and waved her into a seat.

"You want me look around," she shouted in broken English with an accent he couldn't place.

"Yes, please do. Would you like a cup of coffee?"

"In a minute, when I finish look." She plonked her bag on the floor and went off to inspect the house.

The tablets were working; her voice didn't seem so loud. He went through to the kitchen and topped up his coffee from the filter jug. She found him a few minutes later when she swept into the kitchen.

"Help yourself to coffee," he said, flapping his hand in the general direction of the machine.

"This beeg house," she said, sitting opposite him. "It need good woman."

"I had a good woman," Drew said dejectedly.

"Good woman hard to find, why you let go?"

They were talking at cross purposes, but Drew, in his misery, didn't realise that. "She left," he muttered. "She bloody up and left. Took all her clothes and bloody well buggered off."

"Ahh…. The missus we talk about," the woman said, looking sad. Drew suddenly saw that she thought the previous cleaning lady had left.

"Yes…anyway, how much is this lot going to cost me if I take you on."

She went back into the lounge and came back with her bag. "This agency costs," she said, handing him the sheet.

He focused his eyes with great difficulty and sucked in his breath at the price. "Does this include laundry?" he said, trying to stop the small print on the form from wavering about.

"If you want," she said, eyeing the washing machine. "Sophia always do for customers long as machine here."

"OK, Sophia, when can you start?" Drew knew he ought to see the other agency first, but really felt he wasn't up to it today.

"I start a bit today…that if you want. One of my other people go away, have free time now."

Drew hoped she wouldn't make a noise, but the place needed something done, so he agreed.

"You have bad drink last night?" she enquired kindly.

"No, I had a good drink," Drew said, looking at her. Her eyes were black and shiny and smiling. Suddenly, he knew they were going to get on.

"Sophia fix you good. My second husband liked drink sometimes. I fix you dog hair."

"You mean hair of the dog, and how many husbands have you had?" Drew was suddenly curious.

"Three husbands…six children," Sophia said, opening the

cupboards.

"Six!" Drew exclaimed. "My God, you're a glutton for punishment.

"Nights long and cold in England," was Sophia's reply.

The concoction she made for him had warm milk, beaten egg, and a faint smell of whiskey. His stomach lurched, but she stood over him until he finished it all. He managed, much to his surprise, to keep it down and admitted a little later that he was feeling a bit less fragile.

Sophia busied herself upstairs. She seemed to know where all the cleaning stuff was kept without him having to tell her, and to her credit was fairly quiet. When she vacuumed, she closed the doors behind her to muffle the sound. *Yes,* Drew thought, *they were going to get on.*

At twelve thirty, the first gardener turned up. He looked a bit grubby, but Drew thought they all looked like that. He showed him around the garden, and the man kept sucking his teeth and grunting.

"Well," Drew said impatiently. "What are your charges for doing the work on a regular basis?"

"This is a big place," the man said, scratching the stubble on his chin. "Which firm did all this before?"

"My wife did all the gardening," Drew said, moving over into the shade.

"Must have had her work cut out. She decide it was too much for her, I suppose."

Drew didn't feel like giving the bloke chapter and verse and didn't answer. Finally, he came up with a price that Drew thought was astronomic. *I'd rather do the bloody thing myself than pay this grubby sod half of that price,* he thought. *It's a rip off.*

"I'll let you know," Drew said again.

"You won't get a better price for a garden this size," he said defensively.

"I'll let you know," Drew said again and ushered him out.

An hour later, the doorbell rang again. The man standing outside was dapper and grey with a neat little moustache. His overalls were clean and pressed, and he stood ramrod straight, almost with a military bearing. "Mr. Cameron?" he enquired.

"That's me," Drew said, smiling.

"Good afternoon, sir. My name is James Greenham; you called me about the garden."

Drew almost expected him to salute. "Please come in. I'll take you straight through."

"Yes, sir, I looked at the front garden on my way in." He wiped his shiny, polished shoes unnecessarily on the mat and followed Drew out through the kitchen.

"Oh, this is lovely, or it will be when it's tidied." He wandered about, muttering about greenflies on the roses and moss on the lawn. He came back to Drew and stood in front of him. "This is a very well-stocked garden, Mr. Cameron. It won't take much to put it to rights again. It will be a pleasure to work here."

"Come in and have some coffee and we'll talk," Drew said, opening the back door.

"If it's alright with you, Mr. Cameron, I'd prefer tea. My Elsie, the good lady wife, says coffee is bad for me. Makes me hyperactive."

That I'd like to see, Drew thought, hiding a smile. "Do you always do what your wife tells you?" he enquired.

"Oh yes, Mr. Cameron, she's bigger than me. Most people are," the little man said dryly. Drew chuckled and put the kettle on.

It turned out that James Greenham was retired and loved gardening. When he and his wife sold their house and downsized into a flat that was smaller and cheaper to run, he missed the garden so much that he took up doing other people's gardens. This gave him some extra money doing a job he loved and got him out from under Elsie's feet.

Drew liked him, and when the job was priced, he realised what a rip off artist the previous bloke had been. He employed this neat little man and was invited to call him Jim. After he left, Sophia shooed him out of the kitchen.

"He nice man," she nodded, "he work for one of my other people. Do good job."

"I'm sure he will," Drew said with a smile, feeling now that he was at last coming to grips with his upset life.

CHAPTER 14

idway through the following morning, whilst Sophia was blitzing the lounge, the phone rang. Drew was getting paranoid about answering the phone during the day. All the calls seemed to be for Jessica or yet another call from Elizabeth or Cassie. He was fed up making lame excuses to everyone, especially Cassie, who was asking in-depth questions about the state of their marriage until he told her it was none of her business and hung up on her.

Elizabeth missed no opportunity to nail him the minute he walked out of the house, and if he stayed in, she phoned. After her vitriolic attack on him at the motel, she had gone back, pleading with him to give it another chance. Her knowing looks and remarks with suggestive double meanings made him glance over his shoulder at Jim when she caught Drew in the garden. He was sure Jim had got the general drift of the conversation and glared at Elizabeth in embarrassment, trying with a look to shut her up. Now, the element of danger was gone; the novelty seemed to have gone out of the whole thing.

He decided to answer the phone rather than leave it to the machine.

"Dad, it's me," Caro said. "What the hell is going on between you and Mum? I got a phone call from Mum yesterday. She's got herself a job. You told me she was just going away for a few days for some rest. It doesn't seem like that now. I'm not a baby anymore, and I think you owe me a proper explanation."

"Where is she?" Drew said, sinking down on the seat beside the phone.

"I don't know, she wouldn't tell me. All she said was that the situation was such that she would rather not come home for a while. She wanted to please herself for a while, and we were not to worry about her."

"Oh, come on, Caro, she must have given you some kind of clue as to where she is. What kind of job she is doing? Your mother hasn't worked for years. You need some sort of experience to get any sort of work except the menial stuff." Drew's voice was gruff and abrupt, and his foot was jerking up and down with impatience.

Caro was quiet for a moment, and then she said, "Dad, were you having an affair?"

"What did your mother tell you?" Drew snapped.

"That's just it, nothing. But when I asked her if you were playing around again, the pause before she answered was just a fraction too long."

"Again, what do you mean again?"

"Christ, Dad, do you think Marty and I were blind all those years? We knew what was going on. For years, we've been watching you and all your nonsense. We watched all the secret glances, with loads of different women, all behind Mum's back. Marty and I used to take bets on how long it would be before you started to spend the night in town…on business…. We also heard Mum prowling around the house half the night and having a quiet weep when she thought we were asleep. But when you came home she was always happy and smiling for you. We couldn't understand how she managed it. Sometimes Marty and I found it very hard to be civil to you after seeing the strain Mum was under. You really have been a bastard to her for years. Maybe she decided at last to do something about it. I've spoken to Marty today, and he seems to think the affair must be something serious for Mum to leave now after putting up with the shit for so long. Is it?"

Drew felt sick. He felt very sick. As Caro had been talking, he started to tremble. His guts felt fluttery and shivery, and he felt a sheen of sweat break out all over him. His children taking bets as to when the next infidelity was going to take place. It was obscene. He thought he'd been so clever, and all the time, his children were getting more and more disgusted with him. No wonder they couldn't wait to leave home.

"Jesus Christ, Caro…what can I—" Then, to his horror, he started to cry.

There was no sympathy in Caro's voice. "It's a bit late for that now, don't you think? Spilt milk and all that. I've got a couple of days leave due to me, so I'm coming down tomorrow. I think it's about time we did some straight talking. I'm worried about Mum. For God's sake, pull yourself together, and I'll see you tomorrow. Marty's coming over on business soon, and he's trying to bring the trip forward. So you'll have some explaining to do to him too. I don't think he will be as gentle as me. I'll see you tomorrow…be there." With that parting shot, the phone went dead.

Drew sat there with the receiver in his hand for many minutes before placing it carefully back in the cradle. He felt unable to move until Sophia came out of the lounge. He'd forgotten she was there. She took one look at his face, squeezed his shoulder, and, bustling down the hall, said over her shoulder. "Sophia make tea, we talk if you want."

He didn't want to, but she came and fetched him, sat him down at the kitchen table, and poured them both a brimming mug of tea.

The tears were stuck in his throat like a lump of lead, and he had no chance of forcing the tea past it. He just sat, his head full of the things his daughter had said. When Sophia saw the big salty tears start sliding down his face, she moved around the table and he found his head clasped to her ample bosom. The tears were forced out of him in great, wracking sobs that hurt. He hadn't cried for years, not since the night when his children had been born. What a proud dad he'd been. Nothing was going to be too good for his kids. All the time he'd been smiling and laughing with them, they were losing respect for him and dying inside. Like Jessica must have been.

The tears went on for a long time. Sophia held him quietly, like a mother, until his shoulders relaxed and he slumped against her, feeling drained and hot. He finally sat up straight, and Sophia got some kitchen paper off the roll. He blew his nose loudly, feeling more than a little embarrassed and started sipping the tea. He started to try and explain and found it all came pouring out. He told the whole story to this woman, who was almost a stranger. Everything came out like a confession. Sophia clucked and tut-tutted a few times but said nothing until the long, sorry tale wound to a close.

"You love her," was the first thing she said.

Drew hesitated. "I suppose so."

"Not good enough," she said, standing up and filling the kettle again. "While you play with other women, you take away something from wife. I know; my number two husband not able to leave women alone. Every time it start, I know by his ways, and Sophia die a leetle inside. I love him much. I give him my whole life, and two babies, but still not enough. What more I can do? One night I follow heem and catch heem. I smash up whole room in girlfriend house. They took my children, and put me in hospital for nervous people. I stay there one year and half."

Sophia stood with her back to him, looking out of the window into the garden. "My children grow up without their mamma. My leetle one call my sister Mamma. He don't know me then, OK now he older, he understand. My sister have also children. She not watch over my daughter, and she get with child at fifteen year old. She looking for love and didn't understand what happen to her. I bring up baby for her so she finish school."

Drew sat there stunned. How could anyone leave this lovely woman with the glossy black hair and eyes. If she lost a couple of stones of weight, she would be beautiful. She WAS beautiful. In her youth, she would have been incredible.

"What about your present husband?" Drew enquired.

"My Alfie, he wonderful," Sophia said, her face lighting up as she topped up the teapot and brought it back to the table. "He meet me in hospital. He go home first, but visit me all the time. We good friends before lovers. One night it just happen, and he never go home again. He stay always with me. He work now back at hospital, he understand the people."

Drew sat deep in thought while Sophia loaded up the washing machine and switched it on. "Do you think she'll come back?"

"Don't know," Sophia said, sitting down again. "Your wife have much thinking to do. Maybe she find life on own better, maybe not. She not wish you to be with her now. She let you know when ready to talk. Nothing can do but wait."

What other choice have I got, Drew thought.

CHAPTER 15

Jessica walked across the car park towards her car with a spring in her step. This was the first positive thing she'd done for years, and she felt really good. As she got to her car, Viv turned up and parked in front of her. She had arrived for the early aerobics class and was dressed in skinny leggings and a tight vest with a long cardigan over the top. Her streaky hair was pulled back into a high ponytail; she looked glowing and healthy.

"Well, you look like the cat that got the cream," she said, locking her car.

Jessica told her about the job, and Viv gave her a hard hug. She told Jessica how pleased she was for her. They stayed chatting for a while and Jessica battled the whole time to skewer her hair back up. The breeze was blowing it all over her face. She bid Viv goodbye and unlocked her car. She hesitated and locked it up again. She walked along the canopied pathway to the hairdressers. Ann, the owner, was standing by the desk taking an appointment over the phone. She made a note in the book and rung off.

"Hello, what can I do for you? You're Polly's friend, aren't you?"

"Yes, I am," Jessica replied. "I was wondering how booked you are today. I really need a trim, this mop is driving me mad."

"Well, I've got a perm to finish off and a boy's hair to trim. That shouldn't take too long. If you could mark time for forty-five minutes, I could get you in today," Ann said, consulting the large open book in front of her.

"That's wonderful," Jessica said with a smile. "I'll go and have a coffee and sticky bun while I'm waiting; see you later."

After getting herself a cup of coffee, Jessica called Polly and gave her a blow-by-blow account of the interview. She explained she'd be a little late as Ann was going to trim her hair. Then, she proposed the idea of the three of them having a celebratory meal and drink to mark her successful interview. Polly thought it would be great and agreed.

"Hell, I'm so sick of cooking sometimes. I don't care if it's only fish and chips out of a paper."

"I think I can run to something a little posher," Jessica chuckled. "My treat."

"I'd better get out the old gold lame frock then, I suppose. Never thought I'd get to wear it again."

Jessica was smiling as she put the phone down. Her moods were improving. Forty-five minutes later, she was sitting in the chair by the wash basin with the cape around her, waiting for her hair to be washed.

"I washed it this morning," she told Pippa, the junior. "I think it will only need a wet."

"Right. Oh, I'll just wave the shampoo over it."

Pippa had a spiky hairstyle that seemed to defy the laws of gravity.

"How do you get your spikes to stay up all day?" Jessica said, looking up at Pippa's nostrils.

"Extra strong gel. My dad calls it super glue and tells me not to get too near or I'll have his eyes out." Pippa's gentle fingers massaged Jessica's scalp while she rinsed. "What a lot of hair you've got. I hope I've got all the soap out."

Jessica's head was wrapped in a warm towel, and Pippa took her over to the chair by the large central mirror.

"Ann won't be long," she said, going back to clean out the hair wash basin.

"Well, here we are," Ann said, taking off the towel. "How would you like it?"

Jessica stared at herself in the mirror. Her hair hung in heavy, wet strands down her back. "Cut it all off...."

Ann stood back from the chair and looked at Jessica in the mirror. She lifted a wet strand of hair up and let it drop. "Are you sure that's what you want? It's a drastic step, and I wouldn't want you to regret it. It's going to take years to grow it again."

"I'm fed up with it; cut it all off. Polly told me it was dated, and it is. I want to be free of it. I leave myself entirely in your hands. Polly and Viv's hair always looks terrific, so I trust you. You come highly recommended."

"Well," Ann said smiling, "how could I ever let you down now after that fantastic compliment."

As Ann started to cut, Jessica found her eyes filled with tears and had to look away. *Oh God, what if it looks awful? What am I going to do? A new job in the public eye, and I'm going to look like a freak. Don't be so negative,* she chided herself. *Ann knows what she's doing.*

As the heavy strands fell to the floor, Jessica's head felt lighter and lighter until she felt as though it didn't belong to her. She started to stare in fascination at herself. The heavy hair had disguised a wave and a bit of curl. The shorter the hair got, the more the wave developed. Ann thought it was super as it would help to hold the style. Jessica remembered her hair being curly when she was very young.

"A few highlights would look good," Ann mused, snipping away.

"Do it then," was Jessica's brief reply.

After the cut, the hair was roughly dried, and Jessica was taken to another part of the room. The bleach was bluey and was painted onto strands. Then, the hair was wrapped in pieces of foil. Layer after layer, the foils circled her head.

"I'll do the highlighting in several stages to give a sun-streaked effect," Ann shared her plan.

At last, Ann was happy with the various shades and the whole lot of 'gunge' was washed out and the hair conditioned. During the procedure, she instructed Jessica on how to take care of it when she came to wash it.

Finally, it was all finished, and Jessica sat up and looked at this strange woman in the mirror. The hair was cut short but fuller on the top tapering to very short at the back. A few wispy strands had been left longer to soften the neckline. The fringe was soft, and there were wisps in front of her ears. They had a light curl and were feminine and natural. The colour was a variation of dark and light blonde, with some almost white blonde streaks here and there. The style changed Jessica's whole appearance and made her eyes look darker, her cheekbones more pronounced, and her face a different shape.

Ann and Pippa both seemed extremely pleased with their work. When Jessica reached for her pearl earrings, Ann stopped her.

"Wait a minute, I've got just the thing to set off the style." Ann came back with a pair of earrings she had taken from the showcase by the door. They were gold ornamental filigree hoops. Jessica hadn't worn hooped earrings for years. Drew had said they looked tarty. Funny how all the other women he knew wore them.

To hell with what Drew likes or doesn't like, I think they are nice. "I'll take them," Jessica said.

"They do set off the style, and its time I got more adventurous than my boring old pearl studs."

Jessica felt like she bounced out of the salon. Twenty yards down the walkway, she met Alan Todd. He had taken off his jacket and the sun reflected off his colourful waistcoat. He gave a long, low whistle and walked slowly around her. "Well, well, well, I can hardly believe it. You look wonderful. If it hadn't been for the dress, I wouldn't have recognized you. What a change. I'm beginning to think you're far too glamorous for this place. One of our competitors will whisk you away if you're going to come to work looking like this."

Jessica felt the blush spread upwards from her chest and hung her head, feeling like a girl. Alan cupped her chin and lifted her head up. "Don't hang your head. Walk tall and proud, recognise it, use it."

Jessica looked into his twinkling eyes, and at the contact, couldn't look away. She felt a jolt right down to her toes. For long seconds, they looked deep into each other. Suddenly, his black eyes became serious and his hand reached out towards her. This movement broke the spell and Jessica fled to her car, muttering a goodbye. He stood there and saw her drive away.

CHAPTER 16

To say Polly was thunder-struck was an understatement. She was opening the back door for Charlie and had her back to the room.

"Bloody hell, I thought we were going to have to send out a search party for you. You've been gone hours. Come on, you bloody stupid cat, move your ass. I'm not going to stand here all day holding this pissing door while you make up your mind." With a gentle prod from Polly's foot, the cat finally made up his mind…and came back in! "I swear I'll strangle that caaa…. Oh my God, you did it." Polly had finally turned around. "John…John, come and look. She's had the chop!"

John, fresh from the bath and wrapped in a towelling dressing gown, came into the kitchen. "I thought only blokes had that done. Which bit did they chop off?"

Another long, low whistle, which made her think of Alan and she started blushing again. "Do you like it?" Jessica said, tentatively touching the back of her hair.

"Like it…I think it's terrific. Who did it? Ann?"

Jessica nodded.

"Well, she's certainly excelled herself this time. You look great, really great."

John seconded everything that Polly had said, then wanted to know if they could get the show on the road before he died of malnutrition and thirst. Both women hurried upstairs together to get changed, and John opened the back door to let Charlie out before following them.

They went along the coast road to one of the country pubs a few miles away. It was such a lovely evening; they sat outside and ate. John smacked his lips over his first pint and went off to order another. As it was Jessica's treat, she had opted to drive so Polly and John could enjoy a drink. The food arrived, and they ate heartily. After polishing off a large dollop of sticky toffee pudding with cream, Jessica was full to bursting. The evening started to get a bit chilly, so they moved inside. John got into a farming discussion with one of the regulars, and the two friends sat and chatted about nothing in general.

"Just going around the other bar a minute," John said over the top of everyone's head. "Got some machinery I'm interested in."

Ten minutes later, he was back. Jessica was so full she was feeling sleepy and Polly was also quiet.

"Look who I found," John shouted over the noise.

He stood aside to reveal Alan Todd. Jessica sat bolt upright, all drowsiness gone. "Alan, how good to see you. We heard you were down. Come and join us. We'll make room between us. Shove over, Jess. Nothing like a rose between two thorns."

"Yeh…nothing like." Alan smiled, wriggling down on the bench seat between the two women. "Hi, beautiful lady!" he said, turning to Jessica.

"Well, that's nice. I always used to be a beautiful lady. How fickle you are, Alan Todd."

Polly put on a pout and pretended to glare at him. They all laughed, although Jessica felt it was a trifle contrived. Her face was flaming and her thigh was burning through her skirt where Alan's leg lay against it.

What the hell is wrong with me? One look into a man's eyes and I go all silly. Jessica very carefully shifted in her seat to break the contact, but the leg returned and she couldn't move any further along, so there it stayed.

Alan had changed the conservative suit and fancy waistcoat for well-washed denim and a blue sweatshirt. He looked relaxed and at home. He was very good company, and before long, Jessica felt herself loosening up despite the continual press of his leg against hers.

It seemed that Alan's waistcoats were legendary. He had a whole collection of them and was always on the lookout for something different. The company at first frowned on them, but he won them all over in the end, and now the board members looked forward to seeing the next creation unleashed on the unsuspecting public.

"Come back for coffee, Alan," Polly said at closing time. "We see you so rarely that we want to make the most of it."

"Love to," Alan said. "I got a taxi here. Will you have room in the car?"

"We came in Jessie's tonight as we are the paid-for guests. We got our dinner in celebration of her job."

John shouted many goodbyes to the people streaming out to the car park. Polly and John scrambled into the back seat, and Polly squawked.

"Shut up, woman. Can't you remember what to do in the back seat anymore?"

"Not when we've got a nice comfortable bed at home," Polly replied, slapping his hand.

"You two never change," Alan chuckled. "When are you going to slow it down."

"When I'm in a wooden overcoat," growled John, getting another slap from Polly.

Alan's hand lay along the back of the seat and Jessica was sure she could feel the heat from it. She leant slightly forward and concentrated on the road. The two in the back were giggling like school kids, and although Jessica was used to their antics, tonight it was making her feel very uncomfortable. She wriggled in her seat and became aware of a feeling of wetness. She was sexually aroused. She couldn't believe it. She hadn't thought about or needed sex since she left home. Now, all of a sudden the thought was uppermost in mind. She couldn't wait to get out of the car.

My God, I only just hope I can keep away from him. I only met him a few hours ago and I'm getting turned on like something on heat.

Upon reaching home, Polly bustled about the kitchen, making coffee and laying out cheese and biscuits. *Oh, good Lord, this looks like it will be a long session,* Jessica thought, remembering signs from other times around the large table.

"If you'll excuse me a minute, I've eaten so much this waistband is killing me. I'll just go and change into something baggy." Jessica hurried upstairs. *A bit of a reprieve is all I need. Some distance between me and those black eyes.*

She splashed some water on her arms and chest and dug out a baggy tracksuit. Going back downstairs again, she felt more in control. That was until Alan's eyes raked her from head to foot, and he remarked that with the baggy tracksuit and her short hair, she looked small and sexy. She felt a clenching sensation in her groin.

Here we go again, she thought and went with the flow. *At least, I know I'm still female. Perhaps it's time to try pastures new. After all, what's good for the goose and all that?*

CHAPTER 17

Alan had been invited to stay the night. Jessica deliberately stayed in her room in the morning until she heard Polly take the Range Rover around to the front to pick him up. As they came out of the gate, she came down. Chad, the terrier, was pleased to see her and made a fuss around her legs. He was a dog with a streak of misery in him and seemed to take to Jessica, recognising one of his own. As she got less down in the dumps, Chad still stuck by her. She was the only one that Chad had ever taken to, and John was amazed.

"Miserable little bugger nearly had my fingers off last week and all I tried to do was pick him up. Look at him now. Looking at you like butter wouldn't melt in his mouth," John had said.

Jessica bent to smooth her hand over his head. Chad sat down and looked up at her under his eyelids. His stump of a tail wagged and he licked her arm. "You really are a softie, you know. Why do you put up such a macho act with everyone else? You'd get a lot more love if you weren't so aggressive, you know."

Chad's face looked tragic and made Jessica laugh. "What an actor you are," she chided him, helping herself to coffee from the jug.

Knowing Alan had been just down the hall had given her a very restless night. Her body wouldn't behave at all. At one point, she debated whether to go downstairs and make a drink but dismissed the idea as too risky. *What if he heard her and came down?* The state she was in, she would have leapt all over the poor guy. All night, she tossed and turned, her throat as dry as the Sahara, and finally dropped into a fitful sleep at dawn.

John's birthday bash was the coming week. The dinner had been postponed for a week as Barney, the chef, had to attend a funeral in Cornwall and was reluctant to delegate responsibility to the assistant. So, as Jessica would be at work next week, Polly suggested having a shopping trip. She wanted something new to wear and Jessica needed quite a few new things. The clothes she had brought with her had been mixed and matched so many times she was sick to death with them all.

Polly drove into the yard at the same time as John arrived for his breakfast. Jessica started cooking the thick slices of bacon that John insisted on. Polly had tried to tell him about the cholesterol etc, but it fell on deaf ears.

"If you want to eat birdseed for breakfast, then you carry on," he said, eying her bowl of muesli. "I need some substance to keep these weary old muscles working. Preferably something that won't make me fart all day."

So bacon and eggs stayed on the breakfast menu.

The women decided to drive to Bristol for their shopping trip and left the dishes in the sink to do later.

Jessica's new hairstyle took her all of five minutes to organise. A rake through with damp fingers pulled the wisps around her face, and it fell back into place. She applied slightly more eye shadow and mascara than she usually used, and her eyes took on a new depth. She borrowed a bright lipstick from Polly and, feeling pleased with her appearance, sashayed down the stairs.

"You look very sexy," Polly said, eying her up and down. "If it was my week for loving girls, I wouldn't let you out the door."

The shopping trip was tiring but successful. Both women were loaded to the gills by the time they got back to the car park. Jessica had found a wonderful little boutique selling long-flowing clothes that were ethnic in origin, with some bordering on hippy. The colours were muted and blended with subtle beading and embroidery. She was doubtful at first, but Polly loaded her arms up and sent her off to the changing room. They were totally unlike the classic clothes she was used to and gave her a whole new style of her own. The blends of brown, black, and deep burgundy made her hair look even blonder. Everything looked so comfortable and felt even better.

She also bought long ropes of beads and chunky earrings to finish off the outfits and spent far more than she had intended. Her remaining money had been put in the local bank, much to John's relief, but Polly paid for everything as the bank hadn't issued Jessica's cards yet. On the way out of the shop, Jessica stopped dead and looked at a lovely all-in-one catsuit hanging at the end of the rail.

"I've got to try that," she said to a groaning Polly.

She took her size back into the changing room and yanked all her clothes off again. "What do you think?" she asked Polly, throwing back the curtain a few minutes later.

The catsuit was very dark green, lightweight crushed velvet. The trouser part was unstructured and hung fairly loosely from a pleated waist. The shoulder line was gathered and embroidered, and the neckline was fairly high. When she turned around, it was completely backless, and Polly let out a gasp. "Oh, Jessie, you can't miss out on that one. It was made for you. What a turn-on. All modest in front and all sex at the back. Buy it, it's great."

The price was definitely a turn-off, but Jessica bought it anyway. *What the hell,* she thought, *I'm a working woman now.*

Polly's choice for the party was bought a little later after tramping through nearly every shop in Bristol. It was black and very plain but looked super on her. The top was vest-like and fitted her beautifully, and the skirt was calf-length, full and swirly. Pleased with all the goodies, they sat over a cup of coffee and a sandwich with their shoes kicked off under the table before heading home.

"By the way," Polly said as they turned out of the multi-storey car park. "Alan's decided to take a few days' leave next week, so he'll be coming to the party."

Jessica twisted her neck and stared at Polly, who caught the look.

"What?" she said.

"Nothing," Jessica muttered.

"He asked about you this morning."

"What did you tell him?"

"Only that you were trying to sort your life out."

"Did you tell him about Drew?" Jessica asked, feeling suddenly warm.

"No, of course not. He knew you were married from the application form. He just wanted to know how married you actually were. I told him if he wanted to know more, he would have to ask you himself."

"Tell me about him," Jessica said quietly.

Now, it was Polly's turn to twist her head around. "There something here I should know?"

"Just curious, that's all."

Polly looked at Jessica again and saw the flush. Her mouth curved into a grin. "You like him, don't you?"

"Oh, Polly, I just met the guy. Don't make it sound like something from Mills and Boon. All I wanted to know was a bit about him, not his inside leg measurement."

Polly chuckled, "Looking at the colour of your face, I'd say you'd have lots of fun finding out for yourself."

"Christ, Polly, I wish I hadn't asked."

"OK, OK, don't bite my head off. I'm only winding you up."

Polly drove on thoughtfully for a minute. She knew Jessica and sensed a tension in her that wasn't there before she mentioned Alan. *Hope this isn't going to get into a sticky situation, at least not until Jessie's talked to Drew,* she thought.

"John and I have known Alan for a while now, since the complex was started almost. He married late, after a short engagement. His wife didn't like the long hours he worked, and especially the days away putting the complex together. He stayed with us several times over the period the main recruiting was taking place. Every time he came off the phone after talking to her, he was angry and upset. Finally, she decided she could get by without him and went off with a banker several years her senior who had pots of money. Alan went through a lot of soul-searching, played the field a bit, and settled down to work even longer hours for the company. He was eventually offered a place on the board of directors, and since then, he seems to devote all his time to work."

"Has he got any children?"

"He's got a fifteen-year-old daughter at boarding school. He brought her down once during her school holidays. She has his dark colouring. Alan's parents are Italian. Marla is a really lovely young girl. Sensible and grown up. The boys were also home at the time and were nearly fighting over who got her company for the day. Alan loves her to pieces, and she loves him. It nearly breaks his heart every time she has to go back to school."

For the rest of the journey, both women were quiet. Each within their own thoughts. Jessica realised that Alan had crossed her mind on numerous occasions during the day and wondered if she had read something in his look that wasn't there. One deep, meaningful look, a few hours of his company, and she could not get the damned bloke out of her head. She felt an electricity between them. She might be out of practice with the chat-up lines, etc., but she hadn't imagined the chemistry. She'd just have to see what happened when she saw him again.

As Polly switched the engine off outside the house, she twisted sideways to look at Jessica. "My friend, stop me if I'm speaking out of turn, but from the conversation and your red face, I feel that there are some strong vibes running between you and Alan. He's really nice and a very attractive bloke, and God knows, with all the shit you've had from Drew, I wouldn't blame you if you two started something. However…don't use Alan as consolation. I wouldn't like to see either of you get hurt again. You are still fairly fragile emotionally and need a definite decision in your life before you can move on, and Alan has taken a long time to adjust to being on his own. He used a variety of women over a period of time to alleviate his loneliness, and some of them got badly burned by it. All I'm saying is, keep each other company if you must, but don't go in over your heads."

"Your remarks are heard and duly noted," Jessica said, not at all convinced that she would remember any of it.

CHAPTER 18

Drew's meeting with his daughter was fraught, to say the least of it. Caro was colder towards him than he could ever remember. She was relentless in her condemnation of his behaviour and was clearly very upset at the way things had turned out, though it seemed not entirely surprised. Even with her questioning of him, he managed to keep Elizabeth's name out of it. He was pretty low in his children's esteem as it was. If he had brought Elizabeth into it, he would have been lower than dog shit.

They went out to a local bistro to eat later that evening, and the mood lightened a bit among other people. Caro assured him she still loved him. After all, he still was her father, nothing would ever change that. But she really couldn't understand why he continually needed to have affairs.

"You know, Dad," she said over coffee. "I don't think you've really looked at Mum properly for years. She's an extremely beautiful woman. A lot of women her age look older than they are, you know, wrinkled and all that. But Mum looks good. She may not be the fanciest of dressers, but she always looks nice."

"I know," Drew replied.

"Do you, Dad, do you honestly? I frankly don't think you've really seen her for years. You look at her, but you don't see her."

"Of course I do," Drew replied sharply, getting a bit fed up with feeling like a prisoner in the dock and not at all convinced that Caro wasn't right.

He thought his daughter would have stayed the night, but she opted to travel home, preferring, obviously, to spend the weekend with her friends. At first, Drew felt rejected, but then he felt just a bit relieved. He wasn't sure he could cope anymore with lengthy discussions with this grown-up young lady who was his daughter.

After she left, the rest of the evening seemed to stretch interminably before him. He showered and donned a towelling robe meaning to get some work done before the following week. He dug a load of papers from his briefcase but just sat with them in his lap, gazing into space. The jangling of the phone next to him made him jump. He snatched up the receiver, "Hello, yes."

"Drew, it's Adam. I've been trying to get you all evening. Your mobile isn't switched on, so I kept ringing the landline."

"What's the panic?" Drew said, leaning back in the chair, his heart still leaping.

"Bloody Melanie, that's the panic."

"Who is Melanie?" Drew said, wracking his brains for the names of Adam's children.

"Melanie, Melanie, you dumbo. The girl in the ads. Sullivan won't sign anything until we've got her under contract and the bloody girl disappeared. Her flatmates don't know where she's gone, and the agency hasn't got a forwarding address for her. She's done a moonlight, and without that contract, this whole deal falls apart."

"Oh Christ, what the hell do we do now?" Drew ran his hands through his hair. "What about her parents? Have you tried them?"

"They don't even live in this country; they've lived in New Zealand for years. We got hold of their phone number from one of her flatmates and contacted them. They hadn't heard from her in weeks and were beginning to get a bit worried themselves. I covered every lead before I phoned you, but I haven't come up with a thing. I don't know what else to do."

Drew had been present when the commercials were filmed, but

he hadn't really spoken to the girl except to tell her what image he wanted her to project. She was a dark, sultry little thing with a lovely body. Drew had got a lot of pleasure from watching her work. She seemed to interpret his ideas professionally and quickly, but at the end of the day he had left without any further conversation.

He glanced at his watch. "It's too late to do anything tonight. Meet me in the office at ten tomorrow and we'll go over it and see if there's anything we might have overlooked."

"I don't think there is, but we'll have a go. Maybe you can shed some light on the reason for her buggering off. She could have been laughing all the way to the bank, and she's chucking it all down the drain. Stupid bloody girl."

"Yeah, OK, well, I'll see you tomorrow."

Adam hung up, and Drew sat and ruminated on why a model struggling to get known amongst fierce competition would land a chance of a life time and then run away. *Must be something serious.* Drew hoped she was OK. *Better also try the police tomorrow, just in case.*

He picked the papers up and tried to concentrate, then realised how futile it was. *If the girl didn't turn up, all the work would be for nothing. Dam the girl, just when everything was sewn up. What could be so bad in her life? For God's sake. She'd got it made. What the fuck did she want to run off for. Nothing was ever resolved by running away.*

Jessica did, a little voice in his brain said. Drew sat on the floor, and his mind wandered back and forth. Nothing was making any sense. In the end, he climbed slowly up the stairs and went to bed.

Adam was already there when Drew let himself into the office. Everything was so quiet when the phones didn't ring, and the computers had ceased their clattering.

"Christ, Drew, you look a bit baggy around the edges. I thought a holiday was supposed to do you good."

"Good morning to you too, Adam," was Drew's abrupt reply.

"Oh shit, Drew, if you going to give me a hard time, you might as well bugger off back home. I've got enough on my plate without having to deal with prima donnas. It's your own bloody fault if Jessie left you."

Drew's head shot up. "Who told you that?" he barked.

" Oh, for fuck's sake, don't give me all that innocent shit. We knew right from the beginning. All these years, Jessie's never been anywhere without you for any longer than a few days, and suddenly she's gone, and you take leave without going anywhere. It doesn't need someone with a Mensa membership to figure that lot out."

"Huh…I suppose that gabby wife of yours has been running off at the mouth again. You need to put her in her place."

"Like you did with Jessie," Adam shot back at him.

Drew stopped and looked at his friend. In all the time he had known him, Adam had always been on his side. Right or wrong. They only had differences over work, and they never lasted long. Now, suddenly, they were daggers drawn.

"Sorry, mate," Drew said quietly. "I should have known you'd see through all the bullshit. I'm having a hard time with the kids, and I don't even know what to tell them. How can I reassure them when I don't even know where she is? I've had one short note from her and nothing else. She phoned Caro, but she wouldn't even tell her where she is. The only thing I can do is wait. I've tried everyone I know and got nowhere."

Adam's fingers made a rasping sound as they scratched the stubble on his unshaven chin. The sound was loud in the silent office. "Sorry, Drew. Didn't mean to go off at you. I don't know what to say. Cassie said that Jessie knew you were carrying on. She said she'd known for years. I suppose we thought she'd accepted it and learnt to live with it. Is that the reason for her suddenly taking flight?"

Drew sat very quietly. He slowly stood up and stretched his back. "Elizabeth" was all he said.

Adam sucked in his breath, sunk into a chair, and covered his eyes with his hands. Drew watched him, noticing that the hair on the crown of Adam's head was thinning.

"Well, if you were going to break her, that was a sure way of doing it," Adam said, sitting up and leaning back in the chair. "How did she find out?"

"A note I left in my jeans," Drew answered, also sitting down.

Again, there was silence.

"I'm sorry to say, old friend, but I'd reckon this time you've burnt your boats."

"If I could just talk to her. This cut-off treatment is driving me mad. There's so much to sort out, and she can't even be bothered to speak to me. The kids are worried, I'm worried, and she's cut herself off from us all as if we mean nothing."

Adam stood up and walked over to the window. He looked out at the rooftops and thrust his hands deep into his pockets. "People do that. Cut themselves off when they are very hurt." He fell silent again. "Cassie had an affair, you know." The words fell like lead weights.

It was Drew's turn to suck in his breath. "I didn't know," was all he could say.

"I know you didn't." Adam turned around and leant against the window sill. "I really needed to talk to someone at the time, but I didn't think you would understand. I had a feeling your advice would have been to punch the bloke's lights out and file for a divorce. But I didn't want that.

"I love Cassie; I've always loved her. I just wanted to find out the reason for her doing what she did. There's usually a reason, you know. So, I started looking at our marriage, and what I saw made me stop and think. I was so busy trying to claw my way to the top that Cassie always took second place.

"She always looked beautiful but I never told her. The house always looked good, but I was always too tired to notice. Whenever we went anywhere, I always seemed to talk business and left her standing around and excluded from the conversation. So as soon as someone came along who thought she was sexy, feminine, and desirable, she fell hook, line, and sinker."

Adam started to pace about the room.

"Cassie's brother studied at university here before he went back to India to work. I was busy as usual, so Cassie flew over for his birthday on her own. She hadn't seen him for a long time. His best friend from uni was also there. He and Cassie got friendly. Whilst they were there, they saw quite a bit of each other and came back on the same flight. A long flight with plenty of time to talk. Lots of things in common. Language, tradition, places they had been.

"The guy was younger than Cassie and was intelligent and articulate. He was genuinely in love with her and fought tooth and nail to keep her, but then so did I. I started wooing her all over again. I began to really see her and liked what I saw. I couldn't even begin to imagine what my life would be without her and told her so. I had no shame and used the kids, my money, the house, my love…anything to get her back."

"Where the hell was I while this was going on?" Drew said, amazed at how he never had the slightest inkling of the pain Adam had gone through.

"Oh, I don't know." Adam passed his hands over his face. "I think you were chasing around with that Julie piece at the time."

Drew looked at Adam and felt a hollow feeling in the pit of his stomach. *How could you work so closely with someone for a long time and not sense their pain?* He felt a deep regret that Adam had not confided in him. "So she came back."

"Yes, she came back. For a while, the marriage was strange and shaky. I couldn't seem to get the image of her making love to someone else out of my brain. I would keep on seeing them twined together and my eyes kept filling with tears. It was sometimes very embarrassing, and I had to keep on making excuses to leave the room. I thought about pleading prostrate trouble." Adam grinned and then his face seemed to crumple. His shoulders shook and he covered his face with his hands.

Drew could never remember hugging another man before, but this time, he did it instinctively. He grabbed Adam in a tight bear hug and kept on holding him. He felt his own eyes filled with tears, and he let them fall for his friend and Jessica.

Adam gently pushed Drew away and, looking rather shamefaced, remarked that he hoped no one with a zoom lens was watching. Looking at Drew, he saw his face and silently handed him a tissue from the box on the desk. "I'm sorry I acted such a prat. We were talking about you and Jessie, not me. Don't know how I got sidetracked. Cassie and I are really trying hard, and I think we'll make it. It just takes a long time to heal. Cassie's affair was short-lived and was with someone I didn't know. With Jessie, the hurt is double-sided. Not only you but her close friend. That's going to take some forgiving.

"I wish I could reassure you a bit more, but I can't. I know how I felt; it was God-awful and gut-wrenching. You're going to have to face it. Jessie may never come back. I thought about leaving, just running away, but I couldn't. I had to fight, and I'm glad I did, but Jessie might have gone past the point of no return. You'll just have to wait and see."

Funny how Adam's words echoed Sophia's.

CHAPTER 19

After another lot of futile phone calls, Drew decided they should go and see Melanie's roommates. They found the address and headed off to Richmond. The flat was in a large block, and the lift was out of order. The two of them slogged up to the third floor, hoping that when they got there, someone would be home. After two long rings on the doorbell, a sleepy, bleary-eyed girl opened the door to the extent of the chain and looked out.

"Where's the fire, for Christ's sake? You don't even give a girl time to get her knickers on. What do you want?"

"Can we talk to you about Melanie?" Drew said through the crack.

"She's not here," the girl said, trying to close the door.

"I know," said Drew, sticking his foot in the space.

"Get your fucking foot out of my door before I call the cops," the girl shouted, shoving the door for all she was worth.

"Hold on, hold on," Adam said, peering over Drew's shoulder. "She must have told you about us. We've just set up the commercial she's appearing in, and we need to find her to sign the contract, or we'll all be out of a job. We've spoken to you before. You gave us the phone number of her parents."

"What's your name?" the girl said suspiciously.

"I'm Adam, and this is Drew. He was with her while she was filming."

The explanation seemed to satisfy the girl. She closed the door and removed the chain. "You'd better come in then. Though I don't know what else I can tell you, she's been gone all week."

"Does she often do this?" Drew asked.

"Never done it before that I know of. She's usually told us if she's going away on a shoot. Sometimes she's gone a while, but she usually phones."

"Aren't you worried?" Adam said, looking around.

The flat was clean and feminine, with lots of plants and cushions hiding the slightly worn furniture. The kitchen had a clutter of last night's coffee cups, and there was the remains of a pizza in a box on the drainer.

"No. Not really. We share the flat with her, and we're all good friends. But we don't play keeper of the faith." The girl put the kettle on. "Coffee?" she asked, rubbing her eyes. "Sorry about the clutter. We had a couple of people in for a pizza and a video, and it turned into a late night."

"Coffee will be fine," Drew said, sitting down.

"I'm Angie. Our other flatmate who's still wallowing in all the hot water is Sam. Was Melanie supposed to turn up for this contract signing or what?"

Adam took a mug of coffee off the tray Angie plonked on the table. "We told her to be available, and we would let her know which day to come in, but we've been sitting on papers for three days, and she's not around to speak to." He handed a mug to Drew and sat down. "Have you any idea where she might be? Has she got any friends you know of, and where she might stay?"

Angie tucked her legs under her and thoughtfully ran a hand through her tangled hair. "Well, it was all a bit hush-hush, but we got the impression she was seeing a bloke. She usually told us a bit about who she was going out with, but this time, she was very secretive. A couple of times, she'd get a phone call and then go straight out, sometimes very late. The only reason we could think of was that he was married. Sam might be able to shed a bit more light. They were here together last week when I went to visit my family for a couple of days. Speak of the devil."

Sam emerged from the bathroom in a cloud of steam wearing a long robe, with a towel wrapped around her head. "Hello," she said brightly. "Thought I heard voices. You aren't here to evict us, are you? We did try to keep the noise down."

She took a huge basin of a cup from a shelf and made herself a coffee while listening to Angie's introductions.

Drew stood up and put his cup back on the tray, getting an interested look from the slanted eyes of Sam over the rim of the cup. She leant back on the kitchen table and let her robe fall open, exposing a length of pale golden leg. As she was behind the sofa where Adam and Angie were sitting, the gesture was obviously for Drew's benefit.

His glance flicked over her. She noted it and the corners of her mouth curved slightly in a knowing look. Drew sat down again. *Business first,* he thought, nevertheless needing to cross his legs to quell the beginnings of an erection. Her eyes also noted it before she sat on the arm of the sofa beside Angie, covering her legs as she did so.

"Melanie and I did talk last week, and she's seeing this older bloke. She was very smitten by him, but I couldn't tell you his name. She's been seeing him for some time, although it's only lately got serious. I think he's got some sort of flat where he meets her."

"Do you know where the flat is?" Drew said, uncrossing his legs.

Sam's slanted eyes fixed on a spot below the belt of Drew's jeans making him uncomfortable again.

"I heard her tell the taxi driver once. It's something court near the Ealing tube station. That's all I heard before they drove away."

"Thanks very much. We'll check it out. It's the only place left to try," Drew said, standing up and moving away from her eyes.

In the car, the two men studied the London A-Z and, after finding three cul-de-sacs with a court name, headed off to Ealing. An hour and a half of fruitless searching got them nowhere. Finding parking near Ealing Station, they headed off on foot.

"This is a bloody waste of time. It's like looking for a needle in a haystack," Adam muttered.

"Just think of yourself as a private eye on the trail of a beautiful blonde with millions worth of uncut diamonds," Drew replied, striding along on his long legs and beginning to enjoy himself.

"Philip Marlow, I ain't," Adam gasped, breathing hard in an effort to keep up.

"Ah…if in doubt, ask a policeman." Drew headed across the road to two bobbies on the beat.

The smaller of the two policemen didn't know the area too well, and the older man gave them directions to the places they'd already been. Just as they walked away, he called them back. He told them that there had been a block of flats built on a piece of disused ground a couple of streets away. He didn't know the name but thought it might be worth trying.

Drew and Adam set off in the direction given and finally found a new and expensive-looking two-storey block of flats. The paved courtyard had tubs of plants and trees, and there was a security door with an automatic lock.

"What do we do now? We'll never get in the dam place unless we know which bell to ring." Adam sat down on the top step and leant against the doorpost.

"What was Melanie's surname?" Drew said, studying the list of names printed at the side of the various bell pushes.

"I don't bloody know," Adam growled, massaging his calf muscles.

"Didn't you ever hear it?"

"Course I did, but I can't remember what it was."

"If you read out all these names, would it jog your memory?"

"It might, but how do you know it's these flats, and how do you know the place is in her name?"

"Oh, for Christ's sake, Adam, don't be so negative. What other choices have we got? If this isn't right, we've had it till she turns up on her own accord, and by then, we might be in the dole queue."

Drew started reading down the list. After about twenty names with only a few to go, Adam let out a bark. "That's it, Mason, that's it. Melanie Mason. I remember now. Christ, yes, how could I have forgotten."

"Right, let's give it a go," Drew said, pushing the bell.

No answer. Drew pushed it again, but still no answer.

"Looks like she's not here," Adam said, standing up.

Drew pushed again, leaving his finger on the button. A loud click followed by a muffled, tinny voice came out of the grill above the bell.

"Yes, who is it? What do you want?"

"Melanie, is that you?" Drew said into the grill.

"Who wants to know?"

"It's Drew and Adam. We need to see you about your contract."

"Go away. I don't want to see anyone," said the tinny voice.

"Please, Melanie, we've been looking for you for days. No one knew where you were, and they are all worried."

"Go away. Please go away and leave me alone." The grill clicked again and went quiet.

"Oh great. Now we're really fucked up." Adam threw his arms up.

"Quick, move your ass." Drew saw the shadow of someone approaching the door from the inside.

He purposefully walked towards the door just as it opened from the inside. "Thanks, love," he said to the girl in the tracksuit and trainers who came through.

The door clicked shut behind them and left them in a cool foyer with a marbled floor and staircase.

"Shit, the rent on this place must cost an arm and a leg. I thought she was a struggling model." Adam looked around in awe and spoke in almost a whisper.

"Perhaps the boyfriend pays," said Drew, heading for the stairs.

"He must want to get his rocks off pretty bad if it costs him this much," Adam replied, following Drew.

Drew rapped sharply on number twenty-two. "Melanie, open up; we want to talk to you."

There was a scuffling sound on the other side of the door, but no answer. "Melanie, if you don't open up, we'll break it down or call the police."

The men waited a few more minutes, and then Drew rapped on the door again. There was the sound of a chain being removed, and finally, the door swung open. As they crossed the threshold, they got their first sight of Melanie, and their jaws dropped open. Her mouth and nose were swollen to twice their normal size, and one eye was black and completely closed. She wore a robe that was clutched around her and didn't come high enough in the neck to hide the bruises all around it. Her hair was matted and greasy, and she stood hunched over as if in pain. Fat tears rolled down her battered face, and she turned away.

Both men moved at the same time. Adam closed the door quietly behind him. Drew placed his hand on Melanie's shoulder and, turning her round, put his arms about her. She stood within the circle of his arms, her body trembling violently, and cried into his chest without making a sound. Adam stood and looked at the two of them, his hand across his mouth and his eyes brimming. *What manner of man could do this to such a lovely little thing?*

Drew felt a huge rage building up inside him as he held her. He felt his whole body flush with heat with the force of it. "I'll get the bastard who did this. I'll get him and I'll make him pay for every bruise if it's the last thing I ever do."

CHAPTER 20

The day of John's birthday bash finally arrived. Jessica had already started work and, despite feeling a bit disorganised and confused, was enjoying it. Stacey and Alan were taking time out to show her as much as possible, but the complex and the site were so busy that much of the time Jessica ended up coping alone.

After the first couple of days, she had more or less gotten the hang of the basic parts of the computer and didn't get in so much of a muddle. The first morning, she had made a hash of it and wiped out a lot of the details already programmed, making her feel awful and giving Stacey a load of extra work. Alan had made out a handwritten page of simple instructions for Jessica to work to, and she referred to it constantly, learning as she went along.

She was by the door, directing a couple to the coffee shop, when Alan appeared around the corner. He smiled and greeted the couple as they passed him, then turned to Jessica.

"Well, beautiful lady, I think it's about time you took yourself off to do a bit of pampering for the big night, don't you?"

"I've still got some things to finish before I go," Jessica said, turning around and heading back to the desk.

"Oh, I think that can be safely left until the morning. You've had a busy day and coped very well. I reckon you deserve an early off today."

Jessica busied herself at the desk, trying not to be aware of Alan's closeness behind her. *Damn, man, he was making her nerve ends raw with those black eyes.* She turned sideways to move away and brushed against his arm with her breast. She stepped back quickly as if she'd been burned and glanced up, meeting Alan's eyes. He lifted one eyebrow quizzically and stepped back to let her pass.

"OK," Jessica said, reaching under the desk for her bag. "I think I'll take your advice. I could do with a nice long bath."

"If you need your back washed, just whistle. You know how to whistle, don't you?" Alan's lip curled in an imitation of Humphrey Bogart. "You put your lips together and blow."

Despite her confusion, Jessica grinned. "I thought the heroine was supposed to say that. You've got it the wrong way round."

Alan's face became serious. "Say it to me then, Jessie. It's an offer I won't refuse."

Jessica felt the heat rush through her body and made the fastest exit she could to keep her dignity.

At home, John was wrapped in a new pale blue towelling dressing gown, which was a present from Polly for his birthday. The effect was somewhat dampened by the black socks worn with it. Chad had carried his slippers outside in the rain, and they were still drying out, hence the socks.

"The house welcomes the working woman," John said, standing to attention and saluting, his feet turned outwards.

"Oh, John, what a magnificent specimen of manhood you look in those socks," Jessica burst out laughing.

"I thought so, too," John said, looking down at his feet. "It's the muscular legs that do it."

Polly came into the kitchen also in a gown and rubbing her wet hair with a towel. "Hi, Jess, the bathroom's all yours. We've both had ours early."

"You can say that again," John said, nuzzling the back of Polly's neck.

Polly swiped at him with a towel. "Randy, old bugger thought he wouldn't be able to get it up later and caught me bending over the sink washing my hair. The conditioner was left on so long I can't do anything with it."

"You can do everything with it, my love," John said at the back of Polly's neck.

"Christ, you've had your birthday nooky. Now bugger off and let me get ready," Polly replied with a huge grin.

"Nice, very nice. Give her my whole body in a sacred joining of souls, and as soon as she's satisfied, I get cast off like an old shoe."

"That's a very fanciful way of describing a bonk," Jessica chuckled.

Polly and John turned with a shocked "Jessica!"

"Well, Poll," John said, shaking his head. "Sooner or later, I just knew we'd drag her down to our level of English."

Jessica's mouth opened wide as she laughed. She felt good. There was a buzz of anticipation inside, and she didn't have to scan her brain for the reason. She lightly ran up the stairs to relax in a scented bath.

Sometime later, they were all ready to go. Polly had completed the outfit of a black dress and shoes, with a long rope of pearls, matching earrings, and a black and silver fringed shawl around her shoulders. Jessica's green velvet suit was teamed with flat bronze and gold Roman sandals, a selection of bronze and gold bangles, and large bronze earrings.

John stood and stared, then let out a low whistle. "I can't believe it. I feel like a rich oil baron leading out his harem."

"Oh, John, you are an idiot," Polly said with a smug look. "You know how susceptible we women are to flattery."

"Play your cards right, and you can have me tonight," John

growled, nibbling Polly's ear.

On their arrival at the restaurant, they found many friends already waiting for them. As soon as John walked through the door, they all started singing 'Happy Birthday,' and John's smile stretched widely.

"Hello, beautiful lady," said Alan softly in Jessica's ear.

His breath seemed to stir the featherlike strands of hair framing her face, and she jumped as she felt his warm hand in the small of her back. The hand moved over her skin in a caress, and her whole body broke out in goose bumps. She turned around to face him, at the same time taking a step backwards, away from his touch. He wore a pair of casual black trousers, a black shirt, and an expensive-looking dove grey jacket. He thrust his hands into his trouser pockets and surveyed her in a way that made her shiver.

"You look unbelievably good." His eyes met hers in a long look. "I look forward to dancing with you later."

Not waiting for an answer, he moved over to shake John's hand, wished him a happy birthday, and picked up a parcel from the table by his side. "Hope this is OK for the man who has everything, including an incredible wife," he added as Polly joined them.

"I hope this is what I think it is," John said, tearing off the wrapping paper. "I've been relying on you, yes, great. I knew you wouldn't let me down on my birthday."

John almost reverently opened the box of Havana cigars and sniffed them. "Quick, Pol, hide them in your handbag before anyone sees them; I have to pass them round. Be like giving away my life blood."

Alan laughed. "Give them here, scrooge, and I'll put them out in the car."

John tucked one in his top pocket for later and handed the box to Alan.

The musical group hired for the evening was playing background music while friends greeted each other and drinks were dispensed. Huge joints of meat were keeping warm under heated lights, and waitresses moved in and out of the kitchen bearing steel dishes of vegetables and sauces. A vast variety of hors-d'oeuvres were already laid out, and bottles of wine were being corked and placed on each table.

At eight o'clock, John tapped a wine glass with a spoon, thanked everyone for turning up, and asked them to please start the food before Barney had hysterics. The tables were placed at random with no formal arrangement so everyone could mingle. John and Polly sat at a table near the middle with Jessica and Alan.

"Don't glare at me, Jessie," Polly said, catching Jessica's look. "You two are the only singles here. What was I supposed to do?" Jessica gave Polly another glare, and Polly grinned and made the sign of the cross with her two index fingers. "Lordy lordy, if I didn't know you better, I'd think you were trying to turn me to stone."

Alan came over to the table and sat down. People were helping themselves to hors-d'oeuvres, and John poured some wine while they waited for the numbers to diminish a bit. The four chatted, all the time Jessica acutely aware of Alan's presence. She quickly downed three glasses of wine and caught a raised eyebrow from John. "If she hadn't already had it cut off, I'd say our Jessie's out to let her hair down tonight."

"I do hope so," Alan said softly, getting another raised eyebrow from John, who also shot a startled look at his wife.

The meal was superb, and sometime later, before John disappeared outside with one of his cigars, Alan proposed a toast to the birthday boy, told a couple of risqué stories, and the group picked up the tempo for the dancing to start.

Jessica's three glasses of wine on an empty stomach had more than mellowed her, and despite the food, she still felt the effects of them.

She found herself talking much more than she usually did, and John and Polly were amazed at her dry wit and slanted sense of humour. She had always let Drew carry the conversation on previous occasions of celebration, and his overpowering and dynamic personality had kept her in his shadow. Now, for once, she was the centre of attention and was enjoying it. That was until Polly and John got up to dance, and she was left on her own with Alan. She looked at him and all conversation dried up.

"Let's dance," Alan said, smoothing her arm, and she walked on to the dance floor with a feeling of relief. The group was playing all the latest hits, and everyone wriggled, gyrated, and sweated in time to the music. Ties were removed, along with jackets and some of the ladies' shoes.

After several numbers, the group slowed down and started playing a romantic and smoochy song that had been on the charts for weeks. Jessica started to walk back to the table, but Alan's hand stopped her. He stood and looked at her, then slowly pulled her towards him and put his arms around her. She moved stiffly at first, but her arms crept up behind his neck and they moved closer. Her whole body relaxed against him. Her senses smelt his aftershave, her fingers felt the softness of his hair, and her body felt his growing hardness. Her own body responded with a sudden tightening and a feeling of warmth. They didn't speak, just moved in time to the music, their bodied moulded into each other. They became completely oblivious to the rest of the dancers and were aware only of each other.

The music continued into another slow ballad, and they continued to circle. The circles got smaller until they just swayed. Alan let out a groan into her hair.

"God, Jessie, I've wanted to hold you since the first time I saw you. When you came in tonight, I had to put my hands in my pockets to keep myself from grabbing you. I knew you'd feel like this, I've dreamt about it."

Jessica leant back and looked at him. "You have?"

"You know I have," Alan growled, pulling her to him again.

"Yes, I knew," Jessica said softly in his ear. "Felt all your vibrations very loud and clear, but I was scared."

"Of what?"

"Oh, I don't know; the sheer force of it, I suppose. I've been with the same man for so long, I forgot how strong chemistry can be."

"And now you know."

"Yes, now I know."

Alan pulled her back to him and wrapped her even more tightly in his arms. "So what now?" he said against her neck.

Now, it was Jessica's turn to groan. "Shit, I don't know."

"I can't turn off, and I want you so badly, Jessie. Don't run away, will you?"

"How could I run away from you, Alan? There's so much more to be discovered, so many untapped reserves," Jessica said, smiling.

Alan's deep chuckle reverberated through his chest. "Witch," was all he said before the dance ended and the music quickened.

CHAPTER 21

Jessica's hand resting on Alan's thigh in the taxi home was not missed by Polly, nor had the close dancing gone unnoticed. She felt a slight uneasiness but dismissed it. Jessica was a big, grown-up woman now, but Polly still felt Drew's awesome presence had to be exorcised from Jessica's life first.

John was very merry and sang all the way home. However, as soon as he got into the house, he appeared to have trouble keeping his eyes open. Polly half carried him up the stairs, all the while trying to keep him from pulling the top of her dress down. "Goodnight, you two, sleep well. Coffee's there if you want some."

Much thumping came from upstairs, and they could hear Polly giggling. Jessica smiled and put the kettle on. "John seems to get worse as he gets older," she remarked.

"Polly doesn't seem to mind," Alan said, standing behind her and wrapping her again in his arms.

"No, she's never looked at anyone since she met John, and I don't think she ever will," Jessica said, turning around in the circle of his arms.

The kiss was long, slow, deep, and felt as if it could go on forever. Alan cupped Jessica's face in his hands and kissed her eyelids, cheeks, and nose. He ran his tongue over her mouth and down her neck. The kisses got wetter and deeper, and Jessica's legs started to shake. Alan sat in one of the big kitchen chairs and pulled her down onto his lap. His eyes were half closed with desire and his erection pressed hard against her thigh. His hands were warm upon her breasts, and Jessica heard herself moaning. They were both getting more and more inflamed, and finally, Alan stopped her mouth with his finger.

"Christ, Jessie, I can't do this anymore. I'm bursting my zip. We've either got to stop or I'm going to throw you down on this kitchen floor and make violent love to you. I want you like hell, but not on a floor. I want to take time and love you to pieces in a comfortable place."

Jessica felt slippery and wet. At that precise moment, she wanted to be loved so badly that she would have opted for a bed of nails but instead stood up and smoothed her hair. Alan also stood up and, turning away from her, unzipped his trousers and made some adjustments.

"Christ almighty, it's going to take all night for this bloody thing to go down. If my testicles turn blue tomorrow, it's all your fault."

Jessica giggled. "Serve you right. You should have had me while the going was good."

Alan turned to her, his face serious. "No, Jessie, you are one hell of a woman, and I want you like crazy, but not just a quick moment of gratification. I think we'll make very sweet music together, and I intend to make a banquet of it."

Alan kissed her again softly and tenderly, "Goodnight, lovely lady, may all your dreams be sweet ones."

Surprisingly, despite being so aroused, Jessica slept soundly and awoke the next morning alert and clear-headed. She had the afternoon and evening hours at the complex, so there was no rush for work. She showered and dressed in leggings and a baggy top and went downstairs.

John had crawled out of bed at his usual time, and was due back for his breakfast at any minute. Polly and Alan were sitting at the kitchen table chatting over a pot of coffee.

"Good morning, Jessie. Did you sleep well?" Alan said, standing up and pulling over a chair for her.

"Oh, I slept wonderfully, and all my dreams were sweet ones," Jessica said with a sideways look at Alan from the corners of her eyes.

Polly watched the look from Jessica and the returning one from Alan. *Well, Drew, me lad,* she thought, *looks like you've finally got some competition with this one. Hope you can handle it if you ever find out.*

Over the scrambled eggs and toast with John's bacon grilling, the three of them rehashed the previous night's party. The people, the remarks and who said what to who, etc., before getting on to other things.

"Look, Polly, " Jessica said, "I really love being here with you, but now I'm working, I need to find a place of my own. You and John have been so good to me, and I'll miss you like hell, but the boys will be home soon on half term, and you'll have your work cut out without having to squeeze me in. I thought I'd go into a local letting agency and see what they have available."

"Christ, Jessie. Have you any idea how much you'd have to pay to rent a place around here. This is a holiday area and all the properties fetch sky-high prices this time of year. Even in the winter the rents are ludicrous. I know you're earning now, but you've got to have enough money left to eat."

"Surely, there must be something somewhere I can afford," Jessica said, pouring coffee into all their cups.

"What about the caravan?" Alan said.

"What caravan?"

"Didn't Stacey tell you? For the employees who have to work unsociable hours or the ones who are on call, we offer them a mobile home on the site. We have four available, but only two are occupied at the moment. Carl, the German lad who deals with general maintenance, gas bottles, blocked drains, and things, has one, and the swimming coach, who often has to open the pool early, has the other one. If the hairdressing girls have very late or early appointments, they sometimes use one of them, but they both live locally, so it's not often. The other one hasn't been used at all this year, so I'm not sure what state it's in."

"Can I look at it?" Jessica said quickly.

"Sure, I'll take you over this morning if you want," Alan replied.

"I'll come too," Polly headed for the stairs. "I'll just get changed. Can you put John's bacon in the warmer and leave out the frying pan? H can cook his own eggs for a change; I'll leave him a note."

Ten minutes later, they were on their way to the complex, with Jessica feeling a buzz of excitement. However, on opening the door of the caravan, her excitement evaporated quickly. The mobile home smelt musty and unused. The carpets and coverings were dirty and stained, and the doors on a couple of the cupboards were hanging off. The bedroom looked OK, although the full-length mirror was cracked right across. The kitchen area would once have been really nice, but now the floor and cooker were greasy and dirty, and the sink looked like someone had washed an engine in it.

"Good God, Jessie, I didn't realise it was so bad. You can't live here," Alan said in a shocked voice. "I wonder who the hell made such a mess of this last year."

The three of them just stood and looked at the place. Polly went around, opening the cupboards and pulling out all the cushions from the settees. "You know, I reckon with a bit of work, well, OK, with a lot of work, we could make the place nice again. What a challenge this is, a silk purse from a sow's ear."

They stood around thoughtfully for a few minutes before Alan spoke. "Hang on here while I find Carl. See if he can find some time to fix a few things."

Jessica went around and opened all the windows, which proved quite difficult as most of them were stuck fast. Polly turned on all the taps and flushed the toilet, which filled the pan up with rusty brown water.

"Bloody good job. I didn't pee in the loo first. Looking at that, I would have thought I'd got some dreaded lurgy."

Alan came back with a tall, blonde, good-looking young man who turned out to be Carl. He had been part of the team that had built the complex and stayed on a maintenance man. He coped with the everyday problems but the complicated or major ones were dealt with by a local company with skilled workmen.

"What do you think?" Alan asked him after introducing them all.

Carl walked around. "Repairs won't be a problem," he said in a deep voice with an accent. "Smells a bit, though. Have to check up on the drainage. If you want to have a go at cleaning it up, I can do the work in between. These doors and drawers won't take very long. I can get you a new mirror, and I've got one of those shampoo vacuum things for the carpets and cushions. It'll take a few days to dry, though. Should clean up."

"Well, we're going to give it a go anyway," Jessica said with determination. "I've got nothing to lose, and like Poly said, it'll be a challenge."

"Right then," Alan laughed, handing her the keys, "I now declare this abode occupied."

CHAPTER 22

After a hasty discussion, Drew and Adam decided that Melanie had to be taken somewhere safe. She needed to be looked after, and the only place they could think of was Drew's house; Sophia would know what to do. They sat Melanie down, and Adam found the makings of coffee and some pain pills for her and for his own cracking headache.

Drew went through the bedroom to pack up her clothes and to find something for her to wear. After a few minutes, he appeared in the bedroom doorway and beckoned to Adam. Melanie was slumped on the plush velvet sofa with her head back and her eyes closed.

"What's up?" Adam said, walking into the bedroom.

Drew pushed the bedroom door closed and nodded towards the bed. Adam followed Drew's eyes and gasped, his hand once again going to his mouth, this time to prevent himself from gagging. There was a heap of towels laid one on top of the other on the bed, all soaked in blood, and a bowl at the side of the bed filled with what looked like wads of kitchen paper, also all soaked with blood.

"Oh my God, Drew, what is it?"

"What does it look like, you idiot?" Drew snapped.

"Well, I know what it is, but where did it come from? I thought she was just bruised."

"I've got a good idea what's gone on here, but we're going to have to ask her."

"Whaa—" Adam spluttered, looking towards the bed.

"I reckon she's miscarried here on her own," Drew said, moving towards the door to the lounge.

He sat down beside Melanie and put his arm around her. Her head fell onto his shoulder and she started crying again. "Melanie, darling, look at me."

She straightened up and turned her head painfully to look at him.

"Were you pregnant?"

She nodded.

"Have you lost it?"

She nodded again. Drew pulled her head back onto his shoulder again and held her.

After a few minutes, she started in faltering half sentences. "I thought he'd be pleased…went into a rage…punched and kicked me until I fell down…called me names…pulled me along the floor by the hair."

Adam sat down in the doorway opposite, looking white and shaken. "Why didn't you call for help?"

Melanie looked up, one eye completely closed and the other one bloodshot and red-rimmed.

"He paid all the bills, we never had a phone installed, he used his mobile for calls, said he didn't want me running up any more bills. My mobile battery was flat."

Both men looked at each other; Melanie said shakily, "I couldn't walk, and I don't know anyone here."

"OK, my sweet," Drew said, standing up, "let's get you dressed and away from here."

Adam nodded towards the bedroom door, "What about that lot."

"Let the bastard responsible sort it out," was Drew's abrupt reply.

Melanie managed to dress herself and, despite everything, looked like a mirror image of Audrey Hepburn, with tight-cropped black trousers, a baggy black sweater, and flat ballet pumps. She had brushed her tangled dark hair and donned a pair of oversized sunglasses. The flat was obviously for one purpose only and the few possessions that were there, she pushed into an oversized handbag.

Adam had gone off to fetch the car, hoping that he could find his way back. Melanie was leaning heavily on Drew's arm and barely managed to painfully inch her way down the stairs to the lobby. Not wanting to keep her standing outside, Drew sat her on the bottom step and waited by the glass door for Adam.

The door clicked and a girl wearing the tracksuit and trainers came through. She was breathing heavily and her tracksuit top was knotted around her waist. "Going to be a hot one," she said and headed for the stairs. She passed by Melanie, went up four steps, turned, and then came down again. She stood and looked at the top of Melanie's dark head until Melanie became aware of the scrutiny and looked up. The girl looked at the swollen and bruised mouth, the only thing that would be seen under the oversized glasses, and sat down beside her, looking more closely. She looked at Drew with pale blue eyes that were like ice chips.

"Did you do that?" her voice rang out in the marble foyer and bounced off the walls.

Drew was still looking through the glass for the car and visibly jumped.

"You bastard, did you do that?" and the girl flew at him with her hands raised.

"Whoh," Drew shouted, catching her hands as they came towards his face.

Melanie heaved herself up from the stairs and grasped the back of the girl's shirt. "No, no, no," she rasped as loudly as she could.

The girl didn't seem to hear and raised her water bottle towards

Drew. She flexed her arm and the bottle bounced off his head. As the bottle was only plastic, it split and showered Drew with the remains of the water. Drew felt the liquid and, for a moment, until he looked down at his shirt, thought it was blood.

Melanie dragged the girl back towards the stairs with her shirt pulled almost up to her bra. "No. No. No," she said again. "He's a friend, here to take me home."

Drew had never been so glad to see Adam's face peering in the window. He opened the door, mopping his face and hair with his handkerchief. Adam looked from one face to the other in utter bewilderment. "Now, what the hell's going on?" he said.

Between the three of them, they gave the girl, whose name turned out to be Carla, a thumbnail explanation of the events.

"Oh, you poor thing," she said giving Melanie a hug. "These are mostly business peoples' flats and there's never anyone much here at weekends. I only just arrived back from the States yesterday; I'm still on US time."

It turned out she was a showgirl and was appearing, only as a bit player, in a West End show starting rehearsals in a few days.

Whilst they were setting Melanie in the car, Drew had a quiet word with Carla and gave her his card. He nodded towards the car and Melanie's pale face. "I need to know the name of the bastard who did this. Keep your eyes open and call me if you find anything out."

Carla nodded. "To damn right I will."

CHAPTER 23

Jessica and Polly armed themselves with all the trappings of a cleaning company and went to work with a vengeance. They used the machine to shampoo the carpets and upholstery, polish and disinfect the kitchen units, and clean the inside and outside of the windows. Carl got under their feet with his toolbox and long, gangly legs but fixed most of the odd jobs fairly quickly between numerous cups of tea.

"Christ, Carl," Polly exclaimed, watching him put the kettle on again, "not another brew. It's a wonder you aren't afloat. Any more liquid and we shall have to crack a bottle of champagne over your arse and rename you HMS something or other."

Carl just grinned his white-toothed grin that crinkled up his eyes and started packing up the last lot of dirty cups. "While the kettle's boiling, I'll just go and give Luke a ring about the smell from the drains. You can't stay here with that stink. I think something must be blocked in the main drain."

"Luke," Jessica said. "Who's Luke?"

"He's the boss of the maintenance firm that looks after the site," Polly answered, sinking down onto one of the settees and lighting a cigarette.

"Oh shit, now I've got a wet behind; this material's still soaking."

"Well, Poll, I think we've done great things today. Already, it looks liveable in here, but I'll have to get rugs to cover up some areas of this carpet; it looks a bit past it in places."

Polly stood up and stretched her back. "I'll leave you to it then. I'd better get back to another lot of chores at the farm. See you later."

"OK, Poll, thanks for all your help. I'll just wash the floor in the kitchen now Carl has finished trailing through. Should be home soon." Jessica gave her friend a hug as she left and wearily started to fill a bucket with soapy water.

Jessica found the floor cleaning very difficult. It needed some hard scouring and she was really tired. Eventually, it was finished and looked six shades lighter. She stood up, dropping the cloth back into the bucket of filthy water and placed both hands onto the small of her aching back. Two seconds later, the door burst open, and a huge figure came hurtling through the door, knocking the bucket flying. Jessica turned quickly on her heel, slipped on the soapy water, and her feet skidded along the floor taking the legs of a man from under him. He went down like a felled tree and the impact as he hit the ground shook the caravan and rattled the windows. Jessica was hanging onto the sink like grim death to stop herself from going right over, but she finally lost her grasp and joined him in a wet, tangled heap on the floor, nursing a badly bashed elbow.

Jessica took several moments to get her breath back, and then she exploded. "You stupid bloody great oaf, what the hell do you think you are doing. Look what you've done. What the hell do you want barging in here like that? You nearly killed me, you bloody idiot."

Jessica tried to scramble to her feet, pushing up with her hands on a vital part of the man's anatomy, which brought forth a whooshing of breath, followed by an ear-splitting bellow. "For God's sake, woman, get off the wedding tackle. What are you trying to do? Castrate me as well."

Jessica snatched her hands away as if they were burning and promptly slipped over again. Now soaked completely all over. She glared at the man, who, to her amazement, burst out laughing. His face was bearded, and, with a mop of brown hair, was wet. His eyes then started to stream with tears of laughter. He just lay on the floor in the water and howled.

Jessica managed to get to her feet and stood there spluttering with rage. "How dare you just walk in here without knocking. This is my caravan. I could have been in here taking a bath."

This brought forth another huge bellow of laughter from the man, "I thought that's what you just did."

Jessica found herself smiling when she realised how ridiculous she sounded. "Oh, get up, you crazy man. You can give me a hand to clear up his mess. Who are you anyway?"

"Luke Benson at your service," he said, sitting up and mopping his eyes. "Carl caught me just as I was leaving and asked me to check out the caravan. He didn't tell me there was anyone in here."

"Well, for your information, I'd just finished cleaning up. Now I'm back to square one," Jessica said tiredly, her shoulders drooping.

Luke picked up the bucket, "I'll sweep this water straight out the door and dry it all off. It'll be done in no time." He picked up the towel from the dining table and handed it to her. "Go and dry yourself off. You look like a stray cat."

Jessica did as she was told, feeling her face flame when she looked in the mirror. Her baggy t-shirt was soaked and clung to her bra-less top half like a second skin. The whole thing was completely transparent and her cold nipples stood out like organ stops. *Well, at least he'll know there's no padding,* she thought ruefully.

A while later, she crept into the bedroom and pulled on her tracksuit top. Luke was wringing the cloth out on the grass and looked up as she appeared in the doorway. His face split into a grin. "Bit late to cover up now," he said, stuffing the bucket under the van. "Let's go and have a drink to get warm".

Jessica's first instinct was to refuse, but a drink did sound good, and this great brown bear didn't seem to invite a refusal, so she trotted meekly beside him to the bar.

After an hour, they were still sitting there with Jessica in stitches at Luke's dry humour. He talked slowly and moved in a slow, ponderous way, but Jessica felt the quickness underneath the slow exterior and warmed to this large man who made her laugh. As they left, they ran into Alan.

"Oh, I see you've met our Luke," he said, his eyes flicking over Jessica's dishevelled appearance. "Has he managed to fix everything up?"

"Haven't had time to look yet; me and Jessie took a bath together and had to drip dry in the bar," Luke said with a sideways glance at Jessica.

"Oh, I see," said Alan, not understanding at all, but the slight narrowing of his eyes was not lost on Luke, who noted it and moved fractionally away from Jessica.

"Well, see you people around," he said breezily. "I'll get it sorted tomorrow, Jessie," and with a casual wave, he strolled away. *Better tread lightly in the future,* Luke thought pensively. *Seems like Adam's trying to put his mark on that one. Pity, she's a lovely lady; wouldn't like to see her get hurt.*

By the end of the week, Jessica was ready to move in. The lounge had been transformed with a white shaggy rug, some colourful velvet cushions, a white-painted coffee table, and plants in white pots. The bedroom had new dusty pink curtains and rugs and deep pink and cream duvet covers and sheets. All in all, it was really beginning to look like home, and Jessica was pleased. She had invited people she had got to know over for a glass of wine and a few eats as a modest housewarming. Barney arrived carrying several plates of mouth-watering delicacies that disappeared at the speed of light. Alan brought a boxful of vintage wines, which disappeared almost as quickly. Carl carried over a CD player and got the music organised, and Polly and John arrived with a set of saucepans for her, each one containing something to eat. The party was a great success and continued till two in the morning. The surprise of the evening was Luke. He turned up a bit late and carried a beautifully wrapped parcel containing an exquisite lacy tablecloth and a lovely ceramic fruit bowl filled with fruit. Jessica was speechless and very embarrassed, mostly because of the reaction of the assembled company. Apparently, Luke was not known for being too generous with money and had never been seen to give presents before.

"Well, sweetie," Polly said, "you certainly made an instant impression on Luke. What part of his body did you minister to to get such a generous present?"

Jessica felt all hot and glared at Polly, "For God sake, Polly, keep your voice down. Luke's just a friend; you'll have everyone thinking something's going on."

Polly chuckled, "Looking at those limpid brown eyes, I think he'd like it to be. The best bit was seeing Alan's reaction. Talk about looks killing. Then to add to Alan's annoyance, Luke saw him glaring and winked at him. I nearly burst. If you don't watch out, those two will be at each other's throats over you."

Jessica grinned and gave Polly a shove, "Oh, get on with you. Your trouble is too much romantic fiction before bedtime. I'll have to have a word with John to see if there's not something else to occupy your romantic inclinations."

Polly burst out laughing. "For Christ sake, don't do that. I've got a job to get a couple of nights free as it is. I keep thinking as he gets older, he'll slow down. Some hope; he just gets more randy. Anyway, Jess, if you aren't going to continue your marriage, don't you think you ought to contact Drew and tell him so. You can't start a new life if you're going to stay married in name only. If you leave it too long to find a lover, things might heal over."

Jessica's laughter was loud and long, and the group all turned and looked at her.

"Come on, Jessie, share the joke," John said, wrapping his arms around her from behind. "Knowing Polly as I do, albeit not very often in the biblical sense."

This remark brought a howl from Polly.

"It was bound to have been something rude."

"John, you are absolutely correct, and it's not repeatable in mixed company."

"Don't worry, Jess, I'll find out later," John twirled his moustache. "I have ways of making her talk."

The party broke up in dribs and drabs until Jessica and Alan were the only two left. Jessica busied herself, clearing up the glasses and plates, but Alan had other ideas. "Leave it, Jess; I'll help you with all this in the morning," he said, taking a pile of plates out of her hands and dumping them in the sink. "Come and sit with me for a minute."

"Alan, it's late and you should be leaving," Jessica replied. Making it very clear that he would not be staying the night as he had inferred.

"It's OK, Jessie; I'm staying in Carl's van tonight, but I'll be over early to help you with this lot."

Jessica felt as if he'd read her thoughts and was mortified that he had realised in advance his remark would be misinterpreted by her. She sat down beside him, leaving a few feet of space between them, which he soon closed. His arms went around her, and his mouth came down gently on hers. He didn't use any pressure, just a soft brushing of his lips against hers until he felt the tension leave her body and she started to relax. She leant into him, and his kiss hardened and deepened until the familiar tingling started down in the pit of her stomach, and her skin took on a sheen of moisture.

"Jessie, you really are driving me crazy. You must know by now how much I want you," Alan growled into Jessica's neck. "Every time I look at you, my body starts playing strange tricks, and I'm finding it very hard to concentrate on anything with you around. I have to go back to London next week; will you come up and spend a weekend with me soon? I want to make wonderful love to you, but not here. I don't want everyone to be gossiping after I've gone."

Jessica was by now fully relaxed and aroused. Alan's remarks made her move even closer to him, wanting him to be as ready for lovemaking as she was.

"Jessie…. No…don't do this to me. I'm having a very difficult time keeping the blood running upwards to my brain. I don't want to leave you tonight, but I can't have this whole place talking about you. It wouldn't be fair with me going away. I want you like mad, but you don't deserve a bad reputation."

Alan almost tore himself away from Jessica's arms, feeling immediately cold and brutal. Jessica had wanted him to leave, and now she couldn't bear the thought of him going. She stood up, feeling annoyed and frustrated, and turned away from him, moving towards the kitchen. He stopped her and turned her around to face him.

"Please, Jessie, don't turn away from me. Anything going to happen to us is a private thing, and I know it will be special. It's not something I want to share with anyone yet, especially the people here who will start with the smutty remarks."

Alan held her tightly in a brief hug and then stepped back. "Goodnight, lovely lady. I'll see you in the morning."

Jessica watched him walk over to Carl's van and open the door. He stopped in the doorway and waved before going in. Jessica locked her door, suddenly feeling very tired. She switched on the kettle for coffee, thinking over the evening's events. She realised Alan was right, but it still left her feeling very uptight and wound up. Drew would have taken full advantage of the opportunity and damn the consequences, but then you could always lead Drew by the nose where sex was concerned and look where it had got him.

"I wonder where it did get him," Jessica said aloud. "Maybe with all those adoring females around, he doesn't even realise I've gone."

She switched off the lights and moved through into the bedroom. "Well, if he doesn't know by now, he never will," she mumbled into the pillow.

The clatter of a diesel engine starting up sounded noisy in the silence, but Jessica didn't hear it. Luke drove slowly towards the main gate and out onto the main road. *So the prince hasn't claimed the fair maiden yet,* he thought, and a wide grin split his face as he accelerated towards home.

CHAPTER 24

Drew phoned Melanie's flatmates and explained that there had been a problem and she would be staying with him for a while. By the sexy, knowing chuckle on the other end of the line, Drew knew that they had put the wrong interpretation on the situation but didn't feel that it was his place to go into all the details. Melanie would tell them what she wanted them to know in her own time.

Marty arrived with a screech of tyres, and Drew knew what mood his son was in before he stepped out of the car. He opened the door to welcome him, but instead of the usual hug, Drew got, "I'll get my bags out in a minute, Dad. At the moment, all I need is a drink and a shower." Marty said in a clipped voice that was every bit as impersonal as the handshake.

"I'll get them for you," Drew replied, feeling stiff and unnatural in the presence of this large, tanned and well-dressed person who was his son.

Marty threw the keys at him and turned to the drinks trolley. Drew offloaded a couple of large, expensive cases and some duty-free bags and dumped them down in the hall. He walked across the lounge, stepping over Marty's long legs and poured himself a drink. During a brief and uncomfortable silence, Drew could feel Marty's eyes on him and looked up. His eyes were every bit as blue as his father's and were at this moment like two pieces of ice.

Drew cleared his throat. "How's the job going in the Big Apple then? I suppose you feel like a native after all this time."

Marty just looked at his father, the two icicles glinting. "Well, so she finally blew you out, did she?" he drawled, ignoring his father's question completely.

Drew was by now starting to get a bit peed off by his son's sarcastic attitude, which was making him feel like a naughty and immature schoolboy. He stood up. "Quite frankly, Marty, I really don't think this has anything to do with you. It's between me and your mother. We have never told you how to run your life since puberty, and I resent your interference in ours. What good do you think it will do flying all this way just to have a go at me? You could have done it just as effectively over the phone at far less expense."

Marty also stood up, and Drew, for the first time, noticed that his son was taller than him. "What makes you think I came all this way for you? I came over for Mum. No one knows where she is or even if she's still alive. Has that ever occurred to you? She must have been in one hell of a state to leave the way she did after putting up with the shit for all these years. How do you know she hasn't done something silly? Have you even tried to find her, or are you arrogant enough to think that she'll forgive and forget again and come crawling home with her tail between her legs."

Marty's fists clenched and unclenched, and he spun on his heel and marched over to the patio doors, sliding one back fiercely and stepping onto the patio outside as if he was afraid of lashing out.

"Of course, I've tried to find her, you stupid bugger. Do you think I haven't been worried, too? This country might not be as big as America, but it's a bloody big place to search for someone who is obviously hiding. None of her friends know where she is, and unless I hire a private detective, where would you suggest I start?"

"God, Dad. Elizabeth…how could you? She was Mum's friend. The only real one she thought she had. All the other people were your business friends and hangers-on, just there for the parties, but Elizabeth was Mum's pal, or so she understood. Of all the women you had to screw around with, why did it have to be her? Surely you could have stayed further away from home than the next-door neighbour?"

"That's not your business, Marty," Dew yelled, wondering how his son knew about Elizabeth.

"Yes, it is," Marty yelled back. "Damn you, Dad, it is my business. It's always been our business what hurt Mum—mine and Caro's. We've watched it for years and spent a lot of our time being cheerful for Mum even when we didn't feel like it. Sometimes when you'd found another bimbo to screw around with, we were the ones who helped her get through it until you came galloping home again with your stupid grin and your slushy bunches of flowers, which, by the way, Mum always binned as soon as you went back to town."

"Your mother and I had many happy years together, before and after you were born."

"Happy…you call that happy," Marty interrupted in a loud voice. "She always did exactly what you wanted her to do. Otherwise, you went all moody and sulky like a little kid. She always had men trying to chat her up, but she was constantly looking over her shoulder to see where you were, and they never got past first base. She is an interesting and entertaining woman, but when she's around you, she becomes like a pale grey shadow. If she did have an opinion on anything, you always talked her down, even in front of other people, so in the end, she always agreed with everything you said. Happy, you must be joking."

"I think you've said enough," Drew snapped, his face flushed and his breathing rapid. "You have really overstepped the mark this time. Who do you think you are talking to me like this? Without me, you and your sister wouldn't have half the things you have always taken for granted. A good education, holidays, money to do what you want, a lovely home. There are thousands of kids who would give their eye teeth for just a small part of any of this."

Marty again interrupted. "We are not talking about material things. Don't you think we know what we've got? Don't you know we'll always be in your debt for all the opportunities we've had, but we aren't talking about this. There are families with a hell of a lot less who stick together through thick and thin because they love and respect each other, and not just out of gratitude. Mum stuck it out with you when you had nothing, and she would have carried on loving you with or without money, you know that, but during the years, your success pushed her further into the background all the time. She should have been side by side with you, not one step behind."

"Your mother never wanted a career," Drew blustered. "She was content to stay at home and be a housewife and mother. She never wanted to go back to work, even when you and Caro moved out."

"How do you know? Did you ever ask her?" Marty shot back, face thrust forward to his father.

"She would have told me if she wanted to go out to work," Drew said defensively.

"OK, Dad, then answer me this. What did you say to her when she told you she'd like to take a course on creative writing?"

"For Christ's sake, Marty, how in hell am I supposed to remember that?"

"Yes, Dad, you'll remember if you try. Think back to one of Mum's birthday's not so long ago. We all went down the Thames on a boat and had a slap-up meal in the Dorchester. Mum said what a lovely time she'd had, and you asked her what she would like you to buy her for her birthday. Anything she wanted. Can you remember what her answer was?"

"I dare say YOU can," Drew snapped, remembering all too well.

"Yes, I can," Marty snapped back. "She said she would like to go to night school. There was a course starting in creative writing that she would like to join, and you burst out laughing and told her not to be so silly. She had surely done enough creative writing keeping in touch with her mother. What you really meant was some clothes or jewellery. She never mentioned it again and threw all the college books she'd collected in the bin the next day.

"But tell me something, Dad, did you ever see her wear the gold pendant you bought her?"

Drew stared at his son. Marty's chin still jutted out aggressively and his hands thrust deep into his pockets. His eyes were startlingly blue in the daylight, and he needed a shave. He was a familiar stranger. "I didn't realise how much you hated me," Drew said quietly.

"I don't hate you, Dad," Marty replied, turning away. "I thought I did…I thought I did for a long time. That's really why I took the job in New York. You started talking down to me like you do to Mum, and I couldn't stand it. I didn't want to go away. I was very lonely and miserable at first. I didn't know anyone and was very much the new blue-eyed boy at work, you know, a director's son and all. I missed Mum and sis' but I had to get away. To run away, I suppose. If we had been more of a family, I would never have considered going. Still, now I've made my own life and my own friends, and it's not so bad. Lots of the older guys I work with spend their lives chasing one female or another, even when they've got a lovely wife at home. It's a bit like chasing their own lost youth or something. It's all a bit sad really that they can't accept that everyone's got to grow old."

"Is that how you look at me now? Someone chasing a lost youth," Drew said slowly, not really wanting to hear the answer.

"I don't know, Dad. All I do know is that Mum deserves something better than what she had. Someone out there is looking for a woman like her, someone who will love her to death and care for her."

"And you don't think it will be me," Drew said softly. "You don't think it will ever be me anymore, do you?"

"Dad, you won't ever change. You might change for a while, and Mum would be very happy, but if you went back to your old ways, she would never have the strength to leave again and would spend the rest of her life miserable. So maybe it would be better if she never took the risk and stayed away."

Drew poured another drink and gazed unseeingly out of the window at the tidy garden, his anger now gone. "I'm sorry, Marty, I'm sorry for everything. I can't turn the clock back and change anything, but I can try to change if you and your sister will give me a chance. If it's not too late that is. But first, we have to find your mother. If she needs her own life, then so be it, but I have to know she's alright. I'll leave her in peace, but I have to have peace, too, and for this reason, I have to find her. I'll contact a private investigator in the morning."

Marty turned and looked at his father for the first time in many minutes. They both took a step forward at the same time and reached for each other. For the second time in his life, Drew wrapped his arms around another male and found his eyes once again filling with tears. "God, Marty, what a mess. Please help me."

"Would anyone like a cup of tea," said a small voice from the doorway. They both turned to see Melanie looking small and very bruised, peeping through the door.

CHAPTER 25

Drew returned to work the following week and had to admit a feeling of relief to be doing something constructive. All the traumas and upsets had given him a sense of uselessness, and to be back on familiar ground gave him new energy.

After the initial shock of Melanie's appearance and the subsequent explanations, Drew was surprised and very touched to see Marty take Melanie under his wing. He seemed to grow another two inches in height and became protective and understanding. He managed to achieve what all the others had failed to do and escorted Melanie to see the doctor. The physician insisted on X-rays, and after the reports, plus a thorough examination, pronounced her clear of any major damage and prescribed lots of rest.

Sophia and Jim also took Melanie to their hearts and found her things to do around the house. She liked to help Jim in the garden, who indulged her, all the while watching in case she damaged any of his handiwork. In the end, he had to admit, she was gentle and careful and seemed to attain a kind of peace from even the most menial tasks.

"Nature's power of healing," he said, making Sophia huff and puff about her wonderful healing food doing the job quicker.

True to his word, Drew found the name of a well-recommended investigation agency and arranged for an appointment. He gave them the names of everyone he had already contacted, a recent photograph of Jessica, and full details of her description. He had no idea how long they would take to find her, hoping it wouldn't be long. Apart from the need to know she was alright, the agency's fees would be liable to bankrupt him if it took too long.

Sullivan and his board of directors had been constantly in contact over the absence of Melanie and the fact that the all-important contract had not yet been signed. Rather than bluff anymore, Drew set up a meeting to try and grab a bit more time from them. If they saw her face now, it would probably blow everything. Sullivan's secretary informed him that Mr Sullivan's personal assistant, Max Duffield, would be keeping the appointment as the man himself was otherwise engaged. Drew was very surprised to discover that Max was, in fact, female.

Maxine Duffield had tawny copper-coloured, wavy, shiny hair and a well-toned body clad in a cream-coloured silk suit. Drew would have sworn the hair colour came out of a bottle till he noticed the pale skin with its scattering of freckles and the copper/blond eyelashes and brows. The lady was all efficiency and very businesslike. Drew realised his charm was going to count for nothing with this one. He felt he couldn't tell her the complete truth, but he had to come up with a plausible excuse all the same. He settled on a car accident, which would account for the bruising but wouldn't alarm the powers that be.

"Has she broken any bones?" Ms Duffield rapped out.

"No, just bad bruising," Drew replied, also in a clipped tone.

"Then, if she can walk, why wasn't she able to be here?"

"She didn't want to frighten the horses," Drew replied.

He intercepted a glare from the ginger-coloured eyes, a silence, and a small crinkling in the outer corner of the eye, which made him relax a little. *So she is human after all,* he thought.

"Would you like to see her? She's staying at my house at the moment."

The eyes narrowed, losing their crinkle.

"My housekeeper and my son are taking care of her."

She leant back in the chair. "Yes, to be on the safe side, I think I'd better. That would put Mr. Sullivan's mind at ease, not to mention the board of directors."

"Why don't we make it this weekend? Perhaps I could take you to dinner and we can discuss the details in comfort."

"Mr. Cameron, this visit will be to ascertain the health of our model, and the rest of the business can be discussed in the comfort of our offices."

"As you wish."

Stuffy old cow, Drew thought maliciously as he smiled and walked her to the door. "My secretary will inform you of my address, and you can confirm the time I can expect you."

"Thank you, Mr. Cameron. I'll look forward to it."

Drew smiled again and closed the door behind her. "That's more than I fucking will," he muttered aloud, bringing a puzzled look from Joan, his secretary. "Well, Drew, old man. What a fun weekend to look forward to, a sick girl, a worried son, and a visit from a miserable, bloody woman."

The intercom on his desk buzzed.

"Mr. Cameron, I have Elizabeth Smyth on the line. I know you told me not to put her calls through, but she said if she didn't speak to you now, she is going to come into the office and cause a scene."

Drew's secretary was a smart, single lady in her fifties and had been with him for years. She obeyed all his instructions without question and was loyal down to the last tinted brown hair on her well-groomed head.

"How many times has she phoned Joan?"

"Dozens of times, Mr. Cameron, but this time, she won't take no for an answer," Joan said in a very flustered voice, which was totally unlike her.

"Has she upset you?"

"Well, to be honest, she has called me a few things, which were not very nice."

"OK, Joan, I'm sorry she is such a pest. Put her through and I'll try to get her off your back."

"Drew, darling," Elizabeth said in a syrupy voice which made Drew grit his teeth. "Why don't you answer any of my calls? I stayed away like you told me. I went to my sister's, and when I came back I saw Marty at your house and some gross, fat old woman. When I phoned you to find out what's been happening, the crone at your office kept making excuses."

"For your information, the crone you refer to is my secretary, who was carrying out my instructions," Drew answered her in an abrupt and businesslike tone. "What's more, I would suggest you take your spite out on someone else in future. I will not have a member of my staff upset by you."

Elizabeth's voice changed to a screech. "Why, you fucking bastard. How dare you refuse to take my calls. Who the hell do you think you are? I'm involved in this, too, in case you've forgotten. At the end of this, I stand to lose every bit as much as you. Anyone would think it was all my fault. It takes two to screw, and I don't remember holding a gun to your head."

"For Christ's sake, Elizabeth, stop shouting."

"Stop shouting, stop shouting. You haven't heard anything yet. I've been sitting on hot tin tacks waiting for Will to appear at my sister's with my suitcases and divorce papers at any minute, and when I finally buck up enough courage to come home, I can't even phone you to find out what in hell's been going on. Anyone would think you were the one that's been shit on, not Jessie. Walking around being holier than thou like a wronged husband. I'm not the only one you've been screwing around with, not by a long chalk, but it looks like I'm the one who's going to carry the can for it all."

"Of course you aren't. It seems my family has known for years what a rat I am, and everyone has been waiting for this to happen."

"Do they know about me?"

Drew's pause was answer enough.

"Oh God," Elizabeth groaned, her anger turning to panic. "I can't stay in this house now. What am I going to do? Our mortgage is nearly paid off, and there's no way Will is going to sell up and take out another one without knowing why I want to move. We've lived here for years, and when he wanted to move before, I'd always fought against him. Mainly because of you. I'd never get him to move now. Can't you sell up? After all, if Jessie's not coming back, you won't need such a big house anyway?"

Drew's face tightened into an ugly mask. "Why you scheming, bloody bitch. You've got a nerve. If you hadn't written that stupid note, we wouldn't be in this mess, and now I'm supposed to sell up to bail you out. You self-centred cow. You've got no chance."

"And if you hadn't been such a stupid fucking bastard and had got rid of the note like you were supposed to, we wouldn't be in it either. You're as much to blame as I am, and just because your life is screwed up, you've got no reason to drop me in the shit as well."

"Oh, for fuck sake, this is getting us nowhere."

Drew covered his eyes with his hand. He had the beginnings of a raging headache and wanted this conversation, if that's what you could call it, to be over.

"Well, come on then, Drew, you're supposed to be the big, brainy, clever man. Tell me what I should do. You've got your son staying with you, who knows about us. You will have your daughter visiting you, who also presumably knows about us, and I have to come and go to my house, constantly running into them. How am I supposed to play it? Wear a veil, stay in for the next five years, bluff it out. What?"

"Elizabeth, I don't know. I really don't know."

"Well, you miserable fucking bastard. When you've figured it out, maybe you'll let me know. I have to go on living too." With that, the phone went dead.

Drew sat with his head in his hands for a long time, his headache throbbing with a vengeance. A polite cough from the other side of the desk brought his head up fractionally. Joan stood there with a cup of tea and a headache tablet.

"Thought you might need these, Mr. Cameron."

"Joan, you're an angel. How did you guess?"

"Well, she always gives me a headache," she said dryly on her way out.

CHAPTER 26

Jessica settled into life at the complex like a duck to water. She had never been so busy in her life. The season was well underway, the vans were full, and so were the spaces for the touring caravans. She didn't seem to have much time to visit Polly lately and only saw her at the first few aerobics classes she could manage to get to.

Luke was on site quite a bit. There always seemed to be some work to do that Carl couldn't cope with. Jessica was surprised to see Viv flirt outrageously with Luke every time she ran into him. He took it all in his stride and fended her off by making jokes and ribbing her. Jessica knew with a woman's intuition that Viv was not joking and wondered if Luke was aware of Viv's seriousness under all the banter. She had seen the look in Viv's eyes when she was around Luke and realised it wasn't all a joke.

Carl invited Jessica and Ann to his van one evening for drinks and a chat. They finished up playing cards and Trivial Pursuit. The evening was so successful it became a regular event when they could make it. When it was Jessica's turn to play hostess, Luke turned up, almost on cue, with a couple of bottles of wine. It seemed too much like a coincidence until she found out that Carl had invited him.

Luke was such a dry wit; he had them all in stitches and was invited back the next time. Carl remarked that he had never seen Luke on site so much and asked where all his workmen were. Luke's answer was a bit vague and centred mainly on being fed up with getting stuck in his office all the time. So, from then on, he became a regular member of the group.

Luke's eyes were soft when they looked at Jessica. The looks were not lost on either Carl or Ann, but they weren't seen by Jessica. Ann and Carl talked about it. They had never seen Luke with any female in all the time he'd been working there. He visited a local pub in town for a pint or two and was always on his own.

"I wonder if Jessie knows he's got a soft spot for her," Ann mused to Carl in the coffee shop one day.

"Shouldn't think so," Carl said through a mouthful of Chelsea bun. "Jessie seems to treat him just as a friend. I don't think it has entered her head he might want to be anything else."

"Do you think we ought to tell her?" Ann cupped her chin in her hands. "He might be an older man, but he sure is nice."

"Jessie's a big grown-up lady. She'll find out in her own time, and if she doesn't, Luke will find a way to let her know."

So the social evenings continued, and Luke continued to soften towards Jessica, who continued to laugh at his jokes and treat him like a friend. Until Jessica's first long weekend off came around and she decided to go to London to spend it with Alan. Then, for the first time in weeks, Luke was missing from the site and their games.

"Go and find him, Carl," Ann pleaded. "Did you see his face when Jessie told us? He looked stricken."

"I'm not going looking for him. I work for him. What am I supposed to say? Sorry, boss, the girls sent me to look for you. They think you might be crying. He'd think I was crackers."

"You don't work for him; you work for the complex," Ann snapped.

"Doesn't matter, I'm still not going. I'm half his age; it would look ridiculous, and in any case, it's none of our business."

And with that, Ann had to be content.

Jessica treated herself to a couple of new outfits, a hairdo, and a leisurely evening to pack. She didn't really mind the weekend work but was looking forward to having some time off and also to seeing Alan again. She had missed him and the undercurrent of suggestion that always ran between them. She wondered if the feelings would be the same in a different location. When people were in a holiday atmosphere, they somehow acted differently, which seemed to rub off on the staff. Rules didn't seem to be so harsh, and even though everyone worked extremely hard, there was always a lot of laughter. There was a feeling of fun generated by the holidaymakers they were in contact with. Maybe in the capital city, where the pace was faster and more commercial, Alan would be different. Well, she'd just have to wait and see.

She had decided to go by train instead of driving; Alan was picking her up from the station. He had sounded as excited as a little boy when she phoned and told him. She was sitting with her feet up, painting her toenails, when there was a rap on the door. She hobbled over, toes splayed apart with cotton wool, and opened up to Carl.

"Just came to wish you a good weekend," he flashed his white smile.

Jessica hobbled back to finish the other foot. "Thanks, Carl. Will you miss me?"

"Like a toothache."

"If you're going to insult me, you can do it over a glass of wine. There's a bottle already opened behind you."

Carl poured the wine and sat watching her paint. "Is this all for Alan's benefit?" he asked after a few minutes.

"No, it's for mine. I happen to like red toenails."

"So Alan won't be seeing them over his shoulder then."

Jessica glanced at Carl from the corner of her eye, and her mouth curved in a cheeky grin. "He might."

Expecting an answering smile, she was puzzled to see Carl's face remain impassive and unsmiling. She put her feet down on the floor and turned to face him. "I thought you liked Alan."

"I do," said the unsmiling mouth.

"What then?"

"Nothing."

"Don't give me the nothing routine, Carl. Out with it."

Carl's shoulders hunched, and he swirled the wine around the glass but didn't answer.

"Oh, for Christ's sake, Carl. What the hell's wrong with you? This is the first weekend I've had off, and I was really looking forward to it. Don't tell me you disapprove." Jessica stood up and reached for the wine bottle. "Why is it you young people think you've got the monopoly on all things physical? Life doesn't stop when you are over thirty-five, you know. All the feelings are still there. What's wrong with wanting to be with someone?"

Jessica poured another glass of wine and found she was fiercely gripping the bottle. "Anyway, don't think you're going to make me feel guilty for spending a weekend away because you won't."

Carl drained his glass and stood up. "How could I possibly make you feel guilty, Jessie? It's none of my business what you do."

With that, he put his glass on the drainer, wished her goodnight and left. Jessica stared at the door in amazement. *What the hell was that all about? Anyone would think I was his mother the way he'd carried on,* she thought angrily.

Deep in thought, Carl was unaware of the dozens of different sounds around him. The muted sounds of music, TVs, children's voices, and laughter coming from various directions all over the camp. He didn't really know why he had gone to see Jessica. He'd been having a quiet early drink in the bar, chatting with Pete, the barman, when Luke walked in. The huge man had barely greeted him and ordered a double brandy. Carl saw Pete's eyebrows go up in surprise.

"Well, well, a beer drinker on the hard stuff so early in the evening. Are we celebrating something or drowning our sorrows?"

"None of your damn business," came the gruff reply, stopping all conversation dead.

Pete busied himself polishing glasses at the back of the bar, all the time keeping a wary eye on the broad shoulders at the end of the counter.

In the years gone by, Luke had achieved a reputation second to none for settling every dispute with his fists. His size and strength had made him a fearful opponent for any man, and many had shown a clean pair of heels rather than face him. But as his business had grown and prospered, he had matured along with it and was now more inclined to use a diplomatic approach. Some of the men who worked for him were real hard cases, but they listened to him. They knew if they didn't, he would still be a hell of a man to beat in a fight.

Carl watched him down the brandy and ordered another one. A thought half formed in his mind that if he could stop Jessica from going away this weekend, he could also stop this self-destruct feeling hanging over Luke like a cloud. Without a clear idea of what to do, he found himself at Jessica's door. Seeing her all packed up and ready had finished any possible discussion on Luke, and he had felt stupid and tongue-tied immediately.

Pete looked up as Carl walked back into the bar.

"What's up with Luke, for God's sake? I've never seen him so pissed off. He hasn't got financial problems, has he?"

"Not that I know of. Where is he now?"

"Gone to the pool for a swim, would you believe? Said he wanted to clear his head. More like sink after all that booze."

Carl suddenly felt panic. They had signs up around the pool about swimming after drinking and how dangerous it was. He moved quickly out of the bar and towards the pool. All the lights were on, but most of the residents had gone off to supper long ago. He bypassed the turnstile and cut through the box office door straight into the pool area. He stood at the side of the footwash and watched the strong muscular arms lift and curve in perfect rhythmic motion. The strong kicking feet propelled the body forward in a powerful crawl that was pleasurable to watch. *No problem here,* Carl thought, feeling foolish at being panicky. He turned to go, and then, as the body hauled itself from the water in one smooth streaming movement, he stopped and turned back to look.

From time to time, nature turns out a man whose bone structure and definition of muscle emits a sense of strength and power without any need for bodybuilding or help of any sort. Luke was such a man. His legs were massive columns of power, well-shaped and muscular and all in proportion. His upper torso carried not an ounce of fat, the shoulders broad, and the stomach flat and hard, with muscular definition. The body hair was a thick mat at the top, tapering down to a point below the navel, where it disappeared below the line of his shorts. He lifted his arms to sweep the water from his hair and beard, and the muscles in his shoulders and arms rippled with a suppleness that left the watching Carl with his mouth gaping.

Luke always wore baggy jeans and jerseys, which made most people think that he was a big man covering up a layer of fat. Carl would never have believed he had such a build under all that baggy gear. Luke turned and headed for the changing rooms. Even from the back, he was magnificent. His walk was easy and flowing. His stride long and smooth as he disappeared from sight. Carl went out through the foyer and back to the bar.

I wonder what Jessie would do if she ever got to see him in all his glory. I'm going to make bloody sure she does, he thought, a grin stretching across his face.

CHAPTER 27

The train journey was peaceful and smooth. Jessica's magazine lay unread on her lap, and she gazed at the passing landscape, deep in her own thoughts. Her mind went back to Carl's visit the previous night. Funny how he had managed to put her on the defensive without actually saying anything wrong. Despite what she'd said, he had made her feel guilty. Why this should be, she didn't know. In theory, if she spent the nights with Alan, then she would, in the eyes of the law, be as guilty as Drew. The circumstances might be different, but the outcome would be the same. Adultery. Not a pretty word.

Jessica's mind went into a black, gloomy cloud of depression. She straightened her shoulders and sat upright. *I'm not going to start my weekend like this. I let Drew dominate my life and make a mockery out of our marriage. It's time for me to do what I want without feeling guilty about something lost years ago.*

She took a mirror from her bag and touched up her makeup. Around the corner of the mirror, she caught an admiring glance from a man further down the carriage and felt her spirits lift. *Yes,* she thought with an inner smile, *this is going to be a wonderful weekend.*

With much shuddering and squealing of brakes, the train came to a stop. Jessica pulled her small suitcase off the rack and headed towards the door. As she stepped down, she caught sight of Alan walking slowly along the platform, peering anxiously in every window. He suddenly saw her and his face beamed. He strode quickly towards her and gripped her in a bear hug. She inhaled the familiar aroma of his aftershave, dropped her case, and hugged him right back.

With their arms around each other, they kissed long and hard before walking out to Alan's car, where she got well and truly kissed again.

So much for the makeup, she mused, not giving a damn.

Alan weaved his way through the heavy traffic, talking all the time. "First, we'll have lunch and catch up with all the news. Then I'll show you the hotel, and we'll get all glammed up. I've got tickets for a show and booked a late dinner at a supper club, I know. Tomorrow will be all yours. You can go wherever you want. Your wish is my command."

"Whoa, whoa, I thought this was going to be a nice restful weekend. Already, I'm out of breath."

Alan turned a worried face towards her. "I'm sorry, Jessie. Am I rushing you? I've been looking forward to this time together for so long; tell me if I overstep the mark."

Jessica threw her head back, her mouth wide with laughter. "It all sounds wonderful; I can't wait."

Alan's smile returned, and the black eyes took on their usual sparkle. "Thank God for that. You had me worried there for a minute."

The car turned sharply down a ramp and into an underground car park, gliding smoothly to a halt in a parking bay. Jessica's hand reached out for the door handle, only to be stopped by Alan's warm hand on her wrist. She turned to look at him and was met by hard, hungry lips that threatened to eat her. She found herself responding with a passion that made her writhe in her seat and left her breathless.

"Christ, Jessie, I've been like a cat on hot bricks since yesterday. I keep getting short of breath, clammy hands, hot sweats, and lapses of memory. Do you think you can help me get better?"

Jessica looked into the glittering eyes and felt her insides melting. "When would you like me to start?"

"How about under the table while we're waiting for lunch."

Jessica punched him gently on the arm. "Down, boy, feed me first. I'm going to need the nourishment."

Alan chuckled deep in his throat. "You certainly know how to keep a man dangling."

"That's not a word I would have used to describe your situation," Jessica replied, glancing down below his belt and climbing out of the car.

Alan's laugh was loud in the confined space.

The lunch passed pleasantly. Jessica caught him up with all the news about the complex, Polly, the visitors, and Uncle Tom Cobley and all.

Alan put her in the picture about what was happening at the head office. They had several meetings recently to discuss the possibility of opening the same type of thing overseas, with Spain, Italy, and France being the prime targets. Space for touring vans for travelling holidaymakers and permanent mobile homes booked with travel agents in England. If the plan got the approval of the board, work would start around the clock during the winter months and would be ready to open for next year's season.

Jessica found herself being charged up with Alan's excitement and ideas. They chattered non-stop and eventually ambled back to the car in high spirits.

The hotel was excellent; Alan must have pulled out all the stops. There was a small cosy sitting room with a deep squashy pair of sofas, the usual TV, a gorgeous view all over London, and large baskets of fruit and flowers. The bathroom had every available toiletry, and the bedroom was lush and softly coloured in blue and grey.

Jessica suddenly found herself feeling shy and strange. Her bubbly mood had evaporated and left her jittery and nervous. Alan still talked away, but not quite so fluently. Then, even his chatter stopped as her mood reached him. He walked over and took her in his arms. His mouth was soft and undemanding, relaxing and unwinding her slowly. He didn't speak but smoothed her face and hair. He kissed her throat and neck. His hands ran slowly up and down her back with a massaging and caressing movement. Jessica leant against him, her legs quivering. They sunk down onto one of the sofas, and the kissing deepened. Alan placed a cushion on the arm and slid Jessica over sideways until her head was resting on it and her body lay lengthways. He fitted his body along hers and the kissing continued. She felt his excitement with the increasing hardness of his body and suddenly lost all her shyness as her long, subdued passion took over. She became wanton and demanding. Hardening her mouth on his. Letting her hands roam where they may. Stroking him and gripping him through his clothes until his eyes closed, and he moaned and sucked in his breath.

Jessica became feverish to be naked with him, to feel his skin against hers. She became impatient with his shirt buttons. They wouldn't go through the holes, and he took her hands away and undid them himself. She tore her blouse and bra off and lay across him, desperate to feel him against her. But even that was not enough.

"Get up. Stand up," she demanded.

When he did, she kneeled in front of him, scratching his lower back and sides. She ran her nails around him, up and down his chest and belly, her hands finally stopping at his belt buckle. She quickly undid it and the trouser's hook and zip. Hearing him suck in his breath sharply as he realised what she was doing, she exalted in the feeling of power that his arousal gave her. She eased his trousers and pants over his now fully erect penis and ran her tongue up along the underside. His moan was long and drawn out. He bent to grasp her under the armpits and pull her up against him. He rubbed his chest from side to side against her. His hair rasping across her nipples. With a quick movement, he bent down and yanked up his trousers, holding them up with one hand while the other grasped her around the waist.

He half carried, half dragged her into the bedroom.

The remainder of his clothes were torn off in seconds, and with one tug, her skirt and everything under it were pulled from her body. She lay along the length of him. Their mouths were open, sucking and licking. She pulled him over onto her, ready and impatient. He stopped her briefly to fit a condom and then entered her smoothly. On his entry, their moans were simultaneous and deep. He stayed inside her, unmoving for several seconds. Filling her and opening her even more for him. But this wasn't enough. She wanted him to move and she thrust her hips up at him. Urging him to move, forcing him to move. He was in danger of being too quick for her and exerted every ounce of willpower he could muster to stop the imminent surge. But already her body was curving upward, her eyes tightly shut, her teeth bared, and muscles twitching and shuddering. He watched her face, his whole body as tight as a bowstring, and when she thrust strongly upwards, he let go of all control and took his pleasure with her.

He lay unmoving on her for a long time. Their breathing slowed, the heartbeats slowed, and a small movement from her told him he was getting heavy. He rolled over onto his side, still holding her, discarded the condom, and quickly flipped the corner of the duvet over them. He pulled her head into his neck and his whole body relaxed. His breathing deepened and he drifted into sleep.

When Jessica felt him getting heavy, she stayed wrapped in his arms. Her eyes were wide open and fixed on a pot on the dressing table. Her body felt boneless and satisfied. Why then did she have this small hollow feeling in the pit of her stomach that wasn't filled?

She wanted to move. She wanted to wipe the stickiness from her legs. Her mouth was dry. But she lay still for a decent length of time before she moved her body away from him and got up.

CHAPTER 28

Drew primed Melanie on what to expect over the weekend. The visit had been arranged for mid-morning on Sunday with Max Duffield, and she had been told about the car crash story and was prepared to go along with it.

The rainbow hues of bruises were slowly fading, but even heavy makeup wouldn't cover them completely yet. However, the face was starting to look again like the beautiful one Drew remembered from the filming.

Melanie was still close-mouthed on the subject of the person who administered the beating, and even Marty could get no information out of her without upsetting her, so they let it rest.

Around eleven o'clock, a car pulled into the driveway, and Drew looked out to see the expected Ms Duffield climb out of a white BMW convertible. The formidable lady he was expecting seemed to have disappeared to be replaced by the person who now stood by the car. She wore tight-fitting jeans with a casual white shirt tucked into the top of them and low-heeled white strappy sandals. Her hair was pulled back into a high ponytail on top of her head, and the wind had loosened it to leave wispy strands around her face. The sun glinted on the hair and it was the colour of burnished copper. Drew opened the front door and walked out to meet her.

"Good morning, Mr. Cameron. What a lovely morning. I really enjoyed the drive down."

She entered the house and took off her sunglasses. The ginger eyes were outlined and shaded a smudgy brown, and the white teeth were set off by a deep cinnamon lipstick. Gold hoops in her ears glinted in the subdued light of the hallway, and a waft of light perfume trickled up Drew's nostrils. *Christ, what a transformation*, he thought. His eyes scanned her; she looked like a sleek, tawny cat.

"Good morning to you, too, and it certainly is a lovely morning. Would you like coffee?"

"That would be lovely."

Marty came in through the patio doors and looked at Ms Duffield and then at his father. His eyebrows rose a fraction, to be replaced by two vertical frown lines when the eyebrows lowered.

"Marty, I'd like you to meet Maxine Duffield. This is my son Marty. He's helping to look after Melanie while her bruises heal."

Marty's face was one of relief at the introduction. "I'm very pleased to meet you. Melanie's in the garden. Come on through. We'll have our coffee outside."

Drew wondered at the look on Marty's face while he poured the coffee for them. Then it dawned on him. *He thought that was another of my women. After the description I'd given Marty, he thought that was someone else and not the old dragon we were expecting. Well, screw him,* Drew thought viciously. *Does he think I'd shit on my own doorstep while he's here? What sort of bastard does he think I am? Huh…I know the answer to that already.*

He took the coffee outside; a smile plastered across his face, and he felt like tipping the pot over his son's head.

Melanie was at ease with the sleek, tawny lady, and Max Duffield was very gentle and soft towards their house guest. She leant towards her and looked closely at the bruises, tut-tutting and sympathising. "My sweet girl, even with all that lot, you still have the looks that most women would kill for. I think we can give you a bit more time before we put you to work. Mr Sullivan is not unsympathetic. These accidents do happen. Come in and sign the contracts, and we'll review the situation in a week."

Melanie's smile warmed everyone's heart, and the deal was done. Maxine stayed and chatted with them for another hour.

How could I have got such a wrong idea about her, Drew wondered. *She's charming.*

They all tried to persuade her to stay for lunch, but she declined. "I always visit my daughter on Sundays. With my busy life, it's the only day I truly get to myself, and I like to spend it with her."

The various questions about her daughter were fended off gracefully. They learnt nothing about her other than her name, which was Kate—short for Katherine.

After Maxine left, the whole company seemed to get somewhat subdued, as if the sun had gone behind a cloud. Marty decided to take Melanie to the cinema, and for want of something to do, Drew decided to travel back to London, stopping for lunch on the way to fit in a couple of hours of work at the office while it was quiet. Within an hour, everyone had drifted their separate ways for the day.

Happy families, Drew thought wryly as he backed out of the driveway. *We used to be one.*

With no traffic on the road, Drew decided to drive straight through without stopping and have lunch somewhere in town. He parked with no problem and went for a wander around, something he rarely did. There was a small bistro in a shopping mall that served a pleasant meal; he decided to eat there and read the Sunday papers. The place was only half full, and he enjoyed the food with a decent glass of house wine.

A bookstore was open, and he browsed around there for a while, buying a couple of paperbacks on the best-seller list. He rarely had time to read, but he thought Melanie might enjoy them in the meantime. He strolled out of the store and glanced around him. The place had quite a few people milling aimlessly about. A case of

Sunday, sweet Sunday and nothing to do.

He looked towards the escalator and debated whether to go up to the next floor when his eyes caught and were riveted to the couple travelling upwards on it. They leant towards each other on the same step and were smiling. The man's hand rested on the small of the woman's back in a gesture of familiarity and their hips were touching. He stood dead still, unblinking and unmoving. The woman could have been Jessica's double. Her hair was cropped short and lighter than Jessica's and her clothes were soft and flowing, totally unlike anything that she would wear, but the likeness was uncanny. At the top of the stairs, the woman laughed. That was when Drew moved. His legs felt heavy as if the muscles had seized up, but he propelled himself at a run up the long escalator. There were more people on this floor, and Drew searched each shop with frantic haste, elbowing people out of the way in the process. After a fruitless forty-five minutes of searching, he gave up and sat down on a chair outside a coffee shop, feeling out of breath and shaky. *It couldn't have been her. She just looked like her.* He almost convinced himself until he remembered the laugh. It had been like hearing a ghost.

He made his way slowly towards the street. *Tomorrow, I will phone the agency to see if they have any news for me.* He really couldn't stand this happening to him over the next umpteen years; his nerves would be shot. Not feeling at all like going into the office now, he decided to take a leaf out of Marty's book and go to the cinema. He sat through a box office smash hit for two hours and didn't take in a word.

CHAPTER 29

Jessica was soaking in a warm, bubbly bath when Alan appeared in the doorway looking tousled and bleary-eyed. His dressing gown was loosely tied, and for a moment, his face had a look of panic.

"Oh, Christ, Jess. I got such a shock when I woke up and you'd gone. I hated it when I fell asleep like that. I'm so sorry, love. I was so relaxed and warm with you, I couldn't help myself. I thought you'd got mad with me and left."

Jessica laughed and flicked bubbles at him. "It's OK, no apologies needed. I've had a busy day, and this is lovely. I needed to pamper myself a little before the start of the wonderful evening's entertainment I've been promised."

Alan knelt down on the floor and softly kissed Jessica on the mouth. "Thank you for spending this weekend with me. I've thought about nothing else since you phoned me. Even through some of the meetings, my mind has been seeing you get off that train. Once this week, I even had to read the minutes to get me up to date with the previous decisions. And now you're here."

His mouth moved down over her neck, and his hand caressed her breast, but Jessica sat upright and turned her body away from him, laughing. "Behave yourself, Alan Todd. If you keep playing with fire, we aren't going to get out of this room for the whole weekend."

Alan laughed, too, and stood up, revealing a very healthy erection. "Now look what you've done. I shall be like this all evening now."

Alan knelt down again, searching for her mouth, but Jessica stood up, showering him with soapy water. "Go away, you randy man, and I will see to you later when I've been fed, watered, and entertained."

Alan looked up and grinned. "Think I'll stay here, the view's better."

Eventually, they were both ready. They had chatted away to each other while dressing and were both quite at ease. Although Jessica had circled around a couple of times, out of grabbing distance, when she caught Alan watching her, his black eyes glittering dangerously. It was all very pleasant.

Alan looked smartly casual in navy slacks and a blue striped shirt, topped with a dark burgundy jacket. Jessica looked slim and elegant in a dark chocolate fitted dress with a high polo neck and a long swirly skirt, which she wore with brown high-heeled suede boots. The evening was a bit chilly, so she slipped on a soft suede bolero-type jacket in tan that Drew had bought her in Italy. With Alan wafting Dunhill aftershave behind him and Jessica leaving a cloud of Opium perfume, they both sallied forth.

The evening was a great success. They ate a light salad with a bottle of wine just around the corner from the theatre and arrived in enough time to watch the audience and absorb the excited buzz people always generate at the theatre before curtain up.

Throughout the show, Alan watched Jessica from the corner of his eye. She was completely riveted to the action on stage, and her body stayed motionless as the story of Les Miserables unfolded. Most women he had brought to the shows always fidgeted, crossing and uncrossing their legs, but Jessica was a model of stillness. It took all her willpower to stop herself from leaping to her feet and applauding loudly at the end of the show. They discussed the show over a late and leisurely dinner before catching a taxi back to the hotel in the early hours.

Jessica yawned widely and emerged from the bathroom in a satin gown to find Alan already propped up in the bed and waiting for her.

To be truthfully honest with herself, she had hoped for just a cuddle tonight; it had been a long day. But seeing the look on Alan's face, she knew that was out of the question. She slipped off her gown, and Alan flipped back the bedcover, reaching for her immediately.

"Now we're going to finish what you started hours ago," he growled into her mouth.

Their lovemaking was slow and easy, and despite Jessica's tiredness, she soon found herself responding. Where before she had been the dominant one, it was now Alan's time to take charge. He kissed and nibbled and caressed, and she just lay there, letting him do whatever he wanted. Her occasional moans let him know what she liked. They merged together, and the rhythm was unhurried and deep. Both hardly moving, letting the sensations roll over them, until the last few moments when the pace quickened, and their bodies shuddered and clung. Jessica slept deeply. She realised she was on the wrong side of the bed to the one she usually slept on, and for a few minutes she felt awkward, but she was so tired, she fell asleep still thinking about it.

The next morning, after breakfast in their room, in their dressing gowns, Alan said he had someone he wanted her to meet later. They had a drive through London, quiet now on a Sunday morning, a walk in Hyde Park, the sun warm and the birds singing, lay on the grass and read the papers, bought plastic cups of coffee, in fact, lots of little nothing things that add up to a pleasant time. Later on, they parked the car and walked into a cool and modern shopping centre. Alan informed her he had a surprise for her.

"This has been such a special weekend for me, I wanted to give you a gift so you will always remember it. I want you to tell your grandchildren, Alan was a smashing bloke, good-looking, charismatic, and very modest, and he gave me this."

"Oh, Alan," Jessica said, smiling. "You don't have to give me a present for me to remember this time. I've had such a good weekend;

I'll never forget it."

"But I want to," Alan replied, guiding her towards the escalator.

"Who is this person you want me to meet?"

"You'll see soon, sweet lady."

Over Jessica's shoulder, Alan's eye was caught by a handsome, dark-haired man gazing up the escalator towards them. He turned back to Jessica. "My friend is actually an artist who wants to paint you nude and in abstract. I told him you wouldn't mind."

Jessica threw her head back and laughed.

Smiling into each other's eyes, Alan pressed a bell in a recessed doorway between two shops, spoke into an intercom, and, after the click of the automatic lock, pushed open a heavy door. It shut with a snick behind them to leave them in front of another heavy door. A security camera watched them, its red eye glowing, before another loud click admitted them into a foyer.

"Alan, my friend, it's been too long."

A young man wearing a Jewish yarmulke on his mop of curly hair appeared from the side of them and wrapped Alan in a tight bear hug. "I was so pleased to get your phone call." Turning to Jessica, "And this is the lovely lady you told me about. I'm very happy to meet you. Come in, come in."

They followed him into a workshop where another man, almost identical to the first one, stood up. Alan walked over to the second man and received another bear hug. "Jessica, I'd like you to meet two very good friends of mine. This is Isaac, usually known as Zack." Jessica shook the first man's hand. "And this is Zack's brother, Solly." Another handshake.

"Zack and I were at school together. He has been a friend for many years and is one of the cleverest manufacturing jewellers I know."

"And I'm the other one," Solly added.

"And Solly is the other one," Alan repeated with a grin.

"Come, Jessica. See what I've made for you," Zack took her arm.

She walked over to Zack's workbench. It was a strange-looking arrangement consisting of a large bottom bench, with a smaller bench set above it with a half circle cut out of it and a piece of leather slung underneath to catch the filings from the precious metals he worked with. Laying across the top bench was the most delicate bracelet she had ever seen. It was an intricate weave of fine gold and silver wire in scrolls and swirls, all beautifully intermingled into a two-inch wide fragile looking, but surprisingly heavy, piece of handmade jewellery. She picked it up gently.

"Oh my God, this is so beautiful." She held it up to the light, and the pattern the bracelet created fell across her face. "I can't take this, Alan. It's far too precious."

"'Course you can," Zack said, his chest puffing out with pride at her praise. "It's about time he spent some of his money. He works so many hours, he can't have any time left to spend it. It must be stockpiling like Fort Knox by now."

He took Jessica's wrist and clasped the bracelet. It felt heavy and cold, but the metal gleamed and warmed, and even though Jessica was not a covetous person, she really wanted this bracelet. She should still be refusing it, but the words stuck in her throat.

"We haven't finished yet," Solly said, walking towards her. "This is the other part of the set."

He took her left hand and, on her index finger, slipped a broad ring in the same beautiful scrolled work. The shank of the ring was still open for sizing before soldering. Solly closed the gap until the ring fitted her comfortably and went back to his bench. "This won't take long. Give me ten minutes, and I'll have it ready for you."

"Jessica, my sweet. While I talk business and haggle with my friend here, would you like to find a coffee shop? There's one down on the next level, and I'll join you soon."

Jessica embraced both the brothers warmly, thanked them, praised the gifts once again, and was escorted out. Caressing the bracelet, she walked over to the edge of the parapet and looked down to find the coffee shop. Her eyes were drawn immediately to a tall figure walking towards the doorway. Against the brightness of the sun coming through the glass, his form was in silhouette. Jessica felt herself pale, and a jolt went through her like a shock. Drew. That was Drew. But Drew never came into town on a Sunday.

Giving herself a mental shake, she dismissed it as being someone who looked like him, but realised she was going to have to make contact soon to get things sorted out. She stepped onto the escalator to be carried down to the coffee shop. *When I get back, I'll contact a local lawyer and get some advice. Enough time has passed, and I feel ready to tie up some loose ends now. I wonder if it really was Drew,* she mused as she sat down to wait for Alan. *Well, if it was, he could only have been in town for one purpose; I suppose she got him to stay the night. Now, he doesn't have to come home to me on weekends. He can stay out any night he wants.* Her lip curled with distaste. *Yes, it was definitely time to get things sorted out.*

CHAPTER 30

Drew threw himself into his work with a vengeance. Marty had decided to extend his leave a bit longer in case the investigator came up with anything. Melanie also stayed on after consulting Drew. She was still a bit jittery about going back to her flat in case the still unnamed man came looking for her, and she wanted to spend a bit more time with Marty until she had to start work. She had gone into town for a makeup test at the studios, but despite heavy applications of gunge, the bruises still showed through. Maxine Duffield had seen the proofs and had decided to give her one more week.

Sophia was pleased. She had taken the girl to her heart and had invited both Melanie and Marty around for an Italian dinner with her and her Alfie. Drew drove them to the house on his way to his club. He stopped off to meet Sophia's family.

Alfie was a burly man with brown hair, a good-looking face, and a quiet manner, totally unlike anything Drew had imagined. He had pale blue eyes, and his face was tanned, unlined, and lit up when he looked at his wife. Sophia was the boss of the kitchen and family, but despite his gentle attitude, Alfie was definitely the boss of the house.

"Mr. Cameron, I pleased you in my home. Come, sit down. I pour you nice glass of Italian wine."

"Just one, Sophia, I'm driving," Drew looked around.

The room was dominated by a magnificent fireplace. It was built from a very white stone and went from floor to ceiling and from one side of the room to the other. There were cavities in it for books, plants, photographs, TV, etc. A gas log effect fire was in the centre, topped by a beautiful beaten copper chimney breast. The carpet was deep red, as were the curtains, with a cream leather lounge suite. The whole room was warm, lived in, and well-loved. Drew sat down and felt immediately at home.

Alfie's voice was deep and resonant. "Sophia's told me a lot about you, Mr. Cameron."

"Not too much, I hope," Drew answered with a grin.

"We have no secrets. Sophia is my wife and my best friend. We've been through some very bad times together, and now we realise how much we have. Everything I have, I owe to my wife, including my sanity."

Sophia bustled in with a tray of drinks and caught the last part of Alfie's reply. "Don't listen him, Mr. Cameron. He owe me nothing. He take on me, my kids and all the troubles I have, and put all together to make family. He work long days to put home together. He owe me nothing."

Sophia sat on the arm of her husband's chair, and his arm went around her ample hips. "What do you think of this bossy woman of mine then?" he asked Drew

"I think you are a very lucky man," Drew replied warmly.

"I'll be even luckier when I've tamed her," Alfie squeezed her hip. "I've spent many a tiring hour trying to break her spirit, but after all these years, I think my technique must be all wrong."

Sophia ruffled her husband's hair and glanced at him coyly out of the corner of her eye. "You always enjoy Sophia's spirit. If you too tired I always find way to put life in your bones."

"Wicked woman in front of guests," Alfie laughed, slapping her rump. "Get you to the kitchen."

On that cheerful note, Drew took his leave. He had arranged to meet Adam for a drink at the club. With the pressure of work, they had both been so busy they'd been passing each other in the doorway. Cassie had gone to visit her mother, who had just come out of hospital, and the two men had decided to dine at the club and catch up on their lives in general. Adam had asked a couple of times if Drew had heard from Jessica, but apart from the negative answer, nothing else had been said.

The first thing that Drew noticed when he entered the club was the new barmaid. She was a pretty little thing with a mane of streaky blond hair and a voluptuous figure. Her eyes stared straight into his, knowing and seductive. "What's your pleasure, sir?" she asked with a smile.

"Something springs very quickly to mind, but in the meantime, I'll have a whisky," Drew leant on the bar and used his blue eyes to good effect. He detected a small blush from the pretty cheekbones and chuckled. "I might have been around sooner if I'd known they'd changed the bar staff."

"I've only worked here a couple of weeks." Knowing eyes locked again with his.

"And what do they call you, pretty thing?"

"I'm Ellen."

"And I'm Drew," feeling a touch on his sleeve and a clearing of his throat. "And this is my friend Adam."

"Pleased to meet you, Miss. Look out for Drew, though. He's been known to gobble up good-looking barmaids for lunch."

Ellen showed small white teeth in a coy smile. "Thank you for warning me. I'll make sure I keep away from his mouth."

Adam moved away from the bar towards a table. Drew followed him, sitting down quickly to hide the bulge in his trousers. The first moment of eye contact had given him an instant hard-on, and he would have liked to pursue the chemistry a bit more before Adam arrived. It had been a long time between sessions, and after the disastrous events of the previous encounters, he had been a bit shy of anything physical. *However, it was time he dipped his toe in the water again or dipped something anyway,* he thought, turning his attention to Adam. "Well, Adam, my friend, what's new?"

"Just going to ask you the same thing," Adam looked at him over the rim of his pint glass. "Seems you are the one whose life is ever-changing."

Drew spent the next half an hour bringing Adam up to date on things in general, who listened quietly.

"I would have thought the investigation people could have found something out by now. Jessica was always so steady and predictable; who'd have thought she had the imagination to plan her escape so completely at such short notice."

Drew snapped his glass down on the tabletop. "Escape! God, Adam, you make it sound as if she was in prison."

Adam wiped his mouth with the back of his hand and put his glass down before replying. "Maybe she didn't realise she was in one till she was on her own. It's possible to feel lonely and trapped even when you're in the middle of a crowd of people. Sometimes, it takes years to start to feel differently. Closeness is a mental feeling, not a physical one."

"Since when have you been an expert on therapy?"

Adam stood up. "Since I had to look at myself through someone else's eyes. Since I had to try and see what other people saw when they looked at me."

"You and Cassie?"

"Yes. Me and Cassie. I wanted to put things right between us, but I couldn't do that without seeing what was wrong in the first place. Maybe it would be good for you to give yourself a hard look from the inside. Be honest and brutally frank about the shitty side of yourself, and try to do something about changing it. Anyway, I'm going for a pee. While I'm gone, you can leer at the barmaid a bit more and get the menu."

Drew did as he was told and got her phone number as well.

The lunch passed pleasantly enough. The subject of work dominated as it usually did on these occasions, but Drew found, unusually, that his mind was not on it. He had been working a lot of hours recently, but the cut and thrust of the advertising business didn't seem to be giving him the buzz it used to. He put it down to the outside pressures dulling his edge, but he caught himself scanning the situations vacant pages last week. It had been a day when nothing had gone according to plan, and he was feeling tired and irritable. *How nice to have an undemanding job that was also fun,* he thought. *Something like…. What, for Christ's sake!* He used to think his job was fun. Whatever was the matter with him today? Too much sexual tension. He leant back in his chair and let his mind wander to past liaisons and memorable pleasures. Yes, he definitely had to give the whole thing another go.

He came back to the present to see Adam looking at him strangely. "For God's sake, Drew. Am I talking to myself, or what? You haven't heard a bloody word I've said for the last ten minutes. Where were you?"

"Changing my job," Drew answered, watching Adam's jaw drop.

"W…when?" he stuttered.

Drew laughed. "Don't worry, old son. It was only in the mind."

"Thank Christ for that," Adam said, relaxing. "Thought for a minute you were serious."

"One day I might be," Drew said, surprising himself.

Drew said goodbye to Adam in the car park, sat in his car, and waited. Eventually, the side door opened and Ellen came out. She headed across the members' car park and over to the visitors' side.

Her key was in the lock of a small Fiat when Drew's hand covered hers, making her jump. "Shit, you frightened me to death. Fancy creeping up on a girl like that."

Drew laughed and apologised. "Just wanted a few words before you left. I'd like to take you out one evening. Thought I'd find out when you're free."

Ellen turned and leant on the car, the open body language telling Drew that his attentions were not unwelcome. "Boy, you don't let the grass grow under your feet, do you? When did you have in mind?"

Drew moved closer. His body almost touching hers. "How about tonight?"

Her brown eyes locked with his again before she turned and got in her car. He watched her drive away before returning to the other car park with his trousers feeling once again uncomfortably tight and a grin on his face.

CHAPTER 31

Alan very reluctantly put Jessica back on the train on Monday morning. "I've got this awful feeling that this is the only time we're going to spend together."

"Oh, Alan, don't be silly. You have to go to work today, and I have to be back tomorrow. We've had a lovely weekend and thank you again for my lovely present."

"A beautiful gift for a beautiful woman," Alan replied, his eyes warm on her face. The train started to move, and Alan walked along beside it, not wanting to see her leave. "I'll ring you," he called and waved as the train picked up speed.

Jessica leant back in her seat and watched the last of the station disappear behind her. It had been a busy couple of days and she was feeling a bit gritty-eyed. *She must have gotten out of the habit of sleeping with someone,* she thought. Last night, she had tossed and turned despite the prolonged lovemaking and the late hour. Even though she had enjoyed Alan's company, and he was an excellent lover, she was glad to be on her own again. She sat and went over the weekend in her head. She realised that Alan had been totally relaxed with her, but she had always felt a knot of tension around him. Maybe it was because it was all new, and she thought she ought to be on her best behaviour. A wry grin touched her face. Best behaviour! That was a laugh after her wanton carry-on the first evening. *No. It had to be because it was the first time since Drew. Well...whatever, she had had a wonderful time, and she would sort it all out later.*

The campsite was completely full when she arrived back, and

everyone was pleased to see her. She didn't feel like giving a blow-by-blow account of the last couple of days and was very non-committal until they all got the message that however much they ribbed her, she wouldn't be drawn. After a while, they gave up and went back to work.

Jessica decided to spend the rest of her day catching up with her washing and cleaning the van, ready for the rest of what looked to be a busy week. She shoved her dirty washing into a plastic sack and headed for the laundrette, hoping it wouldn't be too busy. She chatted to a couple of mums trying to catch up with a heap of sandy towels and spotted Luke coming across the complex. She walked to the door and waved at him. Her arm dropped to her side as he turned quickly on his heel and walked away in the opposite direction. She could have sworn he saw her. *How strange. Maybe he didn't.* She shrugged and went back to the laundry. She finished all her washing and cleaning and was lying in a nice hot tub when someone knocked at the door.

Damn, double damn. Why had they waited until she was in the water? It was always the way. Sod's law. "Who is it?" she called, wrapping a towel around herself.

"It's me, Carl."

"Oh, Carl. I might have known it would be you to get me out of my bath. Hang on a minute."

She opened the door, clutching the too-small towel up under her armpits.

"Well, well, well, Venus arising from the deep. Nice to see you back. Have a good time."

"Yes, thank you," she answered briskly.

"Ok, don't bite my head off. I just came to see if I could take you to dinner. As you're still on official time off, and it's my first evening free for four days, thought we could go and sample Barney's cooking."

"Oh, Carl, that would be nice, but as you can see, I'm hardly ready to go anywhere."

"No, no, I don't mean right now. It's too early. You finish your bath, put on something glam, and I'll call for you later. I'll book a table, and we'll have a drink at the bar first to whet our appetite. How would that suit you?"

"Wonderful."

"Good," said Carl, his white teeth gleaming at her. "I'll come by about eight."

Jessica climbed back into the bath and stayed there for another half hour until she was in danger of falling asleep. *I mustn't be too late tonight,* she mused, washing her hair. *After a heavy meal, I shall be hard-pushed not to doze off over the dessert.*

Later, feeling fresh and more alert, she dressed in an ivory-coloured flowing muslin dress with multi-coloured sandals and an embroidered shawl tied around her shoulders. She swept her hair forward in loose tendrils along her cheeks and added a pair of fine hoop earrings in gold. Carl gave a long, drawn-out whistle when he saw her and held out his arm for her to hold in an old-fashioned and gallant gesture, quite unusual in a young person. She felt flattered and touched by his attention. Barney fluttered around them when they arrived and, after taking their orders, left them at the bar.

Carl was an entertaining companion. He made her laugh with some of his stories about the visitors. He had been called out to one of the vans by a family who had a dripping tap that was driving them crazy. He promised to fix it during the afternoon whilst they were out but walked in to catch two teenagers making love on the couch. The boy was so startled he fell on the floor, and Carl was so surprised he fell backwards out of the door. The girl burst into tears until Carl assured her he wouldn't say anything, and then she started flirting with him until he was scared the boyfriend was going to punch him.

Then the father raised a riot because the tap still dripped.

At the end of the story, while Jessica was still laughing, a gruff voice at her side remarked that it must have been one hell of a weekend.

"Luke!" Jessica said, her mouth still wide with a smile. "How nice to see you."

"Is it really?" Luke replied, unsmiling.

Jessica's smile died on her face. "What's wrong?" she asked, touching his arm.

"Nothing a few bevies won't fix," moving away from her hand.

Oh, Christ, thought Carl, *I don't need this tonight.*

Jessica looked at Carl, who made a wry face. Just then, the waitress asked them to be seated, and with several backward glances, Jessica allowed Carl to lead her to their table.

"Is there something wrong?" Jessica said, still looking over at Luke's hunched form.

"Who knows," Carl answered around a mouthful of food. "Luke's so deep you could find a home for that Scottish monster in his mind."

Jessica's appetite suddenly deserted her. Each mouthful of Barney's wonderful food was chewed and swallowed with difficulty. She constantly glanced over, and it seemed Luke was downing his drinks at an alarming rate.

"Please, Carl. Can't you do something? There's obviously something wrong."

"Why does everyone think I've got any influence over Luke? He's a big man, and I'm young enough to be his son. I can't tell him what to do. Just relax and enjoy the meal; Luke will be alright."

"What do you mean, everyone? You said, everyone. Who else is worried about him?”

“Oh, for God’s sake, Jessie. He went on a bender last week. Stacey wants me to talk to him, you want me to talk to him; it’s not my business. Why don’t you see what’s bugging him, and we can all get on with our own lives.”

As Carl got crosser, his accent became more pronounced until he was almost impossible to understand.

“All right, I will,” Jessica said stiffly and stood up.

“What a bloody evening this turned out to be,” Carl muttered and carried on with his meal.

Luke turned his head when she touched his hand and then turned back to gaze down into his drink. “Your food’s getting cold.”

Jessica slid onto the bar stool next to him. “I don’t appear to be hungry anymore.”

“I’m sure Carl will be pleased when he gets the bill.”

“What’s wrong, Luke? I thought we were friends. Maybe I can help.”

Luke’s laugh was more like a bark. “No, Jessie. You can’t help.”

“Why can’t I? You can talk to me. Sometimes it helps just to talk.”

Luke turned and looked at her. Jessica felt herself move back at the anger she saw in his eyes. The gentle eyes had disappeared to be replaced by glaring rage. “You would be the last person I would talk to, Jessie.”

“Why? I don’t understand.”

“No, Jessie. You don’t understand. Perhaps you never will.” Luke drained the rest of his drink and stood up. “Goodnight, Jessie. See you around.”

She watched his broad back disappear through the door and

returned slowly to her table. Carl had sent her food back to be warmed up in case her appetite had improved. On looking at her face, he knew that the effort had been wasted. "That bad, eh?"

"It seems his anger is directed at me. What have I done?"

"I'm sure I don't know," Carl cast his eyes down as he replied, in case she read the understanding in them.

"Well, one way or another, I'll find out."

"Maybe you will, and maybe you won't." Carl picked up the menu. "How about a dessert and another drink?"

CHAPTER 32

The bright moonlight through the willow tree cast a pattern across Ellen's naked form. Drew was still breathing heavily after the frantic exertions of the last few minutes. Ellen sat up and said, "I'm getting cold."

Drew knew he should have wrapped her in his arms, but now his body was satisfied he was eager to get away. They had spent a pleasant enough evening, but even though the physical attraction was very strong, all in all, she was an empty-headed young thing without much personality.

He learnt she was engaged to a builder who was away on contract work. She had now fallen out with her parents and was living with her sister. More than that, he didn't really want to know. They had spent the evening touching and exciting each other with eye contact and kisses. She knew about this place by the river and was as urgent to be alone as he was. By the time Drew had parked the car up a farm track, he took the blanket from the back seat and walked across the field. With Ellen kissing and touching him, his erection was threatening to burst his trousers. They both tore their clothes off with an urgency bordering on frenzy, and Drew entered her immediately. The sex was fast and furious, and he took her without much thought to her gratification. Thankfully, she was carried along with him and seemed to enjoy the haste as much as he did. The problem that Drew had carried around like a millstone for months was non-existent, and for that, he was grateful to her. At that moment his feeling of relief was so overwhelming it brought tears to his eyes. He sat up and put his arms around her in a tight hug.

"You were wonderful. I feel like a teenager again out here in the open. Thank you for a lovely time."

Ellen turned and looked at his face in the gloom. "That sounds like this will be the only time. Will I see you again?"

Drew thought about bluffing but decided against it. "Ellen, you're a lovely girl, but apart from the fact that I'm far too old for you, you also have a boyfriend."

"So you used me then."

"Oh, come on lovely, we used each other. You enjoyed it as much as me. Let's just take it for what it was. Instant lust, and leave it at that."

Ellen sat still and quiet for a while, then turned and grinned at him. "It was bloody good though, wasn't it?"

Drew chuckled. "Come on, you randy thing, get your clothes on before you catch cold."

He returned her to her car, kissed her softly, and drove home feeling good. The house was in darkness. It seemed everyone was already in bed. He made himself a cup of coffee and wandered up the stairs feeling relaxed and tired. Max Duffield was calling again tomorrow to look at Melanie's face. He hoped she didn't arrive too early. He felt like sleeping for ten hours.

It seemed like only minutes before he dragged himself back from a deep sleep by a loud rapping on the door.

"Come on, Dad. Are you dead or what? Breakfasts ready."

"Yeah, Marty. I'm awake."

The door opened.

"I've been shouting up the stairs for ages. I thought I'd better make sure you were still in the land of the living. Melanie has cooked a huge breakfast, and it's getting cold".

Marty was already showered and dressed, and was carrying a cup of coffee. He plonked the cup by the bedside and threw a dressing gown across Drew's feet. "Come and eat first, or Melanie will be cross."

"Melanie doesn't get cross," Drew mumbled, struggling into a sitting position.

"Huh, you don't know her like I do," Marty replied, heading for the door.

"Obviously not."

Drew walked naked into the bathroom, splashed water on his face, cleaned his teeth, drank his coffee, and descended the stairs in his dressing gown as instructed. Melanie had cooked the lot. Bacon, eggs, sausages, mushrooms, heaps of toast, and a large pot of coffee. Drew ate like a racehorse and sat back in his chair holding his stomach.

"Christ, what a blow-out. I might not move all day."

"I'm sure Max will just love looking at your hairy legs sticking out of your dressing gown," Marty said dryly.

"If she looks hard enough, she might even see something else sticking out from it," Drew answered, belching softly.

Melanie giggled, her hand in front of her mouth, but Marty just glared at him with eyes narrowed.

"Oh, for God's sake, Marty. Lighten up a bit. I'm sure the illustrious Ms Duffield knows by now what little boys are made of."

With that parting shot Drew headed upstairs for his shower. He returned sometime later dressed in jeans and a soft white jersey, to find Max already there and sipping coffee.

"My, you're an early bird this morning."

"Hello, Drew. Yes, as I told you before, I like to spend the day with my daughter, and I like to make the most of the time."

His eyes ran over her with interest. She was dressed in black tight leggings, heeled black ankle boots, and a fluffy black jersey. Her hair hung loose around her face, and she looked about sixteen.

"Our girl's bruises look much improved this week. I think we can put her to work on Monday."

Drew took the cup Melanie brought him, sat down in the armchair, and stretched his long legs out before him. "I think you're right. She's certainly back to her beautiful self now," Drew replied, smiling.

Melanie was sitting on the floor leaning against Marty's legs, a gesture that was not lost on Drew, nor for that matter, Max, who looked at them with warm eyes.

"Yes, she certainly is beautiful," Max replied, standing up. "See you bright and early Monday morning in my office, and we'll take it from there."

"You're not going already," Drew said, standing up.

"Fraid I have to. Time is ticking by, and I've still got a few miles to drive."

"Where does your daughter live? How come she doesn't live with you if you're so fond of her?" Drew asked as he walked her to the car.

"My, my, questions, questions," was her only reply.

"Sorry, I didn't mean to pry. I'm just interested in you, that's all"

"In me or my personal life?"

"Both, I suppose. You seem so different when you're at work. All efficient and uptight. I couldn't believe you were the same person when I met you again."

Max turned and looked at him, her hand on the top of the open car door. "Am I always efficient, uptight? No, I don't think so. You probably thought so because I didn't respond the way I was supposed to when you came on to me."

"Came on to you! When did I ever do that?"

"The first time I came to your office. You were all smiles and blue eyes, and I was supposed to be bowled over by that. But when I wasn't, you got the impression I was a hard and frigid female."

Drew could hear himself blustering. She had quite taken the wind out of his sails with her frank diagnosis of him, and he couldn't think of a thing in his own defence. Max threw back her head and laughed. Her eyes screwed shut and her mouth opened wide with mirth. "Oh, Drew, your face. You really don't like the truth about yourself much, do you?"

His head drooped downwards, and he thrust his hands in his pockets, looking and feeling rather dejected. "Sorry if you thought that. I suppose old habits die hard. Like most men, I react to a lovely woman."

Max hesitated, one foot already in the car. "What have you got planned for the day?"

Her question took him by surprise. "Same as most Sundays lately. Not much. Why?"

"Would you like to keep me company and come and meet my daughter?"

Drew was not aware his jaw had dropped until Max started laughing again. "Don't look so amazed. I'm only a dragon Mondays to Fridays."

Drew grinned. "I'd love to. Let me say farewell to the kids. I think they'll be glad to see the back of me."

Her driving was precise and efficient, much like the lady herself. Drew leant back in the seat and relaxed. The day was overcast and the top was on the car; the taped music was low and lazy.

"Where exactly are we going?"

"You'll see soon enough."

The journey passed mostly in a comfortable silence. She didn't chatter or volunteer much information at all, and after the initial small talk, they both lapsed into silence and just listened to the music. Finally, they turned into a narrow road and then into a long driveway leading to a large old house. *Very impressive,* Drew thought as they continued towards the house through vast, well-kept grounds bordered with flower beds all in full bloom. The car drew up outside a huge front door with wide stone steps leading up to it.

"It's a school," Drew said, seeing the sign on the wall.

"It most certainly is," Max answered with a smile.

"Is your daughter a boarder here?"

"No, she's a teacher."

"A teacher!" Drew said with surprise. "How old is she then?"

"Kate is twenty-two now," Max answered, opening the car door.

"Christ, I thought she was a little girl. You don't look old enough to have a daughter that age."

"Just goes to show what clean living does for you."

As Max straightened up from the car, a whirling dervish came running down the steps and threw herself into Max's arms. Max picked her up and swung her around in a tight bear hug before putting her down and looking into her face. No words were spoken, and Drew watched in amazement at Max's hands fluttering around like butterflies in the time-honoured language of the deaf. The two women turned towards him.

"This is my daughter Kate. As you can see, she is deaf."

Drew looked at Kate. She was smaller than her mother. Her figure was slim and neat, and her hair was a red-blond. Her wide smile showed white teeth, and her eyes crinkled at the corners like her mother's.

"She is very pretty," he said to Max.

Kate's long, tapered fingers worked quickly, and Max watched them and smiled. "She said thank you very much, and you are very handsome."

At Drew's expression, Max laughed. "It's ok, don't look so startled. Kate also lip reads. As long as she can see your mouth, she will know what you are saying. Come on. Let's go inside".

Drew followed somewhat reluctantly behind. He suddenly had a feeling of misgiving. In all his life, he had never had any contact with people who had any form of disability, and whilst not going out of his way to avoid them, he had never actively sought them out either. He was sure that this was going to be a difficult afternoon.

"Come on, slow coach," Max called over her shoulder. "Come and meet the rest of the gang."

Drew smiled a rather wan smile and went through the big front door.

CHAPTER 33

The weather had turned showery and windy, and the holiday visitors hung around the complex in droves. The staff all had their work cut out, keeping some of the youngsters from vandalising the place behind their parent's backs. Most of it was boredom, but some of the damage was caused by a deliberate wish to destroy. Tim Allard, the deputy manager, had quite a few set-to's with aggressive parents over the behaviour of some of the children, and a couple of times, after repeated warnings, they were asked to vacate the site. It always left a bad feeling, but the constant damage to the toilet blocks, laundry, and pool changing rooms were causing the other visitors to complain and costing the complex a lot of money to put right.

Despite the continuing repair work, Luke's large body was conspicuous by its absence. Even some of the more major repairs were being carried out by his workmen, some of whom were taken off other jobs to be there. Jessica pondered many times about his attitude, but could find no reason for it. She constantly looked for him and even asked one of his men where he was keeping himself. All she got was a shrug of the shoulders and the reply, "I dunno."

Feeling rather down in the dumps, she agreed to go to a local flower show and fete with Polly and John on her day off at the weekend. She hadn't seen Polly for a while, and while John was getting showered and changed, the girls caught up with some of the gossip. Polly already knew about her weekend in London and wanted a blow-by-blow account. Jessica told her as much as she deemed necessary, and Polly read between the lines as she always did.

They sat at the kitchen table with the coffee pot between them, and Polly lit a cigarette. She blew out a stream of smoke, leant back, and said, "You don't really feel anything for Alan, do you?"

"Whatever makes you say that?"

"If you did, you would have had more excitement in your voice when you were talking about him, and besides, you would have been over to me before now telling me how wonderful he was."

Jessica's face had a thoughtful look as she digested what Polly had just said. She poured herself another cup of coffee before replying. "I must admit, I never felt entirely at ease with him. Perhaps it was just because it was the first time I had been on intimate terms with anyone other than Drew for years. I kept thinking I was doing something I shouldn't be. You know, like a naughty schoolchild."

"Will you see him again?"

"Well he is one of the management. When he comes down, it would be hard to avoid him. I honestly don't know."

"See…I knew I was right. If you really had a passion for him, you would be counting the hours."

"Oh, Polly, don't try and pair me off already. I'm still married, you know. I like being a bit independent for a change. I gave myself heart and soul to Drew for the best part of my life, and look where it got me. Maybe I should be aloof and distant like a mature woman of the world and let them all run after me for a change."

"Talking of Drew. Have you contacted him yet? It's been a long time now."

"No, I keep putting it off. I'm scared that once he knows where I am, he'll come down here and cause a scene. You know what he's like. I'm sure he's never going to allow a divorce without a fight. At least he's going to want to talk and that would upset the balance of things here just when I seem to be getting surer of myself."

"Well, you can't keep putting it off. Promise me you'll write to him and the kids. Once it's all out in the open, you can start again properly. Have you definitely made up your mind about divorce?"

"Oh, yes. There's no way I could ever go back now. With every passing day, I'm more convinced of that."

Polly took the cups over to the sink and turned on the tap. "What about Luke then?"

"What about him?" Jessica said, surprised.

"Surely you've seen the way he looks at you. Viv's been after him ever since she first laid eyes on him. She'd like to lay a lot more on him, too, but he's never taken her seriously. Only the other day she was moaning that he doesn't even joke with her anymore since you arrived. How did he take the news of your dirty weekend with Alan?"

Jessica looked at Polly with her mouth open. Polly turned around when she got no reply. "What?... Oh, Jessie, you must be blind and daft if you hadn't noticed."

Jessica's mouth closed with a snap. "You can't be right, Polly. You've got the whole thing all wrong."

"OK, have it your own way," she turned as John came through the door. "At last, I nearly had to come and fetch you."

"That's what I was waiting for. After half an hour, I could still hear you two gabbing, so I got up off the bed and put my trousers on."

"You!... I'm sure your hormones are too active. I shall have to get you seen to, like the cats."

John pinched her rump, picked up the car keys, and, over his shoulder, grinned and told her she'd have to catch him first.

By the time they got to the fete, the wind was very strong, and the huge marquee was flapping wildly. The canvas was cracking and ballooning. The kiddies' roundabout was in full flow, and the pony club lot was out in force. The ladies on the side stalls were battling to keep the goods from blowing away and their skirts from blowing up.

The three of them entered the marquee where most of the flowers were arranged for judging. The noise of the wind and the canvas was deafening. John had to shout to one of the exhibitors he knew to make himself heard. "This is terrible. When are they doing the judging? They'd better hurry before this whole tent blows away."

The exhibitor made a face and put his hands over his ears. "The judges are on their way round now," he shouted. "As soon as he's made up his mind, I'm heading for home before my eardrums burst."

They all went back outside to look around the stalls. Thirty minutes later, the rain started, and they made a dash for the marquee again. Polly and John were ahead of Jessica, who had a couple of carrier bags full of jam, preserves, and stuff. As she got near the tent opening, the flap of canvas that closed the door and was pegged back suddenly came loose and whipped towards her at great speed. The canvas hit her square in the middle of her back, taking her off her feet like a rag doll. She was thrown forcefully against the metal table just inside the tent. Her body landed loosely on the grass, the blood welling from her forehead, and her arms flung out at right angles to her body. Polly was laughing and brushing her wet hair off her face when she turned around. Her smile died, and she turned ashen as she knelt beside Jessica's unconscious body.

"Oh my God, Jessie. Jessie," she screamed, panic in her voice. "John, John, quick, quick. Oh my God."

John also knelt beside her but could do nothing. Jessica was out cold. One of the nurserymen dialled 999 from his mobile. Someone fetched a car blanket, and John took off his sweater and put it under Jessica's head.

"Don't try and move her. Wait till the ambulance gets here in case she'd hurt her back, OK, Polly? For goodness sake, stop crying."

Polly was usually so calm, but she seemed to have fallen apart.

John wrapped his arms around her. "She'll be alright, darling. She's just been knocked out, that's all."

Polly was still crying when the ambulance arrived and insisted on riding to the hospital with her. John got the car and followed as fast as he could. It seemed as if they paced the hospital corridor for hours before the doctor came out. His face looked grim and unsmiling. Polly cried out, "How is she? Is she going to be alright?"

"Well, it's early days yet. The X-rays show no sign of any skull fracture, and the spine has no dislocation, but she's had a whiplash injury similar to car crash victims, and she's concussed. We are keeping her in a neck brace for the time being, and I'm afraid she hasn't regained consciousness yet."

Polly's hand was across her mouth, stifling a sob. "How long before she comes around?"

"That we don't know at the moment, but we are monitoring her very carefully."

"Can we see her?"

"Just very briefly. There's nothing more you can do. I suggest you go home and phone us in the morning."

"Oh, no, doctor. I can't leave her. I must stay."

"No, Polly," John said, his arm around her. "The doctor's right. There's nothing we can do now except wait. She's going to need you later."

Polly's eyes filled with tears again when she saw Jessica. Her face was yellow-white, with a red livid bruise across her brow and a dressing on the wound. One eye was hugely puffed up. Tubes led from her body to a machine that monitored her vital signs, and she looked more dead than alive. After a few minutes, the nurse suggested they leave, and with dragging feet, they went home to a sleepless night. The morning phone call brought no good news. Jessica stayed unconscious.

CHAPTER 34

Drew was lost in thought on the journey home. He watched Max's hands on the steering wheel and remembered them throughout the day, constantly forming quick, precise gestures that brought smiles to the faces of the many children who gathered around her. She told them stories, talking at the same time, for his benefit and also for the ones who could read lips. The stories were about her work and the people who worked with her. She put a comic slant on everything, which made them laugh and kept them entertained for most of the afternoon. Kate added to the stories, and the children's heads were constantly turning from mother to daughter, the chuckles and pure enjoyment of the children coming over Drew in waves. On several occasions, he swallowed hard. The rapt looks on the faces of the small ones really get to him.

Games were organised on the back lawn, and he got roped in for all sorts of things, finishing up totally puffed out with all the running around. Soft drinks were laid out on top of the wall for everyone to help themselves, and Drew tucked in like the rest of them. He helped the teachers to clear up and asked many questions about the school; all were answered with honesty and pride.

Many of the children only went home occasionally as their homes were too far away, so the staff tried to make the weekends special. Kate had been one of the children taught here and had gone on to take her degrees in teaching, and came back to pass on her knowledge. The staff thought the world of her and of Max, too. Max was a director of the school and involved herself as much as she could in fundraising, organising trips, and general help wherever needed.

When it was time to leave, the children clustered around Max, hugging her and kissing their goodbyes. A couple started crying, but Max assured them she would be back, and their tears dried up. To Drew's amazement, the goodbye hugs and squeezes were also extended to him, and he felt his throat tighten again.

"A penny for them," Max said, breaking the silence.

Drew was so deep in thought that he actually jumped at the sound of her voice. He didn't answer straight away. He chewed the side of his nail, looked out the side window, cleared his throat, and finally said, " I couldn't even begin to tell you. My thoughts are in such a jumble I wouldn't know where to start."

"Try," Max replied, turning to stare at him.

"Do you think we could stop somewhere for a drink?" Drew looked out at the countryside. "I would like to talk, but I'd find it easier if it was over a drink. This has been one hell of a day".

"Was it so bad? I'm sorry if I dropped you in it. It must have been very hard to take. I should have told you first instead of forcing it all on you. Some people don't like to be around children that are handicapped."

Drew heard the worried note in her voice and looked over at her. His face split into a grin. "Dropped me in it. I should say you did. The little buggers wore me out. I feel like an old man."

She let out a bark of a laugh. "Oh, Drew. Aren't they darlings? They have had so many hurdles to get over, and when they start understanding, it's like Christmas. I'm so glad you had a good day."

The small pub they found was charming, and they talked ten to the dozen for ages, all about the day, the children, the teachers, and finally about Kate.

"Where's her father? Does he visit her?"

Max's face got tight and drawn, and Drew got the very strong impression that he had ventured into forbidden territory. She sat back in her chair. Her arms crossed in front of her, her body language closed and withdrawn, away from his space and into the past.

"No. Kate's father doesn't visit her. He left us when she was two years old. His freedom was more important to him than a distraught wife and a deaf daughter. Oh, I don't blame him. He was always a bit of a 'jack the lad.' I knew that when I married him. He was the catch of the crowd, and all the girls were after him. It was quite a feather in my cap when I got him. The trouble was he continued to be 'jack the lad' after we were married. I mistakenly thought a baby might settle him; maybe it would have if the baby hadn't been deaf. In his mind, it somehow reflected on him, and he couldn't cope with it, so he left. There, you have it in a nutshell."

Drew looked at Max's downcast face, knowing that what she wasn't telling him was more important than what she had. "How did you manage?"

Max's arms were wrapped tightly around her body now. "My father helped me a lot before he died. He bought us a flat, arranged care for Kate so I could go back to college, and found out about the wonderful school she's in now. John Sullivan is an old friend of my father and also Kate's godfather. He offered me a job in his company, and I worked my way up to the position I hold now."

"John Sullivan, your boss, is Kate's godfather," Drew couldn't believe it. "That dry old bastard."

"That dry old bastard, as you call him, is one of the cleverest and most astute businessmen you will ever find," Max snapped back. "He has one of the quickest and most brilliant minds in the international market, and he's also a fair and just man with a sharp sense of humour."

Drew was remembering Sullivan's deadpan face in the boardroom. "Well, I'll have to take your word for the humour. I must admit I didn't see too much of it".

"No...and you won't when you're doing business with him.

That's how his company profits increase every year. He is very ruthless if he needs to be but is always prepared to give the benefit of the doubt if the occasion warrants it."

They wandered back out to the car. Max seemed to be deep in thought and had closed Drew out without saying a word. He watched her out of the corner of his eye, missing her bright chatter of earlier; he wanted her back with him. Out on the road again, he felt he needed her to break the silence. He hadn't planned what to say but suddenly found himself speaking his feelings.

"Please don't shut me out, Max."

Startled, she glanced at him. "Sorry, is that what I was doing?"

"You've gone into yourself and left me outside."

She was quiet for several seconds. "Force of habit, I'm afraid. A form of self-defence, I suppose."

"You don't have to be defensive with me," Drew said softly.

"Don't I?"

"Of course not. Why do you think you do?"

Again, she took her time answering. "Because you are made in the same mould as Steve, my ex-husband, and that's not good."

Now Drew took his time answering. "Not good for whom?"

"Not good for me. You disturb me. Your reputation is well known, and your domestic situation is common gossip. But you are still so sure of yourself, it's as if nothing touches you inside."

"That's a polite way of saying you think I'm shallow and unfeeling," Drew's voice had taken on a rough note.

"Maybe you are. I don't know you well enough to have an opinion, but I saw you choke up on several occasions today, so I'm sure there must be a heart in there somewhere."

Drew didn't reply but slumped further down into the seat, his chin on his chest. Everyone seemed to be having a go at him lately.

The disappearance of Jessica had opened a whole big can of worms as far as his friends and family were concerned. How come all these years he thought he was popular and well-liked, only to find that as soon as everyone thought he was vulnerable, they couldn't wait to tell him what a bastard he was and always had been?

"Now, who's closed up," Max broke the silence. "If you want me to talk to you, then you must also talk to me."

"What do you want to know?"

"I don't want to know anything that you don't want me to, but I enjoy your company, and I really don't want to be walking on eggshells in case I hurt your feelings. I don't want a love affair with you; I would like a friendship. You know…one of these man-woman friendships that people don't believe is possible. I don't want you as a lover; it would complicate my life too much, and you are married with the possibility of reuniting with your wife. Do you think we could be friends?"

The car pulled up in his driveway, and Max switched off the engine. Drew unfastened his seatbelt and swivelled around. "You are a very lovely woman, Max, both outside and inside. I'm not sure I could keep it all on the level you demand."

"So I was right in my first estimation of you then. Without the constant physical buzz or an emotional high, a relationship would not be possible."

"Well, I can try, but what if I forget myself and try to come on to you in a moment of weakness," Drew's hand was in front of his mouth, hiding his smile.

"Then you would lose a friend and gain nothing."

Drew's smile faded. "OK, friend. Can I take you to dinner during the week to cement this friendship?"

"Sorry, I'm busy all week, but gird up your loins, get fit, and I'll pick you up next Sunday."

CHAPTER 35

Jessica's eyelids slowly fluttered open but due to the bright and painful light, quickly shut again. She was aware of sounds of activity around her without realising what they were. There was a warm weight on the back of her hand; she very slowly opened her eyes a little and glanced down. She saw the top of a head of curly dark brown hair with the forehead resting on her hand. She raised her head to see more, and intense pain shot up her neck and into her head. A groan escaped, and the curly head shot up.

"Luke," she breathed. "What's happening?"

"Jessie...oh God, Jessie," and Luke's large bulk disappeared quickly through the door, followed by the entry of a nurse.

"Well, sleeping beauty, glad you decided to join us again."

A cool hand swept over Jessica's brow as the nurse checked the graph on the screen above the bed. "Your husband will be pleased you're awake. He's been here nearly all the time for the last three days. Slept in the chair for a while but wouldn't go home. When I came on duty this morning, the night nurses told me to leave him with you. I'm glad he was here when you woke up."

The nurse bustled around, and Jessica tried to grasp what she was saying through the pounding pain. The mist cleared when the nurse told her the doctor was on his way and her husband could come back in later.

"But...he's not—"

"Don't try to talk, dear. No, he's not gone; he's still here."

Jessica was totally confused and sank wearily back on the pillows. She couldn't make sense of it all and didn't feel up to trying.

The doctor spent time with her and, between examining her thoroughly, explained what had happened. Jessica could only remember the hard slap on the back and then nothing else until now. The doctor instructed a pain shot for her and left her in the capable hands of the nurse. Later, when she was more settled, a beaming face looked around the door.

"Polly."

"Hello, you. What a fright you gave us all. We've been worried to death."

"Christ, Polly. It's all such a blur. The doctor told me how I got here, but he didn't tell me for how long. What day is it?"

"Today's Tuesday. You've been out of it since Saturday. If you hadn't come round by tonight, we were going to call Drew in the morning."

"That's who I thought the nurse was talking about earlier. She kept on about Luke as if he were my husband. Why do they all think that?"

Polly was looking down at her fingernails.

"Polly, what the hell's going on?"

Polly looked up. "As soon as Luke found out from the office what had happened, he arrived here, and nobody could make him leave. The doctors threatened to call the police, but the nurses, John, and I stuck up for him. He was so distressed we left him with you."

"But why, Polly? Why was he distressed? I don't understand. It wasn't any of his fault. God, my head hurts so much; this is all too much for me to take in."

"Just get well, Jessie. When they say you're OK, you are coming home with me. You just sleep, and I'll be back in the morning."

"Polly…you haven't answered my questions about Luke."

"It'll keep, Jessie."

"No, no, it won't."

Polly sat down again. "Jessie, Luke cares for you. That's all I know. I sensed it the first time he ever looked at you in front of me, but you were oblivious to it, and it was none of my business. That's why he's been staying away from you. He thought you and Alan had a thing going."

"How do you know all this?"

"John and Luke were at school together. They go back a long way, and at one time, they were really close friends. Once, Luke needed to talk to someone and John was there."

"Oh, I see."

"No, Jessie, you don't, but now is not the time. When you feel better, we will settle things. Now I'm going, and you are going to rest. I'll be back in the morning." Polly kissed her cheek and left.

Five minutes later, Jessica was asleep.

Luke sat on the hard bench with both hands wrapped around a plastic coffee cup. His stomach felt as if an iron hand gripped it, and letting go would leave it bruised and painful. He looked up as a shadow crossed in front of him. Polly sat down beside him and gripped his arm. "She's OK, Luke. You can go home now."

Luke looked down at the toes of his size eleven trainers and sighed. "I'm glad."

"Luke, tell me to mind my own business if you want. I'll quite understand, but how can your feelings for Jessie be so strong and she doesn't know? I guessed weeks ago."

Luke leant back and drained the rest of the nearly cold coffee. "How to be a prat in one easy stage, eh."

"That's not what I mean, and you know it. Jessie is like my sister, and she would have talked to me if she'd known."

Luke leant forward to scrutinise his trainers again. "I knew she was still married, and I got the impression she was still making up her mind if she wanted to stay that way or not. I wanted to be around her, but I didn't want her to think it was just for a fling. It's been a long time since I wanted a woman's company for more than a few hours," he glanced over at her with a wry grin, "if you know what I mean."

Polly returned his grin, "I sure do."

"Well, anyway, I thought if I let her do all her thinking and deciding, and if she finally made up her mind to be free of her husband, then I would go all out to get her." His big hands crushed the coffee cup with a loud crack. "I really do want to be with her, Polly."

"I know, Luke. But hiding your feelings hasn't helped much, has it?"

Luke stood up with a jerk. "What was I supposed to do? When I heard about her weekend away with the waistcoat wonder, I felt as if my guts were being torn out."

"And you were too proud to tell her."

Luke sat down heavily. "Not proud…no. I suppose if I had to put it into words, I was jealous more than anything else."

Polly stood up. "One thing I can tell you. Jessie's weekend with Alan was not much of a success by all accounts. They had an enjoyable time, but as far as Jessie is concerned, that's all it was. He was the first and only man since she got married, and it was an entirely new experience for her. I'm not even sure she will see him again other than at work. Maybe I shouldn't have told you, but if you can put it down to curiosity on her part and start again, perhaps you can see how it develops."

Luke stood up and took Polly's arm. "That seems like a good idea to me. Come on, it's late. I'll walk you to your car."

In the car park, Polly looked hard at Luke under the bright floodlights and then gave him a tight squeeze. "Good luck, sunshine. Jessie could do with a bit of happiness. She hasn't had too much to smile about for a while. I reckon if anyone can manage it, you can."

Luke watched Polly drive out of the hospital gates and walked over to his van. He unlocked it, then locked it again, and walked back to the hospital. Jessica was propped up with a mountain of pillows and sound asleep. She looked a better colour but was uncomfortable with the neck brace keeping her rigid. Her hair was sticking up in small spikes, and Luke felt a lump in his throat. She looked small and defenceless; he knew he had to be with her, even if it was only as a friend. The urge to kiss her was so strong he actually took a step towards the bed before he checked himself. She needed her sleep, and anyway, what would he say if he woke her? *Sorry to wake you, Jessie, but I want to climb into bed with you and hold you against me all night. Yeah…that would be great, Luke, old boy. Guaranteed to frighten her to hell and gone.*

Luke turned around and walked back down the corridor, with Jessica watching him all the way to the door.

CHAPTER 36

The next few weekends had Drew looking forward to his Sundays. Marty had gone back to the States, and Melanie had returned to her flat in town. Drew wanted her to get another place in case she was put in danger again. Apart from the business interest he had in her, she had become very dear to him on a personal level. After a long talk with her, they decided it would be best if she told her flatmates what had happened so they could form a united front if it should become necessary. She would still not disclose the name of her attacker, but Drew was sure the other girls would keep an eye on her.

Sam, the sexy flatmate from before, was still making eyes at him, and Drew found it hard to look away on occasions. He was tempted to take her up on the promise her slanted eyes were making but resisted the urge. She was very young and also Melanie's friend. For once, he let the opportunity pass and let his head rule his trousers.

The house seemed strangely sad and empty, and his Sunday visits to the school were something he found he was looking forward to more and more. Max was trying to teach him to sign. She lent him books and gave him a few lessons, but his fingers felt stiff and unyielding. He found himself working his fingers whilst speaking on the phone at work, trying to match the spoken word with the sign. Joan, his secretary, had caught him on several occasions, so he felt it necessary to explain to her what he was trying to do. Her puzzled frown turned into understanding and then into a smile. "Well, I'm very glad you told me, Mr. Cameron. I thought maybe you were learning to play the trumpet," she said dryly.

The previous Sunday, they had taken many of the children to the swimming pool. Two of the teachers had stayed on the side of the pool, watching the children with sharp eyes, but Kate, Max, and Drew had gone into the water and, with the aid of inflatable rings and armbands, splashed about heartily with the kids and had a great time. Max wore a yellow one-piece suit, and within it, her body was curved and lush. She was well-muscled and firm, and her nipples were like hard buds with the cold water. As soon as he looked at her, Drew got the most ferocious and hard-on he'd had for weeks. He couldn't look at her anymore, or he knew it would be impossible to lose it, so he stayed in the water the whole time. Even after the children went to change, he had to swim several lengths of the pool on his own before he could trust himself to emerge from the water.

Christ, this is going to be much more difficult than I'd ever imagined. If we're going to do this on a regular basis, I'm going to have to tie a lead weight on my prick to keep it in its place. He dragged himself out of the pool and made a bolt for the changing rooms, still semi-erect despite the swim.

He and Max were now totally at ease with each other and talked about most things over a drink on the way home. They had stopped at the same pub for weeks now and were being greeted as friends by the landlord. The sexual feelings Drew had for Max were kept strictly in check, except on occasions like today when, no matter how hard he tried, his body betrayed him. The feeling stayed with him and, over their usual drink, somehow transmitted itself to Max, making their conversation stilted and contrived.

When the awkwardness finally killed off the talking, Drew decided to take the bull by the horns. He cleared his throat and started, "Max, about today in the pool."

"Don't, Drew," Max said before he got any further.

"You don't know what I was going to say," Drew said, sitting forward in his seat.

"Yes, I do. I'm not blind, you know."

Drew looked at her and she lowered her eyes. "I'm trying really hard, Max," Drew said, lifting her head up with his fingers under her chin.

"Yes, I know you are," she looked at him. "If this is all too difficult for you, I'll understand if you don't come with me anymore. I enjoy your company very much, and I'd miss you like hell if you decide to stay away."

"I don't want to do that," Drew leant back in the chair. "It's just that we seem to be getting so close that I'm finding it really difficult to keep my hands off you. I want to touch you."

She looked at him steadily for several moments, her ginger eyes troubled. "Drew, you're a good-looking and desirable man, but I've had a good-looking and desirable man, and he took what he wanted and left other people to pick up the pieces. I don't need any complications in my life, and more important than that, I don't need to be hurt again."

"But that was years ago," Drew interrupted. "Surely you don't intend to spend the rest of your life scared of men."

"You still don't understand, do you, Drew? I'm not scared of men. There have been many men in my life since Steve and I parted. Some of them were really good friends of mine. But in nearly every case the relationship changed as soon as the physical thing started. Then the whole attitude became possessive and smothering. Questions on where I was, what I was doing, and who I was doing it with. That's OK if that's what you want, but I'm not ready to submerge my life to be always trying to please someone else."

Drew suddenly thought of Jessica and all the things she'd given up to look after him and the children. "It doesn't always have to be like that," he said, sounding unconvincing even to himself.

"No, not always, but the instances of two people who are

successful in their careers living in sweet harmony without any friction are as rare as rocking horse shit."

Drew cupped his chin in his hand and rested his elbow on the table. His blue eyes were thoughtful as he turned over in his mind what she'd said. "But what about your emotional needs?"

Max flopped backwards against the soft cushion of the chair and let out a laugh. "Oh, Drew, don't be so coy. What you are really asking is, what do I do about my sexual needs? Well you've asked so I'll tell you. Working in a mainly male dominated world, there are many males I know who would be more than willing to become more than business acquaintances. One phone call and I'm sure all my needs would be seen to. However, once the phone call has been made, those people could never be my friends again. Every relationship has to go forward, and once it has, you can't go back to how it was before."

Drew stared at her for many seconds, his eyes wide. Her head tilted to one side, and her eyebrows lifted. A smile curved her mouth as she read the shock on his face. Suddenly, she chuckled deep in her throat. "Christ, if only you could see your face. Why are you shocked that a woman would use a man for her own pleasure? You men do it all the time. I didn't figure you as a person who believed in the old double standards. One rule for men and another for women?"

Drew didn't answer but continued to look at her. Max looked steadily back at him, refusing to feel defensive. He stood up, picked up their glasses, and walked over to the bar. Max watched him. He had an easy grace. His long, well-shaped legs and body unconsciously transmitted sexual undercurrents. He had a look about him that drew the female eye. Dangerous; very dangerous. She had seen his reaction to her today as soon as she stepped from the changing rooms. He turned his body away from her immediately, but not before she saw his eyes travel quickly over her. The shallow water had not quite covered him, and she felt a rush of warmth as she saw his hardness, which he tried to hide. She had splashed around with him, all the time aware of what she was doing to him and exalting in it. *If only he knew,* she thought with a wry grin. It had been a while since she'd been with a man, and Drew's body was turning her on as much as hers was tantalising him. However, stronger for her than the sexual feeling was the feeling of friendship and companionship. She really enjoyed his company; sex always complicated things so much.

Drew came back with the glasses. "Next time, I'll drive. You must be fed up with all this orange juice."

"It's OK," she smiled. "I'd still have to drive home."

Well, she thought at the end of that particular discussion, *but it's funny how I get the feeling it's going to be dragged out again sometime.*

The atmosphere seemed to have lightened a bit on the remainder of the drive. As they pulled into the drive, Max said, "I shall be going to Florida with John Sullivan and a couple of other people next week. I may be gone for two or three weeks. Don't know yet."

"You didn't tell me you were going away," Drew said, surprised.

"Sorry, I forgot. It was only arranged a couple of days ago."

Drew kissed her cheek. "OK, flower, have a good time. Ring me when you get back."

"The children like you a lot, Drew. If you want to go down on your own, they'd love to see you."

"I might just do that."

He watched her car until it disappeared from sight and slowly walked into the empty house. He felt a sense of loss already. "Shit, this woman's going to do my head in," he muttered, walking up the stairs.

CHAPTER 37

For the first few days after Jessica came out of hospital, Polly fussed around her like a mother hen. In the end, Jessica lost her temper. "For God's sake, I'm beginning to feel as if I reverted to childhood in that hospital. The way you're going on, I feel like a little kid. Apart from a couple of bruises, I'm alright. Just because I didn't eat for a couple of days, it's not necessary to keep force-feeding me. Just let me be."

Polly looked hurt by the remark, forcing Jessica to apologise. "Well, I'm sorry, Poll, but you're making me feel like an invalid, and I'm not. I'm OK, really."

"I was so worried about you, Jess. I don't mean to annoy you."

Jessica put her arms around Polly and gave her a tight hug. "I know, and I didn't mean to snap, but I really think it's about time I went back to my own place."

"You don't have to, you know," Polly said, looking near to tears.

"I promise I'll behave." Seeing Polly's eyes welled up, Jessica laughed, "Now, who's acting like a child."

Polly pushed her away, smiling. "Go on then. Clear off. See if I care."

Much as she enjoyed the company, Jessica missed her little place. The caravan had become home to her, and she had made it just how she wanted it. She could relax more there, and she desperately wanted to go back.

John drove her back after supper that night, and Polly said she would stop by to see her the following afternoon until John intervened. "She'll be ok, Poll. Give it a rest, for goodness sake. Jess has all the other people at the site to watch over her if she needs it. Give her some space, woman."

"Oh shut up, you. What do you know?"

"Don't be so snappy or I'll put you over my knee."

"It'll be the last thing you ever did, John Sheldon."

John threw his head back and laughed. "Listen to her. Knee high to a footstool and she's going to duff me up."

Polly laughed, too.

"Go on then, the pair of you. Naff off."

After John had gone, Jessica put her feet up on the sofa, turned the TV on, and thought how nice it was to be home. The soft lights around the walls gave the van an intimate, cosy look, and the large white furry rug and velvet cushions added a touch of luxury.

Not for the first time when she was alone, her thoughts turned to Luke. He had sent flowers to Polly's house and phoned on several occasions to enquire, from Polly, about Jessica. He never asked to speak to her, which she found a trifle strange. When she remarked on it to Polly, Polly just shrugged and said, "I expect he'll come to it eventually."

How odd that she hadn't seen what everyone else had. *It must have been because I was so wrapped up with Alan. Just as well he's still abroad and didn't know about the accident. It might have been a bit awkward to have both of them turn up in the hospital at the same time. I'll go and see Luke tomorrow. Thank him for the flowers and everything.*

Her eyes were starting to get unfocussed, so she cuddled up in her bed and drifted off to sleep, thinking about the curly brown head resting on her hand.

The next day was beautiful. For days, the weather had been

drizzly and chilly, but on that day, the sun shone brightly. Jessica tried to hide the bruises with makeup and nearly succeeded. The swelling had gone, but the eye area was still a blend of blue and yellow. She put on a deeper colour lipstick to try to focus the looks away from her eye. She was bound to get a few remarks, but that couldn't be helped.

She strolled up to the reception to let them know she was back. She was going to suggest that she would start working again from Monday. Stacey was pleased to see her and, after a blow-by-blow account of the accident, was eager to see her back. The place was still full, and the weekend bookings would be coming in the following day. They agreed Jessica would help out for a couple of hours at the busiest time and then back to full-time on Monday.

Stacey raised her eyebrows when Jessica enquired about the whereabouts of Luke's place, but Jessica muttered something about thanking him for the flowers, and Stacey wrote down the address.

It seemed that Luke worked from home. He had a big place, and part of it was built up as an office and yard for the business. Jessica found it without too much trouble and pulled up in front of a sign that said 'Reception.' The young lad at the counter pointed her out to the back when Jessica introduced herself as Luke's friend and that it was a personal visit. "He's in the workshop. You'll have to shout. He's always got the radio on full blast."

With that, he went back to the reception desk. The boy was not joking there. Country and Western music was shaking the roof, and the sound of a tuneless voice was coming out from under a beautiful, gleaming car. The size of the jean-clad legs and the trainer-clad feet could only be Luke's. She shouted but got no response, so she shook the leg of the jeans.

"Fuck off, Kevin, I'm busy"

She shook the leg again.

"This better be a bloody emergency."

The trolley rolled out from under the car, and an oily Luke gazed up at her.

"Sorry, Jess, thought it was Kev," he said, looking somewhat embarrassed.

He scrambled to his feet. He had taken his shirt off, and his body glistened with oil and sweat. Jessica stared at him. He got even more embarrassed and pulled an old t-shirt over his head. Jessica's reaction was every bit as intense as Carl thought it would be. It was a pity he was not there to see it.

"How are you now?" Luke peered at the eye.

"Not too bad. Better than the last time I saw you."

Jessica's nose was assaulted by the smell of the oil covering Luke, and her nose wrinkled. Luke saw the gesture and laughed. "Sorry about the whiff; if I'd known you were coming over, I'd have been clean."

Jessica's voice had become a croak; she cleared her throat and said, "I just came over to thank you for the flowers."

"My pleasure. I'm just glad you're OK."

They stood silently and looked at each other. Now, it was Luke's turn to clear his throat. "If you'd like to come in the house, I'll have a quick shower, and you can make a brew."

"Fine," Jessica said and followed his broad back into the large house behind the workshop.

The house was a revelation. Deep lush carpets in dark blue as far as the eye could see, and huge blue suede-covered settees and chairs. A pair of wide sliding doors led out onto a patio with pots containing a variety of plants framed by white gauzy curtains. Every wall had oil paintings in bright colours and in the middle of the room was a circular fireplace.

Jessica stood and gaped. Luke's face split into a huge grin at her face. "How do you like my humble abode?"

"Well, humble, it's not. Luke, it's beautiful. Did you do it all?"

"Sorry to disappoint you, but a firm of interior design people did it. I chose all the curtains, carpets, and furniture; they suggested a colour scheme and put it all together. The kitchen, though, is all my work. I spend most of my time there and wanted it right, so to make sure it was absolutely right, I built it myself."

She followed him into the kitchen, through a dining room also in blue with a large black ash glass-topped table and six velvet-covered chairs. The kitchen had a masculine feel with its dark wood and copper pans. One end was carpeted in heavy-duty brown, almost completely covered with a heavy old wood table and four ladder-backed chairs. The table had piles of papers scattered over it, and it was obviously in constant use as a desk. The other end was completely functional and dominated by a large Aga in cream, a big American-style fridge/freezer, a microwave, and all the usual kitchen appliances.

"Well, woman. There's the kettle. Get to it."

"Yes, sir," Jessica said with a smile.

Luke pulled his dirty t-shirt off and threw it in the washing machine. Jessica got a funny tingle again as she looked at him out of the corner of her eye. He bent to pull off his trainers, and she took a longer look. *Well, who would have thought it? He looks like a centrefold pin-up. All muscle and tanned skin.* He straightened up, and Jessica looked away. Suddenly shy.

"See you in a mo," he said over his shoulder.

She was very tempted to ask if she could wash his back.

She found everything and made the tea. Luke returned in due course, looking damp and clean and smelling nice. He wore black jeans and a white shirt with the sleeves turned up over his muscular arms. His feet were bare. They sat around the table, drinking tea and talking about nothing in particular. She learnt that he liked to renovate classic old cars in what spare time he got. He found it relaxing and absorbing. The car she had seen was an MGB GT, and he already had a buyer for it when finished. She made him laugh with stories about the complex, and both of them skirted around any personal revelations as if the subject was taboo.

"Can you cook?" he suddenly asked.

"Of course, I can cook. What a funny question."

"No…what I mean is, can you cook for, say…a dinner party?"

"Yes, I can. My husband frequently needed to entertain business colleagues."

There followed a silence as if the mention of a husband had suddenly intruded. Luke leant back in his chair and toyed with a teaspoon. "My tender for work on a new housing estate has been accepted, and I would like to entertain some of the people involved. Usually, in cases like this, I take all the blokes out to a restaurant, but this time, I thought it would be nice to invite the wives and partners as well. I've been thinking that it would be nice to have it here instead. We could eat in comfort, and maybe if everyone gets on, have a bit of a party afterwards. The only thing is the meal."

"How many people will there be?"

"I don't know yet. I wouldn't expect you to do all the work. I'd hire caterers, but I need to sort out the menu, and I need some help. If you would be my hostess for the evening and supervise the food, it would be great."

Jessica looked at him. He seemed to be holding his breath. She felt quite excited about the idea and grinned at him. He let out his breath, "Yeah…great stuff. Thanks, Jessie. I'll start the ball rolling."

He walked out to the car with her, his hand resting on the small of her back. Long after she had driven off, she could still feel the warmth of it.

CHAPTER 38

Drew faced the coming Sunday with a sense of doom. He'd had a brief goodbye from Max but hadn't thought too much about her absence until he woke up this morning. Every Sunday for weeks, he had waited for her with joy and excitement. Now, suddenly, the day stretched ahead without her. It was only now that he realised exactly how much he looked forward to being with her. He was not sure that he could carry off the visit to Kate alone. With dragging feet, he showered, dressed, and made some coffee. He stood by the lounge window sipping the steaming brew when suddenly his eyes snapped into focus at the 'FOR SALE' sign in the garden of the house next door.

When had that gone up? Most nights this week, he had worked on, eaten in town, and travelled home in the dark. He was sure he would have noticed it before. *Wonder how Elizabeth had managed that. Must have taken some fancy talking on her part to get Will to agree to sell the property after all these years.* Drew made a mental note to phone during the week and see what was going on. He picked up a warm jacket and went out to the garage.

He took his time on the drive down. It was so strange to be driving this way without Max beside him. Even though she wasn't really a chatterbox, she made her present felt, and today, it was sorely missed. As he pulled up in front of the house, he was met by Avril, one of the senior teachers. Drew smiled and shook her hand. "Where's Kate today?" he asked as they walked towards the front door.

Avril had returned his smiled greeting but now stopped walking and faced him, her mouth serious and unsmiling. "Before we go and find her, could you come into my office for a few minutes, please?"

Drew's stomach gave a flip. "What's wrong, Avril? Is Kate alright?"

"Yes, she's OK, but rather troubled, I'm afraid."

"About what"

"Let me show you something that will explain."

Avril handed him a letter and sat in the chair by the window, motioning with her hand for Drew to take a seat behind the desk. Drew sat down and took the letter from the envelope. The writing was heavy, bold, and flowing. It went into detail about a life spent travelling, never forgetting, and of an overwhelming urge to see her, and was signed Steve…your father.

Drew looked at the front of the envelope, saw Kate's name, and then looked at Avril. "When did this arrive?"

"During the week, she's been very down since she got it. She hasn't had any contact with her father since she was about four, and she says she can't even remember him. Max, as you know, is in America, and Kate seems to be bottling everything up without anyone to talk to. I wonder if you could get through to her."

Drew stood up, walked around the front of the desk, and then sat on the corner of it, gazing unseeingly out of the window. He ran his fingers through his hair, standing it up in dark spikes. "Well, I can try, but what makes you think I can help? She has lived here with you for many years, and I've only known her for a short time. Maybe she'll think I'm intruding and tell me to mind my own business."

"Maybe she will, but her mother won't be home for another couple of weeks, and by that time, it's going to be a major problem unless we can get her to talk about it."

Drew walked over to the window and pulled aside the net curtain.

A group of children ran around on the lawn, throwing and catching a ball. Their voices were low and guttural, completely different from the high-pitched shrieks of most young children. Drew watched in silence for a few moments. After his first visit here, he had been so aware of all the sounds around him that he had tried to block them out with earplugs and earmuffs from the stereo. With all outside sounds blocked out, all he could hear were strange hissings and noises inside his head. The images on the television were just that. Images without voices. He could not believe how frightening it all was, as if he was not in control of his own life.

"Yes, I'll talk to her. She must be very frightened," Drew said, still watching the children. "Will you stay with us to interpret? My signing is not very good yet."

"Of course," Avril said, standing up. "I'll organise some tea to be sent up."

Kate looked pale and drawn and, much to Drew's surprise, held him in a tight embrace as soon as he entered the room. Her body felt wispy and light, almost without substance. He smoothed her hair and held her gently as if she were a small, frightened animal who might run away. Finally, he held her away from him and looked into her face. "Kate, I've seen the letter from your father. I know you would rather speak to your mother, but I'm your friend, and if you would like to talk about your feelings, I would like to listen."

Kate's head drooped and her shoulders lifted under Drew's hands, giving a huge sigh. He lifted her chin and said jerkily with his hands, "Think of me as an uncle who cares for you," and looked at Avril, who used her hands to correct a mistake.

For the first time, Kate smiled, and her fingers flew too quickly for Drew. Avril translated. "She says you are far too handsome to be an uncle, but in deference to your age, she will gladly think of you as one."

"Cheeky little madam," Drew smiled into her eyes.

The arrival of the tea relaxed everyone, and the talking started, with hands and voices.

It seemed that although Kate couldn't remember her father, she could remember her mother crying over him many times. She could also remember seeing her mother sorting through bills and bank statements and crying over lack of money. In her child's mind, she thought she was the one who had caused all the troubles by being deaf. It was only after a holiday with her mother, grandfather, and John Sullivan that thoughts came out in the form of a traumatic and furious tantrum of guilt and frustration.

Kate hadn't yet started school but had learnt to watch people's mouths, realising that she could understand by their expressions and body language a bit of what was happening. Her mother met a young man on this fateful holiday, and Kate could tell from his face and eyes that he wanted to be with her mother but didn't want her around. When Max had gone out to dinner with her friend one night, and her father and John had just gone downstairs to the bar for a few drinks, leaving Kate safely asleep, the whole drama unrolled.

Waking up and finding herself alone, Kate started to panic. She was crying and frightened. She tried to get the door open, but it was too stiff and the handle wouldn't turn. Kate was never sure if she was screaming for someone because, in her world of silence, she didn't know what screaming was. In any case, no one came to help her. Feeling trapped and very scared, she managed to open the balcony door. She hadn't been allowed out onto the balcony and had no idea it was on the fourth floor. When she looked over and, in the dark, saw the water of the swimming pool, to her, it was the only way to get out of the room and find her mother. She remembered jumping into the pool from the low diving board. She climbed up onto the balcony rail to jump into the water.

Somewhere in all the scrambling, she must have made some noise, and one of the waiters looked up. He shouted, but Kate couldn't hear him. However, the guests did and looked up. Kate's grandfather and John Sullivan craned around the potted plants and looked up to see her balanced precariously on the balcony rail. He froze, his heart pounding in his chest, but John Sullivan was galvanised into action and raced for the stairs.

Before jumping, Kate remembered wearing a special swimming suit. Her mother might get cross if she didn't put it on, so crying, sniffing, and gasping, she went to look for it. She had dragged it up to her waist when the door burst open, and John Sullivan nearly knocked her over in his haste to get to the balcony. He saw her and grabbed her up into his arms, crying and laughing at the same time. This was all too much for Kate, and she started to scream uncontrollably with fright, fear, and shock. She went into convulsions and a doctor had to be called to administer a sedative. In the midst of all this, Max turned up. By this time, Kate was sleeping, and Max's father had been found still slumped in his chair, the pain in his chest so intense he couldn't speak.

John Sullivan chartered a plane and flew them all back, and within hours, Max's father was in the intensive care unit of a private hospital. Kate underwent tests in the same hospital. Max looked like a ghost, and John Sullivan was scared she would be the next one in the hospital, so he set about doing everything in his power to make her life his business.

The specialist doctor dealing with Kate's case had a long chat with them. It seemed that by wrapping her up in cotton wool and being overly protective, Max was not doing her daughter any favours. Being hearing impaired shouldn't prevent Kate from leading an almost normal life. She could easily learn to speak and sign, read and write, and have some knowledge of the world around her. That way, she would never be frightened of everyday things again. She had been completely panicked by the circumstances that she should have been able to deal with had she not been so cosseted.

It was at this point that Max's father, who was on the road to recovery after his heart attack, told Max about the school. Apparently, he had looked into it sometime before but had been reluctant to mention it to her in case it had seemed as if he was trying to take Kate away. After visiting the school with and without Kate, Max knew this was the right place for Kate to be. She contacted Kate's father, Steve, to ask for financial help for his daughter and explain the circumstances to him. She received a curt note back to say that he had no money and couldn't help her. That was when, once again, John Sullivan and Kate's grandfather stepped in. Max had always made sure that Kate knew how much they both owed these two men and, without actually defining it, how little her father had done to assist.

Once Kate learnt to speak to her mother, she asked many questions. Max answered as truthfully as she could, leaving Kate to make up her own mind about her father. Since she had never seen him, his absence hadn't bothered her, but now here he was, and she had to make up her mind whether to let this stranger who was her father into her life.

Drew listened and added very little. After the talking dried up and Kate looked at him, the corners of her mouth turned downwards. "What do you think I should do, Drew?" she asked.

"I think we should put our coats on and do our thinking in the fresh air. What do you think, Avril?"

Avril smiled. "It does seem a shame to waste the sunshine."

The wind was chilly, and suitably dressed, they sallied forth towards the woods at the back of the house. They all walked in silence for a while, and then Drew turned towards Kate. "Have you ever been curious about your father?"

Kate nodded.

"Did you ever wonder what he looked like?"

Again, the nod.

"Did your mother ever prevent you from getting in touch with him?"

A shake of the head.

"Would she be upset if you saw him?"

A pause, then a shrug.

"If she knew you wanted to, felt it necessary too, would she stop you?"

Another shake of the head.

"Answer me honestly, Kate. Is this indecision of yours anything to do with a feeling of disloyalty to your mother? Do you think she would be hurt by your wanting to see him after all these years?"

Several nods.

"And is her reaction the only thing stopping you from getting in touch with him?"

Kate's hands fluttered quickly, prompting Drew to look towards Avril. "My mother gave me everything. I owe everything in my life to her. All the love I ever had has come from her. My father gave me nothing. He never even remembered my birthday. I never even got a card or a present from him, not even at Christmas. I can understand how upset I'd be if I were in my mother's shoes."

Drew ran his hands again through his hair. He stopped and leant against a tree. "If you were in your mother's shoes, wouldn't you be scared your daughter would resent you for stopping her from visiting her father?"

"I suppose so."

"Would you resent her?"

Kate walked slowly away from him, her head down. She turned and her hands moved slowly. "I might"

"And what do you think that resentment would do to your mother?"

Kate nodded in understanding.

"If you don't see him and blame your mother in any way for this, it will be more damaging than seeing him."

Kate had her back to him but faced Avril. Avril's voice stopped and started with Kate's hesitant movements. "I'll see him; I have to see him. Mostly for my own peace of mind but also out of curiosity. I've had this mental picture of him for years, and now I need to see him for real. I won't see him yet, not till Mum gets back and knows about it. I'll write to him first. I don't like him, but I owe it to him to try. Anyway, I'll never like him more than Mum."

Drew walked up behind her and put his arms around her. She turned around in the circle of his arms. "Thank you, Uncle Drew," she said with a smile. "I wouldn't have a problem if you were my Dad."

That remark haunted him all the way home. *Christ, if only she knew what a rotten bastard I am and how I upset my kids for years, she'd never ever give me the time of day.* He got quite a jolt when he realised how upset he'd be if that should ever happen.

CHAPTER 39

Despite the fact that Jessica's neck was still very stiff and her face still bore traces of bruising, the time was hanging heavy with nothing to do, so she decided to go back to work. Stacey tried to talk her out of it, but Jessica could observe she was snowed under. Jessica suggested coming in a few hours a day until the hospital outpatient visit when hopefully they would give her a clean bill of health.

On the third day of her return, she saw Luke's van pull into the car park. As he got out, Viv's car pulled up alongside him. Jessica saw him smile and wait for Viv as she locked the car. Viv was dressed for the gym in skin-tight leggings and a leotard, with a jersey thrown casually around her neck, the sleeves knotted in front. Her body was taut, firm, and exquisite, and very close to Luke's. As she looked up at him, her face was glowing and alive under the mane of streaky dark hair. Jessica tried not to watch but felt her eyes going constantly back to the two of them.

If anyone had asked her what her feelings were at that moment, she wouldn't have been able to define them, but her muscles were tense, and she was very aware of the pumping of her blood around her body. Had she been a student of body language, she wouldn't have looked so long at them. Viv's body language was open and inviting, but Luke leant back against the van with his arms folded in front of his body and was completely closed to her.

They talked for maybe ten minutes before Luke turned towards the reception doors. Viv's hand on his arm made him stop briefly, but after a couple more minutes, he finally walked away. By the time he came through the doors, Jessica had her back to the room and gave all the appearance of putting papers away in the filing cabinet. She turned with a smile as if greeting a visitor. "Hello, Luke. More problems on site?"

"Hi, Jess. No, actually, I came to see you."

"Well, that's nice. What can I do for you?"

Jessica thought how stiff her face felt, as if the smile had been forced up from her feet. Even her voice sounded stiff. Luke must have sensed something as his eyebrows drew together, and he looked hard at her, his face serious. "Everything ok, Jess? You look very pale. Are you sure you should be back yet?"

"That's what I've been telling her all day," Stacey said, coming through the office door. "Why don't you go, Jess, put your feet up and relax. All the bookings are done. Everything is fine for the rest of the day. Go home now, and come in a bit earlier tomorrow if you feel up to it."

Jessica started to protest but got outvoted by Luke and Stacey.

"How about if I take you for a drive out to the beach," Luke suggested. "Put some roses back in your cheeks."

"Oh, I don't think—"

"Yes, Jess. Go on," said Stacey. "Let Luke rattle all your teeth in that old van of his. That should put your neck right in no time at all."

Luke's face fell. "That's a point. I'm afraid you're right, Stacey. Can't take a lady out in that heap. Tell you what, Jess. You go back to your caravan, put something comfortable on, and I'll pick you up in about half an hour in something more comfortable."

Luke turned on his heel and was out through the door and halfway across the car park before Jessica could think of an argument. Stacey rested her elbows on the counter and her face in her hands and watched Luke's long legs covering the ground towards his van. She gave a huge sigh. "I wish I was off for a drive with him this afternoon. Would set me up for the rest of the week."

Jessica laughed. "Oh, Stacey. Don't tell me you've got a secret passion for Luke."

"Yeah, me and quite a few others too."

"Really, do tell me more," Jessica looked at Stacey, who still was gazing out through the glass doors.

Stacey was quiet for a few moments before replying. "Most people around here have known Luke for years. Real hell-raiser he was. If there was a fight, he was always in the middle of it somewhere. He used to go off working all around the country, and then he'd be back again, large as life and twice as handsome. Then, one time, he went off to work in Ireland and came back with a wife. She was the most beautiful girl anyone had ever seen. Jet black hair and the most incredible eyes I have ever seen. Brilliant emerald green. She was small and fragile on the outside and as hard as nails on the inside. It didn't take the community long to suss her out. Luke was her meal ticket, you see. She latched on to him to get away from a rough-drinking family who were as poor as church mice. Luke was trying hard to build up his business and was still spending a lot of time away, wherever he could find work. While he was away, she was knocking around with everything in trousers. Out drinking and dancing every night till all hours. Because of Luke's hard reputation, everyone was afraid to tell him what was going on, so every time he came home and took her out on his arm like she was some kind of lady, everyone was laughing behind his back. Anyway, one night, he went out with some of his mates. They all got drunk and told him. He went ballistic and laid into a couple of them. They called the police and locked him up till he was sober. Nobody pressed charges, so they released him. Once he was sober, he went around asking questions, and it all came out. She disappeared back to Ireland and he divorced her in double quick time."

Jessica also gazed out of the doors, deep in thought. "Did he ever see her again?"

"Well, for a long time, nobody really saw much of him. It was as if he had lost face with the people he knew. I suppose he never was quite sure which of the blokes round here had been with his wife, so he broke contact with all of them. I did hear she turned up once and told him she was pregnant, and he just laughed at her. They said he told her to put all the names in a hat and pick a father for the baby, cause sure as little green apples it wasn't his."

They both lapsed into silence again.

"Anyway," Stacey said, standing up straight, "you'd better start moving; he'll be back soon."

"Thanks for telling me, Stace."

"Well, it was all a long time ago. I was still at school, but all the girls adored Luke, and it was talked about for a long time. Anyway, I would rather you didn't let on I told you. I expect he will tell you in his own good time if he wants you to know."

Jessica hurried back to the caravan, still deep in thought. She showered quickly, there was no time for a bath, and dressed in a white t-shirt and jeans. She had just laced up her trainers when there was a knock at the door. She grabbed up a white fluffy cardigan and opened the door. A beaming Luke stood there dressed the same as she was: jeans, a white t-shirt, and trainers with a white sweatshirt over his shoulders.

"Snap," they both said at the same time and burst out laughing.

They strolled to the car park, and there waiting like some predatory beast was a long, gleaming black Jaguar. Jessica's mouth opened and closed, and Luke started laughing again.

"Luke, this is so beautiful. I've never seen you in this before."

"Well, it's not usually something I carry my tools in. The van's more suitable for that, but if I go anywhere on business, I do like to travel in comfort. I'm so big that I need a big car to fit me."

Jessica sank into the seat and the car purred to life just like its namesake. "Where are we going?"

"It's a lovely day, so I thought we'd walk a bit on the beach and up over the cliffs. Then, if you want to, we'll go and find a nice pub and have some dinner while we discuss the arrangements for this dinner party of mine, which is why I was on my way to see you in the first place."

"Sounds good to me," Jessica said, relaxing into the seat.

The beach had a few people milling around; the fishermen were out in force as usual. Luke stopped to talk to a couple of them, but they didn't look as if they were having much luck. As they walked, he tucked her arm in his, and she tried to match his long strides with her own without much success. Every once in a while, she had to do a hop, skip, and jump to get back alongside him. He watched her antics out of the corner of his eye, trying to suppress a smile, and lengthened his stride slightly until she was almost running to keep up with him. Suddenly, he stopped dead and let out a loud bellow of laughter.

"What?" Jessica said, puzzled but smiling.

"Jess, you are one stubborn woman. I was wondering how long it would take to ask me to slow down, but you'd rather run than admit I was going too fast."

With that, he picked her up and swung her round. He planted a hard, smacking kiss on her mouth, which suddenly softened, deepened, and clung. Jessica was taken completely by surprise and was still smiling when he kissed her. Her smile seemed to disappear into his mouth to be replaced by a pounding in her ears and an overwhelming urge to wrap her arms around his neck. His lips released her but remained slightly touching her mouth.

"Oh Jess, I'm sorry. I didn't mean that to happen." His breath cooled her lips. "I wanted to kiss you, but this is too soon."

Jessica suddenly didn't think so. She pulled his head towards her, her lips finding his. They stayed lips caressing for long moments until Jessica became aware of her neck muscles pulling. She groaned, broke the contact, and dipped her head, rubbing the back of her neck. Luke was immediately concerned and bent his knees to look at her. "Jessie, I forgot you were still sore. I'm sorry I got carried away for a minute,"

Luke sat down on the fine shingle, pulling her down in front of him. He stretched his long legs either side of her and she felt his hands on her neck, kneading and soothing. His hands were slightly rough but warm and relaxing. She sat still, her head forward and enjoyed the feel of the large fingers on her skin. They sat in this way for some time. Jessica could feel her whole body unwinding under the soft massage. At what point she sagged back against his broad chest, and his arms went around her waist, she didn't know, but his head rested gently on her hair, and they sat quietly and watched the sea turn to orange with the setting sun.

She had no idea how long they sat, but she felt him finally stir, his head dipping to nuzzle her neck with his lips. She was aware of his soft beard and also of the sudden hardening of his body. She felt his heat at the bottom of her back and revelled in it. She moved slightly back against him, knowing she would inflame him further, and wanting to. She heard him groan and draw in a deep breath. She turned onto one hip and her arms went around his neck. He groaned her name as his lips came down on hers. The kiss seemed to last forever. They explored each other's mouths and tasted each other in a way only a deep, intense kiss can do. The crunching of the shingle under someone's feet finally brought them back to reality with a look into each other's eyes and a bashful grin.

"Evening," the man said as he passed them. A knowing look in his eyes.

"Evening," they both said together.

Luke's grin stretched across his face, and Jessica's hand went in front of her mouth to muffle her giggle.

"I feel like a teenager who just got caught out," Luke said, standing up and pulling her to her feet. "Another five minutes and he might have had to send for the police to complain about lewd behaviour on a public beach."

Jessica looked at his broad back as he turned away from her to adjust his clothing. "I wouldn't have minded," she surprised herself by saying.

Luke's movements stilled as he turned to look at her. Their eyes met and locked. "Truthfully," Luke said quietly.

"Truthfully," Jessica replied.

Luke's grin split his face from ear to ear, and he let out a howl like a wolf, making the fishermen all turn towards the sound. "Woman, you have just made me the happiest man in this whole country, even though you have no idea what you've let yourself in for."

"Oh, I think I do," Jessica said, looking at him from under her eyelashes.

Luke chuckled deeply in his throat, put his arm around her waist, and the two of them strolled slowly towards the car, stopping every few yards to smooch a bit more.

Even though I haven't eaten all day, Jessica thought, *my hunger at the moment seems to have moved away from food.* She glanced up at the big man beside her and realised she hadn't felt such a yearning for someone since the early days with Drew.

CHAPTER 40

After his talk with Kate, Drew took her out for dinner at a local hotel, and they enjoyed each other's company over a simple meal. His signing was still not very good, but Kate seemed to grasp what he was trying to say. She made her own movements slow and precise. Drew dropped her off at the gates, and she gave him a warm hug before running off up the long driveway. He thought, not for the first time, about how he missed Max's company.

As he turned into the gates of his house, he glanced towards the house next door. The curtains had all been taken down, and the house had already adopted a vacant look. Elizabeth had phoned him briefly and informed him that Will had taken a job in Staffordshire at a reduced salary, and the whole thing was Drew's fault, and she hoped he rotted in hell. *He probably would,* he thought with a wry smile.

He walked towards the front door and the security lights switched on. He saw a small movement as something ran across the front step. He stopped and peered into the shadows. Two large yellow eyes looked at him, glistening in the bright light. He stood still, not quite knowing what it was. A small pink mouth opened and emitted a pathetic little mewl.

"Good grief, where did you come from?" he said, bending down towards the little cat.

The small pink mouth opened again, and the sound was even smaller than the first time. The furry body moved and rubbed itself against his leg.

"Are you lost, little one?" He bent and picked it up.

A soft head nuzzled along his face, and the small body emitted a purr that shook its tiny frame and sounded as loud as an electric drill.

"Come on, you, let's find you some milk."

Drew opened the door and, with the cat still butting his face, walked into the kitchen. He took the chill off a saucer of milk in the microwave and watched the small beast lapping as fast as it could. It splashed the milk all over the place with the force of its lapping. Finally, it finished and looked up at Drew, looking as if it had grown a white beard and whiskers. He laughed. "Didn't your mother teach you any manners? Look at the state of you."

As if the cat understood him, a very small paw came up, and it started washing its whiskers. Drew laughed again and wiped its face with some kitchen paper. The loud purr started once more and the tiny thing started exploring. It has the most unusual colour, almost gunmetal. Blue-grey with white feet and a white bib, and was also very thin.

Drew rummaged in the cupboard and came up with a tin of tuna. He mashed some of the fish up to a pulp and put it down on the floor near the cat. Once again, he was rewarded by a loud purr while the cat pushed the dish around the floor. It licked up every last morsel and instantly curled up on the rug in front of the sink and fell asleep. He watched it for a while, then picked up the dishes and put them in the sink. He left the kitchen and went into the lounge to pour himself a drink. He flipped the TV on and sprawled in the chair. He was just getting interested in the show when the phone rang.

"Meester Drew, it's Sophia."

"Hello, flower, what can I do for you," Drew replied with a smile.

Sophia turned out to be every bit the treasure he had thought she would be and continued to amaze him with her perception and wisdom. He found himself discussing most things with her when he was working at home, and even if she didn't understand the finer points of commerce, she always had some valuable views and was always worth listening to. Her down-to-earth grasp of life somehow put everything in perspective and he couldn't contemplate life without her now. She still 'did' for her other people and refused to work just for him, but she had the entire house running like clockwork, including Jim, who had also developed a healthy respect for her.

"You work home tomorrow?" Sophia asked.

"Just for a few hours until an appointment at lunchtime," Drew replied. "Why? Aren't you coming in?"

"I come early. Daughter not very well, and have hospital visit. I drive her."

Sophia had learnt to drive, and when she passed her test, Alfie had bought her a little car. Her pride in it was almost as great as her pride in her family.

"That's OK, flower. I'll be up early; get here when you like."

"See you in morning then."

Sophia hung up, and it was then he saw the light flashing on the answer phone.

"Hi, Drew, I'm back," said Max's voice. "It didn't take as long as we thought, and not being much of a shopper, and having nothing else to do, I headed home. I'm a bit jet lagged, so I'm going to phone Kate, and then I'm off to my bed. Speak to you soon."

Drew got quite a jolt of pleasure when he heard her voice. He became aware again of how he had missed her. What a pity he couldn't speak to her, but she was probably asleep by now. Wonder if Kate had passed on the news about the letter. A plaintiff meow came from the kitchen, followed by a furious scratching. He leapt off the telephone seat to find his new lodger making a furious deposit on the back door mat.

"Oh my God. I forgot about you."

His voice was loud, and the cat cowed away from him, with its ears flat and its eyes frightened. Drew was immediately filled with remorse and scooped the cat up. The cat nuzzled his neck and forgave him, and Drew was lost.

His gorge rose as he cleared up the mess, but clean it he did. He sprayed freshener around the room, then found an old roasting pan, one of Jim's spades, and by the light of a torch, shovelled up a load of earth and filled the pan, hoping he hadn't shovelled up Jim's seeds. He placed the pan by the door, and straight away, the cat scratched a hole and squatted over it as if letting Drew know that he knew what it was for.

Drew rang Sophia back and asked her to get some cat litter on the way in tomorrow. There was a silence on the end of the line. He waited for the question, but it never came. He felt aimless. He felt lusty. He wanted to feel a female body. It was too late to arrange anything now. He wondered if the barmaid was working at the club tonight. *No, that was not a good idea at all.* His mind turned again to Jessica. It was funny; he could hardly remember what she looked like after all this time. He had called off the investigator and would just have to hope she contacted him in her own good time. Annoyed that he couldn't picture her, he went upstairs and pulled down the loft ladder. He hefted two cardboard boxes down into the bedroom and emptied out years of photographs. He sat for two hours, the time passing unnoticed as he sifted through the memories. Baby photos, school photos, front teeth missing photos, holiday photos. Friends of the kids who had long ago gone their separate ways. Friends of his had gone the same way. Relatives, some of whom he couldn't put a name to, Polly and John and holidays on the farm.

Oh, Christ! Polly. His lungs burned with a long-held breath. The photograph shook in his suddenly icy hand. He knew with a blinding clarity that was where Jessica had gone. He couldn't understand why he had not thought of it before. Suddenly, his bowels felt shaky and he was clammy and cold. Her small phone book was still in the dressing table drawer where it had always been. He dialled the number, then put the phone down before it rang. He sat there, his mind churning. He went back downstairs and poured himself a large whiskey. He took the phone into the lounge, took a deep pull at the whiskey, filled his lungs with air, exhaled, and dialled the number. A well-remembered voice answered.

"Hi, Polly, this is Drew."

CHAPTER 41

They sat very close together in the pub. Luke's leg warmed hers, and they tasted each other's food. Their feeling of ease with each other seemed to have happened almost immediately, as if they had known each other for years. They spoke of nothing in particular. All the serious talking was done without words. They wandered out to the car park, and Luke's large body wrapped itself around hers as they leant against the car. His kiss was soft and deep, and Jessica's whole body moulded itself to him from chest to knee. Without speaking, Luke drove back to his house, opened the car door for her, picked her up, and carried her into the house. He put her gently onto her feet and once again kissed her long and deeply. Still not speaking, they walked up the stairs, their arms about each other's waists. Between the kisses, they slowly undressed each other until they were naked and inflamed. Luke laid her back onto his bed. They kissed and caressed for a long while savouring the feelings that were being aroused. They were in no hurry, wishing to prolong the sensations that started to bring murmurings and mindless whispers from their mouths.

Luke's body was a revelation to Jessica. She had seen him half unclothed but was not prepared for the pure sensual feel of this large man. His skin was soft and fragrant, and the muscles were hard and solid. The down on his chest had no feeling of coarseness about it, and she felt herself drowning in the sheer feel of him. She couldn't get close enough to him and wriggled her body against him, ever closer. Luke looked at her face and felt the breath catch in his throat. Her eyes were glazed and half closed, and her skin was flushed. He slid his hand downwards, and her body arched up towards him. Her juices had flowed and she was open and silky moist. He felt his control slipping with the wantonness of her lust for him. He moved above her, meaning to lie against her, but she thrust her hips upwards with an almost savage movement, and he was inside her. His penis was large and thick, and he drew back slightly from her, suddenly afraid he would hurt her, but her body wrapped itself around him and welcomed him.

Within seconds, she reached a shuddering climax, which took him completely by surprise. He moved slowly inside her until her trembling stopped. Her eyes opened and she looked at him. They were still slightly glazed and the pupils were huge and dark. He kept up the slow movements and nuzzled her lips, the efforts taking all the willpower and control that he had, and was finally rewarded by the age-old response of a woman's body as she became aroused. When once again her hips started thrusting up to meet him, he pulled her tightly into his body, his movements becoming frantic and his muscles were as tight as bowstrings. When she speeded up and the violent upward spasms of her hips signalled her approaching orgasm, he finally let all control go, and his triumphant shouts echoed throughout the house.

They lay in each other's arms, their bodies hot and sticky with sweat but still unwilling to let go. He kissed her hair and caressed her back, trailing his fingers across the dampness. Her hand rubbed along the muscles of his arm and across his shoulders. They both heaved sighs to draw breath into their starved lungs, but still, they clung. Finally, Luke moved, bringing a cry from Jessica. "It's OK, my love. I'm still here. Let's get under the covers before we get cold."

He tucked Jessica's legs under the duvet and then climbed in again beside her, once again wrapping her in his arms. They were still tangled together in the morning, their bodies hot and sticky, but entwined. Luke looked down at Jessica just before she awoke. Her hair sticking up in spikes, her eye makeup smudged under her eyes, and her mouth looked bruised. He had never seen her look so beautiful or felt so happy. Her smudged eyes opened and she looked up at him. He grinned broadly at her, and she shyly smiled back, suddenly coy. She tried to pull the duvet up over her breast, but his hand stopped her. He pulled the cover down slowly and looked at her. His eyes went over every inch of her body. She saw a movement from the corner of her eye and turned her head to watch his growing erection. His hands followed his eyes, and still watching his body with fascination she felt hers responding to his hands. She pushed him onto his back and sat up. His surprised look turned into a broad grin when he realised her intention. For the next half an hour, she took control, and Luke went along with it wholeheartedly, his white teeth smiling at her and finally turning into almost a look of pain as he bared them, threw his head back, and took his pleasure from her.

They showered together and walked around in their underwear. They cooked and ate breakfast at the large table in the comfortable kitchen. Jessica washed up while Luke made some phone calls. When he had finished, Jessica called Stacey to confirm that she wasn't due in until the afternoon. They then sat down on the settee still in their underwear and planned the dinner party, which had got somewhat forgotten. After a while, Luke stood up and stretched, suddenly bored with the arranging. He pulled her to her feet and kissed her soundly. "Come on, woman. Get your clothes on and we'll go out. If I have to look at you any longer dressed like that, we'll never get out of the bedroom."

"Where do you want to go?" Jessica said, following him up the stairs.

"Somewhere," was all he said and started pulling on his jeans.

They drove leisurely along the country roads for about half an hour. Luke sang along with the radio and Jessica relaxed back into her seat with her hand resting on Luke's leg. They turned into a narrow road, and she sat up and looked around. A tractor wound its way across a field, and she felt a stab of guilt. It had been more than a week since she'd spoken to Polly; she really must phone her. Luke turned the big car into a narrow gateway. The hedges on either side were talk and overgrown, and the drive was thick with weeds. As they turned the corner, they were confronted by a rose garden that had gone mad. The bushes grew in a tangled riot of long leafy branches, and the blooms were every colour, and in every stage of flowering. Standing half-hidden behind them was a small cottage that looked rather seedy and run-down. Jessica looked at Luke with her eyebrows raised, but before she could say anything, he switched off the engine, reached under the dashboard, took out a bunch of keys, and got out of the car.

She followed him slowly as he unlocked the door and whipped away the cobwebs with both hands. She followed him tentatively into the gloom to find him battling to get the small windows open. The light flooded into the dusty interior to reveal a small room with a beamed ceiling and rough-plastered walls. The fireplace was carved with intricate wrought iron, and the small windows had leaded lights. Jessica looked around with interest. It was like going back into the past. She followed Luke's broad back through to the kitchen, where he was again struggling to open a window. The kitchen was stone flagstone floored and also beamed, with an old-fashioned range along one wall. An antique wooden dresser festooned with years of cobwebs took up most of the other wall, and the back door was a stable type with an old-fashioned heavy latch. A narrow winding staircase led up from the corner of the kitchen, and Luke had to turn sideways to climb it. His wide shoulders brushed the walls either side, leaving dusty marks on his dark blue jacket.

The upstairs had two bedrooms, one quite large with another wrought iron fireplace and the other slightly smaller with a sharply sloping wall and a skylight above it. Jessica looked out of the dusty window after rubbing one of the panes with her tissue. The land fell away from the house at the back, and there were miles of uninterrupted countryside rolling out towards the horizon. Luke also peered out of the window over her shoulder.

"What do you think?" His voice sounded loud in the small room.

"It's charming."

Jessica sat on the dusty window sill and looked around her. "I've never seen anything like it. I didn't think anything like this still existed. It's like stepping back into the past. I feel I ought to be wearing a long dress."

Luke strolled into the other bedroom, and Jessica followed him. "Who does it belong to?" she said, bending down to look at the fireplace.

"Me," said Luke.

Jessica stood up and looked at him. Luke's teeth gleamed in the gloom as he smiled at her. "Don't look so shocked. People do buy places like this, you know."

"How long have you owned it?"

"A long time now. I bought it because it has a history, but I've never had time to start the work that needs doing. Now I have."

"Luke, it will be wonderful. I only hope I can get to see it when it's finished."

"I was hoping you could help me with it," Luke said, taking her in his arms.

Jessica laughed. "How can I help you? I know nothing about building."

"That's not what I had in mind," Luke said, grinning.

"The structure is sound; the work is all mainly cosmetic, except for the electrics and plumbing."

"Then what do you want me to help you with?" Jessica said, puzzled.

"Decorating and furnishing it. I thought it would be fun to do it personally instead of getting someone in, and I thought you would love browsing around the auctions for suitable pieces. Wouldn't you?"

Jessica heaved a big sigh. "Oh, yes, please. I would adore it."

"Thought so. That's settled then."

Luke started back down the narrow stairs, whistling. Jessica smiled widely and followed him. "I'll tell you the history one day," he said over his shoulder.

They drove back a different way, stopping at a pub for a shandy and a sandwich, and drew up in front of the reception, looking relaxed and happy, with Jessica's face luminous and glowing. She climbed out of the car and turned back in to say goodbye to Luke. She told him that she would be looking forward to seeing him tomorrow. The big car purred away, and Jessica turned towards her caravan. Her face was all smiles, and she came face to face with Drew.

CHAPTER 42

To say that his conversation with Polly was strained was putting it mildly. He didn't know where to begin, and Polly didn't make it any easier for him. After the initial greeting and a polite enquiry into their health, etc., there was a heavy silence. Drew racked his brain for an opening, but when the silence lengthened, he realised he was going to have to be direct.

"Is Jessie with you, Polly?" he finally asked.

There was another long pause.

"What makes you think that, Drew?" Polly replied.

The fact that there was no surprise in her voice and he hadn't got an instant denial confirmed Drew's suspicions. "I know she's with you, Polly. I've eliminated all the other possibilities and that leaves you. I'd like to speak to her, please." Drew's voice took on a sharp demanding note, and Polly replied in kind.

"I'm sure if Jessie had wanted to speak to you, she would have been in contact long before now," Polly rapped.

"Bloody hell, Polly, do you think I haven't tried? I've contacted everyone I can think of. I've even had a private detective looking for her at great expense, I might add; she's just disappeared. Even the kids didn't know where she was. Didn't it occur to you we were all going out of our minds wondering where she'd gone." Drew could feel himself losing his temper.

"That was about the same state she was in when she left you," Polly snapped out. "Going out of her mind."

Drew took a deep breath, fought down his temper, and tried again. "Please, Polly. I won't ask again."

"Oh…what will you do then, Drew?"

"Stop pissing about," Drew almost shouted.

"Maybe that's a warning you should have heeded, sunshine," Polly retorted, not a bit fazed by Drew's tone of voice. "Anyway, she's not here."

"But she was."

"Yes, she was, and now she's not."

"For Christ's sake, Polly, give me a break. You can't keep her hidden forever."

"I'm not keeping her hidden, never was. If your celebrated private dick had been worth his salt, he'd have found her."

"Where is she?"

"Gone."

"But you know where she is."

"Yes, I know."

"But you aren't going to tell me, are you?"

"Like I said, if she'd wanted you to know, she would have told you."

"I'll find her, you know."

"Good luck, Drew. Maybe when you do, if you do, she still won't want you."

"That's a chance I'll have to take. Thanks for nothing, Poll. I thought you were my friend."

"I was, but I was Jessie's friend first."

Drew hung up and found his hand shaking badly. What to do

now was the question. *If Polly knew where she was, she must still be around that area somewhere.* He phoned Adam and explained the situation to him, and that he would be gone a few days, but he'd keep Adam informed. Then, he threw a few things in a suitcase, gave the cat some more food and milk, and wrote a note to Sophia. He shut the cat in the kitchen and locked the house. The traffic was very light, and he put his foot down hard, keeping one eye on the rearview mirror all the way. He pulled into Polly's drive just before midnight. The door opened as he switched the engine off, and a woman stood silhouetted in the doorway.

"Where's Polly?" he said as he stood up.

"She's here," said the woman.

As Drew got closer, he saw that the slim woman with the bobbed hair and slim legs was Polly.

"I've been expecting you," Polly said, turning to let him pass.

"Well, it's for sure I wasn't expecting you," Drew said, stopping to look her up and down. "You're half the woman I remember."

"And you're every bit the man I remember," Polly retorted sharply.

Drew at first thought it was a compliment until he looked at Polly's tight face and realised the remark was derogatory. "Still the same sharp tongue," he said, passing her on his way in.

"Still the same ego," she replied, shutting the door.

The kitchen was as he remembered. He sat down at one of the chairs. Polly busied herself making coffee, and he watched this new slim woman with interest.

"Put your eyes back in their sockets, Drew; you are burning a hole in my back."

Drew allowed himself a wry grin and took the coffee she handed him. "Well, you can't blame me. It was a bit of a shock, after all.

Where's John boy?"

"Gone to a meeting," Polly replied, lighting a cigarette.

"Give me one of those, will you."

"Thought you gave it up."

"I have, but I think this is what you're supposed to do in moments of crisis."

He took a large drag and spent the next two minutes coughing and spluttering. "Ah, that's better," he said when he finally stopped, making Polly smile for the first time since he arrived.

They sat at the big table and talked as time passed. What Polly didn't tell him was that she had foreseen his arrival and had tried to get hold of Jessica. She had phoned the complex and was told that Stacey had gone off duty. The girl that was there, however, hadn't seen Jessica's trip out with Luke. Polly then got her car out and hurtled around to the caravan, only to find it in darkness and locked. She rattled the door and knocked but got no reply. She phoned Luke's number, but it was unobtainable. *Well, now it's going to hit the fan,* she thought, letting Charlie out with the help of a shove. *Still did your best, old girl.*

John arrived a bit later, shouting a loud goodbye to his lift. Polly had phoned him a bit earlier with a brief description of Drew's phone call, hoping that John would try to get home early, but here he was with more than a couple of pints under his belt from the sound of it. *Bugger, I wanted him sober, not all smiles,* she thought grimly. Just as she thought, John was all smiles and greetings for Drew instead of the serious man she wanted to bring some male support into the discussion.

After several cups of coffee and some sandwiches, John got a bit more serious and read Drew the riot act. The talking went on into the night and they still wouldn't give away Jessica's whereabouts. Only that she was back on her feet and had a job. Polly kept giving huge yawns and finally went to bed. John was not far behind, and by mutual agreement, they didn't start talking. They both fell asleep almost immediately, but Drew lay with his hands behind his head and stared into the blackness of a country night.

As soon as he heard John up and about, Drew got up, too. His mind had gone around in circles all night; he felt gritty-eyed and out of sorts. He followed John into the shower and turned it to cold, gasping as the water froze his back, but he got dressed feeling better. John left the house, and Drew made another pot of tea and paced around the kitchen, sipping a brimming mug. He opened the back door, and Charlie came in, rubbing around his legs and sat on the step. The early morning was still and warm. Drew got accustomed all over again to the sounds around him. He heard Polly moving upstairs but was in no mood to face another confrontation so early in the morning, so he shut the door, nearly trapping Charlie's tail in the process, and went out to his car. As he started it, Polly's head appeared at the window. He gave her a jaunty wave and pulled away.

You crafty bugger, she thought. *Too scared to stand and fight, eh.*

Drew meandered around the lanes for a while and finally headed for a favourite viewpoint where he could park, look at the view, and work out a plan of action. He stopped the car and stared at the scattering of buildings and caravans down in the hollow.

"Christ almighty, where did that lot come from?" he said aloud. "That was where we used to go for our picnics. That was John's land."

He stared at it for a few moments more and then started the car to go down to investigate. He drove down the long driveway and pulled into the car park. He looked around him and was impressed at the cleanliness of everything and the modern layout. A woman strolled across the car park. Her tawny, streaked hair was damp, and she had a towel draped around her neck. She was wearing shorts and a skimpy top and had obviously been swimming. As he locked his car, he gave her a long, appraising glance, which she returned. His eyes ran along her legs as she got in a car, very aware of his scrutiny. Viv was very sure of her attraction and tossed her towel onto the passenger's seat, shaking her hair out at the same time. As she pulled away, she gave Drew the once over from under her lashes and was rewarded with a blinding smile. She drove away with a warm feeling, and he walked towards the cluster of buildings with a sure stride.

He wandered about the place for a while until the smell of bacon cooking made his stomach rumble. He ordered a full breakfast in the cafe and, taking his coffee, sat down at a table by the window. He ruminated on the price John must have got for the land and wondered why it hadn't been mentioned. Something like this on the doorstep would have surely entered the conversation at some point. His breakfast arrived, and he gave it his full attention. He sat with a second cup of coffee and watched the holidaymakers going about their morning routine. Kids with scrubbed faces and slicked-down hair, fresh from the shower and squeaky clean for five minutes. A game of cricket was getting organised in the middle of the field. Mums on their way to the laundry with buckets, and men heading for the washhouse with toilet bags and towels.

He decided to see what else was around and spent some time in the small bowling alley, watching them oil the lanes. He had often wondered how they did that and watched the machine glide smoothly along the lanes, leaving a glistening slick behind it. He wandered out towards the campers and smelt again the aroma of bacon on the air. Not so enticing since he was full.

Suddenly, he stopped in his tracks. Over to his left, on a concrete slab at the side of a mobile home, was Jessica's car. He stood stunned. The number was an unusual one that they had remarked on when they bought it, and this was definitely the one. He walked towards it. Perhaps she had sold it. Perhaps she needed the money. He circled the van and stood undecided by the side of the car. There was no one about, and he dithered about from foot to foot. He suddenly turned on his heel and strode towards the reception. The pretty girl behind the counter looked up with a warm smile. "Can I help you, sir?"

"Jessica Cameron, is she working today?" he asked, expecting a puzzled "I'm afraid I don't know her" answer.

Instead, the girl smiled again and said, "I'm here till midday. She takes over from me. Can I give her a message?"

Drew was stunned. *No wonder Polly omitted to mention this place. They knew all along.* The girl's eyebrows lifted as she waited for an answer. "No, no message. I'll catch her later," his smile stretched the tight skin of his face.

He searched all the small shops in the complex. If she hadn't taken her car, she couldn't have gone far. He walked back to the van. This must be hers if the car's here and she's not living with Polly. A tall, good-looking blond approached him. "Are you looking for someone?" he asked with an accented voice.

"Jessica Cameron."

"Sorry, I don't know where she is, but she's working later, so she won't be long. Can I give her a message?"

"No, no message," Drew said for the second time and started to walk back towards reception.

A classic, sleek black Jaguar pulled in, and Drew ran his eyes along it admiringly. A shiny blondish cap of hair emerged from the passenger door and then leant down again to speak to the large bearded man inside. Drew saw a flash of teeth as she shut the door, and his glance took in her trim figure and tanned skin. She turned, her face all glowing, and Drew caught his breath. The smile died on her face as her eyes locked on his.

"Jessie," he said in a whisper.

"Drew," she said in the same whisper.

CHAPTER 43

Jessica never believed it when they said the blood drained from the face when you got a shock, but she sure as hell believed it now. She could feel hers running downwards to her shoes, and her heart began a hard thudding in her chest. Drew took a step towards her, and at the same time, she took a step back.

"Well," Drew began and then had to clear his throat, "look at you. I never would have recognised you."

"How did you find me?"

"More by error than trial," Drew said with a wry grin. "You covered your tracks very well."

"I didn't cover anything."

"No, maybe not, but you certainly didn't leave many clues."

Jessica started to walk towards the caravan, and Drew fell into step beside her. They walked in silence across the grass. Jessica unlocked the van and went inside, Drew following close on her heels as if he was scared she might shut the door in his face. He stood in the doorway and looked around. Jessica watched him from the corner of her eye and saw his face screw up with distaste. It was a look she had seen many times before. She straightened up and lifted her chin, ready to defend this little tin box that had wrapped itself around her and given her a sense of security.

"I presume this is the place you call home now. Bit of a comedown, isn't it?"

Jessica stood and looked at him. He looked pale and had lost weight. He needed a haircut and a shave. "Pathetic as you might find it, this is my home, and if you are going to stand there and insult it, then save your breath and close the door on the way out."

It was Drew's turn to stare at her now. This was not the timid Jessica he remembered. She didn't even look anything like her anymore. Her short hair was something he had talked her out of many times, but he had to admit it suited her. Her eyes looked bigger and more slanted like a cat when he'd caressed its ears. He took in her neat, firm figure and tanned skin and felt himself drawn towards her. He moved to take her in his arms, suddenly needing to assert his dominance over her again.

"Stay where you are, Drew," she snapped. "If you don't want me to run screaming out of here, you'll keep your distance."

He faltered and frowned. This was not going at all according to plan.

"Sit down if you wish, and I'll make a cup of coffee, but don't think now you've found me I'm going to melt into your arms. Those days have gone."

He sat as instructed and watched her as she made the coffee, still not knowing what to make of this woman who was still his wife. Jessica sat down opposite him and leant back against the cushions of the couch. She looked at him steadily over the rim of the cup, and he found himself getting really uncomfortable.

"I don't know where to begin this conversation," he looked down at his feet. "I have tried to find you for a long time now. I was worried about you. The kids were worried about you. Marty came over from America when he heard, and Caro's been on my back constantly. The least you could have done was let us know where you were."

"What would you have done if I had, Drew?"

"I would have come and talked it all over with you."

"That's why I didn't tell you where I was."

"Did you think running away would solve anything?"

"I don't consider it running away. I would class it as escaping from a situation that was threatening my sanity."

"Come on, Jessie, don't you think that's a bit dramatic."

Again, he got silent scrutiny. He felt he needed to fill the silence. "After all, you never wanted for anything. You had a good life compared to some people. You never wanted for anything."

He ran out of steam and his argument sounded pathetic even to him. "Come on, Jessie, for Christ sake, say something. It's like talking to a brick wall."

"Since when did you want to hear anything from me?"

"We've always talked."

"No, Drew, you talked. I listened."

"Well, talk now then. Now's your chance."

"You still won't want to listen. Anyway, it's far too late for talking. About ten years too late. It won't do any good anyway."

"What do you mean, ten years too late?"

"Well, that was when all the little affairs started, wasn't it?"

Drew was silent. He opened his mouth, but she interrupted him. "Don't bother to deny it. I can remember almost to the day. You were very transparent, you know."

Jessica stood up and walked into the kitchen area. She filled the kettle and walked over to him. She took the cup from his hand and spooned more coffee into it. She leant her back against the worktop and gazed out through the small window opposite. "Her name was Sandra; the first one, that is. In those days, I cared enough to find out who they were and what they looked like. After about five, I couldn't be bothered anymore. They all looked similar anyway. You have no idea of the times I've waited outside various buildings for you to come out and see who you came out with. I have followed you on numerous occasions to see where you went. Once, I even waited in the car all night just to be sure you weren't really going to the meeting you'd been in great pains to tell me about. In the morning, you looked absolutely wrecked; no wonder you had an early night that night. The pressures of a rising executive you told me. Oh, you were rising all right. But not at the meetings."

"If you knew all this, why didn't you do something about it?"

"Me! You've got a bloody cheek. Why didn't I do something about it? I think you've got that wrong. You were the one who should have done something. I did everything I could to give you the incentive to stop. I seduced you, gave you sexy massages, bought sexy underwear, and did everything but swing from the chandelier, as well as cooking gourmet meals and keeping the house running smoothly. But it still wasn't enough, was it, Drew? You still had to have your little ego flings. Just to assure yourself you could still fuck with the best of them."

"But I always came back to you, though, didn't I?"

"And I suppose that makes it OK, does it, you arrogant bastard?"

Drew couldn't get used to this forceful woman at all. The old Jessica never swore. "You must have known they didn't mean anything."

"How the hell was I supposed to know that? Every time you started a new fling, I did everything I could to keep you at home. Made up all kinds of lies and excuses, but still, you were like a cat on hot bricks. And every time you got tired of it and came home, you took another little piece of my confidence and self-esteem. If someone repeatedly treats you like nothing, in the end, you believe you are nothing. But all those years, I put up with it because, as you so kindly put it, I had everything I ever wanted. Until Elizabeth. You couldn't even resist shitting on your own doorstep, could you? How you two must have connived and lied to do what you did. And all the time, I was confiding in her. How the two of you must have laughed at poor, old Jessie."

Jessica could feel her throat closing up; she was in danger of breaking down. "Anyway, I have to go to work, so you'll have to leave now."

"Surely you can let them know I'm here and take a few hours off."

"Why should I, Drew? They've been good to me here, and I don't intend to jeopardise that to spend time arguing with you. Now, if you don't mind, I have to change."

"What time do you get off? I'll meet you."

"Don't bother. I shall be coming straight home to sleep."

Drew stood up. "I'll see you tomorrow then."

"I doubt it, I'm going out."

"For Christ sake, Jessie, we've got a million things to talk about. Surely, you can spare me a little of your time. I can't stay here forever, you know." Drew slammed his cup down on the drainer. "Where are you going that's so important anyway?"

"None of your business."

"What do you mean none of my business; you're my wife."

Jessica threw her head back and laughed, and Drew completely lost his temper. He took her by the shoulders and shook her. "You're screwing that big bozo you were in the car with today, aren't you? My God, you didn't let the grass grow under your feet, did you? Little Miss Prim and Proper couldn't wait to get her knickers off."

Jessica put all the strength she could muster behind the slap. It hit Drew fair and square across the face, and he staggered back, shock and amazement on his face. His hand went up towards her, but Jessica stood her ground and lifted her chin. Defiance was written all over her face. His hand went down. "This is not the end of this," he said, making for the door.

"It is, as far as I'm concerned."

Drew slammed the door so hard that the cups on the drainer rattled. Jessica sagged against the table, all the bravado suddenly evaporating. She walked wearily into the bedroom to change. *After such a wonderful morning, how could the day have turned into such a bag of shit?* Her thoughts turned to Luke as she got dressed and found herself smiling. *Luke. Lovely Luke. I'm not a bit ashamed, and I don't care who knows it. Even Drew. No…especially Drew.*

CHAPTER 44

Drew drove out of the complex in a towering rage. He flew around the lanes at breakneck speed and, only after narrowly missing a car coming the other way, slowed down. He skidded into the driveway of the farmhouse, with gravel thrown up in a wave. He slammed the car door viciously and strode towards the front door, only to find it locked. He banged and beat loudly on the thick wood and yelled out Polly's name. Around the corner of the house, in a blur of brown and white, charged a terrible terrier, which immediately fastened itself on Drew's trouser leg.

"Let go, you bloody thing, before I kick your fucking teeth in," Drew shouted, shaking his leg violently.

If Chad understood him, he certainly didn't show it and continued to worry Drew's trouser leg. By now, the material was beginning to tear, and his patience finally came to an end. He started yelling for Polly at the top of his voice. He walked round to the back of the house, dragging the dog behind him. Chad anchored down all four feet and left deep drag marks behind him in the gravel. Drew spotted Polly halfway along the back path and started yelling again. He felt totally out of control, and his language was worse than at any other time he could ever remember. He screamed the vilest swear words he could get his tongue around, spitting with the force of them. Polly turned a shocked face towards this lunatic wild man and, for a few moments, took in the sight of a normally laid-back person walking crab-like, dragging a snarling dog behind him. After the initial shock, she could feel her chest muscles constricting. The spasm moved up into her throat, and the laughter erupted in a loud bellow that doubled her over. Her eyes streamed tears of mirth, and she clutched her sides. As she bent forward, another shocked face appeared over her shoulder. Drew spotted the dog collar under the thin white face of the vicar and stopped short.

"Sorry," the vicar stuttered. A pink glow crept up his neck, "I only called in for a pot of jam for the church raffle."

This started Polly off again, and Drew just stood there, the dog still fastened to his trouser leg. "Sorry, vicar. Didn't see you there."

"So it seems," the vicar returned dryly.

Polly mopped her eyes with the end of her sleeve and walked over to slap Chad on the muzzle. "Let go, you stupid mutt. CHAD…let go."

Chad very reluctantly untangled his teeth and sat down about three feet away, showing all his teeth and most of his gums in a hyena grin. A rumble still sounded in his throat, but he watched Polly warily from the corners of his eyes and stayed put.

Drew inspected his ruined trousers. "What the hell's the matter with that dog? The bloody things gone loopy. It's a wonder I haven't got a chunk missing from my leg as well."

"If Chad had wanted your leg, I can assure you he would have had it."

"Wants putting down if you ask me."

"Nobody did," replied Polly, turning back to the vicar.

Drew strode off into the house, and Polly walked to the gate with the vicar.

"Friend of yours?" he asked.

"Sort of."

The vicar looked at Polly with one eyebrow raised.

"Oh, Bob, it's a long story. He's Jessica's husband and they're going through a bit of trauma at the moment."

The vicar knew and liked Jessica and somehow couldn't relate her to this uncouth man he'd just met. Polly seemed to read his mind. "He's not always like that. He's actually a very charming man. You just caught him at a bad time, that's all."

"If you say so," the vicar said over his shoulder. "Haven't heard language like that since I was an army chaplain. Quite colourful, really. Tell him I give him absolution."

"I think you're a few years too late to save his soul. That went to hell in a bucket quite a number of years ago. But I'll tell him anyway."

Polly could hear Drew stomping upstairs and wondered what had set him off. When he finally came down, now wearing a pair of jeans, she was sitting at the large kitchen table, glasses on the end of her nose, going over some of the farm accounts. He prowled about behind her, not speaking, and finally plonked a cup of tea in front of her.

"Thanks," she said, continuing to look at the column of figures in front of her.

"Sorry about the tantrum. I completely lost it there for a while."

Polly took her glasses off and sat back. She looked steadily at him until Drew cast his eyes down. "I saw Jessie."

"I see."

The silence lengthened. Polly knew Drew of old. He would confide in his own time or not at all. She lit a cigarette and continued to look at him. Emotions played across his face. She had never seen him look so unsure of himself, ever.

"She's changed."

"Has she? In what way?"

Drew sat down on the other side of the table and stretched his long legs out in front of him. "She hit me, you know"

Polly's eyebrows shot up into her hairline. "Jessica did! What for?"

Drew leant his head back and stared unseeingly at the light fitting. He saw again in his mind's eye the glowing, smiling face of his wife as she turned away from the black car and the man who was in it. Even when dressed in casual clothes, there was a sensual look about her. A sexual, alluring look that he never realised was there. He knew as a gut instinct the signs of a woman who is totally aware of her body and its power over a man. A power that only comes from one source.

"I was jealous. She looked so good I wanted to touch her."

"And did you?" Polly stubbed her cigarette out and picked up her cup. "Is that why she hit you?"

Drew shook his head. Again, he was silent, as if trying to form the words he wanted to say into a sentence. "Who is the guy with the black Jaguar?"

Polly sucked in her breath, so that was it. *Luke. She's been with Luke.* "He's a local businessman."

"Are they having an affair?"

"That's something that you will have to ask Jessie."

Drew looked across at her. "You didn't deny it, Polly."

"How can I? I don't know."

"Which means you think they could be?"

Polly stood up, endeavouring to put some distance between herself and those all-seeing, all-probing blue eyes. "I know Luke likes her and that they are friends. That's all I know."

"Luke. So that's his name. Luke, what?"

"Oh, Drew; what difference does it make? What you need to do is talk to Jessie if you want to know about her life. I can't tell you what I don't know. I don't see too much of her now she's working, and anyway, I wouldn't dream of telling her what to do. I'll do all I can, but don't expect me to act as a go-between or tell tales because I won't do it."

"She doesn't want to see me."

"Well, you did give her a bit of a shock."

"Can you arrange something, Polly?"

"OK, I'll see what I can do." Polly went upstairs and Drew heard the phone click as the extension was picked up. He resisted the urge to pick up the kitchen phone to listen in. He got up to let Charlie out, opening the door a crack at first to cast a wary eye for Chad. Some minutes later, the phone clicked again as the extension was replaced upstairs. Polly appeared in the doorway, and Drew looked at her face. It didn't look happy.

"Well?"

"She understands you both have things to talk about. But she would rather not be on her own with you. She's coming here to dinner tomorrow evening. You can talk in private. John and I will make ourselves scarce."

"Tomorrow evening! Is that the best she can do?"

"Well, she has other plans for the morning, but she will finish early from work and come over then."

"Huh, we all know what those other plans are. Don't we?" Drew said bitterly.

"For God's sake, Drew. You really are putting two and two together and making five. You don't know any such thing, and if you intend to carry on like this I shall call the whole thing off. She's coming here to talk, not put up with another of your tempers."

"I know. I know. But I still can't get over how she's changed. She looks so different with her hair short. Her face looks totally altered.

She looks really beautiful. Alive and sexy."

"She always looked like that, Drew," Polly said smiling. "She always turned men's heads. It's that you were so busy eyeing up all the other females, you didn't see that their husbands were doing the same to your wife. I don't even think Jessie realised. She was too busy watching you, watching everyone else."

"She's not going to come back now, is she, Pol?"

"I don't know. Will you change if she does? If not. Don't even try to repair your marriage. Just let her go."

Drew chewed on his lip. "Think I'll go and find John boy. Could do with some hard labour to get my mind off things for a while."

Polly sat down and stared at the farm books. There was no way she could go back to these today; she would have a concerted effort tomorrow. She started gathering them up and then stopped. She thought back to her phone conversation with Jessica. She had made it very clear right from the start that her morning with Luke was more important than a meeting with Drew, and no matter what Polly had said, she wouldn't be swayed. When Polly said she had gone looking for her to warn her of Drew's visit, Jessica had said straight out that she had spent the night with Luke. There was no apology in her voice, and Polly knew that this was not something that would be kept secret. Jessica and Luke were going to be totally upfront with their relationship, and it didn't bode well for any friendly talking. The only thing she and John could do was stay out of the way but not too far away. *Oh well. Time will tell.*

CHAPTER 45

After Jessica put the phone down on Polly, she stood gazing unseeingly out of the window. A head peered around her shoulder, making her jump.

"Penny for them," Stacey said, smiling.

Jessica smiled back. "I can assure you they are worth at least fifty pence."

"Do tell, Jess. It's tea break time and I could do with some gossip."

Jessica was not normally into true confessions, but after working closely with Stacey, she found her a good friend and felt the need to put her in the picture. Stacey had never bombarded her with questions. She seemed content to leave Jessica alone. She took their friendship seriously and was non-invasive. Jessica had always appreciated this, as in the beginning, she wasn't able to talk rationally anyway and would have resented anyone prying.

"My husband turned up here today."

Stacey's mouth opened and snapped shut again.

"Come on, let's sit down and I'll tell you all about it."

Jessica found it was like a cleansing to talk to someone who was completely outside the situation and could look at the whole thing objectively. She told Stacey about her life, her kids, her friends, her husband, the affairs, the escape, and Polly and John, in fact, everything leading up to her arriving for the job. Stacey sat quietly and listened. Only interrupting to clarify a point. The only thing

Jessica didn't tell her about was Luke. Stacey was ahead of her on that anyway. After seeing no lights in her caravan last night and Jessica's sparkling eyes when she got out of Luke's car that morning, it didn't take someone with a Mensa membership to know what had happened.

"So there you have it," Jessica said, winding down like a clockwork mouse. "What do you think?"

"I think you're very brave, that's what I think," Stacey said, leaning back and looking at Jessica with new eyes.

"Brave! That would be the last word I would use to describe me."

"Rubbish. To have gone all through that and still have enough strength to leave. That's got to be classed as bravery."

"Not really, Stacey. The truth of it is, I ran away. If I'd been really brave, I'd have stayed and faced it. But now it's finally hit the fan, and I have to face it after all."

"Do you think you'll go back?"

Jessica pursed her lips reflectively. A few months ago, she wouldn't have had a clue what she would have done if she had come face-to-face with Drew. The feelings she had always had for him were still there, and if he had turned up while she was still vulnerable, she had no doubt she would have gone back. But as time went on, she had got stronger and more independent. She could feel it day by day. Now, she felt she had finally stepped out from his shadow and become a real person. When she stood before him in the morning, she felt no emotion at all. This she found very curious. Surely she should have felt something. After all the years together, she should have felt some emotion, even if it was revulsion. It was only talking about the past hurt that had choked her up, but nothing, no emotion whatsoever for the present.

"I feel different now. I like myself. I like having my own life. I don't think I could go back to living on tin tacks, wondering where

Drew was all the time. I feel I have outgrown him now, if that makes sense."

"Maybe Luke had something to do with it."

Jessica's head shot up.

"Oh, Jessie, I'm not blind. Luke's had a thing about you from day one. We all saw it except you. I'm just glad you finally got together."

Stacey's smile stretched across her face, and Jessica's matched it. "We certainly did that, and it was wonderful."

"Does he know your husband's back?"

Jessica's face clouded over, "I haven't spoken to him, and I won't be seeing him till tomorrow. I don't know how to tell him."

"How much does he know?"

"Not much, really. We haven't talked at all about our past. We seem to be wrapped up in the present at the moment."

"Why don't you go and see him when you finish here? Surely, you owe it to him to put him in the picture."

Jessica felt undecided, but with much urging on Stacey's part, she eventually phoned Luke. As soon as she heard his voice, she suddenly realised it was the one voice she had wanted to hear all along. As soon as she spoke and he knew it was her, his voice went soft and warm, and the need to see him almost overpowered her. Her thoughts must have been telepathic as he said, "Jessie, I need to see you so badly. I've been sat here thinking about you and how stupid I was not to arrange to see you tonight. I was just about to pick up the phone when it rang."

"I'll drive over as soon as I've finished."

"Wonderful. I'll be waiting."

Stacey nudged her in the ribs when she put the phone down. "See how easy it was," she said, grinning. "Give him a kiss from me. Or two or three." She disappeared into the office, singing *Love is in the air*.

On the drive over to Luke's, Jessica felt tense and fluttery. She started rehearsing in her mind what she would say. *How to tell him. How to even start.* As soon as the car pulled up in front of the house, the door was flung open and light spilt out, casting Luke's large shadow yards across the driveway. She walked towards him, and he opened his arms. She walked straight into them as if it were the most natural thing in the world. He hugged her so fiercely her breath came out in a whoosh. Arms around each other, they walked inside. As soon as Luke shut the door behind them, he took her into his arms and kissed her softly, his lips warm and moist. Almost instantly, the passion flared between them, and the embrace became rough and grasping. Jessica almost tore the buttons off his shirt, frantic to feel his skin. His hands went up under her loose top and pulled it violently over her head. He spun her around and unclasped her bra, throwing it to one side, his hands going to her breast, rubbing the nipples with his thumbs. Jessica pushed back against his thighs and felt his hardness. She turned back to him and her hands fumbled urgently with his belt buckle.

"I'll do it," he growled. "Take off your skirt."

Jessica tore off the long muslin skirt, followed by her pants, all the time watching him. He pulled his jeans and pants off in one movement and stood before her, fully erect and proud. Jessica ran her hands over his chest and heard herself making a whimpering noise in her throat. Luke pulled her down onto the carpet and entered her immediately. Her hips rose to meet his thrusts and their rhythm was fast and urgent. Her whimpers became grunts, which in turn became wails—each one increasing in volume. Luke's head was thrown back, a look almost like pain on his face. As Jessica's body arched and tensed with her approaching orgasm, Luke brought her to the peak with a mighty thrust that brought forth a roar from his wide open mouth and a shuddering that shook the whole of his body. He loomed above her rigid, unmoving while the seed tore out of his body until, finally, his senses returned; he relaxed, resting on his knees and elbows, his head dropping and his eyes closed. Jessica opened her eyes and looked up at him. She felt boneless yet exhilarated. What had taken place was awesome and earth-shattering, and she felt the tears sliding down into her hair. Luke rolled over onto his side, turning her with him. He opened his eyes and saw her tears, at first he was startled until he realised the reason was not sadness but happiness and deep emotion. He wrapped her in his arms and held her gently until the tears stopped. They lay like this for some while until the hardness of the floor started to be uncomfortable. He stood, pulling her with him.

"Let's shower and get decent, I've cooked for you."

Jessica smiled. "That sounds good."

"Come on then, the shower's big enough for two."

Showered and dressed in one very oversized, towelling dressing gown of Luke's, Jessica tucked into a savoury chicken and mushroom casserole with a jacket potato and crusty bread. They returned to the lounge and sat close together on the large settee with a glass of wine.

"Luke. Can we talk?"

"That sounds ominous," Luke said, peering around at her face.

He smoothed a tendril of damp hair on her neck and pulled her closer to him.

"No, it isn't really, but it's not particularly good either."

"Then you had better spit it all out then."

And Jessica did. She told Luke almost as much as she had told Stacey, and like her, he didn't interrupt but listened carefully. Unlike Stacey, he could also hear the things she wasn't saying. He'd been there and knew what it felt like, knew the mind-blowing hurt and anger and the feeling of betrayal. He also realised that what they were doing wasn't far removed from what had been done to them, and this was not sitting easy with him. His chest tightened. He couldn't lose her now.

He cleared his throat. "Is there a chance you can get back together?"

He found he was holding his breath. It seemed to take her an awful long time to answer, and the breath was burning in his chest.

"No. No chance at all."

His breath slowly left his lungs.

"But there are things to be cleared up, so I'm having dinner at Polly's tomorrow night, and Drew and I will talk."

CHAPTER 46

The prospect of a whole evening and all the next day with nothing to do gave Drew the heebies. John took pity on him and took him off to the pub for a couple of hours that evening. The following day, after a lengthy conversation with Adam and an even longer one with Joan, his secretary, Drew was once again at a loose end. Polly had gone off with the dogs at her heels to take John his lunch and, if she was honest, also to get away from Drew's long face. On many occasions when she had seen Jessica silently suffering over Drew's antics, she had longed for him to be on the receiving end one day. Now he was, and he wasn't coping at all well. He was fidgety and nervy. His face looked drawn and tense, and the bright blue eyes looked dimmed and pink-rimmed. Polly was really hard-pressed to carry on any kind of conversation with him. He seemed to only take in half of what she said, and she finally got a bit fed up with repeating herself all the time. She made the excuse that John was too far away to come all the way back for his lunch but got the impression the elaborate excuse had fallen on deaf ears anyway.

Drew ruminated on whether to phone Caro but decided it was a bit early in the proceedings, so he phoned Sophia instead. She sounded pleased that he had found Jessica and told him everything was under control, including the cat. After Drew hung up, he mooched about for a while, bored to tears, and then snatched up his car keys and went out.

The sky was a brilliant cobalt blue, and the sun was hot through the glass of the car. Drew opened the window wide, and the warm breeze lifted the glossy, grey-streaked, dark hair, lifting his spirits with it. He drove for some ten miles, the radio playing softly and the summer air swirling through the car, bringing with it the smell of the sea. He turned off down to a stretch of the beach and was surprised to find that it was actually completely deserted. He parked high up on the grassy dunes and walked down a steep pathway. He strolled along the beach in the warm sun for a while, his mind for once completely blank and unthinking. Without any conscious thought about it, he veered down to the water's edge, stripped down to his brief black pants, and plunged into the water. He swam until all his muscles screamed for a rest and finally, wearily dragged himself back on the beach.

He lay in the hot sun for a while until he could feel his skin beginning to burn. He pulled his shirt loosely over his shoulders and walked slowly back along the beach and back up to the car. He rubbed the sand from his feet on the rough grass and pulled on his jeans and canvas loafers. He leant on the bonnet of the car and looked at the vast expanse of sea and beach spread out before him. A movement in the corner of his eye caused him to turn and look. The beach curved round quite sharply, and on the other side of the curve, a couple were running out of the water, laughing and tanned. The man was chasing the woman, and the woman, wearing a very brief bottom half and no top at all, was snaking from side to side, trying to avoid the man's hands. Her body was brown and trim with firm brown breasts and golden streaked hair. The man was large with the body of an athlete and easily caught the woman, swinging her up into the air and into his arms.

Drew wanted to cry out. He wanted to scream at Jessica that he was there and he could see her. His throat closed over in pain, and even if he could have uttered a word, the crashing of the sea would have shouted down his puny cry. So he stood there like a pillar carved onto the cliff and watched another man make love to his wife. Behind the rocks, which Drew could see over the top, he watched her roll over to sit astride him, her head thrown back and her closed eyes turned in his direction. He willed her eyes to open and see him standing there, but the man turned her under him, pulling her body up to meet his own. The act that Drew had taken so much pleasure in for so many years was now the most obscene thing he had ever seen, and he felt the strength to finally move. To turn and retch, and throw up, and retch some more until there was nothing left. Nothing but the tears coming up his throat in painful, wracking sobs that threatened to tear his lungs out. If all the tears he had ever shed in his life, including all the ones caused by his unfeeling mother, had joined together at this moment, they would not have been enough to ease the pain.

Drew lay on the sharp cutting grass for a long time. His chest hurt and was still sharply expanding with dry heaves. His eyes burned even though they were tightly closed, and his throat felt swollen and almost closed up. He could feel the hot sun burning the side of his face, but he still didn't move. The tableaux played again against his closed eyelids, and he groaned and rolled over onto his side, an arm thrown across his face. Finally, he heaved painfully into a sitting position and then onto his feet. He opened up the red-hot car and wound down all the windows. This simple act seemed to take away all his energy, and he slumped down onto the hot front seat, resting his head in his hands. He sat there until the sweat dripped from his face before turning his feet into the car, closing the door, and starting up the engine.

He drove slowly back towards the farm but couldn't bring himself to go back yet, so he drove aimlessly around the country lanes until he glanced at the fuel gauge and saw it was almost empty. The jerk of awareness was the first reaction he had felt since he saw them. He headed the car cautiously back towards the main road and a garage.

When he finally arrived back at the farm, John was already home. He greeted Drew warmly, which closed up Drew's throat again, then sniffed. "Good God, Drew, where the hell have you been? You don't half smell funny."

"John! For goodness sake, what a thing to say to a guest," Polly said, bustling in with an armful of washing from the garden.

"Well, he does. You smell," and John proceeded to sniff again.

To allay any more speculation, Drew told them he had eaten a hamburger and it hadn't gone down too well. In fact, it had come up even better. Polly tut tutted and John laughed. Drew made his escape to his room, not without a very penetrating look from Polly.

He decided against his usual shower in favour of a hot bath. He needed to unwind in some peace and quiet and to wash away some of the grubby memories. He succeeded with the first part, but the visions were as strong as ever. He brushed his hair until it shone with its usual lustre, noting the need for a trim, splashed very soft and fragrant aftershave and deodorant on, and dressed in well-cut pale grey trousers and a grey and blue collarless shirt. His belt and loafers were navy, and he presented an expensively dressed and confident man—on the outside, anyway.

He went into the lounge and poured himself a hefty whiskey. He sat in one of the large armchairs and sipped slowly. He could hear John whistling upstairs and could smell some tantalising aromas coming from the oven. He sat there in the silence and tried not to think of the evening ahead. He had, if he was really honest, been looking forward to being with Jessica again. Now, he was dreading it. Dreading to have to look at her, knowing about her day. Dreading having to eat when his insides were churning. Dreading not being able to confront her with it. Not yet, anyway. Polly walked in in black slacks and a black sleeveless tunic.

"You can pour a nice cold gin and tonic for the cook if you like," she said, flopping down in the opposite chair. "The beef and Guinness pie's cooked, as are the new potatoes, just the veg to do now, and that's it."

Drew felt his stomach clench. "Don't be offended if I don't do the food my usual justice, Pol. My insides feel a bit raw, and I don't want to overdo it and have to run to the bathroom."

Polly took the glass from him and waited for him to sit down and pick up his own glass. "Are you going to tell me what upset you today before John comes down?"

"Nothing upset me except the hamburger."

"Well, you'd better tell me where you bought it. It must have been very bad for you to be affected. In all the years I've known you, you have never gone down with a bad stomach. Over the years, we've all had our share of dodgy seafood, too much fruit, and some funny sausages, but not you. Never you. The constitution of an ox. So what upset you?"

Drew swirled his drink around in the glass, the ice clinking. "I'm sorry, Pol. I can't tell you. Not tonight, anyway. Perhaps never. I'll get all upset if I talk about it now, and I need my wits about me tonight. When I feel ready to share today with you, we'll talk."

"OK, as you like. I know I've been a bit abrupt. As I told you, I was Jessie's friend first, but that doesn't stop me wanting to do all I can to save a marriage. So if you need to talk, well...."

The doorbell rang, and Polly stood up. Drew heard the murmur of voices as the door opened and stood up. Polly stood aside to let Jessica through at the same time that John came down the stairs. While Jessica greeted John, Drew had a chance to study her. Her dress was a long, pale lime green soft jersey. It was cut to cling and then flare at the bottom. The shoestring straps were thin, and there was obviously no bra underneath. She wore a cream lace fringed shawl thrown over her shoulders and knotted on one side. Her shoes were cream lace summer granny boots with the toes and heels cut out. She looked like a clone of the wife he remembered, and if Drew had seen her in a crowded room, he would have been drawn to her side without realising who she was. The light shawl showed her tanned skin to perfection, and her lips and toenails were painted a bright pink. Her many bangles were cream and gold, as were her earrings. She looked stunning, and she knew it, and Drew knew she knew it. Even as his brain remembered the beach, his fingers itched to touch her in the old familiar way. He tightly clenched his glass to keep his hands in place.

Fucking hell, this was going to be even worse than he thought.

CHAPTER 47

The visit to the beach had come as somewhat of a surprise. They had both woken early and, reluctant to get out of bed, had laid, bodies entwined and talked. Luke had to go away for a few days to finalise some details with a firm of architects and also to recruit some more workmen. Jessica admitted to being worried about the coming meeting with Drew, and Luke tried to reassure her by wrapping his arms around her. This proved to be the end of any conversation, as his body responded to her immediately. All the blood rushed downwards from his brain and engorged other parts. As soon as Jessica felt the urgent stirring, her talking stopped, and her mouth curved in a knowing grin. She turned over and met his brown eyes. Heavy lidded with desire and proceeded to entice him further. They made love slowly and leisurely and, finally, much later, got up and showered.

Work had started on the old cottage, and Luke wanted to have a look and take some timber to the carpenter there. He loaded up the truck, and they headed out to the cottage. The sun was blazing hot and Jessica was grateful for the shorts and sandals she'd thrown in a bag last night. Luke was also in shorts, and Jessica couldn't resist rubbing her hand along the soft hair on the muscular thigh.

"Too much of that, woman, and I'll take you into the bushes in a minute."

"Promises, promises."

"Wanton hussy," Luke growled, also rubbing his hand along her leg. "I don't think you're quite ready for love in the great outdoors yet."

"What do you mean, not ready?" Jessica said with a frown crossing her face.

Luke saw the frown. "I just think that you are too much of a lady to go fornicating in the bushes."

"Well, little do you know, Luke Benson. Some of my best lovemaking was done under open skies."

"Tell me more, but not too much, or I might get jealous."

"When I was at college, we weren't allowed boys in our rooms, and none of us had cars, so where do you think we went for our privacy."

"I see. Well, where did you go?"

"Mostly into the park, and sometimes, if you wanted to be very private, into a hay barn that we all knew about, but that was a bus ride away, so it had to be planned first."

"Hardly spontaneous."

"True, but the anticipation was better than any foreplay."

Luke threw his head back and laughed.

He stopped the truck just out of sight of the cottage and took her into his arms. He lifted her chin and his mouth covered hers in a deep kiss. His tongue teased hers and her senses started melting with the gentleness of it. He took his lips slightly away and she felt his breath before she realised he was talking.

"Later, my darling," he murmured. "I'm going to take you down to the beach, a deserted beach I know, and I'm going to make love to you. I'm going to lay your body along mine and feel every curve of you. I'm going to rub your nipples and kiss you all over, then when you are wet for me, and your body starts thrusting towards mine, I'm going to slip inside you."

She was leaning against him with her eyes closed, her breath ragged in her throat, when she felt him pull away, turn in his seat, and start the engine. She sat bolt upright and stared at him. He pulled out onto the road and turned his head to look at her. His face was smiling. "OK, you sexy woman. Let's see how long you can stay on the boil."

Jessica laughed. "You, rotten sod. That wasn't fair."

For the next hour, they toured the cottage. Luke unloaded the timber, in between constantly touching her body whenever the carpenter's back was turned. He followed her up the stairs, his fingers inside the leg of her shorts. The carpenter's apprentice was in front of her, so she couldn't say anything. Luke stood behind the lad as he was telling her of some of the old houses he had worked on. Downstairs, a workman was carrying the timber through the house, and Luke pulled her backwards by her arm, seemingly to give the bloke some room but really to push her hand down onto the front of his shorts to feel his hardness. She was scared the workmen would see and pulled him towards the door. But he was having none of it and got into several conversations about the work being done, all the time touching her intimately whenever he could. It was driving her mad, and the urge to touch him back was more than she could bear. They went into the outbuildings to supposedly look at the renovations taking place on the old fireplaces, but as soon as they were inside, Luke pinned her against the wall, rubbing his hardened body along hers and pulling her t-shirt up. Just as she started pushing against him, he walked away.

Bugger him, she thought, getting cross. *I'll go and sit in the truck out of his way.*

She hadn't been there five minutes when he was dragging her out to look at something else and continued touching her and feeling her until she thought she'd go mad. Finally, he piled her back into the truck and took off towards the beach, a smug smile on his face.

"Still boiling," he said looking at her out of the corner of his eyes.

"You bet I am. Boiling to thump you," Jessica answered through gritted teeth.

"You don't really mean that."

He covered her mouth with his as soon as they stopped, and Jessica groaned, "Enough. You've teased me enough, Luke."

He pulled her t-shirt over her head, and his tongue ran over her nipples. He got out of the truck and walked around to her side. He opened the door and pulled her out. She stood while he pulled her shorts down and stripped off his own shirt and shorts. He was wearing red briefs, which hardly contained his tumescence. He stood and looked at her.

"Well, beautiful, red hot lady. Let's go and cool off. Last one in the waters a sissy." He took off at a run down towards the water. Jessica stood open-mouthed and watched his powerful body dive into a wave and swim out with a fast crawl. She moved slowly towards the sea and went in slowly until the cool water revived her and drew her into it.

Luke appeared back and continued his kissing and teasing, but by now, she had got his mettle and gave back as good as she got, pushing her hand in his pants, trying to pull them off, dipping and diving. Finally they came out onto the deserted beach and fell into each other, needing release from the fever pitch they were now at. Afterwards, they lay in the sun, the heat tanning their skin and drying them until they dressed and drove slowly back to the complex, relaxed and happy. As they drove along the back road, Jessica saw, without really seeing, a dark blue car parked in the dunes. "Funny. I didn't see any fishermen today. I suppose it's someone walking his dog or something."

She hadn't realised she'd spoken aloud until Luke looked at her, puzzled. "The car back there."

"Didn't see it. Anyway, what do you think of the cottage so far?"

And that's what they talked about on the way back.

CHAPTER 48

After two very hefty whiskeys on top of his empty stomach, Drew was feeling decidedly mellow before he even started eating. Polly bustled about fetching and carrying various dishes, and John dispensed the wine. The meal was delicious, fragrant, and cooked to perfection. Drew should have been hungry, but the food was sticking in his throat, and he finished up just pushing the food around his plate. Jessica, on the other hand, ate heartily, and Drew found himself resenting her for it. *Why wasn't she nervous and ill at ease?* She hadn't seen him for months and months, and she should have shown some sort of reaction to him, but he could have been Joe Smith down the road for all the notice she was taking of him. She laughed at the things John was saying and parried a few of her own that made both John and Polly laugh. *Who was this woman?* He didn't know her at all anymore. He couldn't take his eyes off her; she looked like Jessica, and she laughed and talked like Jessica, but she wasn't the woman he had married.

Polly watched them out of the corner of her eyes. The normally talkative Drew was quiet and introspective, and the normally quiet Jessica was outgoing and entertaining. *VERY ODD*, she thought as she cleared away the dishes.

"Come on, John, you can help me load the dishes in the machine, and then you can take me and the dogs for a walk and leave these people to talk."

John heaved himself up out of the chair, groaning. "I've eaten far too much. If I knew we were going down to the hayrick for a frolic, I wouldn't have had that last helping of pudding. Now you'll have to do all the work."

"In your dreams," Polly replied, swiping him with a tea towel.

Jessica smiled at their antics like she always did, but Drew's face stayed straight. *Are you two never going to grow up,* he thought to himself. "Bout time John started to grow old gracefully," he said aloud, pouring himself another glass of wine. He gestured towards Jessica's glass, but she shook her head.

"You never used to mind," she said as she stood up and moved towards the lounge. "In fact, you used to say that I should be as relaxed as Polly and unwind a bit."

Drew heard a note of reproach in her voice, and she was ready to pick up on it. "Never mind, it's all water under the bridge now, and you finished up unwinding enough for both of us," Jessica said over her shoulder as she sank into one of the large armchairs.

"So this is the way this conversation will go, is it? Snipe, snipe, snipe," Drew snapped out, pacing about in front of her. His large, close presence was supposed to intimidate her but failed.

"You wanted to talk, Drew, and I'm here as requested. So, where do you want to start? We can go straight to the divorce and let the lawyers hash out the finances, or we can agree about all that first and make the whole thing as civilised and painless as possible. It's up to you."

Drew's jaw dropped. He thought they might have been able to talk first about what went wrong and whether reconciliation was possible. Perhaps to give the marriage another try before giving up on it, but it seemed she couldn't wait to get rid of him. His ego hit rock bottom.

Jessica saw the look on Drew's face and allowed herself a wry smile. "Oh, come on, Drew. You really didn't think there was a chance of salvaging this marriage, did you? Surely you aren't that naïve."

"I thought we might have talked," Drew said lamely, shrugging his shoulders.

"We are talking."

"But not about us."

"Drew, there is no us. Not anymore."

"How can you be so dismissive? After all these years, there's got to be some feelings left between us."

Jessica chewed her lip and swirled the drink around in her glass. "Yes, I suppose so, but not enough to make me want to start again."

They were both silent, lost in their own thoughts. Drew's throat suddenly closed up again, and he cleared it loudly before speaking. "What happened to us, Jessie?" he said, his voice husky and rasping. "How did we get to this point? We should have had it all. The good life, good times with each other, and lots of years to look forward to."

They both lapsed into silence again. Drew's voice sounded loud in the room when he spoke again. "I'm sorry, Jessie. I would like to say if the clock were turned back, I would be different, but I don't know. Not really. I am what I am, whatever that is. Over these last month, I've had time to reflect and look at myself, and I don't particularly like what I see. However, that's hindsight and all water under the bridge. Now, it's the future we have to sort out. If I have to be brutally honest, I don't really blame you for doing what you did. I treated you abominably, and that last stunt of mine was a real cracker even for me. Let's end this marriage as friends, not only for the kids' sake but also for mine. I've realised the hard way that you were not only my wife for years, but you were my very best friend as well. This is more precious to me than I ever knew, and I would like to keep it. Will you remain my friend, Jessie, despite everything I've done to you?"

Jessica listened to Drew stumbling over the words that were painful to him and felt her eyes filling with tears. She moved swiftly across the room to him, and as he stood up, she wrapped her arms around him. The tears ran down both faces and mingled together in shared grief for something lost forever. They mourned its passing and were closer in their mourning than they had been for a long time. Finally, sniffing and a bit sheepish, they pulled slightly apart, and leaning back against each other's arms, they looked into one another's faces and smiled.

Drew was mortified to feel his instant erection, which was not missed by Jessica. He furtively glanced at her face and tried to move away. Her soft, trembling smile suddenly turned into a huge grin and a trilling laugh. Drew let out a bark of a laugh and wrapped his arms around her again, swinging her around and nuzzling her neck. "See what you can still do to me, you witch. Now get away from me before I forget we are estranged or whatever the word is."

Jessica ruffled his hair and did as she was told, smiling and at ease. When John and Polly returned home, they found the two of them side by side on the big sofa, drinks in their hands and smiles on their faces as if nothing had happened. It was only when Polly's shoulders returned down to where they should be that she realised how tense she'd been on the approach to the house.

"All sorted?" she asked with a bright smile.

"All sorted," they both said in unison.

CHAPTER 49

The feeling of peace after Drew left was soon shattered by the arrival of a tanned and flamboyant Alan. He had communicated with Jessica and frequently phoned her all the time he had been away. She had never found the right time to tell Alan about Luke, and now he was on her doorstep and raring to go. Jessica was totally wrong-footed and felt herself being told of all the plans that Alan had for the two of them during his visit, and he couldn't seem to get a word in edgeways. She seemed to start every sentence with "Alan, listen," before being interrupted with another lot of plans. Stacey watched the panic on Jessica's face and tried not to smile. When Alan finally went flying on some errand, all bright-eyed and bushy-tailed Jessica sank gratefully down into the nearest chair. Stacey handed her a cup of tea, and Jessica looked up at her, her face totally stricken.

"Christ, Stacey. What do I do now? Luke's picking me up later, and Alan's already booked a table at the restaurant. What a mess."

She sipped her tea while Stacey leant against the reception counter and looked at her. "I think I'll run away."

Stacey burst out laughing.

"Well, I'm glad you think it's funny," Jessica said in a miffed voice.

"You'd have thought Alan could have let me know he was coming. Maybe he wanted to surprise you."

"Well, he bloody did that, didn't he?"

"What are you going to do now?"

"How the hell should I know? Get hold of Luke, I suppose, and try to explain that I have to talk to Alan."

"Luke's not going to like it," Stacey said in a sing-song voice as she returned to the office.

Jessica phoned Luke's number but just got the answerphone. She phoned the yard and got Kevin. "Sorry, Luke's busy with a customer. Can I take a message?"

"Can you tell him to phone Jessie urgently at work?"

"Will do," Kevin replied and hung up.

Jessica waited half an hour and phoned the house number again. Still the answerphone. She phoned the yard and got Kevin again.

"Is Luke still busy?" she asked.

"No, the customers gone now."

"Did you give Luke my message?"

"Certainly did," Kevin answered.

"Is he there?"

"No, you've just missed him."

"Do you know how long he'll be gone?"

"Nope."

Jessica was getting annoyed with this abrupt voice. *He was as much help as a chocolate teapot,* she thought, and realised she would get no other information out of him. "OK, I'll try again later."

"You're welcome."

Wonder why he didn't phone her. He must have had some urgent business. She ruminated on the lack of a return call, which was unlike Luke when she saw Alan's car pull into the car park. He stopped to talk to Viv after giving her a swift hug and kiss on the cheek. Viv was dressed in her usual tight gym gear and looked stunning as usual. Her hair was a curly mane that stood around her face in a soft, fluffy halo. Where the sun caught it, it turned even shinier, and she looked like she should have been on the beach in California.

Alan bounded in and produced from behind his back a huge bunch of mixed flowers. Despite her knotted stomach, Jessica had to smile at him. He really was a warm and charming man, and she really did like him.

"Listen, Alan…" she started again.

But again, he was off talking about something else. Jessica missed the first bit of the conversation but picked it up with the words, "…it was all the work we put his way that got Benson's business off the ground."

Jessica's mouth opened. "Wh…wha…what did you say, Alan? Sorry, I wasn't listening."

"Benson. I've been over to see him. He was hardly civil. Had some more work to discuss with him. Stuff that's got to be done during the winter. With a lot of building firms in the doldrums during the winter months, you'd have thought he'd snatch my hand off. Instead, he was rude before I'd even opened my mouth."

Jessica felt her mouth go dry and swallowed several times before she could speak. "Why, what did he say?" trying to keep her voice even.

"He wanted to know what I was doing here and how long I'd be staying as if I had no right to be here. I told him I had a dinner engagement for tonight, but could we arrange for a meeting tomorrow."

Jessica came over all hot, and her face burned.

"Then he said he couldn't make it tomorrow. The meeting would have to be this evening. When I told him my date was much too important to break, he went slamming into the office, shouting that

I'd have to find someone else to do the work then. Well, if that's his attitude, I probably will."

Alan went on through to the office and greeted Stacey. The door shut behind him and Jessica stood stunned and unmoving. Her head was pounding and she was still very hot. Finally, she moved towards the telephone. Her need to speak to Luke was overpowering. Again, she got the answerphone. Then again, she got Kevin.

"He's gone off on business," he said.

Jessica's knees started to shake. "When? For how long?"

"He left about ten minutes ago. He just said he'd be back in a few days. Is there anything I can help you with?"

"No thanks," Jessica's hand shook as she replaced the receiver.

He wasn't due to go away till next week. He had purposely run off when he saw Alan. He hadn't even given her a chance to explain. She thought they had something really special, but he wasn't even prepared to stand with her, but just ran off. Her feelings of upset turned to feelings of rage. She felt abandoned and hurt and very near to tears.

Alan came out of the office all smiles. "Well, pretty lady. Why don't you go and get dressed up for a wonderful evening out?"

Jessica managed a tremulous smile, picked up her handbag, and made her way back to the caravan, where she managed to make a cup of coffee before bursting into scalding tears.

CHAPTER 50

At the back of Drew's mind was a persisting sense of loss. Even though Jessica had agreed to everything he suggested about the settlement, he still had this feeling of loss. A feeling he should have fought for her or made it impossible financially for her to leave him, but instead, the two of them had split everything they could in half and agreed on most of the other things. *The house was worth a lot more than the original price they'd paid, so Jessica would be fairly wealthy. The car was hers, as was any pieces of furniture she cared to pick, plus half of any money held or invested.*

He consoled himself with the thought that the lack of finances hadn't kept her with him before, and it was impossible to fight for her when she had obviously gone her own way already. *No…this was the best way. Clean and friendly.* The feeling of loss remained, however, he rationalised.

He drove back towards London, lost in thoughts. Not the least of them a dread of telling the children, although they were hardly that anymore. He knew they would blame him, and he also knew that the relationship he had with them would be damaged. Still, he'd have to deal with that the best way he could. At least they would know where Jessica was now. He allowed his mind to wander to the thoughts of Max. He had phoned her briefly from Polly's in case she wondered where he was and was looking forward to seeing her more than he cared to admit. He also wondered if Kate had seen her father yet or if Max had vetoed it.

Suddenly, he found that his driving became more positive as he neared home. He was actually looking forward to getting his life back on an even keel again.

He pulled into the drive and was surprised to see the front door open. As he walked towards it, the cat came bounding up and then stopped short and started backing away, ears flat when it saw him.

"It's OK, puss," he said, bending down to stroke it. "It's only me."

The cat sniffed his hand, remembered him, and rubbed itself against his leg, the purr rasping in its throat.

Sophia was in the kitchen singing in Italian, in a rich contralto voice, and didn't hear him. He stood and listened, the cat still rubbing his leg. Suddenly conscious there was someone in the room, Sophia stopped singing and whirled around, her hand on her breast.

"Meester Cameron. You neer make my heart stop."

"Sorry, Sophia. I was listening to you sing."

Sophia smiled. "You like?"

"I like very much. You have a wonderful voice."

Sophia almost glowed with pleasure, and Drew was again struck with the beauty of this woman.

"The leetle blue kitty like it."

"You were singing for the cat?"

"Steel only a baby. Babies like sung to."

Drew smiled at this warm, lovely woman who sang to baby cats. "I'm not a baby, but you can sing to me any time you want to."

They both laughed. Over a pot of coffee, with the cat on his lap, Drew told Sophia about the past few days. She listened, nodding occasionally but not saying anything. When he had finished talking, she nodded again and, much to his surprise, kissed his cheek.

"What was that for?"

"For being very nice man."

Drew's eyebrows lifted. "Am I?"

"You treat wife good. I proud of you. Now you go forward with life again."

He wandered around the garden. Jim had certainly licked it into shape. There were flowers everywhere he looked, and the patio was surrounded by pots and tubs, all in riotous colour. The hedges were all neatly clipped, and the paths were free and clean. The house was spotlessly clean and tidy, and the cat, so he was informed, was now properly litter-trained and flea free. Sophia constantly called the cat 'the blue kitty.' Over the next few days, this was shortened to Blue, and Blue it stayed.

Drew caught up with his messages, had a long conversation with Adam, putting him in the picture with the past few days, and caught up with the work situation. There was another large ad campaign in the pipeline, and Adam had been working flat out on it after phoning Max first. They arranged to meet for dinner the following day. Drew was touched when Max admitted she'd missed him and was looking forward to seeing him. *She must be,* Drew thought when he put the phone down. *It's the first time she's ever agreed to meet me during the week.*

He phoned Marty in America, not caring what the time was, only to let him know his mother had been found and was OK and that the marriage was to be amicably ended. Marty sounded very thin and far away, not at all the strong telephone link they normally had. Drew promised to write to him all the details, expecting Marty to want them over the phone now but was surprised when he agreed to the letter. After he put the phone down, he wondered if he'd interrupted something as Marty sounded so distracted. Thinking about it, Drew remembered Melanie was filming over there and had told him she was going to spend some time with Marty. Drew smiled to himself. He remembered Marty's protective attitude towards Melanie and his gentleness with her and felt proud of his son.

He thought of calling Caro the next day and meeting her for lunch. She would want to know all the details, and he didn't want to spend any more time on the phone tonight. He settled down to some work after Sophia had gone, but for some reason, the scene on the beach started to replay itself. Details that he had seen but hadn't been aware of were now thrown into sharp focus. Jessica's glossy, slicked-back wet hair, Luke's heavily muscled thighs, Jessica's teeth-baring with pleasure, drops of water sparkling in Luke's hair, the sand clinging to Jessica's skin when she stood up, the white untanned line on Luke's legs from shorts. The whole kaleidoscope of sun, sand, and water. Drew's eyes filled, and for the last time, he allowed himself to cry for his lost life.

CHAPTER 51

The meal was more difficult than Jessica could have imagined. She really didn't want to be there; her mind was elsewhere, and she was finding it very difficult to concentrate on the things that Alan was saying. Eventually, he realised that something was wrong, and his conversation died whilst he looked at her searchingly, a frown between his eyebrows.

"Are you going to tell me what's wrong, or are you going to let me go rambling on trying to keep some kind of conversation going?"

"Oh, Alan, I'm sorry. You caught me a bit on the hop. I've just seen my husband, and we've spent the last couple of days sorting out years of baggage."

Jessica spent half an hour telling Alan about Drew's visit and wildly exaggerating everything to make her attitude believable. Alan was a very shrewd man. He let her ramble on until the whole diatribe petered out. He covered her hand with his smooth, warm one, and she looked across into his eyes. The twinkle always present in those brown eyes was rather subdued.

"Now, would you like to tell me the rest of it?"

Jessica started to bluster.

"What do you mean the rest of it? How much more do you think there is?"

"Quite a bit more than you are telling me. We were fairly close the last time we were together, in case you had forgotten, and now I feel like you're miles away from me, and I don't know why. Don't you think you owe me a little bit of an explanation?"

Jessica stared at the tablecloth for several minutes. Alan remained silent and continued to massage the back of her hand soothingly. Finally, Jessica made up her mind. "While you were overseas, Luke and I have been seeing each other. I was going to tell you, but I never seem to get the right opportunity, and then you took me completely by surprise by turning up."

"I knew you were seeing him. The only thing I didn't know was how serious it was."

"You knew!"

"Gossip has a habit of moving very quickly. Of course, I couldn't resist rubbing it in by informing Luke of our date tonight. I thought you would probably take this opportunity to tell me, and I was greedy enough to want one more evening with you before bowing out gracefully. Back as far as your grand caravan opening evening, I knew Luke had singled you out. I knew as soon as I left, he would pressure you. The fact that he was successful lets me know that our relationship was never going to get off the ground."

"Alan, I'm sorry. You are such a lovely man. I only wish it could have been different."

"So do I, but if the chemistry's wrong, there's nothing you can do. You were still very vulnerable then. You were undecided about your life, and I was a welcome distraction. An ego booster if you like, but turn the clock back, and I'd settle for that weekend again, even though it's the only one."

Jessica's eyes filled again.

"Hey, pretty lady. Don't cry. You've done the evil deed, and I've let you off lightly. Be happy with your Luke."

"He's gone away."

"Where?" Alan said, the frown back between his eyes.

"I don't know. As soon as he saw you he took off without even speaking to me. He thought so much of me he ran off at the first sign of competition."

"From what I know about him, that doesn't seem like Benson. He's never been one to run away from anything. Totally out of character, that is."

"Well, he's gone anyway."

"He'll be back. He'd be crazy to leave you behind."

"Well, I might not be here when he gets back. If he can do this once, he can do it again. I'm not sure I want someone who keeps running out on me."

"Where will you go?"

Jessica looked at the tablecloth again. Her shoulders lifted in an exaggerated shrug. "I don't know"

"Jessie, don't do anything hasty. You might lose far more than you'll ever gain. Life has a habit of making things right if you give it a chance."

"Rubbish," Jessica exploded. "How many chances does it want? I've spent half my life waiting for life to treat me fairly and it never has. I'm not ever going to give it a chance to kick me in the teeth again. When my divorce settlement is finalised, I'll have enough money, my own money, to do what I want, where I want, and with whom I want for the very first time, and I'm not going to waste any of this time dancing to some man's tune, or bowing to his whims. Not anymore."

With everything she said, Jessica's shoulders got squarer, her chin went higher, and her tears dried. *If Luke wanted her as his equal, as his partner, which is what she had thought, he was going to have to convince her or find someone else.* She really needed more time to grieve for her lost marriage before deciding in what direction her future life would go.

The rest of the meal passed more pleasantly after the difficult things had been said and were out of the way. Alan thought secretly that Jessica's mood was rather too brittle and excitable, her voice slightly shrill and sharp, but nothing he said or did calm her down, so he just went along with it.

They strolled slowly back to Jessica's caravan after the meal. Alan declined the offer of coffee, and Jessica was relieved. He kissed her softly on the cheek and smoothed his hand over her hair. "Goodnight."

"Goodnight, Alan. Thank you for everything."

As the night wound on, Jessica sat gazing into space. Her thoughts had gone full circle, and she was no nearer peace of mind. All she was sure of was that she needed some time alone to think everything through.

As the dawn broke, she walked over to reception and unlocked the door. She typed out a long letter of explanation to Stacey and a shorter one to Alan. She used the office phone to phone Drew, who sounded sleepy but soon was fully awake as she talked. She then phoned Adam's number and asked to speak to Cassie. She heard the surprise in Adam's voice as he handed the phone over to his wife. Like Drew, Cassie listened to what Jessica was saying and didn't ask too many questions. Jessica locked up the office again after leaving the letters propped up against the kettle. *The first place Stacey would go,* she thought with a smile and went back to the caravan to pack.

ACT TWO:
Survival & Success

CHAPTER 1

The magnificent sunset turned the sea to orange, then red. The birds wheeled lazily overhead, and Jessica lifted the glass of red wine to her lips, savouring the tart taste on her tongue before swallowing. Her legs resting on the balcony rail were brown and smooth, her hair bleached even blonder by the sun, and cut as short as boys. The computer sat on its table in the shade under the awning, and the fronds of the tall plants waved gently in the light air.

Jessica sighed contentedly. Her third novel was well on its way, and the second one was still on the best-seller list. Suffering a bit from writer's block, she had withdrawn from the area around the computer until she was ready to start again afresh. She went back inside and headed for the shower. The lounge was cool in shades of beige and white, the only colours coming from some of the furnishings and paintings. The holiday bungalow belonging to Adam and Cassie that she had run to more than 18 months ago was just down the road, but after the success of her first novel, she had paid them an extra six months' rent as a thank you and bought her own. It was more private, standing on its own grounds and with a private road with security gates. Now the public knew about her; Drew didn't like the idea of her being so isolated with no security and set about fixing it up. He was still her best friend and had moved into a different dimension, too. He was more stable and happy than she had ever seen him.

She showered leisurely and changed into loose cotton trousers and a vest top. She added a smoky eyeshadow and a bright lipstick and poured another glass of wine while she waited. The gates had a code that had to be tapped in and was changed each week. The light went on to show the gates had opened and she went back onto the balcony and watched the car coming up the drive. It slid to a halt in front of the double front doors and the driver's door was flung open. "I hope you're ready. We're running a bit late."

"Ready," Jessica said, picking up her bag. She ran lightly down the stairs and across the hall. She locked the door behind her and tugged open the passenger door to greet a smiling Stacey.

"Got your writing arm on," Stacey said as she turned the car around.

"This book signing is going to be a big one. You're going to have a writer's cramp before the night's out."

"I know," said Jessica wearily.

The second novel had been translated into Spanish, and as she was a local celebrity, half the town would want her signature. This was the third one this month, and she was getting a bit tired with all the smiling. However, she was still a new enough author to be eager and grateful to meet the public. Without them, she'd be an awful lot poorer.

The large department store was cool and air-conditioned, and there was already a crowd waiting. Jessica plastered a smile on her face and got on with it. Much later, over a welcome drink, she caught sight of a half-familiar face, one that she seemed to have seen many times over the last few months. He looked away, and Jessica thought she must be getting paranoid. He was probably a local who just happened to be in the same place as her on a couple of occasions. She stood up and stretched.

"Ready, boss," said Stacey, appearing as if from nowhere.

What a treasure she was, Jessica thought for the millionth time. She had taken her on as her secretary as soon as she could afford her, and now she had proved to be invaluable. "Yeh, ready, Stace. Let's go home."

Stacey dropped Jessica and drove off after giving her a big hug. "See you in a week's time, flower. Got to go and pack if I want to catch that plane tomorrow."

"Really don't know why you can't stay with me when you're over here."

"Because I would be a distraction when you're writing, and I would then be in trouble if you missed a deadline."

Stacey was flying back to England the next day. She had several meetings planned to book Jessica on various chat shows and also a couple of radio programmes. It had taken a lot of persuading to get Jessica to go back, and Stacey didn't want her to have a change of mind. Hence, the hurried departure.

Jessica had been almost a recluse for the whole time she had been away. Shut in her own private world, she saw only her family, who visited often. Drew had taken over most of her public relations work, tirelessly promoting her books and making the public aware of her. He had tried on many occasions to get her back to the UK, all to no avail. He bribed her with everything he could think of, from a room at the Dorchester to high-profile TV shows, but she always refused.

When she had run to Spain all that time ago, she had yearned for Luke so badly it was like being in physical pain all the time. She couldn't believe she could need someone so much after such a short time together. For the first few weeks she prowled around aimlessly, not doing anything except think about all the things that had happened in the last year. She cried scalding tears until there were no more left, until at last the demons were exorcised. Only then did she start going out to walk on the beach and visit the local markets. On one of these solitary visits, she spotted a reconditioned computer and printer. It was in good working order, and on a whim, she bought it. It sat in the corner of the lounge for some time before she sat down at it. She started writing down all the feelings she had gone through to reach her present state of shaky self-control. The writing took on the form of a journal, a kind of diary. She called it 'My Year of Soul Searching.'

In the beginning, it acted as a catalyst, offering a pouring out of things long bottled up. Then somewhere in the writing, it became more of a story based on experience. When she had finished, she read it as though she were someone else and realised it was quite good. On a whim, she sent it to Drew. Not only for him to have an insight into the way things had seemed to her through the years but also as a work of fiction. He phoned her ten days later. He had read it, been deeply touched by it, and passed it on to a publisher friend of his, who sold it almost straight away to a well-read and respected magazine that serialised it over six weeks. The public lapped it up and the magazine paid handsomely for the rights to it and called for more. The piece went out under another name, so all the communications went through Drew.

Jessica wrote two more short pieces, which were immediately snapped up, and then started a full-length novel. She wrote from early morning through the day and sometimes well into the night. She ate when she was starving and bathed when she remembered. Finally, it was finished. She felt totally drained, and the large stack of pages sat on the table for days before she could bring herself to phone Drew. He flew over and spent hours reading the whole book from start to finish. At the end, he looked at her, smiled a broad smile, walked over to her, gripped her in a tight bear hug, and then said, "Jessie, my girl, you are going to be a wealthy woman."

CHAPTER 2

Luke pulled the collar of his coat higher under his chin. The heavy sea mist had put droplets of water all over his beard and hair, and the chill wind cut like a knife. The huge Lurcher dog matched his pace, her muzzle touching his big hand every few minutes. She looked frequently up into her master's face, sensing his mood, and quietly plodded alongside him, keeping her frolicking play for another day. Luke walked often on this part of the beach. It was the same beach he had been with Jessica back in those halcyon days when it seemed his life was beginning again.

He had made some stupid mistakes in his life, but running off was the one mistake that wouldn't go away. Oh, he had tried. He had got roaring drunk and found himself a variety of ladies, most of which he had treated abominably, but nothing even came close to a relationship, so, in the end, he had given up trying and learnt to live with the pain. He should have trusted Jessica. Trusted her to tell Alan about them in her own way. He should have realised she hadn't had time to talk to Alan when he had come to see him instead of going off half-cocked. Never in his life had he ever run away from a situation, so why in the hell did he pick that time to start.

He stopped and looked out to sea. His mood today was as black and dark as water. The large dog sat down by his side all the time, looking up at him and waiting for a word to acknowledge her presence. Luke looked at the sea for a long time, his body still and unmoving, and his mind on another plane. He absentmindedly stroked the dog's bristly head, and the plump, damp tail wagged across the pebbles.

It was the cottage that had brought on this mood. The old cottage had started when Jessica was here, then put on hold, and finally restarted as a labour of love. Now it was finished but she wasn't back. Polly had been approached to help with the furnishings. All the auction sales that he hoped Jessica would go to had been attended by Polly. She knew Jessica's tastes so well and furnished it with all the charming things Jessica would have bought. The cottage was originally started with Jessica in mind. Somewhere nice to live instead of the caravan. Something of her own while they got to know each other. Now it was finished. Where was she? All this time, no one had ever told him.

He nearly went mad when he got back two days later and found she'd gone. All Alan would say was that she wanted to be on her own. He even phoned Drew and had to admit the man was very nice about it. Drew had opened up a bit, sensing how upset Luke was, and told him that Jessica thought Luke had run out on her when she cared for him. She felt she needed time to get her life together and that he was sure she would contact Luke when she had sorted herself out. That made Luke feel even worse. For a long time, he was lethargic and uncaring until his business started to suffer, and he finally pulled himself together. At the weekends and in his spare time, he started working on the cottage again. It was for Jessica, only for Jessica. He couldn't visualise anyone else in it now it was finished and waiting.

He turned on his heel, startling the dog, and began walking back. He drove to the cottage, wanting to be in it instead of his own place. The garden in the front was trim and tidy. The paths had all been re-laid, and roses climbed up the walls. The windows with their leaded lights gleamed in the dim light, and the white shutters set them off to perfection. Luke used the heavy brass key to unlock the front door and threw it open. He had lit a fire before he left, and the flickering light highlighted the lovely old fireplace and the beautiful brass renovated sconces on the walls. He closed the door and leant against it before flipping on a switch. The soft wall lights brought the interior to life. The carpet was a deep red, and the settee and armchair had been completely re-upholstered in a rich brocade of red and gold. The antique dresser took up nearly the whole back wall and was stocked with willow pattern plates, cups, and serving dishes. The old range in the kitchen had been replaced with a cream Aga, and old pine units were interspersed with rows of copper-bottomed pans.

Luke took his coat off and hung it on the back of a lovely old ladder-back kitchen chair that was one of a set of four that stood around the old scrubbed kitchen table. He poured himself a whisky to warm himself up a bit and walked back into the living room. He sat down heavily in the armchair. The dog had spread itself out in front of the fire and lazily thumped her tail a couple of times without moving anything else.

"Well, Gertie, old girl. What the hell do we do now, eh?"

A few more thumps. Luke looked fondly at the dog. She was so ugly, she was beautiful. She had been found in the shed at the back of the cottage by one of the workmen. He had gone inside for his toolbox and met this huge, whirling, growling dervish. It scared him half to death, and he locked the door and phoned Luke on his mobile, sounding like a gibbering idiot. Luke went round to get some sense out of it all and opened the shed door on a pitiful wreck of an animal that was trembling and shaking. Her coat was coming out in handfuls, the sores on her back and sides were diagnosed as cigarette burns, and the piece of rope tied tightly around her neck was nearly strangling her and had embedded itself in her skin. Luke was horrified and sickened. He spoke softly to her for a long time and finally coaxed her out of the shed. His workmen were all nearly in tears and wrapped her in a dust sheet so Luke could pick her up. The vet's bills when they finally got her tranquilised and treated were enormous, but by then, Luke had established himself as her guardian angel, and her devotion to him was absolute. The vet said in fun that the whiskers on her chin reminded him of his Aunt Gertie. So Gertie she was. Not a very elegant name for such an elegant dog, but a rose by any other name.

Luke sat and looked at the flames for a while longer. Finally, he raked out most of the ashes, prodded a groaning Gertie out of the way, and put the heavy mesh guard in place before letting himself out. He drove home in a pensive, slow fashion, the radio playing softly, and Gertie again asleep on the old blanket in the back of the van. Piles of paper littered the large table in the kitchen. Quotes for the next stage of the housing complex and ads for the workmen he needed scribbled on scraps of paper waiting for him to phone them in. Paint charts and carpet samples heaped up in one corner, and rolls of architect's plans on the floor. Luke made himself a cup of tea and sat down to deal with some of the more urgent items. He had just got into it when the phone rang.

"For God's sake, mate, don't you ever check your machine," said a familiar voice.

"That you, Kev," Luke said, recognising the voice and smiling.

"'Course it's me. Who do you think it was?" the voice sounded as if it was coming from the inside of a drum.

Kevin had left for a contract in Germany quite a few months ago, and although Luke was sorry to see him go, the opportunity had been too good to turn down. Apart from a couple of postcards, Luke hadn't heard from him for a while. Kevin had done some good work on the cottage, and Luke had confided in him for the want of someone to talk to.

"How are you mate? How's Germany? Speaking the language yet?"

"I'm not there anymore. The contracts finished and I moved on to a new one with the same company building luxury apartments in Spain."

"Spain! You lucky sod, all that sunshine. Can't be bad. Anyway, how—"

"Listen, mate," Kevin interrupted. "There's a reason for this call and I haven't got much battery left. She's here!"

"Who's there?"

"Jessica. She's here. In Spain. Living a few miles away in a smart villa."

Luke's stomach contracted, and his body tensed.

"Luke, did you hear me? Hello, hello!"

"Yes, Kev. I heard you. Is she…OK?"

What he really wanted to know was if she was with someone, and if she was happy, but he couldn't bring himself to say it, but Kevin read his mind. Knowing from their previous conversations how Luke's mind worked concerning Jessica, he answered his unspoken questions. "She's living on her own and is quite a famous writer now. I can't believe you haven't heard of her. She's quite a celebrity and has been doing book signings and stuff. I've asked about a bit, and apparently she arrived here about two years ago, but nobody saw much of her at first. Kept herself to herself for ages. She was living in a rented place belonging to some English friends, but when she got famous, she bought her own place. She's only ever seen with her secretary. No one's ever seen her with a bloke."

Luke made up his mind in a hurry.

"Tell me where you are and a phone number where I can reach you. I'm coming over. I'll book a flight tomorrow. I want you to rent a car for me and pick me up at the airport. I have to see her for myself."

After the phone call, Luke worked into the night, blocking out all thoughts of Jessica until his work was finished. He packed, sorted out his passport, and dozed for a couple of hours until the travel agents were open and his foremen were on site to receive his instructions. Then he moved. He dropped Gertie off with Bill, his foreman, who had a rescued greyhound that Gertie thought was her brother and was happy with. By lunchtime, he was on his way.

CHAPTER 3

dam looked ruefully at the hair tangled in the teeth of his comb. "Bloody hell. Look at that lot. If I'd started collecting all this hair when it started coming out, I'd have got enough for a toupee by now."

Drew smiled and finished drying his hands. "Well, if you had, you'd be able to answer truthfully that you still had all your own hair."

Drew brushed a hand over the shoulder of his suit and straightened his tie. "Ready for the off, then?"

"Yeh, let's go for it," Adam replied, throwing a kiss at his reflection in the mirror. "We can only get shafted."

"Not if I can help it," Drew said over his shoulder as he threw open the washroom door.

"From your lips to God's ear," Adam replied, catching the fast-closing door before it cut his hand off.

Well, he seems to have been listening up to now, Drew thought. Cutting the ties with the company he had been with for so long and starting up a new agency with Adam as his partner had not been an easy decision. But once the wheels were set in motion it proved easier than he thought. The other directors had found the money to buy him out and later also Adam. Their shares had been worth a lot more than their initial outlay, and the directors knew that it was mainly due to very long hours and hard work from Drew and Adam in the past.

The new company was not solely advertising, but had branched into public relations and agency work too. Drew had wooed a young go-getter with a small but impressive list of clients to come and work with him. Ashley Mead was a whirling bundle of nervous energy. With dark hair, dark eyes, and always impeccably dressed, he worked tirelessly for his clients. Although none of them were big stars yet, they were very rarely out of work. Ashley got them bit parts in soaps, small parts in sitcoms and plays, and even parts in commercials. Anything to keep them in the public eye until their big break came along.

Good-looking in a lean, sultry way, Ashley always had different girls hanging on his arm. They never seemed to last long. Most of them gave up trying to compete with the mobile phone always clasped to his ear and moved on to someone who talked to them occasionally. The other coup, as far as Drew and Adam were concerned, was the inclusion of Max. She took a lot of persuading and finally only agreed to work for them as an independent PR agent. Her old mentor, John Sullivan, was retiring, and the chairman's position had passed on to a senior director voted in by the other members. Although Max liked the new chairman well enough, the loyalty factor was not there anymore, so she had no guilt about leaving. She decided she didn't want to work exclusively for Drew's company and would act for clients who contacted her direct, as well as those who were referred through the company. The arrangement was working quite well with the company getting a percentage from both Max and Ashley for anyone taken on their books through referral.

Drew's relationship with Max had gone from strength to strength. They had continued to see each other on weekends and sometimes in the week for many months. When Drew had come back from Dorset and the confrontation with Jessica, Max had been the first one he had turned to. They had gone for a picnic in the country, and in between the cold chicken, salad, and fruit, he had told her everything. She listened and nodded, occasionally probing further with a word or two but letting him talk. He found that after he had told her about the meeting with Jessica, he continued on with the things that had been haunting him in the past. Fragments of all the previous years that he had hardly even thought about, let alone put into words, now came pouring out of him. If Max was surprised at this sudden outpouring she didn't show it. She just sat and watched his face and listened.

Sometime later, when the sun lay low on the horizon, and Drew's words had trickled to a stop, he gave a rueful and embarrassed laugh. "I've never had the time for people who like the sound of their own voice too much, but Christ, both your ears must be numb by now. I'm sorry, Max. I don't know what got into me. Once I got started, I couldn't seem to stop. Next time we have a picnic, you'd better include some sticky toffees to glue my teeth together. Maybe then you'll get a word in edgeways."

Max drained the last of her coffee from the plastic beaker, carefully placed it back in the basket, moved onto her knees, reached over, and kissed Drew long and hard. His eyes flew wide open and stared into her golden ones which slowly closed as the kiss deepened. Without any noticeable effort on either part, within minutes, they were lying side by side on the blanket. Their bodies touched all the way down and their limbs intertwined. Max felt her loins tighten and twitch with an incredible rush of moisture, the like of which she hadn't felt for a long time. Drew's erection was awesome and concrete hard. He pulled Max in towards him with his hands on her bottom, and she groaned deep in her throat with the feel of him. The world ceased to exist around them. There was only one way out.

Drew stood up suddenly, and started to throw everything back in the picnic basket. It all went in haphazardly with no thought for leftover food or drink, just frantic urgency to get done. Max knelt on the blanket, tousled and flushed, and watched Drew. Her eyes were still sleepy and half closed, looking up at him with naked desire still in them. She noted his bulging trousers and half-unbuttoned shirt, and her loins tightened again. He almost ran across the field, slammed the basket in the boot, and ran back. He pulled her to her feet and folded up the blanket, tucking it under his arm. With his other arm around her, he walked quickly towards the woods in the corner of the field. The sun had gone down, and the twilight was still and quiet. Drew laid the blanket on the ground in a soft place between the trees and turned to Max. Her eyes glistened in the gloom, and her fragrance drifted towards him as he kissed her lips and held her to him. She was the one who moved back, but just far enough to unbutton the rest of his shirt and slip it off his shoulders. Her lips nuzzled his chest, and he sucked his breath in sharply. He pulled her blouse over her head and unclipped her bra, frantic to feel her body against his. The kisses started again. They knelt on the blanket. Their mouths fused together and finally Drew could stand it no more. He had to be inside her, or he was going to burst. He laid her on the blanket and moved over her.

Her voice was shaky and husky. "Drew. Wait! Wait!"

"I can't. I'm bursting. Let me love you, Max. I've waited so long."

"I know, Drew. I know. But I don't take the pill or anything. Have you got something to use?"

"No," he said in a strangled voice. "It's been so long now that I've got out of the habit of carrying them."

Max was glad with his answer in one way, but for herself, she could have screamed in angry frustration. She rolled over and snuggled up to him. He turned and kissed her, and immediately, their passion flared up again. He put her purposefully away from him, but she came back and took him in her mouth.

"No, Max," Drew's voice was still strained. "I want you."

"I know, but I don't like leaving you like this."

"I'll live," Drew stood up and pulled on his trousers.

"Come on, sweet pea. Get dressed. We have some unfinished

business to attend to."

They drove out onto the main road and Drew turned away from the direction of home and headed further out into the country. About five miles on, they turned into the car park of a small hotel. He had been here before to meet an old school friend who had been passing through. He remembered the place as being comfortable and fairly quiet.

Max looked slightly uncomfortable when Drew booked in with no luggage, but the guy on the desk hardly looked at them, and when Drew came back out a few minutes later to get a bottle of wine from the bar, the man was just walking out of the door with his coat on and another person was at the reception. A visit to the men's room in the bar contained the dispenser he was looking for, and he re-entered the room whistling and with a happy smile on his face.

The shower was running; Drew stripped and wrapped a sheet around him like a toga, poured a glass of wine, and waited. Max came into the room in a cloud of steam. Her hair was piled on top of her head, but wisps had fallen down and were curling around her face and on her neck in damp tendrils. Drew looked her up and down, his erection back with a vengeance and handed her a glass of wine. They both sipped slowly and looked deep into each other's eyes. Max looked downwards briefly where his erection was pushing the sheet outwards, put her glass on the table, dropped the towel she had wrapped around her, placed her arms up and behind his neck, and slowly pushed her tongue between his lips.

Drew growled deep in his throat and tore off the sheet. His penis stood out proudly and he sat on the bed, pulling Max astride him. Once again, their kisses got more and more intense until they became frantic for more. He laid her on the bed, prepared himself, and entered her. Her body was slippery inside and out, and her heat seared him. She wrapped her arms around him and arched her back.

"Come soon, sweetheart. I'm very high."

Before he finished saying it, her body was tightening in spasms, and guttural sounds came from the back of her throat, changing to hoarse cries. This was enough to push him over the edge and his orgasm tore from him in mind-blowing bursts that were nearly painful.

Much, much later, they lay in the tumbled bed wrapped in each other's arms, drinking wine and eating food that Drew had fetched from a takeaway, and really got to know each other. They knew each other already as friends, now they did it as lovers. For the first time in many months, Drew was at peace with himself.

CHAPTER 4

Jessica put the phone down. Her face was unsmiling and pensive. Stacey had got her quite a few TV appearances on the morning shows, chat shows, and even radio. She should be pleased that so many people had read her books and knew her, but she had awful misgivings about the whole thing. She had spent so much time on her own over the last couple of years that being thrust into the limelight made her feel almost physically sick. She had never been the centre of attention in the whole of her life, and she wasn't sure she wanted to start at this late date. She poured out a glass of her favourite red wine and went out onto the balcony. She sat on the low wall and looked at the sunset. The writer's block seemed to have lifted, and she had spent a productive day typing; the tension in her neck and shoulders let her know just how long she had been sitting.

She finished her wine and quickly showered. A walk on the beach should relax her, so she dressed in shorts and a brief top and got the car out. The local beach was usually busy, but most of the tourists had gone back for dinner, so she had most of the beach to herself. She walked slowly along the water's edge, her shoes in one hand and the other hand in her shorts pocket. The tide was in and the far end of the beach was now closed off, so she sat on a rock and watched the waves lapping the rocks. She hadn't realised how long she'd been sitting there, deep in thought, until she looked around and saw it was nearly dark. She made her way back up the beach and into a small beachfront restaurant. Pieter, the German proprietor, greeted her warmly, as did his beautiful Spanish wife, and they engaged in happy conversation whilst Jessica waited for her meal to arrive. The speciality of the house was seafood dishes, and Jessica ate here so often, she knew the menu backwards.

For some reason unknown, tonight she felt very alone. All the other tables seem to be occupied by couples, all tanned and in a holiday mood. A few strange looks were directed towards her table, making her feel uncomfortable. She ate quickly and left. Normally, she would have gone home, but tonight, the option did not appeal to her, and she drove out onto the highway. She had no clear idea where she was going but found herself outside a hotel that was familiar to her. The English brothers who owned it had held a party in her honour a few months ago on her birthday. She went into the bar, feeling the need for company, and was pleased to find not only the brothers but also a couple of other familiar faces there. She spent a pleasant evening there and walked back out to her car, smiling at the parting banter and feeling much more light-hearted than she had earlier.

As she backed the car out, she glanced over her shoulder, and her eye was caught by a figure standing by the side entrance. It was the same person that she had seen on many other occasions and who looked familiar to her. She just wished she could remember who he was. She was so busy looking behind her that she almost backed into another car and jerked the clutch, stalling the engine. Embarrassed, she restarted the car and drove hurriedly away. A few more seconds, and she would have had the shock of seeing the large figure of someone even more familiar unloading his bags from the boot of another car in the car park.

She found sleep very elusive and got fed up with tossing and turning. She finally got up and made a pot of tea. The stars were bright, and the still night air warm and pleasant; she sat outside and sipped her tea. She still felt very restless and tried to analyse the reason for it. She was worried about the return to the UK, but it was more than that. It was this feeling of loneliness that she couldn't come to terms with. She had enjoyed her solitude, but now, suddenly, she wanted to be with people. Perhaps, at last, her self-imposed exile was ready to end. *Yes.*

She sat up straight. She wanted to buy new clothes and go out. She smiled and stretched her arms above her head. Tomorrow she would book her flight and phone Stacey to pick her up from the airport. Back into the world, she'd go. The rest of the book would have to wait. She went back to bed and slept like a log. She booked an afternoon flight and just packed a few things; after all, she was going on a shopping spree. By lunchtime the taxi was carrying Jessica towards the airport.

The ringing of the telephone sounded loud in the empty house. When the answerphone clicked in, the voice that left the message was very hesitant and unsure. "Jessie…ah. It's me…ah…Luke. I really need to see you…ah. I'll phone later to see if you are back…ah…if not, I'll leave you a phone number of the hotel…ah…I'm not sure of it at the moment. Please be there, Jessie. Ah…hope to speak to you soon."

The second message an hour later gave the name and telephone number of the hotel. The third message was a plea to phone. The fourth message at ten that night was the same plea but a bit slurred.

By that time, Jessica was already with Caro and Drew in a fine restaurant, catching up with the news. At eight o'clock next morning, Luke sat in his rented car and looked at the front of the house through the gates. He had pressed the intercom button until his finger was numb and shouted until the maid from the house next door had shouted at him from the balcony. He was just about to ring again when a smart grey-haired man walked out from the next house and called him. Luke had a job to understand heavily accented English but eventually gathered that Jessica had gone away. She had left a key with this neighbour so they could just keep an eye on the place for her as she didn't know how long she'd be gone away. The man didn't know where she'd gone, but she'd gone to the airport so it must have been far.

Luke slumped down in the seat of the very hot car and felt like crying. All this time to find her, and he'd missed her. He couldn't believe it. He drove back to the hotel and went straight into the bar.

Jessica had a lazy morning and met Stacey for lunch. Stacey was excited and smiling and told her of all the interviews and bookings that were already set up, and the money she would get. Jessica couldn't believe how quickly Stacey had got it all done, and promised her a nice bonus.

After lunch, they hit the shops. Even though Jessica now had money, she still looked out for the bargains. Some of the prices in the high-class shops stopped her in her tracks. She knew she would never spend that much on an outfit however nice it was or however rich she was. Stacey sighed and tutted.

"No, Stacey. Old habits die hard. I would never feel comfortable in something costing that much."

Stacey gave in and went around the bargain basements. She had to admit that Jessica added style to everything she tried on. And inexpensive or not, all the clothes looked great. They arrived back at Caro's, loaded to the gills and dead on their feet. Drew was introducing her to Max at dinner tonight, so she decided to rest a bit before changing. She hadn't met Max before, but she knew how Drew felt about her and was looking forward to finally meeting her.

Several times her thoughts had turned to Luke and his close proximity, but she pushed these thoughts to the back of her mind. She still hadn't decided what to do about that yet. Still, she drifted into a doze, thinking of warm brown eyes and a furry chest.

CHAPTER 5

Even though Drew and Max had been more or less a couple for the last year, she still insisted on keeping her own place. Most weekends they spent together and also a few evenings in the week, but Max needed the cushion of her flat to return to. Drew thought it unnecessary and tried to persuade her to move in with him. He had sold the big house and bought a smaller one nearer to town. He bid farewell to Jim, who didn't want to take on the much smaller new garden but recommended someone who would, however, he still kept Sophia with him. Now that she was driving, she didn't mind the journey over and Drew was glad. He really couldn't visualise his life without her now.

Max and Sophia hit it off right from the beginning, spending many hours chatting and laughing, sometimes at Drew's expense, which he took all in good spirits. Sometimes, he got a bit stressed out and a bit ratty and irritable with Max. She would take it for a while and then quietly pick up her things and return to the sanity of her flat. He would simmer and stomp about for a while, and then when he had calmed down, he would start missing her like hell and phone her to apologise. She never held a grudge and would return the following evening as if nothing had happened, usually bearing bags of nice goodies to cook.

If he wanted to tell her what was on his mind, she would listen and make comments if she thought he wanted to hear them, otherwise she stayed silent and just nodded in the right places. At first, this was hard to do. She had achieved her present position by being forceful and knowledgeable, and to take a back seat was rather foreign for her until she realised that Drew was asking her opinion on more and more occasions and taking a lot of her ideas on board. This was also a first for him too. Some of his arrogance had been knocked out of him, and he was finding that listening and valuing someone else's views gave him a larger insight and a less one-sided perspective. A period of adjustment, enhanced by a lusty need for one another and a simple feeling of togetherness, gave them both a feeling of contentment and peace.

Even though Drew had been to Spain on numerous occasions, Max had never gone with him. Jessica had known about Max from the start and had been happy for him. His more laid-back attitude was due in some part to his new lady, and his visits to Spain had been usually for business and very brief. Hence, the omission of Max's presence.

Drew was due to arrive to shower and change, so Max took the opportunity to have a leisurely bath and spend a bit longer than usual on her makeup and hair. She had had her burnished gold hair subtly highlighted to give it a lift and it was worn tonight up in a loose knot on top of her head. She was wearing black and had used brighter makeup to compliment it. Her tawny eyes were deepened with dark, smoky brown shadow, and her lips and nails were a shimmering coral.

She heard the door slam as Drew rushed in like a whirling dervish, hooking off his shoes, pulling off his tie, and throwing his jacket onto the settee all in one second. He was talking nineteen to the dozen and wrestling with the buttons on his shirt. Max turned on the dressing table stool and looked at this man who had broken down all her carefully guarded defences and a lump lodged in her throat. His shirt was half hanging out of his trousers, his belt was undone, he had pulled one sock off, and his hair was all standing on end; he looked beautiful. She never got tired of looking at him. She watched him when he was asleep. The curve of his mouth, the shape of his eyebrows, the frown between them, his ruffled hair. Once or twice he had opened his eyes, somehow feeling her scrutiny, and pulled her close to him before falling asleep again.

She watched him again now, her love in her throat and eyes. Alerted by her stillness, he looked up and his chatter stopped. They just gazed at each other for several seconds before Drew dropped to his knees in front of her. His hands gently went to the sides of her face as he looked into her eyes and saw something there that made him suck in his breath. "Say it, Max. I can see it in your eyes. Just say it, please."

In all the time they had been together Max had never told Drew she loved him. She had felt it from the time they had spent their first night together, but she had never told him. It was as if by voicing her feelings, she would leave herself vulnerable and easier to hurt, so she didn't say it. Drew told her nearly every day and was sometimes very upset when she didn't return his declaration, but something always held her back. *It was just words,* she told herself. *I show him how I feel in lots of other ways, why does he need the words?* Tonight, the words were in her mouth and nothing she could do would make them go away.

"I—" She cleared her throat, but the lump stayed. Her eyes welled with tears. "I love you, Drew. I love you to bits."

The grin spread across his face from ear to ear, and he grabbed her in a tight bear hug.

"Drew…stop it, you're going to mess me all up."

Drew sat back on his heels. "You have just said the thing I've been waiting a year for. I feel like messing you up completely for the whole night. I feel like I've just won the lottery."

He hugged her again but felt her pull away. "OK, my lovely, beautiful darling. I'll keep my distance now, but just wait till later."

Max watched him strip off the rest of his clothes and head for the shower. *Much more of that, and I wouldn't have been able to wait for later,* she thought as she turned back to the mirror and repaired her smudged lipstick.

Feeling as if her tension had all disappeared and her body was loose and flowing, Max felt herself looking forward to the night and meeting Jessica. *I think I'm going to like her,* she thought as she stood up. And she did.

CHAPTER 6

Luke woke up with a pounding headache. He hadn't left the bar until the early hours and Kev had finally let him get on with it and went to bed. He had told Kev what had happened and then set about drowning his sorrows. Unfortunately, it hadn't worked. He felt even more down in the morning, and the hangover certainly didn't help.

He went gingerly down to the pool, his head feeling like lead, and was glad that it was almost deserted. The sky was overcast and it looked like rain, hence the absence of sunbathers, so Luke took the opportunity to work his headache off. He swam lap after lap in a lazy crawl that still covered the length of the pool in a deceptively fast time. He hauled himself out to see Kev sitting in a lounger, watching him with two pots of coffee on the table in front of him. As Luke walked towards him, he poured a brimming cupful and handed it to Luke without speaking. Luke drank it thirstily and poured a second one before sitting down.

"What do I do now, mate?" Luke said, leaning back, his arm over his eyes.

"What do you want to do?" Kev asked, watching two mini-dressed girls walking across the pool area.

"I wished to hell I knew. Do I stay in the hope she'll be back soon, or do I go home and carry on waiting?"

"Perhaps if you find out where she's gone, it might help," Kev said, catching the eye of one of the girls and smiling.

"Just tell me if I'm cramping your style," Luke said irritably, catching the look.

"No worries, mate. There'll be another batch along next week."

Despite himself, Luke had to smile. Maybe that was the best way. Play by numbers. Love 'em and leave 'em. No…he'd tried that and it didn't work. *Maybe when you're young, but as you get older, it doesn't give the same buzz.* He stood up and swallowed his drink. "I'm going to shower and think about it. I'll see you later."

During the shower he finally decided to stay another day to look around. Mainly, if he was honest, to go back to Jessica's home, but also to enjoy a bit of sunshine and look around with a view to any future developments going on in the building scene.

He drove back to Jessica's gates and looked at the simple white house shimmering in the watery sunshine. He leant on the bonnet of the car and stared through the gates for a long time, trying to visualise her in the garden and on the first-floor balcony. He saw a movement out of the corner of his eye and turned to see the grey-haired man from next door heading his way. The man seemed quite chatty this morning, and Luke explained that he was a friend of Jessica's and had hoped to see her whilst he was here on a short visit. The man struggled a bit with his English but managed to get through to Luke that she had gone back to England to appear on TV. This was all the spur that Luke needed. He shook the man's hand and thanked him again and again before jumping in his car and heading back to the hotel.

Kev was sitting on another lounger in the pool area in deep conversation with the girl from the earlier encounter. Luke tapped him on the shoulder, and they both looked up at him, shielding their eyes against the sun.

"She's gone back to England," was all Luke said.

"So you're off again then?" Kev said, standing up.

"As soon as I can get a flight."

"I'll run you to the airport when you're ready. How did you find out?"

"The next-door neighbour," Luke said, heading for the patio doors. "See you when I've booked my flight."

As it happened, there wasn't an available flight until the next day, and Luke had to cool his heels until then. It was going to be an intolerable wait, so he took Kev and his new friend to a slap up dinner, making sure he went easy on the drinks. As the two girls were together on holiday and sharing the same room it was hardly fair to leave one behind, so it turned out to be four for dinner. They turned out to be good company and the little blonde who was with Kev's friend never missed an opportunity to touch Luke's hand or snuggle up to him. She rubbed his beard, ran her fingers through his hair, and combined this with lots of eye contact. In the past Luke might have taken her on, but now he just found it amusing. He caught Kev's eye on a couple of occasions and gave him a rueful grin. The girl was very miffed when she realised that she was getting nowhere and set to work on the Spanish barman. Luke took this chance to make a quick getaway.

By two o'clock the next day, he was on a plane back to Bristol with Jessica's face looking at him from the pages of the English newspapers. There was a story about her rise to fame. The story chronicled her life in Spain as a virtual recluse and her first short story, which led to her subsequent novels. The story said she went to reside in Spain because of her broken marriage, but Luke knew that he had something to do with Jessica's disappearance even though they didn't say so. Her picture was fuzzy and unclear, but Luke was so starved for the sight of her that it looked beautiful to him and he found his eyes constantly straying to it throughout the flight.

He'd left his car at the airport and was quickly on his way back home to make his plans to see Jessica again. Polly would know where she was staying. She couldn't refuse to tell him now. After all, it wouldn't be too difficult to find out if her face was plastered all over the daily papers. He would make a cast iron plan to see her, and, judging from her responses, he would go from there.

CHAPTER 7

Drew and Stacey had worked together on the publicity for Jessica's new book, and her first public appearance was on a show going out in the middle of the morning. It was hosted by a brother and sister and was very popular. They had started off as co-presenters of an early morning show and had progressed on to a slot of their own, running throughout the morning and carrying everything from cookery to keeping fit, yoga, and up-to-the-minute topics.

The couple appeared to be squeaky clean and always cheerful, although on arrival at the studio the tension was thick enough to cut with a blunt knife. Jessica felt a bit awkward, and even though Michael broke off the conversation and greeted her warmly, the atmosphere still felt more than a bit sticky.

Michael Swift had the charm and looks of a sometime previous surfer. His hair was longish and tousled and streaked with what was probably once blond, natural or not, and now the streaks were grey, natural or not. His teeth were very white and the ear-to-ear grin looked spontaneous but didn't reach his grey eyes. His sister Christy looked as if the smile she gave Jessica almost tore her face apart, and the hand she extended was limp and cold.

"Welcome, Mrs. Cameron, how lovely to see you. I'm sure your new book will be as huge a hit as your last one, which I thoroughly enjoyed."

Jessica smiled and was about to say something in the way of thanks, but by that time, Christy was heading for the other side of the studio, where she accosted some spiky-haired chap with a set of headphones draped around his neck. Jessica glanced at Drew over her shoulder, who made a wry face and shrugged.

"She's full of sweetness and light this morning. I should have liked to have been a fly on the wall a few minutes ago. I wonder what the argument was about."

"Nothing that should affect the interview with your wife, or should I say ex-wife," came Michael's voice from behind them.

Jessica could feel her face flaming with embarrassment at being caught out, but Drew turned quickly, smiling and charming as only he could be, to defuse the situation with a quip at his own expense. Michael regally nodded his head by way of an apology-accepting gesture, and Drew decided there and then he didn't like the guy. He was slimy and insincere despite the surface charm, and Drew hoped he wasn't going to give Jessica a hard time on her first appearance. He looked over at Stacey and was not surprised to see a look of disdain on her face. She caught him looking at her and smiled.

"Quite the royal highness, isn't he," she said. "Seeing as he once worked as a barman."

"Maybe it was at the Kings Arms and it rubbed off," replied Drew.

"More like the Pigs Head," Stacey mused dryly as she went off to find Jessica.

Drew's mobile phone shrilled in his pocket, so he made his way over to the door where the signal was better. Marty's voice came through loud and clear, and Drew was overjoyed at such a good connection.

"Well, seeing as I'm only ten miles along the road, it's not surprising," came back Marty's laughing reply.

Drew spluttered and stammered, and Marty put him out of his misery. "I wanted to see you and Mum, so I thought I'd come over for her big day and maybe get a party going later. I'm still on USA time, so I'll be jet lagged whatever time I get to bed."

Drew let out a whoop and several of the studio people turned round to look, including Jessica. He beckoned her over and handed her the phone. She said a tentative hello, and he watched her face light up as she listened. Still with a wide smile, she reached into her pocket and found a hankie to dab at her eyes. He watched her and his heart warmed towards this woman who had been around him for so many years. She had always been able to laugh and cry at the same time. Her face was so familiar to him but somehow different. It was as if the time away from him had changed her in a subtle way that he couldn't quite put his finger on. She was still the same person, but she now seemed to have a sense of aloofness about her, as if her personal space had grown and he was outside and not within it as he used to be. She was very much his friend now, and sometimes, when he hadn't seen her for a time, she was almost a stranger, and he didn't like that. He didn't like that one bit.

On a couple of occasions, he had tried to get close to her again. A while ago, after a hot day on the beach in Spain and a balmy meal under the stars with a bottle of wine, she had nearly let him back into her bed. At the last moment, she had fought him off like a tiger, almost as if he had attempted physical rape. She alarmed him so much with her panic that he had kept his distance for the rest of the visit and confined the conversation to just business. Before he flew back, she had sat him down and talked to him. She asked him not to do that again because she was still vulnerable and it would be taking advantage of a situation that could never go anywhere. He had started to do the usual Drew reassurance 'you can trust me' line until he looked at her face. For the first time since he'd met her, he saw disgust there. Disgust that he could still be spinning the same line and expecting her to believe it.

"You wanted to prove to yourself that you could still have me. It was the power thing again. Once you had my body, you thought I would be yours whenever you felt like it, then you would have walked away."

Drew started to bluster and deny what she had said, and then he saw the disgust for him come back again. Jessica's eyes were the coldest he had ever seen them; her lip curled and her whole body shrank away from him. "You haven't learnt anything from this whole situation at all, have you? Had you shown one bit of remorse for all the past years, I would have given you the fuck of your life, but you can't have me anymore, Drew. I'm armed against you now. Maybe we can be friends in the future, but not right now. Go back to your bimbos and the illusion that you are still a young stud. I don't need you anymore. I need a grown-up and caring man who will look at me and know that he wants to be with me and no one else. I don't want to be forever looking over my shoulder to see if you are making eye contact with someone behind me. Now just bugger off back to England and let me get on with my life."

For a long time, they had no contact, at least no direct contact. All the business concerning Jessica had been done through Stacey as the go-between. Even the money details from the sale of the house and the first serialised book had been conducted through her. Drew had lost his temper on a couple of occasions and demanded to speak to Jessica, but Stacey was adamant. There was no getting by her no matter what he threatened, and in the end, he gave up. Later on, the animosity mellowed into an uneasy truce and finally into friendship. Even though Drew considered Jessica his best friend, he still got the feeling of aloofness every time he was near her, like a mental suit of armour. He had learnt to accept it, but he didn't like it.

He put his arms around Jessica's shoulders and hugged her. Her perfume wafted up his nose and he felt his body immediately and surprisingly, tense with desire. Without looking at him, Jessica sensed it and moved slightly away.

"Our son is on his way, how wonderful. I can't wait to see him," Jessica said in a trembling voice.

She made a show of mopping her eyes and blowing her nose and was saved from looking at Drew by the makeup girl calling her into her room. Drew stood confused and embarrassed. *How could Jessie be so attuned to him that she knew he was aroused?* Even though she would once have been able to look at his face and know, the distance that had been between them had desensitised that side of the relationship, *or maybe it's like riding a bike,* he thought. *Even though you don't do it anymore, you can still remember the wind in your hair.*

The security guard beckoned him over. "There's someone waiting to come in. Hasn't got a pass. Tall bloke. Says he's your son."

When he saw Drew's smile, the guard turned on his heel. "You'd better come and sign him in then."

So Drew went off to greet his son.

CHAPTER 8

The interview went well up to a point. Christy, despite the earlier thick atmosphere, was bubbly and friendly. She had obviously read the book and not just skimmed through it before the show as some of the other interviewers had. Michael, on the other hand, was a different matter. An integral part of Jessica's novel was an older woman's short-lived and steamy affair with a much younger man—something that happens to many women at some time in their lives, which could either be wonderful and fulfilling or destructive and soul destroying as in Jessica's story. Time and again, Michael came back to this storyline. No matter how many times his sister and Jessica pinpointed other important parts of the book, he kept on bringing the conversation back to the sex scenes as if it was giving him some lascivious pleasure.

"How much of this book is gleaned from your own life?" he asked.

His eyes reminded Jessica of the lizards that sunned themselves on her balcony. Their eyes were also grey and unblinking. "Fiction is exactly that. Fiction. It's a story made up from the author's imagination. If the story is interesting enough, the public will want to read it."

"Parts of the book are," throat clearing, "rather risqué. Surely some of this is far too graphic to be a figment of your imagination."

Jessica looked away from his lizard eyes and concentrated instead on the mouth. Slightly petulant when not smiling, but now gleaming at her like a dentist's dream. "There are very few women who have been married that haven't at least tried most of the things described in the book." She looked at him from under her lashes in a deliberately flirting way. "But then you wouldn't really know that would you, not being married."

There were a few sarcastic chuckles from some of the technicians and cameramen, which were clearly heard by Michael. His smile became fixed and hard. "Come now, Jessie, surely you can't have written it all from imagination. I believe you have a palatial villa in Spain, and they say the Spanish men are very fiery, much like the character in your book."

By turning the tables on Michael, even though he had been giving her a hard time, Jessica realised she had made an enemy. "Books are written about all sorts of things. If a book is written about medical problems, the author doesn't have to suffer from all the ailments to write about them. Likewise, wartime and period dramas, and those on traumatic family relationships, are all from the mind of the writer, and not necessarily their life."

A few more sticky moments followed before the interview drew to a close and the morning transmission went on to the next item—fashion. The couple moved over to the other side of the set and even before Jessica had removed the microphone from her jacket, Michael was chatting up one of the fashion models standing off camera, running his hand along her arm, and leaning towards her. *What a smarmy sod he is,* she thought, moving into the shadows where she knew Marty was waiting.

Marty wrapped her in a tight bear hug and gave her a big smacking kiss. She stood back to look at him, but the smile nearly died on her face. Her son was tanned a deep golden brown but was so thin his clothes hung on him. Marty saw the looks from his parents and put his arms around both of them in a three-way hug like he had done when he was a little boy. "Come on, let's find the hospitality room and have a drink; I'll tell you all about it."

Marty had extended his client list to such an extent it had threatened to swamp him. He was invariably the first one in the office in the morning and the last one to leave at night. His daytime food was taken either at his desk or on the run. His evening food was out of a can or packet as he was always too tired for anything else. The only respite he got was on the occasional visit from Melanie, who was filming the summer advertising campaign from a variety of beaches, boats, and cliff tops in various locations. If she had a break, and was within a few hours from him, she came to visit. They were best buddies and enjoyed each other's company immensely, but as soon as she left, Marty threw himself back into long working hours again.

He developed a cold that seemed to drag on forever, which worried Melanie. She nagged him to go and see a doctor, but instead, Marty spent a fortune on a motley assortment of medicine, which did no good at all. His cold went to his chest and he wheezed and coughed and sweated until he finally found it impossible to get out of bed one morning. Melanie tried to reach him at work and left numerous desperate messages on his answerphone until he summoned enough energy to phone her back. As soon as she heard him, she took the next plane and was in his apartment in three hours. She called the doctor, who diagnosed chronic bronchitis and pleurisy and immediately put him on medication. Marty's temperature soared, and he sweated and shivered until Melanie was desperate and called the doctor again. He prescribed stronger doses of antibiotics for Marty and instructed her to keep him very warm and make sure he had plenty of fluid until the medication started to take effect.

Melanie made him soup; he ate four spoonfuls. Toast, of which he had three mouthfuls, and cereal, of which he ate four flakes and drank the milk from the bowl. The second night, he was very restless and wheezed and muttered in his sleep, constantly throwing off all the bedclothes. Worried he might get cold, and by then, totally exhausted, Melanie wrapped the blankets tightly around him and lay down beside him on the edge of the bed. During the night, Marty woke up. His fever had gone down as the drugs had finally taken hold, and he felt considerably better. He was lying on his side and was amazed to discover Melanie curled into the curve of his body like a small purring kitten. He gently placed his arm around her and she made a definite purring sound and pressed even closer to him. He found himself smiling and caught his breath with the sheer feel of her. Even through the layers of clothes, her body seemed to fit him, and the erection came out of the blue and was painful in its intensity. He lay as still as a statue, scared to move in case he woke her, and she felt his hardness. *She had always been his pal, and he felt protective and brotherly towards her, so how come his body had reacted like this?* He lay and thought about it, willing his penis to lie down and behave, but it seemed, if anything, to get even more rigid until a small groan escaped from his tight-lipped face.

Melanie stirred as she came up out of sleep and turned over until she faced him. As if she sensed his scrutiny, she opened her eyes. They gazed silently and solemnly at each other, and without either of them seeming to make the first move, their lips met and clung. Marty's illness, in fact, everything in the world outside of the bedroom, disappeared in the mists of time, leaving them isolated. It was as if they had suddenly seen each other for the first time. Neither could ever remember removing any clothes, but as soon as their naked bodies touched and moulded together, it was as if they were old lovers and knew each other's bodies intimately. Their lovemaking was slow, deep, and unhurried, and at its climax, the tears ran down Melanie's face into her hair. Marty looked at her face, soft with love and wet with tears, and knew he could never let her go.

For the next few days, the walls of the apartment were the edges of their world. Melanie cooked simple food with whatever ingredients were there to avoid having to go out, slowly building up Marty's strength and discovering each other all over again. They bathed together, soaping each other's bodies, talking, laughing, and drying hurriedly not to get the bedclothes wet when they dived onto the bed to make love. Marty phoned his office and arranged to take some overdue leave, and the two of them took off towards the sea and sun for a few days.

They lazed around the beach during the day, went back to the hotel, made love, got dolled up for dinner, and went home early to be on their own again. It was as if they couldn't bear to share their joy with anyone else. When Marty got the telephone call about his mother's visit to England and her first television show, they both instantly agreed that they had to be there. It was only on the plane that they decided to tell Marty's family about them. He knew they would be pleased; both his parents adored Melanie, although they would be surprised to find out they were more than just friends now. Before touching down at Heathrow, they had hired a car. During the ride, Marty phoned Caro, telling her the news and swearing her to secrecy. They arranged to meet her at the TV studio for a family get-together. She promised to get there as soon as possible, hopefully before the end of the show.

Jessica listened to Marty's abbreviated story and, looking at his glowing face, read between the lines. She smoothed back his hair and fiddled with his shirt collar, constantly touching him. It seemed so long since she'd seen him, and now she wanted to make up for lost time. She listened to him talk, noticing how deep his voice sounded as if now he was part of a couple and responsible for someone else an extra masculine hormone had kicked in.

"Where is Melanie anyway?" Drew said looking behind him as if he expected her to be standing there.

"Well, she went to park the car as I was in such a hurry to see you both, but she should have been here by now."

Drew stood up, "Well, as we are going on to a family get-together, maybe we had better go and find her. It doesn't seem much point parking if we're leaving soon."

As they all rounded the turn in the stairs, they saw Melanie talking to Michael. Obviously, the show had finished as he had changed into jeans and a sweatshirt. A holdall was on the floor by his feet and he had his hand on Melanie's shoulder, his over-white teeth gleaming with a wolf-like grin. The three of them stopped on the stairs as if sensing all together that something was wrong. Melanie shook Michael's hand off, hissing something at him, the look on her face hateful and venomous. They all heard Michael laugh and saw him place his hands on her waist. Her hand flew towards his face, but he caught it before it made contact, gripping her wrist and making her cry out. At this point, Marty's long legs were racing down the stairs towards them just as Melanie's knee made contact with Michael's groin. He let out a howl of pain and let her go. As soon as he released her, she started running towards the door. Marty ran after her, shoving the tottering Michael to his knees in passing. Melanie ran like one possessed, tears streaming down her face. She ran out through the doors and across the road to the car park with Marty trying to catch up and Drew close behind. Running through the doors, Marty shouted her name, but the end of the name was cut short as his body was thrown high into the air and over the back of a black London cab, landing spread-eagle and with his neck twisted at an impossible angle.

Melanie didn't see Marty's body hit the ground or hear the dull, heavy thud, but she did hear the screaming of the tyres as the white-faced cabbie stood on the brakes. After the car slewed to a halt and its engine stalled, Drew, Jessica, Melanie, and several other passersby stood in frozen, disbelieving silence, almost like tableaux in the waxworks. Tableaux that would be evermore engraved on the memory. Around the corner and into the silence came a young woman, dressed to the nines with a cheery grin on her face.

"What's everyone doing out here," she said in a cheerful voice, her grin widening.

In unison, the heads of Drew and Jessica swivelled around, and the last thing Jessica saw before the blackness closed over her was her daughter's happy face, and the last thing she heard was a high keening animal sound coming from the mouth of Melanie.

CHAPTER 9

Jessica swung her feet to the floor at the side of the bed. Her head felt as if it was full of cotton wool; there was a funny ringing noise in her ears, and her mouth was as dry as an old shoe. She sat there for several minutes, trying to put the pieces together. She was still wearing the hotel towelling bathrobe, and she felt hot and sweaty. Suddenly, the memory of the past events all came back in a rush and her stomach knotted in sudden and cramping pain. She staggered over to the bathroom in a crouching position and just made it to the toilet before her bowels opened in a rush. She sat there dizzy and sweating, tears streaming down her face as the remains of the mind-numbing injection the doctor had given her finally cleared her system, and the memory of her son's death replayed itself yet again. The hospital said that he had felt no pain. His neck had been broken and he was dead before he hit the ground.

She had sat by his side at the hospital and talked to him for a long time. All little details about her life and all the things that had happened to her since she had seen him last. All about the hopes she had for his future with Melanie, all the time holding his still warm hand while a white-faced and stunned-looking Drew looked on silently, his eyes locked on his son's face. When people came to take Marty away and told her gently to go and get some rest, she turned into a kicking, screaming lunatic. All the grief and fear, all the love and destroyed hopes came out as one blinding outpouring of red rage. She tore at the nurses with her nails, punched and kicked out at Drew, or anyone else who tried to part her from her son, until in desperation, they all held her while the doctor hastily jabbed a needle into the first available piece of skin. She sank weeping and defeated to the floor, wrapped in Drew's arms.

Caro, who was grey-faced and couldn't stop shaking, helped Drew get Jessica into a cab and back to the hotel where a doctor was waiting who administered a knockout shot to an uncaring Jessica, and she knew no more. She slept, watched over by Caro while Drew went back to the hospital to make the arrangements. Caro knew that she should be on the phone, informing the family and friends of the death, but the tears were so near the surface, and all she could think about was that her lovely brother and best friend was gone. Her mind kept running over the things that they had done when they were growing up. The pictures played in her mind like the jerky frames of an old movie. All the mischief and nonsense she had got up to and always blamed Marty. He always took the blame for her, and when she had been bullied at school, he'd sorted it all out. How she never knew, but he obviously had information about the girl gang that tormented her because suddenly, without any reason, the gang left her alone. He also intervened when a local lad was constantly chasing after her and making her life a misery with his unwanted attention. Marty just had a quiet word in his ear and he drifted away. *How was she going to survive without him in her world?*

She sat quietly remembering him, her eyes dry, gritty, and aching, and her throat tight and sore until Drew came back. He had called Sophia to help him with Melanie. She was still emitting whimpering cries deep in her throat, and her eyes were like saucers, huge and unblinking. He remembered how she looked at Marty from the foot of the bed while Jessica was talking to him. Drew stepped back to make way for her to move closer, but she stood rigid and unmoving, still whimpering. He asked the nurses to see to her until he could settle Jessica and get back.

He had called Sophia from the hotel, and both she and Alfie were there when he got back. They were sitting all together in the visitor's room, and even though the whimpering had stopped, Melanie hadn't said a word. Sophia's kindly face was worried as she watched Alfie smoothing and soothing Melanie. He crooned to her in a low voice, and her head finally slipped onto his shoulder. He had spent years working with disturbed people and realised that this lovely young girl was in very deep shock. They all walked slowly out to Sophia's car. Alfie sat her gently in the back seat and tucked the car rug around her, climbed in beside her, his arm once again going around her shoulders.

Drew had explained what had prompted the series of events and Sophia had listened without interrupting. "Something here we do not know about," she said quietly. "She knows this TV man who frightened her."

"Don't know," said Drew, rubbing his hands wearily across his eyes. "But as sure as hell I'm going to find out."

"I will phone her people over the sea when I get home and try talk to her when Alfie makes her better," she said, gazing with soft eyes at her husband through the car window.

She turned and gripped Drew in a tight bear hug. Her soft body enveloped him and she smelt like flowers. He wanted to stay in her arms and cry like a baby. Something he had never been allowed to do all his childhood, and now the need for it nearly overwhelmed him. But once again, the habits of a lifetime prevailed, and the tears got pushed down into his soul.

Much later, when Jessica finally came back to the world, the hotel bedroom door was ajar, and she walked barefooted and silently into the sitting room. Drew was standing in the darkened room, gazing out at a dark city from five stories up. His hands were thrust deep into his pockets and his back was hunched over as if some of the air had been let out of his body. He had removed his shoes and jacket, and his tie was hanging loose from his half-unbuttoned shirt. Caro was asleep on the couch, a blanket thrown over her. Her face was still yellow/grey, and in sleep, her hair stuck up in spikes like it had always done. Jessica looked fondly at her daughter and knew there would be nothing she could say that would comfort her.

She must have made a small sound, which alerted Drew, and he turned around. Jessica's breath caught in her throat at the sight of him. His handsome face had aged ten years; he looked older than his age for the first time ever. She walked quickly across the room and put her arms around him. They stood leaning on each other, quietly drawing strength from each other as they had on numerous other occasions, but this time, there was just not enough strength to salve the pain, and they drew apart.

"I've just sent for some coffee and sandwiches," Drew said quietly.

Jessica made a face.

"Neither of us has eaten all day, and we are going to need all the strength we can for the next few days. Please, Jessie, eat something."

When the tray arrived, Drew stood over Jessica while she ate. She had to admit, the food did help to settle her stomach and the coffee was even more welcome. Between the two of them, they managed to wake an exhausted Caro and force two sandwiches and a glass of milk down her before tucking her up in the other bed.

"Go home, Drew," Jessica said, fetching his jacket. "I'll call you a cab; Max will be worried."

"Yes, she will. She wanted to come over, but I told her I'm going to need her more when I get home."

Drew walked slowly across the hall to the lift and waved briefly before the doors closed. Jessica climbed back into bed and prayed that the night would soon be over.

CHAPTER 10

The funeral was the worst day of the family's life. It was every bit as bad as Jessica thought it would be. Friends jetted in from the US, looking grief-stricken and jet-lagged, and Drew looked about ready to collapse without Max's arm around him. Caro and Jessica were held together by Polly and John and Adam and Cassie, all of whom had known Marty since he was a toddler and had seen him through spotty puberty and even spottier girlfriends into the man he had become. The vicar who performed the service was the same one who had taught him at Sunday school (which created a battle every week just to get him there) and had confirmed him and given him his first communion. Marty had never been religious but had crept off to Midnight Mass occasionally at Christmas and New Year, and also the Harvest festival service which was always attended if they were around the West Country at that time. Jessica could still hear Drew and Marty's lusty voices belting out the harvest songs about all being safely gathered in.

Later on that day, Jessica was still clutching a flower from one of the wreaths on Marty's coffin. Her mind had gone back to the past when Marty, Caro, and Polly's boys had built a tree house during one holiday in the woods. The woods were deep and full of birdsong with a view of the sea from the tree house. Long after everyone else was fed up with it and went off to do things more exciting, Marty could still be found sitting peacefully up there with a book or a sketching pad. Some of his pencil sketches were so good they had framed them, and some still hung in Polly's hallway. When Jessica had had another of her rows with Drew and he was snappy, restless, and bored, she had gone looking for Marty. The two of them had sat peacefully in the tree house quietly listening to the birds and the distant murmur of the sea, when Marty suddenly expressed a wish to be buried there in the woods. Jessica was shocked at someone so young even thinking about dying and saying so.

"People die at any age, Mum. You don't have to be old to die," Marty said.

Jessica wrapped her arms around him. "You aren't going to die for years and years yet, silly boy," she had said.

Funny how that memory had come back to haunt her during the service.

"I'd like to come back with you, Polly," Jessica said after most of the mourners had gone. "I want to take Marty back to the woods."

Drew looked at her with a puzzled look on his face, but Jessica had told Polly about it at the time, as it was such an odd statement, and she immediately understood. Jessica walked away and let Polly explain to Drew. The thought of reliving that memory again was just too much. Polly found her later and said that Drew and Max would come down, bringing a devastated Melanie with them. Adam, Cassie, John, Polly, and Polly's sons all expressed a wish to also be a part of a small and intimate farewell. And that was the way it was.

CHAPTER 11

After everyone finally went back to their homes, Jessica stayed on with Polly. The newspapers were full of all the details for days, and all her TV and radio shows had been cancelled. She didn't feel ready to go back to Spain just yet and started spending time in the rickety and derelict treehouse. John was so worried about her safety that he and his son Ben had spent half a day laying new planks for the floor and pulling down part of the unsafe wooden roof.

"Christ, Jess, that ladder has got half its rungs missing, and you could have fallen through the floor at any time. I don't want you going up there again until I've fixed it," John said sternly.

He caught a look from his wife which went with an almost imperceptible shake of her head. He looked at Jessica and saw her chin go down onto her chest. Her nerves were so near the surface that the slightest thing brought tears to her eyes.

"Sorry to shout at you, sweetheart," he said, putting his arm around her and giving her a squeeze, "but I'd never forgive myself if you got hurt."

Jessica gave him a tearful smile and went across the kitchen to open the door for Charlie, the cat. She followed him out, then nearly tripped over him as he dashed back in again between her legs. He then sat down on the step.

Polly followed Jessica outside and also nearly tripped over Charlie. "That bloody cat gets worse, I swear, he does. I'm going to take him to one of those animal psychologists, that'll be a laugh. It would take them the rest of their lives trying to sort him out."

They walked to the end of the garden in silence and leant on the fence at the bottom, looking across the fields. Jessica broke the silence when she cleared her throat. "I know I'm a bit of a damper, Poll, but I can't seem to move on. I feel that I'm near Marty while I'm here. Over the last few years we only ever seem to be in touch through the phone and mail. Apart from a couple of holiday visits, I haven't seen much of him. I suppose we teach our children to be independent and then we lose them."

"We never lose them," Polly said, lighting a cigarette. "They stand on their own two feet, but we never lose them completely. What's that old Chinese proverb—'If you love something, set it free? If it comes back to you, it's yours. If it doesn't, then it never was.' Marty always came back. You know he did."

"I know," Jessica said wearily. "But I lost so much of his life when he was so far away. I can't help feeling that if only we'd been closer—"

"What...." Polly said sharply. "You could have stopped him being hit by a car? Our lives are peppered with 'if only.'"

Jessica ran her hands through her hair until it stuck up in spikes like her daughter's. "OK, Poll, point taken."

For the next few days, Jessica took to walking. The weather was hot and humid with the threat of thunderstorms, and she carried a lightweight haversack with a rolled-up waterproof coat, swimsuit, sun cream, and a towel. She tramped along lanes and fields, breathing in the scents of England, catching up with familiar things that she had been without. The delicate wild flowers and the myriad of insects (including some with a savage bite) floated in the beams of the sun like airborne seeds. When the air got still and the heat was damp and oppressive, almost suffocating, she headed towards the sea, where she'd strip off and dive into the almost icy water. Refreshed and cool, she would watch the sun go down in a red ball, staining the sea orange and red, before making her way back. She was finding it difficult being with people at the moment. Always in times of stress, she sought to be alone. She needed the time to sort out her thoughts and get back on track again.

It was during one of these solitary walks that she came across the cottage. It looked vaguely familiar, but even though it jangled a bell in her head, she was sure if she had seen it before, she would have remembered it. The garden was a bit overgrown, and the cottage had an unlived look about it. Taking a chance, she pushed open the gate and walked up the gravel path. She walked around the house, deliberately making a lot of crunching noise on the gravel. She was sure that if there was anyone inside, they would have heard her and come outside to investigate the noise. Taking an even bigger chance, she peered in through the kitchen window. The house looked like the ones that had their picture reproduced on postcards. This one certainly depicted a typically English country cottage and was utterly charming. She went all around, peering in every window, just wishing she could see inside. Reluctantly, she finally left it behind and strolled along the narrow country road that ran past it. She constantly looked back at the cottage; in the pink glow from the dying sunset, it looked like a painting.

At supper that night, she mentioned it to Polly and John. John's mouth opened, "Well—"

But before he said anything else, Polly jumped in. "I think I know who owns that cottage."

John's mouth closed, and he took a sip of his beer. He tucked into his food, head down and eyes well away from his wife's face.

"Then how come there's no one in it? It's so beautiful, and it must be worth a fortune."

Polly looked at her friend and noticed that she had no idea about the cottage. She had only been there once when it was in a bad state, and that was years ago now. "Seems that it brings back sad memories for the owner. I think it's in the hands of a letting agent at the moment."

Once again, John's mouth opened and shut with a snap at a look from under his wife's eyelashes. Jessica carried on eating and Polly held her breath.

"I wonder if I could get the key. I'd love to look around it. I've been your guest for too long already, but I'm not ready to go back to Spain yet. I think I might have the rest of the summer here and go back in the autumn. I've a book to finish, which shouldn't take too long. Walking around, I've had the idea for a book churning around in my head, and this would give me some solitude to make a start on it."

Polly's breath whistled out through her nose. "I'll see what I can do."

She caught her husband's eye with a look of pure mischief. "Devious woman," he muttered under his breath as he took the dishes over to her at the sink.

By the following afternoon, the key was in Jessica's possession, and she had made an offer to rent. Little did she know that she could have had the cottage rent-free for as long as she wanted. She arranged for Stacey to bring the rest of her luggage from London, especially her laptop with her book draft on and a new printer. By the end of the week, she was sleeping under the sloping eaves of the most charming country cottage she had ever seen, and the agreement to keep away, which Polly had insisted on, was nearly killing Luke.

CHAPTER 12

rew was the quietest Max had ever seen him. In the beginning, she had stayed away from him because she thought he needed space, but he looked so grey and old that she couldn't bear to be apart from him any longer. Except for the tears at the hospital, Drew had been stiff upper lip all the way. Max, despite being a forceful and independent lady, could cry with the best of them when the occasion demanded, as had her father, brother, and ex-husband. This silent suffering was painful to see, and she felt so helpless at not being able to reach him. She frequently woke up in the night and found his side of the bed empty and cold. She either found him sitting in the dark with a drink in his hand or at his laptop working. She wanted him to talk to her, tell her his thoughts. She felt if he opened up to her, it would start the healing process, but as soon as she got onto anything personal, he closed the door on her. Adam got the same treatment at work, and even though they were both worried, they had to respect his wishes, so they left him alone. In the circumstances, it was the worst thing they could have done.

Drew had the weirdest sensation of being outside himself. It was a three dimensional thing of seeing himself as if he were another person in the room with him. The only time he had ever felt anything like this was when he had taken a small amount of LSD at university. It wasn't an unpleasant feeling, but it stopped the pain inside or at least dulled it a bit. He tried to work, but his thoughts kept getting in the way. He was trying to put some information into his computer and found he was typing in his thoughts. When he read them back, they were garbled and incoherent. He quickly wiped them off. The face in the mirror was not him either. Every time he shaved or combed his hair, an old man stared out at him. It was all very strange, but he tried to do his best.

He had an important meeting with a client. Adam tried to talk him out of it, but he insisted on going. Four hours later, the client phoned Adam to find out where Drew was, as he hadn't shown up. Twenty-four hours later, a frantic Adam, with agreement from Max, Cassie, and Caro, finally called the police.

"Do you think we ought to contact Jessie," Adam said slowly.

"No," said Caro and Cassie at the same time.

"He might have just gone out on a drunken binge or something." Even as Cassie said it, she knew it was unlikely, as did everyone else in the room.

"No…I don't think so. Dad was a sociable drinker. I've seen him down vast quantities when he's with a crowd, but apart from the odd one or two, he never drinks on his own."

"I know, but these are different circumstances," Adam said, roaming restlessly around the room.

Max said, "He's been so strange lately. It's been several weeks since the accident, and I haven't seen him shed a tear yet." Her voice broke into a gruff croak, and she cleared her throat. "He's bottled everything up, and it's killing him inside. Half the time, he can't concentrate on what's being said to him. Sometimes, I've had to repeat the same thing two or three times before it registers."

Max dug in her bag for a tissue, blew her nose, and dabbed her moist eyes.

"Yes, I've noticed all that too. I didn't want him to see this client. Apart from his lack of concentration, I thought he might not remember the client's instructions, but he got so angry with me when I said I would go that I gave in to him."

"Why didn't any of you tell me this," Caro said loudly and

angrily.

Adam hastened to put his arm around her. "Come on, love. You had enough on your plate already coming to terms with it all, as did your mum. No one wanted to keep anything from you; it's just that we hoped it was a temporary thing, and it was Drew's way of grieving."

Everyone lapsed into silence, busy with their own thoughts. They all visibly jumped at the shrilling of the telephone. They had all originally met in Drew's office, but as time had gone on, they had all moved into Max's comfortable flat, knowing that this was where Drew would come back to.

"Hello…. Yes…. Oh my god…. Thank you very much, George. Thanks for letting me know."

All eyes were on Max as she turned slowly away from the phone. "The whole of the foyer and the road outside is crawling with press," she said quietly.

Caro's hand went across her mouth to hide her gasp

"Bloody hell," Adam shouted. He thumped the back of the sofa, "How the fucking hell did they find out so quickly."

For once, Cassie didn't pick him up on his language. "The police probably put out a call on the radio, and the press picked it up," Caro said knowingly. They all looked at her, and she shrugged her shoulders. "I used to have a boyfriend who always had his radio tuned into the police channel," she said by way of explanation.

"What do we do now," Max said quietly. "If Drew wants to come back here, he's not going to run the gauntlet of that lot."

"I suppose they are only interested because Mum's famous now and because of Marty's death." Caro suddenly burst into tears.

"Caroline darling, please don't; you'll have us all going," Cassie sat on the floor beside her and cuddled her.

Caro's sniffs slowly stopped, and Max made coffee while they all tried to decide what to do.

"Well, sure as God, we can't do any more than the police, so I say we should all go and get some sleep. We shall be the first to be told any news," Adam said with a face-splitting yawn.

Once the decision had been made, they all started to get their things together, yawning, using the bathroom, and finishing up the coffee. George had told them to use the back service lift and he would take them through the basement to a waiting taxi. Caro was spending the night with Max. Just as they were about to leave, the phone rang again, and they stopped in their tracks. Max answered, tapped some buttons, and put the receiver back. A digital message came up on the small screen of the phone. Tapped out by Katie on the special phones that were for impaired hearing, "Mum, don't worry, Drew is with me and safe. He just keeps saying he wants to be with the children. We have all seen trauma like this before, and we know what he's going through. He says at the moment he wants to be left alone to come to terms with everything. Don't worry, we'll take good care of him."

Max beckoned them all over to read the screen over her shoulder, and Caro started crying again. Max tapped out a return message.

Katie answered, "I will keep you informed about him…but at the moment, he needs some rest. He's been crying now for five hours and has only just stopped, but he's going to be fine. Don't worry. I love you and will call you again soon."

After the call, they all just stood and looked at the instrument as if it was going to tell them something else.

"I want to go and see him," Caro said, her lips pouting as if she knew they would all object, but nevertheless, defiant despite the tears running down her face.

"No, Caro," said Adam. "You heard what Max's daughter said; give him some space. You've given some to your mum, and now you must let your dad grieve in his own way, too. It's just a pity they couldn't grieve together."

Cassie looked up at her husband. His voice had been forceful and decisive. Caro listened almost as if he were a surrogate father. "OK, Uncle Adam. I'll do what Dad wants, but whose shoulder do I cry on while they've all gone away?"

"Mine," Adam said briefly. "Or failing mine, your Aunt Cassie like you always did when you were growing up."

Caro smiled through her tears, "You've got a deal."

CHAPTER 13

Jessica had her office rigged up in the largest of the two bedrooms where she could look out over the fields. The view seemed to be one she had seen before, but she thought it was probably similar to the one from Polly's place. She spent a few days pottering in the garden, pulling out weeds and trimming the roses that had run riot. She was feeling very down, and being outside had a calming effect on her. She was still getting very bad dreams and frequently woke up bathed in sweat with her heart racing.

John came over and cut the two small lawns for her as there didn't appear to be a mower in amongst all the other bits and pieces in the garden shed.

"I'll have a word with the landlord about a mower," Polly said, pointedly ignoring a look from her husband.

"I can do that, Polly. I have to go into town to stock up on everything. As soon as I start writing, I won't want to go out much."

"It's OK. I like to call in on the landlord from time to time, just for a chat; I can ask him then."

On the way home in the car, John voiced his misgivings about Jessica staying in the cottage without knowing all the facts. It was rare that Polly ever got criticised by her husband; she slewed around in the seat to look at him.

"Well," John said by way of explanation, "if she'd wanted to contact him, she knew where to find him all this time. And if she wanted to see him, then why did she swear you to secrecy about where she was so he wouldn't find her?"

"The time wasn't right then," Polly said abruptly.

"And now it is?" John replied with a bark in his voice. "Now it's time to restart a relationship just after she watched her son get killed? Come on, Poll, where's the logic in that?"

Polly's head sunk down onto her chest. "I just know; that's all," she said quietly.

"Know what, woman? Know that she needs someone? Of course, she does; anyone can see that, but what about Luke in all this? I reckon the bloke needs a bit more than just being around to put the pieces back. He did that once before and she dumped him."

"She didn't dump him. The timing was wrong; she was still smarting over Drew."

"And now she's doing more than smarting. Anyway, Poll, I'm not going to get into fights over this. I love you, and usually, anything you do is OK with me, but this time, I feel I have to express my views, and so, if you do anything to push those two together, you do it without my blessing. Everyone must find their own level before they can move on, and Jessie is not levelled out yet, and besides, Luke has waited for her for so long now, a bit longer won't change things."

Polly again swivelled in her seat. "How did you know that about Luke?"

"Good God, woman. Do you think the female of the species has a monopoly on all the intuitions and emotions? I've got eyes, you know. I watched Luke over the last couple of years the same as you have. I've heard him constantly asking you where Jessie was. I've seen him hurting."

Polly's hand crept over onto John's knee and she gave it a loving squeeze. John swatted at her hand, "Get ye off me, wife. You're not getting around me like that. I'm still cross with you. Although if you move your hand up a tad, I might be inclined to forgive you a bit."

Polly threw her head back and laughed. As he had said, she rarely did anything to meet with John's disapproval, but when she did, she heeded what he said because it was so rare. *Well, my lambs, looks like you're on your own,* Polly thought to herself.

After Polly and John had left, the place seemed very quiet. It was late afternoon, and the sun was going down in its usual blaze of glory. The summer weather had been fine for quite a while now and, apart from a few torrential outbursts, the days had been mostly warm and sunny. Jessica sat on the front doorstep with a glass of chilled wine and listened to the sounds around her. A distant car, bees still buzzing, a bit of birdsong, and in the background, the sound of silence. She leant against the doorframe, her shoulders slumped, and the first words of the new book played themselves over in her mind. She finished her wine and went inside, putting on a pot of coffee. She knew from past experiences that she would need it. The first hot cup she took with her upstairs and switched on the laptop. While it was firing up, she changed into a caftan for comfort and then sat down at the keyboard.

The pattern of the days and nights turned her body clock upside down. The words tore out of her, tumbling out in a torrent to get onto the page. She poured all her grief into the most heartrending love story her mind could put together. She cried tears for every chapter on the page, turning a mother's love for her son into a powerful and passionate love between a man and a woman. The story was happy, sad, poignant, bittersweet, and, by necessity, tragic.

As with all her writing, she slept when she was tired and ate when she was hungry, regardless of whether it was pitch dark or bright sunlight. Sometimes, if she was on a roll, she forgot the simple things like cleaning her teeth. Polly brought her nourishing, wholesome meals (most of which were eaten cold many hours later) and tiptoed around doing the washing up and the cleaning jobs, although downstairs, the jobs were minimal as Jessica only came down for about an hour a day.

Stacey kept in touch with Polly for progress reports. Excited that

Jessica was writing again but not daring to ring her mobile phone for an update, she picked Polly's brains for details. Jessica kept all the typed pages close to her, and Polly only got the occasional peek when Jessica was in the bath, and she knew she was safe. Even though the bits she read were all out of context, from the powerful words and even more powerful storyline, they brought a lump to her throat, and she put them very reluctantly away, itching to read more but not daring until Jessica gave her permission.

Getting towards the end of the book, the storyline was becoming so emotional that Jessica found herself crying almost non-stop. Feeling drained and washed out, she opened a bottle of cold white wine and took a frosty glass of it out into the velvety darkness. The evening had turned into night, and even though it wasn't late, the darkness was almost complete. The moon was a bright ball in the night sky, and clouds scudded quickly across it, throwing the night from black into light grey. She looked up into the sky and felt the soft air on the tight, dry skin of her face. During one of the light periods, she looked towards the grass outside her gate. Her eyes were caught by a movement there. She took a few steps forward, thinking it might be a fox or a badger, only to be confronted by a huge dog with yellow eyes. She was petrified and stood transfixed while the dog continued to walk towards her. Her heart pounded in her chest and she gripped the wineglass so hard it was a miracle the stem didn't break. The dog slowly kept walking towards her, and just when she thought she would be savaged and the scream was nearly up to her throat, the dog sat down. Jessica could feel her legs shaking, and her instinct was to run, but she was afraid if she did that the dog would catch her before she got to the door. The two were perfectly still, eying each other warily. Suddenly, the dog moved, and Jessica jumped. But it laid down almost at her feet with its paws together and its large hairy head resting on them. Its eyes turned up to look at her, and she saw that the plume at the end of its stringy tail was thumping the ground. She continued to look at it for a few more minutes, still not moving. "Christ, you stupid mutt. You almost gave me a heart attack."

At the sound of her voice, the tail beat even faster. She tentatively reached down towards the large head, ready to snatch her hand back in a moment, but the dog's soft tongue warmly licked all over the back of her hand. *How could she have been frightened?* Its face was smiling, or so it seemed. After a few moments, the dog turned its head at a sound somewhere behind it and loped off back the way it came. Jessica watched it until the darkness swallowed it and then went back inside. She smiled to herself at the thought of her fright and, after comfortably drinking a second glass of wine, felt her eyes closing. She hurried upstairs to bed, knowing if she lingered, she would fall asleep in the chair. The book would be finished in the next couple of days, and then she could sleep all she wanted.

CHAPTER 14

Kate stopped at the top of the sweeping semi-circle of steps, leading impressively up to the front of the house. She absently plucked a dead head off one of the plants in the stone pots lining the entrance, her eyes all the time on the solitary figure sitting on the bench under the trees. The handsome, charismatic man was still there somewhere, but he seemed to have gotten lost underneath all the grief. The white teeth rarely flashed a smile, and the laser blue eyes seemed somehow dimmed and dead.

Kate walked softly towards him across the grass. Her burnished hair gleamed like a new penny as she moved into the sunshine. The dreaded freckles had multiplied and her skin under them had a healthy golden glow. She wore a long, green tube skirt that accentuated her slimness, a floral chiffon blouse in shades of green tied in a knot in the front, and flat gold sandals on brown feet with pink nails.

Drew looked up as she cast a shadow over him, squinting against the glare, his mouth curving into the tight kind of smile that's more polite than welcoming.

"Hello, you," Kate said into his face, also moving her hands at the same time.

"And hello, you," Drew answered.

His head moved back to the front again, cutting off the lines of communication but reaching for her hand with both of his. They sat looking out across the grounds for a while until Kate gently pulled her hand from his and knelt down in front of him so he couldn't turn away. She slowly signed to him, knowing that he still found some of the words hard to understand.

"I would like you to help me."

"How?"

"We have a boy here who is prone to violent behaviour. He was badly abused by his father, who thought he was retarded as well as deaf."

"What do you want me to do?" Drew said reluctantly, not wanting to be disturbed from his thoughts, and trying to break the contact by looking over her head.

Kate didn't let him get away with that and raised herself up further on her knees until her face was on the level with his and he had to look at her. "I want you to be my bodyguard."

His eyebrows shot up, and he let out a mirthless bark, which was the closest to a laugh she had heard so far from him. "What am I supposed to do, go in front of you with a chair and a whip? I'm sure the boy can't be that bad."

"He can be very scary. You have to do everything in slow motion. Any sudden moves, and he thinks he's going to get beaten again and flies into a frenzy to defend himself."

Drew shifted sideways on the seat to move away from her penetrating gaze. Kate just moved with him, not allowing him to slide away from her.

"Ok," Drew signed, his mouth drooping at the corners, for all the world like a little boy told to do his homework.

Kate shot to her feet pulling him up with her. She hooked her arm in his and almost dragged him towards the steps of the house.

"I have to bath him and get him ready for bed. Not an easy task on most occasions. He is very strong and frightens me, but it's my turn this week."

The room was devoid of any toys, ornaments, or personal effects of any sort. Kate saw the puzzled frown on Drew's face as he looked around.

"We can't allow him to have anything sharp or heavy. He uses it all as weapons or throws it and it gets broken."

Drew nodded, looking at the boy. He was of slight build, blond, with light and startlingly icy-grey eyes that looked almost unreal. The eyes were staring unnervingly now at Drew, and he got the feeling they were looking inside him, but then the gaze shifted and the eyes stared down at the floor. The boy, Thomas, sat cross-legged on the bed, slightly rocking back and forth. Kate sat down beside him, bending down to look into his face. She made a washing movement with her hands and pointed to the door. Thomas stood up, and Kate walked slowly over to the three-drawer chest at the side of Drew. She took clean pyjamas from the drawer, a wash bag, and a towel from the cupboard above it. The boy followed quietly behind her to the bathroom across the hall. Drew watched all this and wondered, *why the hell Kate was so frightened. The boy was as quiet and docile as a harvest mouse.*

Kate washed the slender body and the pale blond hair, but even when she blew bubbles for the boy, no smile creased his face. Clean and dressed, they walked him back into the room on either side of him. Drew took the washbag and towel from Kate and crossed quickly in front of the boy to put it away in the cupboard. The boy's fists came up and he immediately started screaming. His feet started kicking upwards towards Drew's groin, and it was only a split-second defence movement that prevented Drew's wedding tackle from being kicked into touch. The boy was like a whirling dervish, flaying fists and kicking feet. Drew dropped the bag and towel and attempted to grab hold of the boy, all the time avoiding the lethal kicks.

Kate was plastered against the wall with her palm flat on the red alarm button. Drew wrestled the boy to the ground and, with great difficulty, used his superior strength and weight to sit on the boy, all the while tightly holding his arms. He held on for grim death while the boy expended all his energy uselessly and grew tired. As Drew looked down at the boy, he looked deep into his icy eyes, and for a fleeting moment, a split second, he saw terror. Pure gut-wrenching terror. In this boy's silent, uncommunicating world, there was no knowledge of love, just fear and survival. The look was gone in the blink of the blond eyelashes, but Drew's breath was caught in his throat. The eyes were defeated now, and without thinking, Drew scooped the boy up into his arms and held him. The boy's reaction was to immediately struggle, his fists thumping Drew's broad back, but Drew held on, and slowly, the boy relaxed into Drew's arms and allowed himself to be held. Drew stroked his hands across the boy's back, soothing and loving. He stroked the blond hair and rocked the slim body that smelt of soap and shampoo.

Kate's hand in the air stopped anyone from entering, and the staff, who had raced up the stairs at the sound of the alarm, now listened to the heartrending sobs coming up from the soul of the boy. For the first time in his life, he felt love flowing out from another person into him, and even in his silent world, the feeling deafened him with its emotion. The tears were the first ones he had ever shed outside the darkness of the night and, for the first time, gave him release.

The staff drifted silently away, touching Kate on the shoulder as they left. Her face was wet with tears as she looked at the two people still knelt on the floor. She went quietly out and shut the door behind her, knowing that Thomas had found his friend and Drew had found his way back.

CHAPTER 15

Jessica tore into the last chapters of the book, and just when she thought that within a few hours, it would be finished, she hit a block. The ending she had foreseen didn't seem to gel. She deleted several pages, re-wrote them, and then deleted them again. She felt drained and her head ached. On a whim, she decided to get some fresh air. There was still an hour or two before dark, and she had a sudden urge to see the sea. Throwing on a pair of cut-off jeans and a white t-shirt, she threw a sweater over her shoulders and, deciding not to walk, headed out towards the car she had hired.

The beach was fairly deserted. A few fishermen were scattered along the front of the beach and were concentrating more on reeling their lines in and casting them out again than on a woman out for a stroll. She was glad of that. She really didn't feel like making inane conversation. The sea was a bit choppy and the tide was high up on the beach. She took her shoes off and the sand felt warm under her feet. The gulls were wheeling overhead and she could feel her headache easing. She walked far along the beach to an outcrop of rocks and sat down. The peaceful ebb and flow of the sea was soothing; she sat for a long time with no coherent thoughts in her head at all. A fisherman further along watched her from the corner of his eye, his fishing line totally forgotten.

The air started to feel fresher and she pulled her sweater on. She stood up and turned to walk back along the higher part of the beach just as the large dog on the other side of the rocks caught her scent. A few yards further on, she became aware of a presence behind her and turned around just as the large dog came up alongside her. The long, scrappy tail waved slowly, and the great head dipped, the eyes looking up at her, almost asking if it was OK to be there with her.

"Hello, you," Jessica said, a smile lighting her face. "Where did you spring from?"

The head went up and the tail wagged the whole body. Jessica looked back up the beach or the bit she could see around the rocks. It didn't seem as if the dog was with anyone. Perhaps it was just out for a walk like she was. She caressed the rough, shaggy head and the dog leant its heavy body against her.

"What an old softy you are, and to think you scared me last time."

The tail beat the back of her leg.

"Come on then, let's walk, it's getting cold."

The two of them walked leisurely along the length of the beach. The dog stayed close—almost touching her and its warmth was surprisingly comforting. As she reached the end and started to enter the car park area, the dog's head lifted and turned back over its shoulder as if to a sound. Jessica watched as it loped back up the beach and felt strangely bereft. She got thoughtfully back into the car and drove home, wondering about the dog but feeling peaceful and refreshed. She worked into the early hours. The end of the book had now come together and was finished, bar the tidying up.

The dog joined its owner and the two of them headed for home. Luke was anything but peaceful and refreshed. The sight of Jessica had rocked him back on his heels and he had felt himself tensing up to go running to her. The sight of the dog greeting her had brought him to his senses, and he had ducked back behind the rocks. His promise to Polly was the hardest promise he had ever had to keep. But Jessica knew where he was, and he had to trust Polly when she said that it was imperative that Jessica made the first move. He could see the logic in it and couldn't risk losing her again. That really would kill him, so he kept his distance. Well— nearly. He kidded himself he was just watching over her with his nocturnal visits. The dog nearly gave him away. She looked so scared the first time she saw Gertie he thought she was going to scream. Then, he would have had to reveal himself. He grinned ruefully and looked down at the dog, who looked up at him, her heart in her eyes.

"*The Hound of the Baskervilles*, you certainly ain't."

The dog smiled and bounded off in front.

Luke had a very restless night, but Jessica fell into bed as the sun was waking up and slept like a baby till the evening. As soon as she woke, she emailed Stacey that the book was finished and she arrived the next morning. Jessica left Stacey sitting at the kitchen table, the laptop in front of her, deep into the story and with a crumpled tissue in the palm of her hand.

"I'm going to get groceries."

A grunt.

"I'll cook us a nice supper."

Another grunt.

"John and Polly are coming over."

One last grunt.

Jessica smiled. That was a sure sign that Stacey liked the story, otherwise, she would have made some comments or suggested some amendments. "See you later then."

No answer, just a nod.

Jessica had taken stock and the place really did look like Mother Hubbard's cupboard. The bags of supplies filled the boot. She stopped off before the supermarket to book a hair appointment and had been warmly welcomed by Ann who slotted her in later that day, making sure she left time to chat as well. She knew about Marty and thought Jessica looked far too slender but kept her own counsel. *The last thing a woman needs is to be told she's not looking well, even if she knows it, especially with the past few months she'd had.*

Jessica did know how much weight she'd lost by the fit of her clothes, but with the scrappy diet she had been on while she was writing and all the grief before that, her appetite seemed to have deserted her. Maybe she would get used to being that much thinner, although when she'd looked in the mirror to apply the first makeup in weeks, she certainly didn't like what it was doing to her face.

"I'll get some cream," she said to the mirror.

She stretched up her neck and leant forward to look at it. "Huh, maybe I'd better make it a polo neck jumper."

Despite her poor appetite, she was looking forward to cooking for her friends and enjoying their company after the long weeks of solitude. Whilst she was going through her wardrobe for something that fitted her, she suddenly thought how complete it would be if Luke was also there with them. The thought stopped her dead in her tracks.

CHAPTER 16

Once Drew's grief had assuaged itself, he started to feel a bit better. He still didn't feel quite ready to face the world quite yet but relaxed with the children. They knew he was sad and tried to cheer him up the best way they could. He watched their lessons, took them for walks in the woods, poking about in ants' nests and letting tiny woodlice and various bugs crawl on his hand so the children could see them. The boys would let them run over their fingers laid across Drew's palm, but the girls looked at them, craning their necks and folding their hands behind their backs.

Kate was going to see her father for a couple of days. As Drew had predicted, Max had been reluctant to let her make the initial contact with him but had seen the need for Kate to know and meet her father. Although the two had a very uneasy first few meetings, eventually, Steve had overcome his stiff formality and got used to speaking to his daughter, knowing she could read his lips; he had even learnt to sign a little. Max had to interpret in the beginning, which made the meetings a bit fraught, but now Kate seemed to enjoy his company, although they would never be close, more like good friends.

Steve had a family of his own, and his wife couldn't understand why he had cut all ties with his daughter and had not wanted to be in her life at all. With her urging him on, he had finally made contact and was glad he had. As he got older, he had many sleepless nights thinking about the past and regretting a lot of it, but with his understanding wife behind him, he was a lot more content and happy to now be a small part of his daughter's life.

Drew had been invited to stay in Kate's room whilst she was away, but he knew he needed to get back to his business soon. They were still a small company, and every person was needed to keep it running. Adam was prepared to carry Drew's workload for a bit, but he would need him back before he was swamped trying to keep both workloads going.

Drew kept in touch by phone and email but knew within the next couple of days, he would head back. Max was busy and had not intruded on his grief, although he knew she would have been here like a shot if he had asked her. She knew that this was something he had to come to terms with by himself. Caro had wanted to be with him, but he had gently and carefully explained to her that he needed some time to get himself back on track and ready to move on. She had reluctantly agreed and had gone back to her flat, knowing her friends would be there for her. They knew and liked Marty and would support her if she needed it.

Drew had invited the headmistress of the school, Mary Miles, to a pub dinner in the village. It was to thank her for her patience with him and also because he liked her. The school was her whole life and had been since she started working there as a helper thirty-five years earlier. Her brother had been deaf and, because of this, was thought to be unteachable and unfit to be in the local school. Mary's parents had heard about this teaching school for the deaf and had brought her and her brother down on the train from Surrey to look around. Mary's father had been a solicitor and could afford the fees. Mary also stayed on as soon as she saw the deputy headmaster, and he saw her. She was only sixteen at the time and persuaded her father to let her help at the school to be near her brother and also to be near the deputy head. If her father thought it strange, he never said so, and she started as a helper and then qualified as a teacher. She and Arthur were married when she was nineteen. Sadly, they never had children of their own. Instead, the children they taught became their family. Mary's friend, helpmate, and husband had died suddenly of a heart attack five years back, and since then, she has been running the school with the help of her brother and a loyal band of teachers and helpers.

Over a delicious dinner in the warm, friendly atmosphere of the pub, Mary turned out to be an entertaining companion. Her dry wit had Drew laughing long and loudly, turning some of the heads at the bar. She told him stories of the early days at the school and of her husband. He loved to go fishing, but in all the years, he had never caught anything. He would spend hours sitting by the river with nothing in the keep net. It got to be a bit of a joke among the other fishermen. "The only thing was," Mary said, leaning forward on her elbows, "his heart attack happened while he was fishing, and for the first time ever, he had a fish on the line. It turned out to be the heaviest carp anyone had ever caught. He was so excited he died. The other fisherman thought he'd just fainted."

Drew covered his mouth with his hand. After all, it didn't seem quite proper to laugh at such a tragic story.

"Go on, laugh," Mary said, smiling. "The other blokes did at the funeral. They said it was the happiest death they'd ever seen."

Now Drew did laugh and he warmed to this lovely and gentle lady with her wicked sense of humour. No wonder the children all loved her. He drove Mary home and enjoyed the remainder of the evening over coffee in the small sitting room that was comfortable and warm and was out of bounds to non-invited guests.

Mary kicked off her shoes and tucked her feet under her in the big overstuffed armchair that was obviously her relaxing place.

"Well, young Drew," she said, resting her elbow on the padded arm and her chin on her hand. "And when are you going back to the real world?"

Drew took a deep breath, then let it out slowly and leant back in his chair. There was a brief silence. "Tomorrow," he replied.

"Sudden decision, was it," Mary said, straightening up.

"Sort of. I thought about it earlier and knew I would have to move on. This place has been a lovely healing balm for me, and I thank you for that from the bottom of my heart. I don't know how I would have gotten through it all without you and the children. My whole family was falling apart before my eyes and I was trying not to join them, but it got too impossible in the end. I knew I had to be away somewhere to grieve by myself. I've never found public emotion very easy, even in front of my own family."

"Are you OK now?"

"As OK as I can be given the circumstances."

"You know you are always welcome anytime, on your own or with Max."

Drew stood up, kissed her cheek, thanked her again, and went to bed. At the crack of dawn the next morning, he was gone, leaving a large donation for the school in Mary's office. By eleven the next morning, the peace of the school was already a distant memory. A long meeting with Adam got Drew quickly back in the loop, and he'd just settled down to some quality work time when his mobile rang.

"Dad, when are you back?"

"Hi, darling, I am back. I was going to phone you later."

"Dad, can you meet me for lunch?" Caro sounded a bit strung up.

"Darling, I've got such a backlog—"

"Dad, it's important," Caro cut across his sentence.

Drew thought about the mountain of work and sighed. He'd have to work very late anyway. "Look, I'll pick you up and bring you over here. I'll order a takeaway and pay for your taxi back. That way, I can save a bit of time."

"Fine. Whatever. I just need to run something by you."

Drew picked her up at the loading bay at the back of the shop, kissed her briefly, and shot out into the traffic. He thought how lovely his daughter looked, if you could call ratty jeans, a short-cropped top, and an oversized leather jacket lovely. Her hair was a glossy brown bob that glinted with copper highlights Drew didn't remember seeing before. She had Jessica's colouring but was blessed with Drew's cornflower blue eyes. The contrast of the dark hair, olive skin, and blue eyes was startling and had developed into a real head-turning combination as she had grown out of puberty and into the young woman she was now.

His gaze flicked over her and noted the slightly paler skin and dark smudges under her eyes. It all added to give her a waif-like look, and Drew knew she was missing her brother. They used to phone each other twice a week and Caro had been over to the States on many occasions. He had been her big brother and she had loved him unconditionally all her life.

"I know you'll do anything for a free lunch, but what's so all-fired important you couldn't tell me over the phone," Drew said, taking a fast left-hand corner, cutting in front of a white van, and getting a blast of a horn and a two-fingered salute.

"You are never going to find out driving like that," Caro replied, taking her outstretched arms away from the dashboard.

The pizza had arrived and Drew took it into his office.

"I just have to make a quick phone call. Get some plates from the kitchen and I'll be with you."

She started to walk towards the kitchen when Ashley Mead, mobile phone clamped to his head, as usual, came out of the main office. He paced up and down, speaking in a rapid rat-a-tat-tat into some poor red ear at the other end. He stopped his pacing and looked up. His dark eyes locked with Caro's blue ones and the look seemed to go on forever. A jolt ran the length of Caro's body. Ashley stood unmoving before snapping shut the phone on the poor, unfortunate soul at the other end. In the stillness Drew walked out of his office and caught the heavy tension full force.

"Got to go," Ashley said, almost diving for the door.

Drew watched the blush creep up his daughter's face, and she moved jerkily towards the kitchen. He groaned inwardly. *Oh, Christ, no, not him. Oh, Caro, not him.* He looked towards the closed door. *Going to have to have a quiet word,* he thought. *Oh, please, not more traumas.* The string of broken hearts behind Ashley would stretch up the M1, and he was damn sure his daughter's wasn't going to add to the list. He'd have to tread carefully, though.

Drew and Caro sat on either side of Drew's desk and devoured the pizza. Wiping his mouth and hands, Drew leant back in the oversized leather chair and looked at his daughter. "OK, out with it then; I've got loads to do today."

"Well," Caro said, also wiping her mouth and leaning back. "While you were away, I was contacted by a girl called Carla, who you met a while back."

Drew started to feel hot under the collar as he wracked his brains over the name, thinking it might be an ex from an old liaison and not wanting to hash this over with his daughter. "No, the name doesn't ring a bell," he said abruptly, sitting up and casting his eyes down towards the papers on his desk.

Caro caught the sudden tension and smiled a wry smile. "It's OK, Dad. You can stop what you're thinking. This was the lady you and Uncle Adam talked to at the place you found Melanie. You met her just after she came back from America. She joined a new West End show and because of the heavy schedule of rehearsals, matinees, and evening shows, she rarely watches TV or reads the papers. However, she picked up a paper someone had left on the tube and read about Marty's death."

Drew still looked puzzled. "I still don't see the connection."

"Well, she lost the card you gave her and couldn't get in touch."

Drew frowned and scratched his head. "Darling, you still aren't making sense."

"Well, the flat she stays in belongs to her father. He's something big in the stock exchange and just uses it when he's in town overnight. Carla has her own key and uses it when she's in London. The flat you found Melanie in is the one up the stairs from her and she reckons she knows who owns it. She wouldn't talk to me; she only wants to talk to you and wants you to contact her as soon as possible."

Drew sat back in his chair and his breath whooshed out of this body, puffing out his cheeks as he thought of the significance of this.

"What's it all about, Dad?" said Caro, leaning forward and watching her father's face.

Drew sat thoughtfully for a minute or two before replying, "This may be of no importance whatsoever, or it could be just the information I need to settle a few loose ends."

"Now you aren't making any sense," Caro said, standing up. "Carla made me promise to give you this information as soon as you come back and also to phone her, preferably late mornings when she's up and about. Here's her phone number. I've got to go. I daresay I'll find out about it all sooner or later."

Drew walked her to the door, noticing that she hesitated and gave the office a swift once over with her eyes. He knew she was looking for Ashley and groaned inside hoping that she would forget all about him, but knowing that it was very possible she wouldn't any time soon.

Sitting back at his desk, he wondered if Carla would still be there or had already left for her matinee show. *To hell with it.* He couldn't wait a whole day and dialled her number. The phone rang and rang. Just as he was about to put down the receiver, a breathless voice answered.

"Hi, Carla, it's Drew."

"Drew, who?" was the reply.

"You spoke to my daughter and asked me to phone you about the flat upstairs."

There was a pause as the penny dropped. "Oh, crikey, yes. I remember you now. Sorry just got out of the shower and not really with it yet. How are you and how is your friend now?"

"She's fine, although the death of my son has hit her hard; they were very close."

"Poor love. She's had a few rough deals, hasn't she?"

"We all have this year, I'm afraid."

"I know; I read about it in the papers. Anyway, time is rushing, and so must I, but the reason I wanted you to call is because my dad has been staying here for a while, and we got to talking about this and that. I asked him if he knew who owned the flat upstairs as there seemed to be a lot of different girls going up and down. After all, with the price he paid for this place, I'm sure he wouldn't want something tacky going on right on his doorstep. I didn't say anything about the other incident, but he seemed a bit worried about all the implications. Anyway, as he knows some of the other tenants he did some asking around, and it seems the upstairs flat is owned by that Michael guy who is on that TV chat show with his sister. It seems they actually live in the suburbs, so I presume they only use the flat occasionally."

Drew hadn't realised he had been holding his breath but then let it out in a big sigh. "Carla, you are a star. Thank you so much for this. I can't tell you how grateful I am that you took the trouble to contact me."

"No trouble. Sorry it took so long, anyway, must dash, hope the info helps. Keep in touch."

Drew sat back in his chair and absorbed what she had said. *Was that smarmy bastard the one that had been involved with Melanie?* He could well be. But he was so high profile that anything about him would be almost impossible to prove. He sat going over possibilities for over half an hour, then sat up straight, stood up suddenly, and headed out the door. Annie on reception visibly jumped as the door banged open and, Drew came striding out. Her mouth was full of sandwich, and she started spluttering as it went down the wrong way. Whilst Drew was pounding on her back, he was yelling for Ashley.

"He's out," Annie rasped out, her eyes watering. "And I think you've broken my ribs."

"He's always bloody out; what time is he due back?"

"About now," said a voice from the doorway. "What's all the commotion."

"I want to see you in my office," Drew said.

"What have I done now?" Ashley said, closing the door.

"It's what you are going to do. Sit down."

Ashley sat and waited while Drew paced up and down. The face of Caro swam before his eyes, and he had a horrible feeling Drew was going to warn him off. He hoped not. He hadn't stopped thinking about her the whole afternoon.

"Who do you know in the tabloid press? A reporter who digs all the dirt on celebrities."

"Whaaa—" Ashley spluttered.

"You know the sort. Scoops about all the things the public loves to read about."

"Well, I know a couple who are always looking for a big story. There's nothing they like more than to put someone on a pedestal and then spend weeks tearing them down. Who are we talking about anyway?"

Drew sat down and leant across the table. "I didn't want to tell you the whole story, but I can see you need to know some of it to be able to get the ball rolling. This is told to you in complete confidence. No one, apart from my family, knows the full story, and there are names that will need to be kept out, and if a mention of those names ever appears, I will know who leaked them, won't I?" Drew's laser blue eyes bored into Ashley's brown ones.

Ashley leant back in his chair away from the blue lasers. "The things I know about people I know would make your hair curl. Your secret will be safe with me." Ashley's whiplash brain suddenly clicked into gear and realised this was an opportune moment. "A favour for a favour."

"What," Drew said, startled.

"I will get you what you want. If there is any dirt to be dished, I know the man, but I would like a favour in return."

"More salary, I suppose."

"Maybe we will talk about that later, but for the moment, I would like to ask your daughter out."

Drew's mouth opened. "You've got a bloody cheek. What is this, blackmail?"

"Certainly not. I would have asked her anyway, but as you are my boss, I thought I would forewarn you."

"And if I say no."

"I shall still ask her, and besides, you can't answer for her anymore."

"What if I fire you?"

"Then I'll go to the agency down the road who have been head-hunting me with lots more money for over a year now."

Drew tried to stop the smile, but it crept out. "I knew you would be trouble the day you started."

"Is that a yes then?"

"You hurt her or break her heart and I will break you. And that's a promise."

Ashley's white teeth gleamed at Drew. "Yes, sir, I hear you. Now, what's this secret, and who is the celeb who will be crashing from his high tower."

Drew told him the story from the meeting with Sullivan and the contract with Melanie, to the information he had got from Carla. As Ashley left Drew's office, he was already dialling a number on his mobile, and Drew had a tight, excited feeling in his stomach that some just deserts were going to be dished out.

CHAPTER 17

Stacey sat curled up in the red brocade chair in front of the fire. Jessica watched her face for some sort of reaction as she skimmed through the book. Speed reading was something of an art, and Stacey had mastered it. Jessica got tired of sitting still and pulled on her old trainers and a jersey. The weather had been very wet, and even though it had stopped raining today, there was still mist in the air. She called out a goodbye aimed towards the lounge door and, receiving no reply, shrugged and went out.

She walked briskly down the road for about 300 yards and then cut off across a bridal path towards the cliffs and the sea. Deep in thought, she sensed, rather than saw, a movement from the corner of her eye. She kept walking at the same pace, but her heart seemed to be beating a bit heavily, realising she was alarmed. She tried to look out of the corner of her eye without turning her head in case there was someone in the bushes and stopped dead. There, pacing along beside her, was the large ginger dog. As soon as she stopped and turned around, the dog sat down, its tail thumping the wet grass behind it, and its face smiling. Jessica put her hands on her hips and smiled back at it. "Bloody mutt," she said to the hairy face. "You are determined to give me a heart attack."

The tail thumped again.

"Come on then," she started walking, "If your owner allows you to roam around on your own, you might as well keep me company."

The dog loped happily along beside her, and Jessica found herself talking to the dog. She walked along thinking aloud, and the dog's brown eyes constantly looked up at her as if it understood every word. She climbed up the cliff path and sat on a tree stump at the top, looking out to sea and catching her breath. The dog sat down beside her, its long pink tongue hanging out of the side of its mouth. She scratched the dog's neck under its collar. Among its bristly hair, she saw a round-name disc and bent to read it. The dog's wet tongue licked her ears and made her shiver.

"My name is Gertie," she read aloud. At the sound of her name, the dog gave a sharp bark, making Jessica jump. She threw her head back and laughed. "Who in hell would call a dog Gertie."

"I would," said a deep voice behind her.

Jessica leapt to her feet and spun around. Luke stood and looked at her. Drinking her in with his eyes, taking in every detail of the face he had longed so often to see. Jessica's hand flew to her throat. Her heart seemed to be beating heavily at the base of her neck, and as she looked at Luke, she realised she had known this moment would come and had been afraid. Even though the thoughts of Luke had been pushed down into her sub conscience, the strength of feeling she'd had for him was still there. All that time ago when she'd run away, she'd known when this moment came she wouldn't be sure of her reaction. In her mind this scene had been played out many times, and each time in a different way. She had dreamt of slapping him and shouting at him. She had dreamt of meeting him when she was on the arm of some handsome man and ignoring him. Now as she looked at him and saw the emotions playing across his face, she knew that in all her wildest dreams, she could never have dreamt a meeting that was so right.

Luke's hair was shorter than she remembered, and droplets of moisture glistened in it. His beard had gone, revealing a strong, tanned face in which his brown eyes almost glowed as he looked at her. His jeans and heavy jersey added to his size, and Jessica had forgotten the sheer physical presence of the man.

As if of its own volition, her body moved towards him. Without a word being spoken, he opened his arms wide and she walked straight into them. He held her gently at first, and then his arms tightened around her as if he wanted to scoop her right inside him. She felt his chest expand with several huge sighs, and his body seemed to be trembling beneath her cheek. She turned her head up to look at him and their eyes locked. Jessica's breath caught in her throat when she saw the love, naked and unashamed, shining in his eyes.

She stretched up on tiptoes to kiss him, and as soon as their lips touched, it was as if the floodgates had opened. The kiss immediately deepened and held. It seemed to go on forever without either of them wanting to break the contact.

Eventually, Luke straightened up. His smile was shy and a bit bashful. "Sorry, Jess. This is not really how I wanted it to be. I wanted to turn up at your door with flowers and take you out and catch up with all the news of our lives and tell you how many millions of times I have imagined kissing you and taking the time to get to know you properly."

Jessica laughed. "Well, we can still do all those things, can't we?"

"I think we need to. Last time we were together, it was all so fast and furious, and because I didn't know you well enough, I made a stupid mistake and you ran away."

Jessica stepped back from him and absentmindedly scratched Gertie's head. She took a few steps away and stood for a moment gazing into space, her mind going back to that time that was so long ago now. "I suppose at the time, it did seem like running away. I felt you should have given me a bit of time to sort things out, but looking back, I think I had a lot of issues that needed to be dealt with before I could really move on. The time I spent away got my life straightened out and also gave me time to start writing and also to settle a lot of inner turmoil. I thought about you so much. In the beginning, I thought I would never get over being away from you or have a night's sleep without waking up in the middle of the night and missing you."

Luke shuffled the earth with his foot. *If only she knew what I've gone through trying to find her, and then having her on the doorstep and having to stay at a distance.* He couldn't tell her now, but he would sometime. He cleared his throat. "That kiss was not one between friends, so have you still got feelings for me, or shall I walk away."

"Can you?"

He felt like something was tearing inside his chest and he took a deep breath. "If I have to."

"Oh."

"But it would break me into pieces."

"Oh."

Both of them were silent, deep in their own thoughts and facing away from one another. Gertie looked from one face to the other, her tail quivering, sensing the tension and not sure if it was good or bad.

They both turned and spoke at the same time, laughed, took a step forward, and Luke's arms went around her again. She stood quietly within them, feeling the warmth of his body and the beating of his heart. Luke's chin rested on the top of her head and they stood like that for several minutes. Jessica moved back and very slowly put both arms around his neck, brought his head down to hers, and kissed him long and hard until her legs ached from standing on tiptoes.

"I have some things to do over the next few days. I have just finished a book and life will be a bit hectic, but if you can bring me flowers and takeaway food, maybe we can catch up on our lives. Mine has been rather sad for a while, but I have a feeling it might be getting better. If that's all right with you."

Luke gave a big sigh, a big grin, and let out a whoop making Gertie bark. "Lady, it's more than all right; it's absolutely great."

They strolled back to the cottage, hand in hand, to see Stacey.

She still had red eyes and sniffed a lot until Jessica explained the reason to Luke, who nodded in understanding.

"Darling Jessie," Stacey said, stopping to blow her nose. "What a lot of money you are going to make when this book comes out. It's a cracker and I can't wait to see it in print. We've got so much to do. Have you thought about the cover, and the launch date, and—"

"Whoa," Jessica said, laughing. "We can get into all this tomorrow. For today, I've got other plans."

"Oh yes, yes, of course," Stacey looked flustered. "I'll be back tomorrow then."

She gathered up papers, her handbag, and a motley of other stuff. Luke laughed and took the pile of stuff from her and put it all down on a chair.

"Not so fast. We aren't sending you away. We just meant we are going to put the book on the back burner for tonight and take you out to dinner. It's been such a long time since I've seen you. Jessie whisked you away from the office and I didn't know you'd gone until Carl told me."

"Yes, I'm sorry. Jessie made me an offer I couldn't refuse and the next thing, I was on a plane to Spain and the rest, as they say, is history. I felt bad about leaving so suddenly, but the office was in good hands with Zoe."

"Yeh," Luke said. "Nice girl, nice figure, too."

Jessica punched him on the arm.

"What. A man can look, can't he?"

"Not now I'm back, he can't."

Luke's face softened as he looked at her, and Stacey looked away, feeling like she was intruding into an intimate moment.

"Are you really back."

"You betcha," Jessica said, linking one arm through Luke's and another one through Stacey's. "Come on, I'm starving. Let's plan where we are going to eat."

CHAPTER 18

The weekend looked to be a fine one and Drew phoned Max to plan to spend some time with Kate. Max was very lukewarm about the idea as Kate's father was picking her up that evening, and she didn't want to run into him.

Kate had met her father some months ago after discussions with Max, and even though she didn't know him at all, they soon forged a bond. Steve was trying very hard to understand what his daughter was saying. At first, Kate had acted as an interpreter. However, because of the strained atmosphere between her parents, Kate asked Max to let her be alone with her father, and she would take her chances with the understanding bit. If push came to shove, she could write down anything important.

Max knew it was difficult for Kate. If she was going to get to know her father, she shouldn't have to feel like piggy in the middle of her parents. The truth was, Max took one look at Steve and a lot of the old feelings for him came flooding back. He hadn't gained an ounce of weight, and even though his brown hair had a smattering of grey now, it was still thick and cut in approximately the same style as it had always been. Within minutes of being together, Max knew that Steve still had strong feelings for her, too.

If she had known that he had regretted leaving her and his daughter every day of his life, and even though he had re-married, no one had ever come close to taking her place in his heart, she might well have understood his tension around her. Steve looked at the woman he thought of every day and fervently wished she had got fat and wrinkled or was changed and different; maybe then he could have shrugged his shoulders and put her to the back of his mind. But here she stood, even more beautiful than he remembered. Her hair was piled up on top of her head, with a few strands falling around her face. His fingers itched to reach up and twist a shiny copper wisp around his finger, but he clenched his hand against the urge. She wore faded denim jeans that clung to her slim thighs and a white cropped top that showed a lean and tanned midriff.

He reached out to shake her hand and, on contact, looked into her face. They both saw the other's reaction and, despite the years, still seemed to be in tune with each other's emotions.

"Hello, Max." Steve's voice was soft and caressing.

"Steve," Max answered abruptly, breaking eye and hand contact immediately. Her heart thudded heavily in her throat, and as she held out her hand towards Kate, it was visibly shaking. "This is Kate."

He looked at his daughter and saw some of the features he remembered. The bright hair, the freckles, the dark arched eyebrows, and the full, generous mouth. He held out both his hands and she took them. "Thank you for seeing me, Kate. You don't know how much I've looked forward to this day. Please forgive me for all the years I've been away from you. I know I can never make them up to you, but I'd like to spend as much time as I can getting to know you now if you'll let me."

Kate looked up into his face, released her hands from his, and wrapped her arms around him in a tight bear hug. He held his daughter to his chest, breathing in the fragrance of her hair, and felt the tears spill over onto his cheeks. Max walked away, feeling the lump in her throat and not wanting to show any more emotion in front of him. She stood and looked out of the window, shaken and jittery. Never in her wildest dreams could she have imagined the strength of feelings still between them after all this time. She had spent years hating him for what he had done to them, and now the hate seemed to disappear as soon as she looked at him. The whole thing was ridiculous.

The next hour was spent with Kate's hands fluttering quickly and Max reading them and translating to Steve. Kate watched her father's mouth and read his lips, except when he got emotional and dipped his head when Max took over again. All the time they were talking, she was physically aware of him right through to her toes. Drew turned up later on while they were drinking tea in the dining room. Max was pleased to see him and greeted him more warmly than she would normally have, meeting Drew's bemused face and raised eyebrows with a bright smile. Steve watched the two of them together and knew that they were lovers. The way they were at ease with each other and the way they touched without any awkwardness showed him that they knew each other very well. He felt his stomach contract with a jealous spasm and looked away.

For the next two meetings, the tension between them was a tangible thing, and Kate, with heightened senses, felt increasingly uncomfortable and was forced into requesting for her mother to stay away. Max didn't know whether to be glad or sad but respected her daughter's wishes and stayed away.

She kept herself busy, and when Steve phoned her at work, she told the receptionist to say she was in a meeting. He phoned twice more only to get similar excuses from the receptionist. After that, the calls stopped. Once again, Max didn't know whether to be glad or sad, but one thing she did know was that she had to stay away from him. She had no wish to start with him again, even though he appeared to have changed and was now well off and successful. Her relationship with Drew was important to her, and besides Steve was married now. She had found out the details from Kate who talked willingly now about her father. Steve's wife was quite a beauty by all accounts. American from the south, with a daddy who was a big something in the oil business. *Trust Steve to marry money,* Max thought spitefully.

It was only when she was low from worrying about Drew after Marty's death that she allowed Steve to see her again. She opened her heart to him and found him sympathetic and understanding. When he took her home, she had drunk nearly a bottle of wine with the meal, and the need for him again took over. Steve pushed her away from him. She went straight back at him, her mouth and hands all over him, but he was strong and determined.

"No, Max. Not like this. You're upset and you've had too much to drink. I'm not going to take advantage of that."

"Why, Steve?"

"Dammit, Max, you know why. Don't do this," he replied, pushing her hands away again.

"For Christ sake, Steve. What's the matter with you? I've never known you turn away from a bit of sex before," Max's voice was cutting as she lost her temper.

Steve walked towards the door. He turned around to face her, his hand on the handle. "You just don't get it, Max, do you?"

"Get what?"

"Whatever we had is still there, but it's all too late. Drew loves you and my wife loves me, and imagine what this would do to Kate."

"What do you want then?"

"I want us to be friends. I want us to be civil and adult."

With that, he went out through the door, quietly closing it behind him.

Max was thinking of this last meeting while driving to meet Drew. They were going to eat at the local inn and talk about his plans for the future, whatever they were, and then to see Kate a bit later in the weekend after her dad had left.

Drew stood and embraced her. She was so pleased to see him, and even though he didn't look at all well, she held him tight and felt her love for him flowing out towards him. *Whatever happens in my future,* she thought, *I hope it includes this man.*

CHAPTER 19

Once Jessica was back in Luke's life, she completely occupied his mind. He couldn't get enough of her and seemed to be thinking about her every waking moment. He hated to be away from her, and his day didn't begin until he was with her again. He moved some of his things into the cottage, and they spent their evenings in dressing gowns, in front of the fire with a glass of wine after a delicious meal, which was usually cooked by Luke.

As Jessica was still working on the final draft of the book, a lot of her day was spent in front of the computer, rewriting some of the chapters. She hated doing this, having to change anything of her work. Feeling that the mood she was in when she wrote it had been transmitted onto the page and would somehow be destroyed if it was changed in any way. But after what seemed like endless arguments, she finally came to a compromise and changed some of it. Stacey had said that it was tighter and more graphic, with some of the words trimmed away, but Jessica still wasn't happy. She and Stacey had quite a few heated arguments over the phone until, at one point, Luke looked at Jessica's white angry face, with her hair sticking up in angry spikes, and took the phone away from her.

"She'll work it out, Stacey, and call you back," he said calmly and broke the connection.

"How dare you do that," Jessica screamed at him. "You have no idea what this is all about. The final draft is due at the publisher's, and I still haven't finished it. How dare you hang up on Stacey? We were just in the middle of sorting it out."

Jessica flung herself into the kitchen and started to bang and crash the pots and pans. Luke sat back in the chair, gazing into the fire and draping his arm over the side of the chair, absentmindedly pulled Gertie's ears. The canine's eyes glazed over in ecstasy, leaning against the chair and grunting with the sheer pleasure of it all.

"How long do you reckon we ought to leave her before she dents all the pots, Gertie old girl."

Gertie partially opened one eye, moved one ear back towards the sound of his voice, and slipped even further down towards the prone position. The crashing of the pots grew fainter and still Luke sat gazing into the flames. A shadow cut out the light from the kitchen as Jessica stood in the doorway. Still, Luke didn't move.

"I'm sorry," said the little voice from the doorway.

Luke didn't move.

"Are you cross with me?" Jessica moved towards him and stood at the other side of Gertie's sprawling body.

"Yes."

"I'm sorry," Jessica said again. "It all seems to be getting a bit fraught lately."

"I noticed," Luke said, still gazing into the fire.

Jessica hovered about in the centre of the room, looking at Luke out of the corner of her eye whilst pretending to tidy the pile of newspapers on the coffee table, her anger now dissipated. Luke suddenly stood up, making Jessica jump and take a step back. He took her hand and pulled her towards the narrow stairway.

"What are you doing?" Jessica said, pulling against the firm grip of his hand.

"Only one thing I know for relieving tension that doesn't involve pills or violence."

Jessica looked at the broad back going up the stairs in front of her. "What's that then?" she felt her face curving into a smile.

"As if you didn't know," Luke turned her around to face him.

All the time looking deep into her eyes, he slowly unbuttoned her blouse and slipped it from her shoulders, unbuckled the belt of her jeans and slowly and sensually pulled it from the loops, and kneeling down in front of her, removed her sandals and after that, her jeans. Jessica slipped her feet out of the heap of denim and kicked it to one side. She buried her hands into the soft brown hair level with her breast and felt the goosebumps break out all over her body as his lips and tongue caressed her midriff and belly. Sinking back on his heels, Luke moved his attention lower down and she felt her panties being eased down her thighs, followed by the wetness of his tongue. Her breath was rasping in her throat now and she pulled at his hair, willing him to stand up.

As he unfurled his length from the floor, Jessica wondered again at the sheer size of him. She looked up at him while she unbuttoned his shirt and pulled it out from his trousers. She unbuckled his belt and pulled it slowly towards her, noticing the large bulge pushing out the front of the black cords. She knelt in front of him and removed his shoes and socks before unzipping him and sliding the tight trousers down his muscular thighs. She caressed him through the cotton of his pants and, standing up, removed her bra and rubbed herself over the soft hair on his chest. He sharply sucked in a deep breath and let it out in a moan.

They kissed deeply and long until as if by an unspoken agreement, they both moved towards the bed. Their lovemaking was slow and satisfying. Luke knew that this was the release of tension she needed, and he rolled them both over onto their sides, pulled the duvet over them, and held his woman tenderly, his own emotion very near the surface, and his eyes started to close with the feelings of happiness and pleasure.

Much later, when she was sleeping deeply, he crept downstairs and damped down the fire, dragged Gertie's basket out, and locked everything up before going back into the warm bed and curling his large body along Jessica's back.

CHAPTER 20

Drew was looking drawn and thin after meetings with his fellow directors and associates. He had had a long meeting with Max, had talked things through with her, and despite her arguments had stuck to the decision he had already made in his mind. He had felt restless for a long time now. Discontent with his life and jaded with his work. That feeling had been magnified a thousandfold after the death of Marty and then his work with Thomas and the other children over the last few weeks. He felt for the first time in years that he was doing something worthwhile, and he wanted to continue with it. The decision to sell his share in the business that he had spent so long building shocked everyone around the table except Max.

Adam rested his head in his hands. "I can't believe what I'm hearing. All the work we put into this venture when we broke away on our own. I thought this was it until early retirement, and now, just when we're doing so well, you drop this bombshell."

Drew rested his hand on Adam's shoulder and gave it a squeeze. "My heart wouldn't be in it if I stayed, and our clients would sense that. You know we have to believe in them to be able to get them the best deals. Sometimes, fighting all the way. Frankly, I don't think I can do that anymore. For years, I've been wheeling and dealing, telling myself that I was doing it for my family. All the days and weeks away, and all the distractions that brought, which I won't dwell on. This was supposed to give them everything they wanted, when all the time I was really only doing it for me, and all my family really wanted was a reasonable standard of living and me spending time with them."

"But we can arrange less hours for you. You only have to say," Adam said, running his hand through his thinning hair.

Drew's laugh was a short, sharp bark. "It's a bit late for that now, don't you think? My wife left me and carved out a successful career; my daughter has made her own life, which doesn't include me, and my son is," Drew lifted his hands, palms up, "gone." He sunk wearily down onto one of the chairs. "Why in hell would I want to take time off."

There was a silence around the table as everyone was lost in their own thoughts. Finally, weeks later, after three other board meetings, several meetings with the accountants, and a company audit, Drew was paid most of his portion of the business, but he retained shares as he was reluctant to cut all ties.

He cleared his office, feeling close to tears. Even though it was what he wanted, so much of him had gone into the success of the business, years of his life, all the headaches, stress, and late nights. Never would he have thought he would walk away from it in this way—could walk away. *Funny, the cards life deals you sometimes.* He stood in the middle of his office, soulless now without his belongings, and took a last look around.

"Drew, old son," Adam said from behind him, "can you come into the boardroom for a minute or two."

Drew put down the box he was holding and followed him. The boardroom was filled with people. All the employees of the company, the directors and associates, clients and friends. People they had done business with in the past, people he hadn't seen for years. They all started to applaud as soon as he entered the room. Drew was amazed. In the seclusion of his room, he hadn't heard any of these people arrive. *Where had they all come from, and how were they all contacted?*

He turned and looked at Adam's smiling face and felt the tears well up under his eyelids. Adam gripped him in a big bear hug, and Drew could feel his friend's body trembling with emotion. They held each other for long moments while they both composed themselves, the applause growing to a crescendo. Finally, they broke apart, and Drew was immediately surrounded by well-wishers and outstretched hands. The buffet, beautifully laid out by the caterers, was devoured, old acquaintances were renewed, and news caught up with, and eventually, the party started to split. Some had to journey home, some were staying in hotels overnight, and the lively ones continued on to a club till the early hours.

Adam and Cassie and Drew and Max went dancing. Drew was still not back to his old self after the traumas of the past months, so he took Max home, and they made beautiful love. It was the best for a long time, and Drew, for the first time since Marty's death, drifted off into a deep and dreamless sleep, his arms around a sleeping Max.

CHAPTER 21

Melanie and Caro leapt onto the platform and were wrapped in a tight, fragrant hug from Jessica. She had been asking them for weeks to come and visit now the book was finished and she had her life back. Since Marty's death, the two girls had grown close and had decided to share a flat. The big move had taken place a few weeks ago with Jessica paying the sale price. She wanted the girls to have every opportunity for a happy life, including not having to worry about a mortgage. The flat was big enough for each of them to have their own space, two bathrooms and a shared kitchen. It was almost like having two separate apartments on one floor. The builders had worked on the arrangements, the decorators had done their bit, and the girls had put their own personal touches themselves.

Drew had stumped up for the building work and decorators. He had a bit more free time at the moment and was constantly in and out bossing around the workmen. Sensing that his involvement would delay the work, Caro sent him away in the end. "For goodness sake, Dad," she said, hands on hips, "if you don't let everyone alone, they'll all be walking out and nothing will be done. They all know what they're doing. Go away. Find something else to do."

He went off with his tail between his legs, and the work was finished in time, and it was done properly in spite of all his grumbles. Jessie was kept up to date with every step, and even though she hadn't seen the flat yet, she felt she knew it intimately already.

The girls looked well. Melanie had taken quite a time to get over Marty's death after spending quite a few weeks with Sophia and her family. Her parents had come over to spend some time with her, but if the truth were known, she had nothing in common with them anymore. The family had split their ways so long ago they were almost strangers. Melanie felt a lot closer to Sophia than her mother. Their lives were different from hers in every way now. They had never met Marty and could only imagine what she had gone through after his death. Because she hadn't really known him that long, they seemed to think her grief didn't go very deep, and their attitude was that she would soon forget.

Melanie was actually glad when they went back. She felt guilty for feeling like that and talked it over with Sophia. They sat around the comfortable lounge, a pot of tea and warm scones on the low table, and talked. After the down to earth wisdom of Sophia, the situation didn't feel so bad, and Melanie felt able to get on with her life. Since her other flatmates couldn't keep her room open for her while she was away, she now found herself without accommodation. As her modelling had been put on hold, she wasn't earning any money and her savings were minimal. Hence came the idea from Caro. From the initial tentative talks, the whole thing snowballed, and now it was all done.

Jessica drove them back to the cottage; her Mercedes feeling like silk and purring like a kitten. She had always wanted something fast and classy, and with Luke's help, she had done the rounds of all the dealers before settling on this beauty. The girls exclaimed, "Wow! Super. Fantastic," and all the other superlatives that only made her glow even more.

The spare room in the cottage now had two single beds, and all the writing accoutrements had been pushed into the corner. The girls were completely bowled over by the place. After they had unpacked and had tea, Jessie took them for a drive along the coast road and a walk on the beach, culminating with a visit to Polly and John, who were expecting them all for supper. They all sat around the large kitchen table, talking nineteen to the dozen, when John walked in with Ben and Jack. Both his sons were taller than him and looked tanned and fit. The boys took an immediate interest in Melanie and Caro and sat down alongside the girls at the other end of the table, engaging them in a deep conversation about music, videos, and surfing the net.

John looked at them and raised his eyebrows. "Look at those two. One look at a female and they come out in a lather. No self-control, I say." He swept the hair from Polly's neck and nibbled it. "Don't know where they get it from."

Jessica threw her head back and laughed, and Polly swatted behind her with the tea towel she was holding. "Get off with you. You stink of dung."

John pulled his jersey up and sniffed it. "I can't smell anything." He addressed the rest of the group. "I don't smell, do I?"

They all said together in chorus, "Yes."

John grinned and headed for the stairs. "I suppose you can't all be wrong. Want to play with the soap, Pol," he looked lecherously at her.

"Bugger off," was her reply, and they all laughed.

The boys also went off to get changed; they promised the girls a walk down to the pub later as there was a local group playing who were very good.

They were all doing various tasks around the kitchen in preparation for supper when Luke turned up. Both the girls knew about him, but they hadn't met him. He seemed to fill up half the kitchen with his bulk. He greeted Polly warmly and kissed Jessica. The girls looked at him curiously from under their lashes until he turned and looked at them as Jessica did the introductions. The corners of his warm brown eyes crinkled, and his even white teeth smiled and welcomed them. There was such a warm feeling emanating from this big man that both girls liked him immediately.

The meal was chatty and noisy; at times, it seemed like everyone was talking at once. John was a past master at throwing a controversial remark into the conversation, waiting for someone to rise to the bait, and then sitting back with a smug smile on his face whilst havoc broke loose.

Eventually, they all strolled down the road to the pub. The group from a local village was belting out the music. Towards the end of the evening, they started playing well-known classic pop songs, and everyone joined in. All things considered, it was a good evening.

Ben and Jack were going off early to a car rally the next day, so they rang for a taxi. They also invited the girls to join them. Even though Luke hadn't slept apart from Jessica for weeks, either at his house or the cottage, in deference to Caro, he got the taxi to take him home. Jessica saw him leave with regret. She had gotten used to cuddling up with his warm body behind her or lying against his back with her arm draped across his middle. The bed would seem lonely without him.

Caro watched her mother's face and saw the fallen expression. As they walked into the cottage, she draped her arm across her mother's shoulders. "Why has Luke gone home? I thought he stayed with you now."

Jessica stopped and looked into her daughter's face. She would never get used to the fact that her little princess was all grown up and understood these things called relationships. Her perplexed looks forced Caro to laugh. "Oh, for goodness sake, Mum. He's a lovely bloke, and he loves you to bits. He must have hated being sent away. Please don't do it again. Anyway, I was looking forward to seeing him hanging out of that undersized-looking dressing gown behind the bathroom door."

Jessica chuckled and pushed her daughter playfully with her hip. "You've got no chance. That's a sight for my eyes only and viewed by anyone else by invitation only."

"Spoilsport," was all Caro replied, making Jessica laugh again.

Settling back into the darkness of the taxi, Luke cast his mind back to a brief part of the conversation around the table regarding the circumstances surrounding Marty's death. Nobody really wanted to talk about it, but when the conversation turned to the TV show, which was the reason Jessica had come back, it seemed to naturally follow on to the tragedy. From what Luke gathered, the reason for Marty running out into the path of the traffic was because he was chasing after Melanie, who was running from that Michael 'Whatsit' from the show. As soon as that part entered the conversation, Melanie stood up and walked away from the table. At the sight of her face, they all unanimously agreed that they would not pursue that subject anymore and quickly talked about other things until the tension eased. It was the only uncomfortable part of the whole evening. Luke, walking behind with John on the way to the pub, opened the subject again. John has also been dwelling on the same thing, so they deliberately dropped behind out of earshot.

"What do you reckon that fellow said to her to make her react so violently?" Luke said, zipping up his jacket and thrusting his hands in the pockets.

"Whatever it was, the girl's not telling."

"No, but even that seems odd. If he had insulted her or been crude, you'd have thought she would have said by now."

They walked in silence for a few yards. "Jessie said, 'Melanie tried to slap him and he laughed at her.' That's when she started running from him."

"Didn't the police ask what it was all about?"

John also buttoned up his jacket. The nights had a chill to them now. "Apparently, because Melanie nearly had a breakdown, the police couldn't seem to get anything out of her. The TV bloke said he just made a sexist remark and she took it the wrong way. Because everyone was concerned with the funeral, etc., the reason for him running out like he did seemed to be immaterial. After all, people do it all the time. Step out into the paths of oncoming cars and all that."

"Still, from what Jessie said, this TV bloke was a smarmy devil and tried to trip her up on a number of occasions during the interview. She didn't like him at all, and Jessie's very easygoing. Usually takes everyone with a pinch of salt. I've never heard her say she dislikes anyone."

"Yes, that's true. Jessie always sees the best in everyone. I think it's because of this attitude that, for years, people thought she was an insipid woman without a mind of her own." John gave a bark of a laugh. "But boy, has she proved everyone wrong on that score. She's become a woman to be reckoned with, and frankly, I've never seen her look better. She's self-assured, beautiful, and knows her worth. But then you knew all that from the beginning, didn't you." John looked at Luke from the corner of his eyes and saw the flash of white teeth. "I've never known you wait for anyone or pursue anyone like you did Jessie. Why?"

The teeth gleamed again, "Chemistry."

"Can't knock that for a reason. Best in the world."

They walked towards the pub door, where Polly was yelling at them to hurry up.

"Still, I'd like to talk a bit more about that Michael bloke sometime. I think there's something else here, and knowing what it is might make Marty's death more understandable."

"I'll be in touch soon," Luke said, then turned and kissed Jessica's flushed face as she waited for him in the doorway before pushing through the crowd to the bar.

CHAPTER 22

Drew watched Kate work with Thomas. The boy had come on in leaps and bounds. It was as if he had been marking time and was now in a rush to catch up. His capacity for learning was phenomenal. He demanded exclusive attention from all the teachers, driving them to call a meeting to determine what to do to cope with him. He soon realised that tantrums were not the way to get anything, but a happy smiling face was, and he soon had all the teachers wrapped around his finger. Some of the other children were getting resentful, and the meeting was to try to sort out some sort of rota to help them deal with it, as well as other matters regarding the running of the school.

Drew took over from Kate to allow her to meet up with the other teachers. She smiled at him as she rose to leave. "I'll let you know what we decide to do," she signed as she left.

Thomas looked up at Drew and smiled his brightest smile, genuinely glad to see him. Drew's hands told him in a hesitating way that the weather was too nice to stay in, and so they were going for a walk. Thomas ran to his room for his coat and Drew waited for him by the front door. Through the glass side panel, he watched with interest as a small, racy BMW slid to a halt just at the side of the steps. The door opened and a pair of long denim-clad legs emerged, followed by the rest of the body dressed in a black t-shirt and a short black suede jacket. The classy-looking woman swept the long blond hair back with a flourish of her hand and reached back into the car for a black briefcase, in the meantime allowing him a good look at her small, tight rear end.

She headed up the steps towards him and he backed away from the door, anticipating a smack on the nose. He wouldn't have been far wrong if he had stayed where he was. The door was literally flung open, and the long-legged blonde came striding through in high-heeled black boots. She glanced at him from the corner of her eye as she strode past and then slowed down and stopped. Turning on her heel, she looked at him, head slightly on one side. "Don't I know you?" she said after a slight pause. "Who are you?"

Drew heard the plummy voice, sensed the arrogant attitude, and responded in kind. "Who wants to know?"

"I do," the upper crust chin lifted and she looked at him down her nose.

Drew was beginning to enjoy this. "And who might you be?"

"Oh, for Christ sake, I haven't got time to play games," and she turned on her high heels and started marching down the hall.

The door to the staff room opened and Miss Bowen, the secretary, looked out. "Clara dear, I thought I heard your car. Come on in; we were expecting you." She then spotted Drew standing there and asked, "Hello, Drew dear. Going out?"

He was tempted to say, *no, he was going for a bath,* but this fluttery little woman, who was everyone's idea of a maiden aunt, would probably be terribly hurt by such a flippant remark. "Taking Thomas out," he said by way of a reply.

"Ah. Well, enjoy the day," and she bobbed back inside.

The statuesque woman looked at him for a few moments longer, her head again slightly on one side, before entering the room and shutting the door with a firm snick.

Thomas bounded down the stairs, his coat flying open and a scarf trailing on the floor behind him. Drew buttoned him up and they headed towards the woods at the edge of the grounds. They both learnt from these excursions into the outdoors. Learning to sign the names for things like leaves, flowers, birds, squirrels, and a multitude of other things they came across, followed up by looking for them in the many books in the school library.

Whilst Thomas was running ahead, diving about among the trees, burning off the excess energy natural for a boy of his age, and for the first time enjoying his life, Drew's mind again turned to the tall blonde. She was right to think she knew him. He also recognised her but couldn't remember from where. He racked his brain; it was there at the edge but annoyingly eluded him. If he pushed the thoughts away, he would remember eventually. He started running towards Thomas, who broke into high laughter and sprinted away. Drew forgot everything but the enjoyment of the chase.

In the staff room, the meeting progressed regarding the many details to be sorted out for the smooth running of the school. They arranged for one of the older pupils to take Thomas under his wing. The boy was a bright scholar, and they were all sure he would enjoy teaching the boy as much as Thomas would enjoy learning. That way it would release the teachers from Thomas' constant demands. However, uppermost in everyone's minds was the financing for the essential repairs and improvements paramount for the upkeep of the old house. There was damp showing in some of the bedrooms, necessitating a roof inspection and possible costly repairs. The bathrooms badly needed retiling, the kitchens needed new equipment urgently, and the furniture in some of the recreation rooms needed repairing or replacing. Nobody wanted to put the fees up for the parents who could afford to pay, and they were not going to get a grant from anywhere, so it was again a case of prioritising the most essential work and hoping for additional funds from somewhere.

Miss Bowen bustled in with the tea and a large fruit cake she had helped cook earlier, to be met with a gloomy silence and despondent faces. Everyone was lost in their thoughts about the future of the school. Kate rapped on the table and they all looked at her. "I'm going to phone my mother to see if she has any ideas, and I'll also ask Drew. They work with a lot of wealthy people and maybe they know of a way to raise some cash."

Clara signed quickly, "Who's Drew?"

Miss Bowen read Clara's hands and said, "Drew is Mr Andrew Cameron, a friend of Kate's mother. You saw him when you came in. He's helping us with Thomas and spends time with the children when he can. He's had his own personal traumas to deal with and has left his London business because of them."

Miss Bowen's voice stuttered to a halt as she realised she might have said too much and given away private details. She was relieved when the others nodded and agreed.

Clara snapped her fingers. "I knew I'd seen him somewhere before. His company used to deal with the advertising for my late husband's business before the takeover. Thanks to the advertising, the business sold for so much. My husband's health was not good even then, and the rise in the share prices allowed him to sell for a good price and spend his last months in peace."

Kate had been reading Clara's lips and signed again, "My mother is now a partner in the business, but Drew sold out after his son's death."

Clara leant back in her chair, chewing her lip thoughtfully. A plan was forming in her mind involving Drew and all his contacts, and also all her many contacts among the aristocracy. *Well, Lady Clara,* she thought, *surely having a title must be worth something.* A smile curved her full mouth. *A benefit with TV and film stars, contacts courtesy of Drew, mixing with a smattering of lords and ladies, courtesy of me.* The smile widened.

Larry Flowers watched the smile and felt his chest tighten with longing. He was a tall, angular man with thinning hair, a terrible dress sense, and a heart of gold. He had also been in love with Clara from the first time he had seen her. She had never given him any more than a cursory glance and the odd word—and never would—but just the thought of her being in the same world as him was enough.

The others had also noticed the smile. "Are you going to share it with us, whatever it is?" a young trainee teacher called Judy said.

"All in good time," Clara said mysteriously. "All in good time."

The meeting broke up, and Clara hung around playing with the children for as long as she could. Finally, more than an hour later, with no signs of Drew returning, she decided to go. She sought out Kate and confided in her she needed to speak to Drew regarding her fundraising idea. She swore Kate to secrecy and arranged to return the following day at a time when Drew would be available. He was house hunting in the area and had arranged to meet the estate agent there at three. Clara intended to get there first. There had to be a way of getting her idea off the ground, and she would use every trick in the book to do it.

CHAPTER 23

After another small piece of re-writing, Jessica's book finally went off to the publishers to be printed, and the advertising hype got started. She had approved the cover of the book, and it was already appearing in some advance publicity articles. Jessica had used the writing of the book as a catalyst for her grief, and even though some of it had been altered, the main re-writing had been towards the end of the book. Jessica was glad about that. Every time she read the first half of the book, she ended up in floods of tears, her son's tragic and untimely death sharply back in the forefront of her mind. Luke knew that the grief had to come out and mainly left her alone at these times, but always hovering around not far away just in case she needed him. He remembered reading somewhere that some of the world's best literature had been written at a time when the authors were sad or depressed. From what Stacey had told him, this new book was going to be a massive bestseller.

The phone calls had started in earnest regarding book signing dates, television shows, and radio interviews. It seemed like Stacey was permanently on one end or other of a phone that was almost super glued to Jessica's ear. Luke knew it was something that he would have to get used to, but he missed their long walks, cosy chats, and leisurely dinners in front of the fire. He had handed a lot of the running of his business over to his manager, but as Jessica was frequently travelling up to London for meetings and whatever, he started spending more time back in his office.

He was still in touch with Kevin, who had made leaps and bounds and now had his own small building business in Spain. The scope for quality houses for people retiring to Spain and also timeshare accommodation for an international company was ripe for some investigation on Luke's part, and Kevin had been asking him to come over. He had tried to talk Jessica into a short trip over before the real onslaught started, but he could see that it wasn't possible. However, when she decided to stay over with Caro and Melanie for a few days instead of travelling backwards and forwards, Luke decided to go to Spain to have a look around and weigh up the possibilities of starting up with Kevin. The winter months were a busy time for the building trade. This enabled the properties to be ready for the summer visitors and Luke knew that this was the time he would have to go if any contracts were to be tendered for.

Jessica gave him the villa keys to check that everything was OK. A security firm regularly checked the residence, but it was the perfect place for Luke to stay while he was there. He had only seen it from the outside and was looking forward to seeing inside the place where Jessica had hidden away for so long and where she had first started writing.

Jessica drove him to the airport, and they clung together. Their goodbye was painful and, for Jessica, tearful. They hadn't been apart for months and she really wanted to go with him. She wanted to be with him to show him around her house and garden. She wanted to take him walking on her favourite beach and for a drink in her favourite bar. The restaurants who knew her and cooked her favourite foods would have been overjoyed to meet him. They were never happy that she was always alone and would have wrapped Luke in their warmth and kindness. All these things made her regret not going with him. She had tried very hard, but there were just too many things to rearrange. It just hadn't been possible at all, so it was with a very sad face that she waved him through the departure lounge and dragged herself back to her car.

Caro and Melanie had cooked a beautiful meal, and their bright faces, happy smiles, and chatter went someway to cheering her up.

However, she only really cheered after a phone call from Luke as soon as he had landed, telling her he loved her and was missing her already and promised to phone her every day.

After the meal, Jessica intercepted a very meaningful look from Melanie towards Caro. Then Melanie very pointedly said that she would do the washing as Caro wanted a chat with her mum. Caro looked down at her hands when Melanie squeezed her shoulder, walking by her chair. "Everything will be OK. I know." With a smile at Jessica, she went out into the kitchen.

Jessica was intrigued and sat quietly watching her daughter. After a lengthy silence, while Caro cleared her throat and wetted her lips, she finally said, "Caro, whatever it is; for goodness sake, spit it out or we'll be here all night."

Caro sat up straight, squared her shoulders, looked into her mother's face, and said boldly and defiantly, "I'm pregnant."

Jessica felt her jaw dropping open. Her heart seemed to miss a beat, and she sat back in her seat and looked into her daughter's lovely face. Caro's eyes looked frightened even as her chin went up a few inches. "Darling, that's wonderful but I didn't even know you were seeing someone seriously." Jessica sadly realised that she had been so busy she had lost touch with her daughter for quite a few months. "Is it someone I know?"

Caro's chin went down and started to tremble. "It's no one you know, but Dad does. It's someone who works in his office, or rather his former office."

"Your father knows you are pregnant?" Jessica said in a shocked voice.

"Not yet. I wanted to tell you first."

There was silence for several long minutes whilst both women were lost in their own thoughts.

"Do you want this baby, Caro?"

"Oh yes, Mum. I really do."

"Are you sure?"

"Very sure."

"And the father, does he also want it?"

Caro frowned. "I think so."

Jessica leant forward in her seat. "Not good enough, Caro. This is a very important decision that will affect your whole life. Or at least it will for about 18 years or more of it. Being a single parent is hard work and not a choice to be made lightly. Why are you not sure of the father's feelings?"

Caro stood up and began to pace back and forth, something she had always done when she was thinking right from the time she was a child. It was as if it was impossible to think sitting down. Sure enough, the thoughts in her head were transferred into speech. "His name is Ashley Mead. He works in Dad's office as a personal agent for some very big names. The first time I saw him, something clicked, but I didn't think he would even notice me except maybe because I was the director's daughter. He is always busy on the phone, with lots of evening functions to attend as well."

She paused in her pacing and chewed the side of her thumbnail. Another trait from her childhood. "He managed to wheedle my phone number out of Dad's secretary and called me up. We talked for hours and made a date to meet. He took me to a lovely, quiet bistro, and we were still there at closing time. He even switched off his mobile, which is the ultimate act of commitment as far as he is concerned." Smiling at this thought, Caro stopped and stared into space, her face alive and glowing.

Jessica looked at her daughter's face. She had seen that look before. It was the look on the faces of people who were in love. Caro faced her mother. "We have seen each other every day since. It's like we are soul mates. We spent several days in Paris when he had to go over for business and it was the most fantastic and romantic time I have ever had. He is five years older than me and has had hundreds of girlfriends, which worried me at first, but after spending so much time with him, I know that with me, it's something different."

Jessica's first thoughts were ones of dismay. He sounded a bit of a Jack the Lad, and even though her daughter had had numerous boyfriends, she had never seen her like this, and it was disturbing. *Was she going after someone who was like her Dad?*

"You still haven't said why he is unsure about the baby."

Caro started pacing again. "He has always had such a busy life and none of his other relationships have ever lasted very long. I think he's a bit scared of the strength of his feelings and the responsibility of a family even though we have talked about our future."

"I see," was all Jessica could say.

"Mum, I love him so much and he loves me."

"Why didn't you take precautions until he was sure," Jessica ran her hand through her hair. "What happens if he decides the commitment is too heavy?"

Caro sat down and looked into her mother's eyes. "Because it wasn't planned. It happened on the spur of the moment. He had never pushed me into sex, but one day, it was such a wonderful day that it was so right."

Jessie knew how that felt. "So what if he decides it isn't what he wants?"

"Then I shall be the best single mum in the world and you will be the best grandma."

Jessie's hands reached across the table and clasped her daughters. "Then so be it," she said, smiling. "Hell, a grandma, how about that? Don't know what your dad's going to say about being a granddad. That will fizzle the lead out of his pencil."

Hearing the laughter, Melanie came back into the room and all three women stood in a group hug with tears in their eyes.

"When am I going to meet this Ashley then?" Jessica said, stepping back.

The two girls exchanged glances. "Tonight, as soon as I phone him," Caro said, reaching for her mobile.

"Well, I'd better go and powder my nose then."

Melanie touched Jessica's arm as she turned for the bathroom and Caro went to the bedroom with the phone. "I'd just like to say Ashley's a lovely guy. He thinks the world of Caro and the only reason she hasn't said anything before was because of her dad. He tried to warn Ashley off, and at the time, Ash was scared he'd lose his job. I think Drew likes him, and even though he's not part of the company now, Ash has so many contacts personally that I don't think the company could afford to let him go. Certainly, not over a private matter, anyway. You know me by now and I would have said something to you if I thought Caro was going to get hurt. Myself, I think Ash will come up to the mark. He's just got to get used to the idea first."

When Ashley turned up half an hour later and Jessie saw the look on his face when he greeted her daughter, she caught her breath and felt the absence of Luke like a sharp pain. It was the same look she had seen earlier on Caro's face and the one that Luke saw on hers. She knew at that moment she was going to have to accept this relationship or pick up the pieces.

Thankfully, her daughter's lover was a charming and likeable man. He was very charismatic, and by the end of the evening, he had wormed his way very firmly into Jessica's heart.

CHAPTER 24

Drew drove back into London early to try to miss the worst of the traffic. He wanted to see Jessica while she was there. Even though he had cut ties with the company, he was still deeply involved in the promotion of Jessica's books. Stacey worked closely with him on all the publicity aspects and, between the two of them, managed to cover all available media coverage. Due to his business engagements, for the first time, he had not actually read Jessica's book yet. He hoped to rectify this in the next couple of days. He had also had a message on his mobile from Ashley about 'the pedestal toppling.' That subject was one he was very eager to find out about.

He was going straight to Caro's flat to meet Jessica and Stacey. He wanted to get up to speed on the launch plans so far, get a copy of the manuscript to peruse later in his hotel room, and meet Ashley in the afternoon at a private place of his choosing. He was looking forward to the day. Since pulling out of the company, he had been very laid back. His days seemed to be split between school and house hunting; he was looking forward to a bit of hustle and bustle for a change.

The journey went quite well, apart from a bit of a jam in the usual places, and he arrived in good time. He had stopped on the way and bought several bunches of flowers and some croissants and rang the doorbell in good spirits. Jessica was still in her dressing gown and had wet hair when she answered the door. Her face broke into a happy smile when she saw him. "Drew, how lovely to see you, and what lovely flowers. Come in. Caro's taken the day off and is still in the shower. Melanie's got a photo shoot today along the Thames somewhere and has already left. I'll put a pot of coffee on."

Jessica bustled about finding a vase for the flowers and chattering about the book. Drew watched her. He had heard from Stacey that Luke was back in Jessie's life and he could see the change in her already. She had got her glow back. Drew felt a pang of jealousy, which he pushed away.

"Just excuse me for a few minutes while I get dressed."

Drew poured a cup of coffee and munched on a croissant while he gazed out of the window at the road and rooftops from the kitchen window.

"Hi, Dad. You're here early."

"Thought I'd beat the worst of the traffic," Drew said, turning around.

He gave his daughter a tight hug and leant back to look at her. She also looked glowing and a bit bashful, not meeting his eyes. "What's wrong sweetheart?" he said, sensing something not quite right.

"I'm fine, Dad. Is that fresh coffee? I'm parched." She pulled away and poured herself a cup.

Drew looked at her and wanted to ask again what was wrong. She seemed very tense. After taking one sip of her coffee, she pulled a face and tipped it down the sink.

Jessica came through the door with her hair dry and shiny and dressed in jeans and a pink tee shirt. Sensing the atmosphere she crossed over to the coffee pot and poured a large mug full.

"What's going on?" Drew said, feeling a bit alarmed. "I seemed to have walked into a strained waft of air here. Have you two had a fight?"

"No," Caro and Jessica said together.

"What then?"

"Dad, bring your coffee and let's go in the lounge. There something I need to tell you," said Caro.

Now, Drew was feeling decidedly uneasy and must have showed it.

"It's OK," Jessica said, linking her arm with his. " It's nothing bad."

Drew sat on the sofa bolt upright and ill at ease. "Come on then, out with."

Caro sat on the chair opposite and leant back, and Jessie stood behind her with her hand on her daughter's shoulder. "Well, you know I've been seeing Ashley and we've got quite serious."

Drew interrupted, "Don't tell me you want to bloody marry him," and started to laugh. "You must have more sense than that. He'll probably promise anything to get you into his bed."

Caro's eyes filled with tears and she rushed from the room. Drew looked totally gobsmacked and stood up, staring at the slammed door. "What the hell have I said now?"

Jessie gave out a sigh. "You never learn, do you? Why couldn't you just sit and listen for a change instead of putting in your two pence worth? She's been on hot bricks since she got up this morning planning what she wanted to say, and you've mucked it all up already."

Drew sat down again. "What's so important she had to make out a script before she could talk to me? We've never had a problem before. Can't you tell me what it's all about?"

"Yes, I could, but I'll have to check with Caro first." Jessica disappeared out of the door.

Drew paced about while he waited. Finally, Jessie and Caro came back. Caro was sniffing and twisting a tissue between her fingers.

Drew walked over to her and wrapped his arms around her. He led her over to the sofa and sat her down. Kneeling in front of her, he tipped her chin up so she was looking at him. "OK, sweetheart. I'm listening now. Talk to me."

"Please, Dad, don't say bad things about Ashley. I love him and we are going to have a baby."

Caro's chin went up even higher in defiance. Drew rocked back on his heels. He could feel his mouth drop open in shock. He stood up and thrust his hands into his pockets. He felt like punching the wall with anger. Jessie saw the look she recognised all too easily. "Caro sweetheart, I need to talk this over with your dad. Go and make us a fresh pot of coffee and bring it through here along with those nice croissants your dad brought."

"But I need to be here," Caro said, her face white and her voice quivering.

"You can be, sweetheart, in a little while."

After Caro reluctantly left the room, Drew sat down and put his head in his hands. "I can't believe it. How could she be so stupid? I warned her about him. She's just a child."

"Oh, for God's sake, Drew," Jessica exploded. "She's 23 years old. When I was that age, I already had two children, and if you remember, my parents warned me about you, too. And as for being stupid, that's one thing your daughter definitely isn't.

"She loves Ashley and he loves her, and whatever happens, she wants this baby. I want her to have it, too, and I will love being a grandparent, and I'll help her all I can. So you see, we don't really need you or your approval, but it would be so good for Caro if she had it. After all, you might actually like being a granddad."

After this outburst, Drew sat quietly. Unbidden, mental pictures slipped into his mind of the time his children were born and the feelings that flooded through him the first time he held them in his arms. Suddenly, he wondered if he would get the same feelings when he held his grandchild for the first time. He could feel his throat closing up. He looked up at Jessica and smiled. "I wonder how Max and Luke will feel about sleeping with grandparents."

Jessie laughed, knowing it would be OK. Just at that moment, Caro came in with the coffee.

The morning passed quickly with both Jessica and Drew getting into the swing of being soon-to-be grandparents. They swapped stories about the little things in their children's lives that had made them laugh and left indelible memories, going quiet from time to time when the stories were about Marty. But, by and large, it was a good morning, and Drew left feeling buoyed up and happy.

He contacted Ashley on his mobile when he got to his car. He deliberately didn't mention about hearing the news as he wanted to be face-to-face with Ashley when they talked about Caro and the baby. Even though he had now accepted that Caro was going to have the baby, he still wanted to sound Ashley out his feelings about it all. It would make no difference to the outcome, but for Caro's sake, it would be so much easier with the baby's dad around.

They arranged to meet in the coffee shop around the corner from Drew's old office. Parking was a headache as usual, and Ashley was already there with a pot of coffee when Drew got there. After some general chit-chat about what was happening in the office and in Ashley's world, Drew straight away ploughed in about the baby. "I ought to punch you on the nose," Drew said, faking an angry laser-blue stare into Ashley's face.

It kind of took the wind out of his sails when Ashley burst out laughing. "You're a bit late, mate. Caro already phoned and told me you knew about the baby and were OK with it. So the angry father act won't work now."

"I'm not worried about the baby. With a doting grandmother and all the other friends who will be on hand, it will be pampered to bits. No, I need to know about you. Are you going to be there for your child or are you going to be swanning all over the place and leaving my daughter on her own? I told you before what would happen if you hurt her. So if you don't want to make a commitment and accept your responsibilities, you had better be honest and tell me now."

Ashley was tempted to throw some details about Drew's life at him. Some of his old exploits had been common knowledge around the office, and Caro had told him the reason her parents had finally split up. However, this did not seem quite the time to antagonise his potential father-in-law. "I love Caro and I want to be with her. I'm already flat-hunting for a bigger place. I still need to be in town for work, and Caro doesn't want us to live too far out or she's not going to see me till late by the time I travel home. Later on, when the baby is older, we are going to have to move into somewhere with a garden, and away from all the traffic and stuff, but for the moment we will rent somewhere. Trouble is, when the baby comes, with a buggy and shopping and stuff, we really need somewhere on a ground floor, and that's like looking for gold dust."

Drew listened to all this and knew from the expression on Ashley's face that he was taking it all seriously, hoping that the novelty wouldn't wear off any time soon. "Are you getting married then?"

"Of course, I wanted to arrange something right away, but your daughter wants to be a slim, beautiful bride and not a fat, pregnant, beautiful one. There was nothing I could do to change her mind, so it's been postponed until after the birth and she's got her figure back."

"Yeh, my daughter is a stubborn girl."

"You can say that again. Anyway, can we get on to the other subject in hand? I've got an appointment later."

"Fire away, I'm all ears," Drew said, waving his hand at the waitress for another pot of coffee.

"Well, first off, I'm not going to tell you the real name of the bloke who I'm dealing with, so for the moment, we'll call him Fred Smith. He thinks I've picked up some rumours from one of my contacts about Michael Swift, and he's digging as deep as he can to see if there is any truth in any of them. So far, it seems there is quite a lot of dirt already sticking to him. The woman everyone thinks is his sister is really only his adopted sister. No one knows who his real parents were, but he was adopted when he was about five years old. The Swifts already had a daughter, Christy, and the two were brought up together. Fred Smith talked to one of their old neighbours, and they thought that there was something a bit unnatural about the relationship between the two kids. They said they looked a bit too close. Nothing they could put their finger on, just an uncomfortable feeling around them. Apparently, the school was worried about it, too, and had a meeting with the parents. One of the teachers, long retired now, remembered how Michael was always chasing the girls, and locked one in a cupboard with him. She complained to her parents about him, and there was a bit of a furore. The upshot was that the parents took him out of that school and enrolled him in an all-boys boarding school. Academically, he knuckled down and did very well, although he made up for it when he came home between terms."

"But this is all ancient stuff," said Drew.

"I'm just giving you the background. Hold your horses; we're getting there. Anyway, they both seemed to disappear for several years. The general opinion is that they went overseas. Both the parents died within months of each other, and the two of them sold up the house and left. Fred said he tried but couldn't find out where they'd gone, but he's still trying. Anyway, they suddenly surfaced again about nine years ago. Michael got a job as a presenter on a local radio station and was such a hit that he progressed upwards onto a regional TV station, where he lost no opportunity getting his sister into every show he could. He's apparently always been a good talker, so eventually, he moved onto bigger and better things."

"How about something to eat?" Drew said suddenly. "All this coffee is rumbling around in my guts something awful."

Ashley got a menu and they ordered some toasted sandwiches, sticky buns, and a pot of tea.

"What do you reckon about him and his sister? Does your guy think there was something incestuous there or is it just gossip," Drew said, his mouth full of sandwich.

"Don't know, really, although I think it's a bit more than gossip. Most of the details have come from very reliable sources not people who normally scaremonger."

"So what more is there, or is this as far as he's got?"

"He is talking to a lot of showgirls and models, and it seems Swift promises them contracts for modelling jobs and acting jobs if they are nice to him. So far, that is as much as he's got. None of the girls seem very willing to spill the beans on him completely. It's like he has some sort of hold on them. He thinks they are scared of ruining their careers if they talk too much. Swift's almost a national celebrity. All his visits to the front line with the army, trips to the famine-torn countries to report, etc. The public thinks he's wonderful, so I suppose some little girl is not going to be believed if she tries to say he's a bad man. The only way to do it is for all of them to come forward with their stories at the same time, but Fred doesn't think that's very likely."

"So what now? We don't seem to have anything to go on so far," Drew said, running his hands through his hair. "It's been quite a few weeks now and all we have is some ancient history."

Ashley poured out the last of the tea, which looked cold and stewed and drank it, then pulled a face. "Fred's still digging. He's convinced there's a lot more to it than he's got. He can sense a story from ten miles away, and he wouldn't keep pursuing this if it was a waste of time, so we'll just have to be patient for a bit longer. He'll get back to me when he's got anything else. He's like a dog with a bone."

Ashley stood up. "Got to go, going to be late. Are you coming round to the flat for dinner tonight? I think Jessica's cooking."

"Probably," Drew said. "Although I've got a fair bit of reading to do for the rest of today. Can't promote a book if you haven't read it."

They parted company with a handshake and a "thank you" from Drew.

CHAPTER 25

Luke was missing Jessica like hell. he arrived at her villa in a taxi after an uneventful flight. The ground floor of the villa had two garages and a large storage room housing a ride-on mower and other garden tools. He switched off the security alarm at the front door and went up the stairs to the living area. He stood and looked at the huge, airy lounge and could almost see Jessica in it.

The walls were all painted white, with a white tiled floor and several large comfortable sofas and chairs covered in white calico. In the centre of the arrangement of seats was a big, thick, brightly coloured rug with a white-painted glass-top coffee table on it. On the walls were paintings in bright hues—a flamenco dancer, a golden beach with azure seas, an orange sunset—and there were cushions in all colours and fabrics heaped on the sofas. On a white wooden corner unit was a large TV with a DVD player and a music system. The room's wide glass doors opened onto the veranda, which ran around the whole first floor and there were shutters for all the windows. These kept out the sun on hot days and were able to be double-locked for security. The room was huge, uncluttered, and cool.

Luke wandered through to the bedrooms. All three large bedrooms were also painted white with white gauze curtains and were carpeted in deep dark green. The beds were king-size and covered in white Spanish lace and coloured cushions. Each bedroom had its own en suite, and the one adjoining the master bedroom had a big circular Jacuzzi as well as a double-sized shower.

Luke wished he had been with Jessica when this beautiful house had been planned. He probably would have argued with her on some of the things and looking around him, he wouldn't have wanted to really change a thing. It was all perfect.

And he missed her like hell.

The kitchen was completely functional, with lots of cupboards and spacious worktops. He went down a flight of stairs in the corner of the kitchen into a large utility room containing a washing machine, dryer, sinks, etc., and let himself out to the back of the house. He used the bunch of keys to open a door at the side of the swimming pool and went into a tiled changing room with a shower and racks of towels, sun cream, and swimsuits. The door next to it had sun loungers and pool furniture stacked neatly inside. Looking at the covered pool, Luke lifted the cover and saw clear water and a well-maintained pool. He thought it looked too inviting to waste. Returning upstairs, he dragged his swim shorts out of the case and returned to the pool and removed the cover. He powered through the water at a fast crawl. After dozens of laps, he showered and dried off with one of the towels from the changing room before laying on the grass and enjoying the last warm rays of the setting sun before getting dressed.

And he still missed her like hell.

He phoned Kevin and arranged to meet him later for dinner. He scrawled the directions to the restaurant on the back of an old envelope and pushed it in his back pocket. He used the code Jessica had given him to open the safe at the back of one of the pictures. Here, he found the keys to the garage and to the small 4x4 run about she used every day. The keys were also there for the BMW estate car Stacey often used to transport books, cardboard stand-up posters, and visuals used for book signings, etc.

Luke started the Jeep on the second try and drove it around to the front of the house. He checked the gauge for fuel. There was enough for this evening but he would have to fill up before going anywhere else. He decided to unpack before going out. He was travelling fairly light, so he just looked for a spare drawer for his underwear, socks, and t-shirts. Most of the drawers contained a variety of Jessica's tops and shorts; a couple had swimsuits and underwear. The very bottom one caught his eye. It had two shoe boxes filled with photographs.

Luke dragged them out and sat on the bed with one of them on his lap. He supposed he should have felt guilty for looking at Jessica's personal stuff, but he didn't. He looked with interest at a very young Jessica with a super slender body and a mane of tumbled hair. He looked at a slightly older Jessica with her babies. She had a glow about her, with her hair tied up in a ponytail and a face bare of makeup. There were photos of Christmas parties, children's birthday parties, and holidays with a young and plump Polly, a tanned John, and their sons.

Luke went through the photos carefully and with interest. The whole of Jessica's life was chronicled here and he was fascinated. Seeing her in a beautiful glittering evening gown with her hair piled high on her head took his breath away. The sight of her as brown as a nut in a brief bikini held his attention for many minutes, and a large photo of her laying on a rug with her hair spread out around her and a child lying on each shoulder and looking up into her face was just beautiful.

Luke felt a stab of jealousy that so much of her life hadn't included him but shrugged it off. After all, a lot of his diverse life wasn't with Jessica and that's the way it was. You can't change history. *But she's with me now,* he thought, his mouth curving into a smile. *We will just have to make our own memories.*

He placed the boxes on the floor at the side of the bed to check later and prepared to meet Kevin. He was feeling very hungry and was looking forward to something good to eat. He planned to phone Jessica later and catch up with all the news.

He carefully locked up, took the envelope from his back pocket, and drove off into the orange sunset. He was missing her now more than ever after seeing her face looking at him in the photos, but he would enjoy his evening and look forward to speaking to her later. He was whistling when he locked the Jeep and entered the hotel to meet a smiling Kevin.

CHAPTER 26

Jessica was rushed off her feet every day. She had the first hard-backed edition of the book from the printers and was disappointed with the cover. In her mind, she had a very graphic idea of what the characters should look like, and even though she had approved the cover previously, now it was in front of her she didn't like it. After several meetings with the artist and quite a few unsuccessful attempts, they finally agreed on a completely different cover.

Jessica was feeling a bit drained and decided to do some shopping. Stacey was negotiating a spot on a women's radio show. It was an afternoon show, and the general idea was to talk to Jessica about her life, the reason she started to write, and also the inspirations behind her books. Stacey was not quite sure if Jessica really wanted to explain the reason for her recent book. Even though Marty's death was some time ago now, the whole subject was still very raw and fresh in Jessica's mind. The woman that Stacey was to meet had spoken to her at some length on the phone and, for a more private discussion, had arranged to meet her for lunch.

She turned out to be a grey-haired lady who was smartly dressed and had a warm and friendly smile. They ordered lunch and Stacey talked for a while about how she met Jessica and started to work for her. She left out many of the private details, like Jessica running away from both Drew and Luke, her relationship with Luke, and the death of her son. The latter event was well documented and no surprise, but discussing it on air would be Jessica's choice. It was a bad idea to bring the subject up, and then Jessica refusing to talk about it. Better it should be glossed over or just touched on.

Flora Allen, the producer of the show, thought otherwise. "Many of our listeners have faced bereavement and, in some cases, had to come to terms with outliving their children. They also have had to deal with divorce, loss of income, and social standing. They've had to start learning to deal with loneliness and having to resume work again when they have no recent skills. In fact, all the obstacles that Jessica overcame. So really, the franker the interview is, the better for our listeners."

Stacey thought about this and answered slowly. "I do see your point and the interview would be very interesting if conducted on those lines. I will put it to Jessica and see how she feels about it, but I'm afraid the final decision will be hers. She is concentrating on the promotion of her new book at the moment and may not wish to include intimate details of her life in any interviews."

"But surely, as I understand it, the death of her son was the main inspiration for the latest book."

"Yes, it was," Stacey replied, signalling for the bill, "But it will still be Jessica's choice how far she is prepared to go to talk about it."

"Well, let me know ASAP. We are very keen to do this interview, and I'm sure it will help enormously with the book promotion."

Stacey shook Flora's hand, gave her a business card, and told her she would be in touch. Making her way back to the car park, she ruminated on the conversation. An interview on the more intimate details of Jessica's life would be interesting stuff, but once all those details were out, they could never be retracted. From a privacy point of view, not really a good idea. Still, it was Jessica's choice.

Meanwhile, Jessica was having a relaxing browse around the shops. She had bought a new briefcase and an umbrella. Hardly retail therapy. She sat down at an outside table at a coffee bar and ordered a cappuccino. She sat quietly, watching the people go by, until she suddenly became aware of the man at the next table. He was staring intently at her and it was starting to make her feel uncomfortable. She finished her coffee quickly and, picking up her bags, started to move away. The man also got up from the table and stood right in front of her. His face in her face. "What do you want?" Jessica could hear her voice quivering.

She could now smell him. She realised he was a very dirty and unsavoury person, and she was starting to feel afraid. She looked around her, but most of the people seemed to be on the other side of the road. The man grabbed at her bags, and for some unknown reason, she held on to them. The man started yelling at her to let go and raised his other arm to hit her. She could feel the scream building up inside her, and just as her mouth opened, the man was spun around and thrown to the ground. The young waiter had the man's arm halfway up his back and was telling him to stay down. He was joined by another waiter who put his arm around Jessica and sat her down on one of the chairs. She was shaking and the man on the ground was still shouting. Many of the words were unintelligible, and then Jessica realised the attacker wasn't English and was drunk. It seemed from nowhere that a policeman turned up. It transpired later that he was across the street with another policeman arresting a shoplifter. He soon took charge and handcuffed the still-shouting man.

"Are you OK, darling," the second waiter said in a rich cockney accent.

"I think so," Jessie said shakily.

"Let me get you something stronger to settle your nerves." He went back inside.

A police van turned up and the man was bundled inside. The officer took a statement from Jessica and also from the young waiter who had been watching it all from inside.

"Flipping drunken bum," he said, sitting down at the table beside her. "I've already thrown him out once and the bloody bloke came back again. I was just about to move him on when I saw him attack you. Are you OK?"

"I will be," Jessica said. "It all happened so fast I haven't had time to think."

The first waiter turned up with a large brandy and insisted Jessica had a few sips.

"Can I get you a taxi?" the young waiter said in a very well-educated voice. "How far have you got to go?"

"Yes, I would like a taxi, thank you. I think I've had enough of shopping for today. It turned out to be somewhat nerve-wracking."

The young waiter laughed and looked closely at her. "Don't I know you?"

Jessie laughed. "I don't think so."

"I'm sure I've seen you before," the waiter said, a frown wrinkling his smooth brow.

"I'm sure you must see hundreds of people every week. I probably look like someone else."

A taxi turned up and the waiter opened the door for her. Just as the taxi pulled away he ran alongside and shouted. "You're an author. My sister reads your books."

Jessica just smiled and waved before collapsing back into the seat. She was very glad to be back in Caro's flat and poured herself a large glass of red wine. She flopped down onto the sofa and the young waiter's face swam before her eyes. She suddenly remembered with a jolt that she hadn't even asked him his name. She felt bad about that. If it hadn't been for him, she might have been hurt or, at the very least, robbed. She would make a point of going back and thanking him. But it wasn't just for this reason she kept thinking of him. He thought she looked familiar, but she also thought he looked like someone she knew, but she couldn't remember who. She dismissed the idea and went off to have a relaxing bath.

They had all decided to dine out. Drew and Ashley were meeting them later at the restaurant. Bathed and dressed, Jessica waited for Caro to come home. Her mobile rang and it was Luke. It was so great to hear his voice. They talked for about half an hour and caught up with each other's news, all except today's incident. Jessica didn't want to tell Luke about that. He would only worry and want to cut his trip short, and she knew he wanted to explore the opportunities in Spain. He was very complimentary about the villa and repeated several times that he wished she was there with him to show him around. He could see her in every room and told her so. They rang off, promising to speak the next day.

Caro came home looking tired. Jessica made her coffee, and they sat and chatted for a while. Caro had been feeling rather sick in the mornings and, coupled with the tiredness was not feeling her usual self. Jessica could remember during her pregnancies that the first three months were very trying times. She tried to reassure her daughter that it would soon pass and she would get her old energy back. She stood up to take the cups into the kitchen and caught Caro looking at her.

"What?"

"Over the last couple of years, you seem to have completely changed the way you dress. Your style is so much softer than it used to be. I like it."

"Thank you, darling. When I was in Spain, light, soft clothes were so much easier to wear and were much cooler, too. So I started to look for flowing kind of things that didn't make me feel all hot and sweaty."

"But what about the other stuff you wear in the winter?"

"Oh well, I shop around, get things altered if I have to. You know."

"No, actually I don't. Who alters them?"

"There's a lady I know in Spain who's brilliant. I buy things so I have the basic style, and she takes them in, lengthens them, adds bits, and comes up with something totally unique. She's great."

"Humm, why don't you start your own clothing line? You would be really great. Clothes for the older woman that's stylish, practical, and not expensive."

"Yeh, great. When would I have time for all that? I'm still trying to get this book off the starting blocks."

"Oh, come on, Mum. The book's advance sales have already exceeded the last ones, and besides, once you've finished writing it, Stacey and Dad can handle everything else. I could always give you a hand with some ideas. I shall want something to do later when I can't stand up all day anymore and have to stay home. Anyway, I'm going to have a shower. Think about it and we'll talk later."

Jessica thought about it whilst washing the cups. Seemed like a bit of a pipe dream. But still, that's what she would have thought several years ago if someone had told her she would one day be a bestselling author. "OK, I'll think about it," she said.

While combing her hair and renewing her makeup, she stopped dead. She could feel her heart pounding in her chest. She just remembered where she had seen the young waiter's face before. He was the boy in the book she'd just finished. He was Leo.

CHAPTER 27

Drew had spent the afternoon and the early part of the evening reading. He was deeply affected by the book and could feel his eyes welling up on more than one occasion. Just from the part he had read, he knew this was something special. He reluctantly put it to one side to shower and change for the evening. Ashley would be picking him up soon and he was looking forward to something to eat and telling Jessie how great he thought the book was.

He didn't want to be too late tonight, though. The estate agent had phoned and sounded really excited about a house that had just come on the market. It was about thirty miles from his old house and deep in the countryside. He had sold the family home for an excellent price and bought the smaller house, but he had never really felt at home there which was why he seemed to spend much of his time with Max. He had taken Blue over to Sophia's. She loved the cat, but Drew wanted him back. He missed him and his warm company. When he had decided to get something that he could feel more at home in, he started hunting around for something suitable. He had put his house on the market and had an offer almost immediately, so now he needed to find a home in a hurry. He had paid Jessica her half share of the family home quite a while ago after he'd had it valued, but the market had bounced back a bit, and it had sold for a higher price than the valuation, so he owed Jessica half the difference as well. He was going to suggest that the difference in price be put into a savings fund for their grandchild. He had already put his to one side and was sure Jessica would do the same.

Later, after a great meal and lively conversation with Caro and Ashley who seemed to feed off each other with witty banter, he thought how quiet Jessica had been. He had asked her a couple of times if she was OK, but she smiled and just said that the pressure of work was getting to her. He let it go, but he knew there was something more. Usually, once the book was finished, she sparkled and always seemed to have boundless energy as though a weight had lifted from her shoulders. He decided to talk to her at a later time, hoping she would tell him if there was a problem.

The truth was, Jessica couldn't seem to get the waiter's face out of her head. She was completely spooked by it as if it was some sort of omen. She wanted to talk to someone about it; Drew and Luke were the two obvious people, but she didn't think either of them would understand. She would have to go back to the cafe and at least find out his name. Maybe if she saw him again, he might look totally different. After all, she was a bit shaken up at the time of meeting him. She put the whole thing to the back of her mind and concentrated on the conversation around the table. Caro brought up the idea of the clothing line again and they all discussed it at length. The general opinion was that it was a good idea but needed a bit more research first. It could be very costly to set up and, if it all bombed, could mean a substantial loss of finances. Caro and Ashley said they would do some work on it and see if it was viable. Ashley had plenty of models on his books that would jump at some catwalk work especially for a new label that would maybe get them known. It would depend on the production costs. Anyway, it was put on the back burner for the time being. Jessica needed to concentrate on the book first. She also had some ideas for a series of short stories, which might take priority over anything else. The book sales were her income, and she needed another bestseller before she could consider ploughing huge sums into an unknown venture.

Drew said a warm goodbye to everyone. He quietly asked Jessica again if she was OK, but she gave him a bright smile, punched him on the arm, and told him not to keep acting like a mother hen. Ashley caught his eye and said he'd walk out with him. When they were outside, Drew turned to him with a puzzled look. "Something you want to say, Ash?"

"Just that you should get the Sunday papers."

"What!"

"You might find something interesting about our mutual Fred Smith project."

Drew's jaw dropped. "Oh my God. What did he find out?"

"Can't tell you much, only that the pair of them spent their missing years in the Philippines, Thailand, and briefly in Vietnam. The authorities in a couple of countries are interested in their whereabouts. They are wanted for questioning for keeping brothels and for selling young children for sex. They had a variety of forged passports, so the authorities didn't know their real names. Even the names they use now are a bit suspect. It seems that, as a child, Michael was adopted for a reason. The reason being their parents and their parents' perverted friends. Even his so-called sister was not really their real child. It seems she was with the couple when they bought the house, so everyone assumed it was their own daughter. When Michael turned up, it was easier to say he had been adopted than to risk a lot of questions. Fred has dug up some info about him being the son of a prostitute who sold him for her next fix, but that can't be verified."

"Oh my God," Drew said again, leaning against the wall of the restaurant.

The two of them stood leaning against the wall for several minutes. "Where is Melanie in all this?" Drew said, straightening up. "Her name is not going to come out, is it?"

"No. No one knows anything about her. Fred was just investigating this because I told him I had heard things from some of my girls. No names were ever mentioned and won't be."

"I couldn't bear it if her name was dragged through the mud."

"No chance of that. He had so many girls in and out of his flat and dressing room that there must be dozens who will be willing to point the finger when it hits the fan. You know what these wannabe models are like for five minutes of publicity. Besides, now Fred's got his scoop, he will be concentrating on the terrible things the two of them have done overseas."

"Do you think it was him?" Drew said quietly. "You know. That hurt Melanie."

"I don't know, Drew. I don't suppose we ever will unless she decides to tell us."

Drew hailed a taxi and thought about it all the way to his hotel. One thing was certain: he was looking forward to the Sunday papers.

CHAPTER 28

Drew met the estate agent the next morning, expecting another of the usual ordinary houses she had shown him before. She was, he supposed, a good agent, but as a woman and a companion, she wasn't much cop. She was very plain, which wasn't her fault, but the few things she had going for her, which weren't many, were completely obliterated by her terrible clothes sense and general drabness. This morning, her mousey-coloured hair was scraped back off her unadorned pasty face, and she wore a dreadful pair of old-fashioned glasses. Her coat and skirt were a drab grey and looked two sizes too big, and she wore brown, clumpy-looking shoes on her rather large feet.

Drew shook her hand and suggested he follow her in his own car as he had to go somewhere straight after the viewing. He didn't, but he really didn't fancy her company, and he didn't know how far the house was. It turned out to be about 20 minutes from the village high street where they had arranged to meet.

It was quite a pleasant drive through the countryside. The roads were lined with high hedges and tall trees. Drew got a glimpse of a very large, stately-looking house down a long tree-lined drive surrounded by acres of fields. *Hope that's not the place she's showing me,* he thought. *I'd have to mortgage my soul for a pile like that.* Thankfully the car in front kept on going.

It finally stopped by a pair of double wooden gates, which she got out and opened, then swung her car into. The drive led up to a good-sized bungalow. The driveway was gravel and weeds were beginning to push through in clumps. The garden was fairly large and had once been well-kept but now was overgrown, although the shrubs and roses were still blooming. *I'll bet Jim would love to get his hands on this lot,* Drew thought and stopped the car behind the agent's. The bungalow was built in an 'L' shape and looked promising from the outside. He found himself actually looking forward to viewing the inside.

It turned out to be quite a bit larger than it looked from the outside but in dire need of renovation. The large lounge ran from front to back of the house and had double doors leading into the back garden. The old gas fire was dreadful, and the wallpaper and curtains were all mismatched, otherwise, the room had great potential. There was a good-sized dining room off the lounge, leading into a large but worn-out and very dated kitchen. The hallway went off to the right and was wide with three double bedrooms (one en suite) and a large square and dated bathroom. The whole house had a musty and unlived-in air about it but didn't smell damp, and there were no visible cracks or signs of anything nasty.

The agent informed him, in her nasal twang, that the owner's husband had died and the widow had decided to move up north to be with her daughter and grandchildren. She wanted a quick sale to enable her to buy a house there, as her daughter's house was not big enough for her to stay permanently. Her husband had been ill in a hospice for quite a while, that's why the garden was in a bit of a state. It had all got too much for her and she wanted something smaller.

Drew went through the house again and found he was planning how to change things to bring it up to date. He wandered out around the back and side of the house and found a brick garage with a door leading through the back of it into a workshop with racking and benches. At the back of that was a double-sized garden shed, which looked fairly new. The garden at the back was separated into two-thirds and one-third with a fence and gate. The front two-thirds had a patio, grass, and flower beds—all overgrown—and the back third had obviously been a vegetable garden back in the day.

All in all, Drew liked it very much. The price was fairly substantial, but he was informed in the nasal twang that the seller was open to offers. Apparently, she had seen a house near her daughter that she wanted to buy so she was prepared to negotiate as she needed the money.

Drew decided he wanted this place and made an offer. This was a good slice lower than the asking price, but considering the work that was needed to improve the property, he thought it was a fair one. So he informed the agent that if the seller accepted his offer and, subject to a survey and the paperwork, she could consider it sold. This brought forth the first smile Drew had seen, but it certainly was NOT worth waiting for.

He prepared to drive back to London feeling very pleased with himself. He had a good vibe about the house and hoped the seller would accept his offer. He would be prepared to go up a fraction but wished he didn't have to. With the plans for the improvements forming in his mind, he knew it was going to cost him a pretty penny or four.

He had arranged to see Max in the evening. She had promised to cook a nice meal, with a dessert served up between the sheets. It had been a few days since he had seen her, and although they kept up with all the news daily on the phone, he still missed her when they had been apart for a while. She had been viewing the various houses with him, but the pressure of work meant that she hadn't been able to make it today. He wished he had taken some photos.

He had a bit of time to kill before seeing Max, so he decided to call in on Adam. They had also kept in close touch by phone but hadn't seen each other for a while. He wanted to tell Adam about the Sunday papers but didn't want to do it by phone. He checked that Adam was there and they arranged to meet for coffee out of the office. Adam was a bit mystified about the secrecy, but Drew told him he would know soon enough.

He was just about to pull away after a last look at the house when a car stopped right in front of him. He jammed on the brakes, cursing loudly. He jumped out of the car but caught his foot on the car door sill and ended up falling out on his hands. "You fucking stupid bloody idiot. What the hell do you think you're doing?" Drew shouted, brushing off his hands on the seat of his jeans.

"And hello to you too," said the plummy voice that Drew instantly recognised.

The long, slim length of her unfurled out of the low car.

"What the hell are you doing here?" Drew said ungraciously.

"Looking for you."

"Well, you found me. What do you want?"

"To talk to you when you've calmed down."

"I was calm till you nearly crashed into me."

"I didn't want you to drive away."

"You certainly prevented that, all right."

Lady Clara ignored the last remark and reached into the car for her bag. Straightening up, she said, "We had a meeting of the school governors and teachers, and we desperately need to raise funds for the school. Kate suggested I have a word with you to see if we could enlist your help."

"Don't know how I can help," Drew said abruptly.

Clara leant her long length against the car, swept her hair back, and stood looking at him.

"Well, I don't," Drew said crossly. "I don't know anything about fundraising."

"Are you always this bad-tempered, or do you have to go away and practice?"

"Good God, woman. You've got a bloody cheek. You nearly

caused an accident. You scared me half to death, and then you expect me to be all sweetness and light and stand out in the middle of nowhere, talking about something I know nothing about."

"OK, then, let's go somewhere where we can talk. It won't take long. Just follow me."

She got back into her car, started it up, and proceeded to turn around without giving Drew time to say anything. His jaw dropped. "Bloody woman," he said aloud. "Who does she think I am? Some sort of lackey to follow on behind her."

He got back in the car, slamming the door hard, still feeling irritated, and followed on behind. Ten minutes up the road, she turned into the long tree-lined drive he had seen earlier, and Drew's jaw dropped once again. The stately house, he was admiring not long ago, was looming larger and larger the nearer they got. Impressive wasn't the word. It was truly awesome. He pulled up behind her and just gazed up at the house.

"Come on. Stop gawping and let's go and have some tea," she said from the other side of the car and started striding out towards the large front door.

Drew followed slowly, looking around him. "Wow. Is this all yours, or are you renting?"

Her laugh was low and husky. "Oh, it's all mine now. It was my husband's family home for generations and it came to me on his death as there are no other relations. Unfortunately, I also inherited a lot of debt as well. So now most of the upstairs rooms are booked by visitors, and a couple of the larger downstairs rooms are used for conferences and wedding receptions. It keeps the wolf from the door."

Drew followed her into a huge hall with a grand staircase curving its way upwards. It was something he had only seen before in Hollywood movies. Her heels clacked across the parquet floor to a door at the side of the staircase and unlocked it.

"These are my own private rooms. The visitors are not allowed in here that's why the door is kept locked."

Drew followed her down a narrow passageway leading into a lush and comfortable lounge. The furniture was old and mellowed with years of beeswax. The fireplace was floor-to-ceiling and in aged marble. Deep sofas in faded velvet were matched by the velvet curtains at the full-height windows.

"Take a pew. I'll put the kettle on," saying that, she disappeared through another door.

Drew wandered about the room, looking at the many photos in silver frames and the great view from the massive windows. He ran his hand over the beautiful furniture and looked at the oil paintings hanging at various heights on the walls.

Clara returned with a silver tray and a silver tea service. He sunk down into one of the deep chairs, feeling speechless. "I don't really know who you are. You look familiar, though."

"I'm Lady Clara Ffoulks-Ward. You were my husband's publicity agency before he died."

Drew grinned. "Edward Ffoulks-Ward was your husband?" he said, amazed.

"You sound surprised, or are you just being polite by not mentioning the difference in our ages."

Drew picked up his teacup and took a sip. He pulled a face and put the cup down.

"Don't you like Earl Grey?"

"Never knew the bloke, but his tea tastes like wet talcum powder."

"Acquired taste, a bit like me," was the dry reply.

"And were you an acquired taste for Edward."

"Why don't you come right out and ask me if I married him for his money?"

"Because I'm too polite."

Clara's husky laugh followed Drew's last comment. "Shall we stop fencing with words? I need your help to raise some funds for the school, hence the kidnapping tactic. I've been giving it some thought and I've got some ideas if you are interested enough to listen."

"I know nothing about fundraising, but fire away if you want."

"That doesn't sound very gracious, but I'll see if I can arouse your interest." Clara leant back and gazed into space. "I was thinking of holding a black and white ball here. This is a beautiful house and has a large ballroom which is rarely used. We would charge a goodly sum for the tickets, and have some gaming, namely roulette. The idea is to buy £100 worth of chips for, say £25, and the one with the most chips left at midnight wins the prize, and all the money goes into the fund. We would have to make the prize a good one, like a holiday somewhere exotic, or something similar. We would need high publicity, which would be down to you, and lots of well-known faces. I know lots of the polo crowd and a good smattering of the landed gentry and politicians, but we also need some film and TV celebrities and famous faces the public know to get maximum coverage."

"This is all going to cost a heap of money, so where's the profit in it for the charity?" Drew said, risking another sip of the tea.

"Well, the idea is to get everything for free or as much as possible. The companies who subscribe in any way will get lots of publicity in the program and by mentions in the papers, etc. We could probably get *Hello* magazine interested as well. The prizes will have to be begged from as many sources as possible. The holiday will have to be from a big holiday company. Maybe some good jewellery and perfume for the ladies competition. Luxury hampers from some well-known stores. Magnums of champagne, maybe a box at a race meeting for the men. The list could be endless. If we could run a kind of auction for the bigger prizes, we could raise some serious money. The catering could be done locally, with the cost coming out of the ticket money. Wine could be bought in bulk and put on all the tables, but the spirits or any other drinks can be bought at the bar. Plus, we could add some beautiful girls and good-looking guys to sell the betting chips. That could increase sales and we would get their photos and details in the program, creating some publicity for them."

As she talked, Drew was leaning forward, taking in every word and feeling an exciting buzz in the pit of his stomach. She'd sold it to him. "You can count me in," he found himself saying. "I only hope I can be helpful. The school is very close to my heart."

"I know it is," Clara said, tucking her feet up under her on the velvet sofa. "That's why I wanted you on board, also, for your contacts. I don't think the school has the foggiest notion of how to raise funds and they desperately need money, and soon."

They sat and fired each other's enthusiasm up for the next hour over a decent cup of ordinary tea until Drew remembered about meeting Adam and made a hasty exit, promising to be in touch soon.

CHAPTER 29

Jessica agreed to do the radio show and answered most of the questions as honestly as she could. She refused to be drawn on her relationship with Luke and, when asked if there was anyone in her life, was very vague. In a break for the news, she made it clear that this was a very new relationship and this was a subject that she wished to avoid. After getting an agreement from the interviewer, the rest of the program romped along and was written favourably about in the following day's papers.

The book hit the bookshelves and immediately shot up the bestseller list. The sales were going so well that she decided to go over to Spain to spend a few days with Luke. She missed him and the last few weeks had been manic. She was feeling tired, and the English weather hadn't helped. The rain had poured down for days, and she really felt she needed some warm sun on her body to dry her out. After such a long time away, she was definitely missing the blue sky and the golden beaches of Spain. She arranged to spend a couple of days with Polly first. She also wanted to look in on Gertie. Bill and his rescued greyhound were the only ones Gertie would stay with, and he and the whole family loved her to bits. Bill was with Luke when they found her and had openly cried at the sight of her on the vet's table. He and his wife had helped nurse her on the days Luke had to be away, and when they introduced Sid the greyhound to Gertie, he lay down by her side and there he stayed. He moved to eat and go outside but was soon back to lie down by her again. The first time Luke brought her around to Bill's house after she had had her stitches out and got a clean bill of health from the vet, the two dogs chased around and around as if they knew that everything was OK at last.

Jessica had heard the story from Luke before when they went around to Bill's for supper one evening. As soon as Gertie saw they were turning into Bill's driveway, she went mad; Sid was running around in circles as soon as he saw the van. It was quite comical seeing the two large, streamlined and elegant dogs acting like two overgrown puppies.

Jessica knew that Luke was missing his dog and had asked her to look in on him if she was going to Polly's. He had intended to be home in a couple of days, but there was someone he wanted to meet first. Some wealthy landowner or something, that's when Jessica had decided to join him. If he was extending his stay she might as well grab the opportunity to go and spend it with him.

But before going down to Polly, she had arranged for the family to have dinner all together as she wouldn't have time otherwise, however, there was something else she had to do first. She packed two copies of the new book into one of her largest handbags and called a taxi. The rain was still relentless, so there was no one sitting outside the coffee shop when the taxi pulled up. Even the smokers had found somewhere dryer. She entered a dimly lit room that had only a handful of people in it. The cockney chap that had brought her the brandy was down the other end of the bar. The other bartender asked for her order, and she pointed to the broad back at the other end and asked for a word with him.

"Hey, Ernie. Someone here to see you."

Ernie walked towards her with a beaming smile. "Can I help you?"

"I came in to thank you for rescuing me a few weeks ago."

Ernie looked at her, his head on one side. Suddenly, he beamed again. "Now I remember you. The lady who had a run-in with the drunk. How are you?" A thick, podgy hand shot over the bar and shook hers in a firm grip.

Jessica smiled. "I'm OK, thanks to you and your assistant."

"Can I get you a drink?"

"Thanks, I'll have a coffee, please, and will you have a drink on me."

"No, I'm fine, thanks, but I'll take for a beer for later."

He brought the coffee and Jessica introduced herself. All the time, she was itching to ask where the young man was.

"I believe you are a well-known lady. I don't do much reading but the wife does. She does most of the cooking in the daytime cause it's only light meals, but we have a chef for evenings, so she goes home. Gets fed up with the TV, so she reads. She's read all your books."

Jessica took one of the books out of her bag. "What's your wife's name? I brought the latest book with me as a thank you."

Ernie beamed again. "She'll be chuffed as nuts with that. Her own signed copy. She'll be telling all her friends about it. Her name's Joanne, but everyone calls her Annie."

Jessie wrote "To Annie with best regards" and signed it.

After chatting over her coffee about her book signing, her life in Spain and the weather, she finally got around to asking about the young man.

"Oh, he'll be here in a bit. He's been in court today, but they'll be adjourning soon."

"In court," Jessie said, a bit shocked. "Why, what's he done?"

Ernie let out a bark of a laugh. "Oh, he hasn't done anything. He's a law student, and when he's not in class, he likes to sit in the courts. Picking up a few tips, I shouldn't wonder. Fancies himself as the next Perry Mason."

"Oh, I see," said Jessie, smiling.

"Yeh, Tyler is a real brainy git. Parents sent him to the best schools and stuff. Father is a partner in a big stock broking firm in the city. You might have heard of them. Called Applegore and Dancing. His father is Arthur Applegore and thought his son was going to follow him in the business, but Tyler had other ideas."

"Why is he working here then? I would have thought he didn't need the money."

"No, he doesn't, although he wants to earn some money of his own. Also, he likes to meet the public. Says he gets an insight into what makes them tick. You know, after all, his high-class friends, he says he needs to meet the general public; that way, he can be a better lawyer."

"I see," said Jessica. She looked at her watch, conscious of the dinner, wondering if she could wait any longer.

"Talk of the devil; here he is now."

Tyler walked through the door carrying what looked like a heavy backpack and looking just like she remembered him. His hair was slick with rain and he took off his padded jacket and shook it out the door. His jeans were the baggy sort that the younger lads seemed to favour. It had caused Drew to expound at length about tatty underpants hanging out of the back of trousers until Ashley turned up in casual clothes with the dreaded pants, in red, in full view at the top of his jeans. Everyone looked at Drew. He turned blotchy pink and just cleared his throat, causing Jessica and Caro to burst out laughing.

"Hello there," Tyler said in his cultured voice, recognising her immediately. "How are you? Got over your scare."

"Yes, I'm fine now. And thank you for all your help."

"No problem. Damn bloke was a nuisance for days. Since the police moved him on he seems to have found somewhere else to hang out now. Can I get you a drink?"

"I've had a coffee, thanks. I have to go soon; I'm out for dinner tonight."

"Heard about your new book. Causing a bit of a stir."

Jessie dug the second book out of her bag. "I've brought a copy for your sister. I'll sign it for her if you like."

"Got mine already," shouted Ernie.

"Can you address it to Olivia, please?"

Jessie signed the book and handed it over. She found herself staring at Tyler. Luckily, he was greeting some customers and his face was turned away. It was so uncanny looking at him. All the time she was writing her book she had the image of this face in her mind. *Where had it come from? If his sister read the book, would she link Jessica's description of the main character to her brother?* She felt she wanted to know more about him. The thumbnail information from Ernie had just whetted her appetite. But she could hardly give him the third degree. He would wonder why she wanted to know.

He turned back to her. "You'll have to excuse me. I need to get changed for work, but please come and see us again; I'd love to talk to you."

That could be a good excuse for another visit. "And I would love to talk to you, too," Jessie said, hoping he didn't think she was coming on to him.

"Take care. Bye for now," and he disappeared out of the back door.

"Bye, Ernie," she shouted.

Ernie came bustling up. "It's chucking it down out there. Shall I get you a taxi?"

"That would be great. Thank you."

All the way back in the taxi, she thought about Tyler. She had no idea why she was so fascinated by him other than the likeness to her character Leo. Well, she would put it to the back of her mind. Maybe she would talk it over with Stacey.

The dinner was great. Jessica hadn't realised how hungry she was until she walked through the door and smelt all the lovely aromas emanating from the kitchens. Caro had got her appetite back and did justice to everything on her plate.

Ashley looked at her empty plate.

"What?" said Caro, smiling.

Ashley smiled back. "Good to see you eating. I was getting worried. That's the first proper meal I've seen you eat for weeks."

"Now I'm going to start eating for two. I shall be as fat as a house soon."

"You'll still be beautiful," Ashley looked at her fondly.

Drew and Jessica looked at each other, feeling oddly, a bit embarrassed. Max just smiled.

Ashley turned to look at Jessica. "Got some costings on that clothing line we talked about."

Jessie had forgotten all about it. "Are they in print?"

"Yeh. Got them here." He handed Jessie a large brown envelope.

"I'll look at them while I'm away."

"What clothing line?" said Max.

"One, we want Jessie to start," said Ashley.

"Great idea," said Max.

"You think so," Jessica said, looking at the fat bundle of papers in the envelope. "Crikey, Ashley. I'm going back to Spain for a break. It'll take me bloody ages to plough through this lot."

"Well, Luke will be out all day wheeling and dealing, so what are you going to do all day but lie in the sun and read? So instead of a trashy novel, you can read how to make lots of money."

Jessica was still looking at the pile of papers. "I've already got lots of money." Then she looked around at everyone and smiled from ear to ear. "I've got lots of money."

"Yes, you certainly have," said Drew and kissed her cheek. "Have a really good break with Luke and we'll keep you posted about how much more you are making when we get the bestseller list for the month."

ACT THREE:
Love … & Ever After

CHAPTER 1

Gertie lay on the grass under her umbrella while Jessica lay beside her and read, or rather, tried to read, a weighty pile of papers. The thick wad was a film script. Jessica had insisted on total script control, or the picture wouldn't get made. She had always hated it when readers couldn't connect the book with the film as the producers had ruined the story completely. She was determined it would never happen to any of her books. She had been back in Spain for over two years now. She had gone back to London for the birth of her grandson Toby Martyn Mead who had arrived tipping the scales at 7lbs 6ozs in April and was now nearly 18 months old and asleep upstairs.

Caro's simple but beautiful wedding had taken place the following September, and the week after, Jessica, Stacey, and Drew had a meeting with a British film company that had pursued Jessica relentlessly for the film rights to her book *An Obsession to Die For*. She had held off for a long time, not wanting to commit her work to be changed into something different than the words she had written. She only agreed to allow the film if its script was true to the book with no changes. She also wanted to choose the actors for the main characters. This caused quite a furore among the producers of the film company. They would be investing big money and wanted a well-known face to ensure the success of the film. They suggested several well-known "stars," but Jessica stood her ground.

"There has to be good actors out there who can carry these roles, and I want to find them. I would like my book to be filmed, but not with big stars who will want to act it their way and not mine. The young stars of the Harry Potter films were not big stars when they started, but they turned out to be fantastic and are now very famous."

The two smartly suited men shuffled their papers, looked at each other, coughed, and the older one said, "OK, leave it with us. We'll get back to you."

Drew intervened, "You had better make it quick. We have others scrambling for the rites to this book. Jessie won't change her mind on this. It's her way or no way." He stood up and continued, "I will expect to hear from you by close of play tomorrow. We have other meetings and Jessie is going back to Spain next week."

The three sat quietly for a few moments after the production house representatives left.

"What do you think?" Jessica asked.

"I think you'll get what you want," said Stacey. "They've pestered the hell out of you for months, so they aren't going to let it go now they've got this far."

"I agree," said Drew. "Let's face it, the book's a bestseller. You've made your money from it. Anything else is a bonus. Anyway, what have you got in mind for the actors?"

"Can I take you two for a coffee?"

Drew looked puzzled. "What do you think is on that tray over there?"

"Ahh, but this is somewhere special. I just have to make a phone call."

Jessica very strangely went across to the door and made the call out of earshot. She walked back and picked up her coat and bag. "OK, let's go."

"Where are we going?" enquired Stacey running to catch up whilst trying to get her arms in her coat.

"You'll see," Jessica said, holding her arm up for a taxi.

Once in the taxi, Jessica said, "You two read the book. Did my description of Leo paint a picture in your mind of what he should look like?"

"Of course," said Stacey.

"OK, keep that face in your mind."

"Why?" they both said together.

"You'll see," said Jessica again.

They all lapsed into silence for the rest of the journey.

They walked into the bar to be greeted by a smiling Ernie. "Jessie Darling. How lovely to see you again. Back from Spain for long?"

He came around the counter to give her a hug. The other two stared, amazed. *Who was this person and how did Jessica know him?* Jessica introduced the two of them and gave them a very brief explanation of how she had met Ernie.

"Yeh, and since then, she's called in regularly when she's in town. Me and Tyler always look forward to seeing her. She's like a breff of spring, she is."

"Where is Perry then?"

"Go get Ty, will you, Amy," Ernie said to the barmaid.

She went to the door and shouted, and they heard a muffled reply. Ernie was getting drinks all round. Wine for Jessica and Stacey and a beer for Drew, who was just about to take a sip when Tyler came through the back door. His glass stopped before it got to his mouth and he just stared. He put the glass down untouched and watched the young man walk towards Jessica with his arms outstretched and his white teeth showing in a huge grin.

"Jessie. How great to see you. When did you get back?" he said in his lovely voice and wrapped his arms around her.

"Oh, last week. Had some business to sort out. How's the exams?

Finished yet?"

"Yes, thank God. What a nightmare."

"How do you think you did?"

"Don't know. OK, I think. Have to wait and see."

"Tyler, let me introduce you to some people who want to meet you."

Drew had finally picked up his pint. He switched it to his other hand and shook Tyler's hand.

"Can you act?" he asked instantly, making Jessica laugh.

"Act," said Tyler, frowning.

"Tyler, have you got a few minutes to sit down and talk to us?"

Tyler looked around at the few people sitting around. "As you can see, we're rushed off our feet. OK, Ernie?" he said over the bar.

"Bugger off, mate. You're always under my feet anyway," Ernie said with a smile.

They spent half an hour telling Tyler the reason for the visit. He really did fit the description of Leo. Uncannily so. Apparently, his sister had said the same thing after reading the book. They said they thought if he could get up in court and talk in front of the public and all the legal lot, then that was a form of acting, and this could be a great deal more profitable even if it was just this one film. They left him thinking about it.

Jessica smiled as she remembered the jubilation she had felt when she got his phone call, accepting the deal. The only thing left was to sell the idea to the film company and find someone to fit her idea of the girl in the story.

Gertie moved her position under the sun umbrella and Jessica was brought back to the present. She leant back and listened to the silence. The day was still and quiet, but leaning back in the lounger, she was conscious of the whisper of the water running through the pool filter, the drone of insects, and the far-off sound of a plane ferrying tourists to or from their holiday. As she looked around the lush garden and sparkling pool, an unexpected feeling of loneliness washed over her. This was not the first time this had happened recently, taking her off guard every time.

Luke was involved in some large building contracts in another part of Spain. He came back as often as he could, but they were against the clock with everything running close to a deadline, so he was working long hours and needed to rest when he wasn't working. She tried to understand, but there had been some heated conversations between them on a number of occasions. She had argued that with all her money, plus the substantial sum he had already made, they could have more time together; he didn't really need to work so many hours. It was as if he almost resented the fact that she was wealthier than he was and was determined to make as much money as he could in case she thought he was sponging off her.

When she said this to him, Luke told her not to be so ridiculous, but she could see by his taut expression that she had hit a nerve. For the first time since they had been together, they spent the night on opposite sides of the bed. The next morning, Luke left early before she was awake, and with the dispute still not resolved. That really hurt her and she didn't phone him for several days. She pushed herself to the limit, spending long hours at the keyboard punching out pages of the new book, telling herself that that was the reason she hadn't called him—because she was busy. Knowing all the time that it wasn't true.

Soon, Caro, Ashley, and young Toby arrived for a visit, and she was so pleased to see them. When Jessica blustered over the reason Luke wasn't there to greet them as well, Caro looked strangely at her mother but kept her own counsel. She surmised quite quickly that something wasn't quite right, but in the chaos of Toby running from room to room, Gertie furiously wagging her tail and getting in everyone's way, and the general unpacking, she left it to be discussed later.

For the next couple of days there was never an opportune moment to bring the subject up. Jessica spent all her time with her beloved grandson. As the novelty of being with grandma had dulled down to a less frantic level, Toby was overtired. He went off for a nap, and Caro and Ashley, grabbing the opportunity to spend some time on their own, had gone to the beach.

Jessica moved the lounger into the shade and went up to the kitchen for a cool drink. She looked in on Toby, but he was out for the count. She went back to the pool and sat on the end of the lounger, gazing into space. The last year had been very busy but rewarding. She had got her way over the film script, found Jilly, a young dancer who had managed to get a place at RADA, for the part of Anya, and was pleased when Tyler, who had already been contracted to play Leo, hit it off with Jilly immediately. The film was in pre-production and the final scripts were on the grass beside her.

Jessica just couldn't fathom this lonely feeling at all. She had everything she had ever hoped for, and more. Why the hell did she feel as if there was a gaping hole somewhere in her insides? She still loved Luke and he was so much part of her life, but she did not seem to be such a big part in his anymore. She hadn't envisaged spending so much time apart and it was in some way damaging their relationship. She had spent years in her own company. First with Drew, then with her writing, and now again with Luke. Now, she wanted to go out and enjoy things. See a bit of the world. She wanted to visit places she had read about and be a tourist. Get close to Luke again. Spend some of her money before she got too old to bother.

She got up suddenly, startling Gertie, and waded into the pool. She lazily floated about, looking up at the azure blue sky and told herself how lucky she was, but still, the feeling of being alone didn't go. *Damn, Luke.* If he couldn't come here, then she would go to him. She would enjoy every minute of this family visit, then when they had gone, finish the book, which was in its final stages, and go and see him. It would be a chance to see a different part of the country and have some leisure time.

She was just drying herself off when she heard Toby's wail. She smiled and hurried into the house to see her grandson.

CHAPTER 2

Drew and Max were having a barbeque. It was a hot but brilliant day with lush green trees and grass, a myriad of colourful flowers—thanks to Jim, and just a slight breeze. A lovely summer day with bees buzzing and birds singing. The very best that England could offer.

Drew's house had been a long time in its renovation, but now it was a fantastic home and he was proud of it. The house had been gutted and completely refurbished with a large extension and a beautiful conservatory. Jim had travelled down each week with Sophia and had transformed the garden from a builder's yard into a landscaped wonder. Drew had employed a team of helpers to do some of the heavier work for him, but the design layout had all been Jim's. It was now a year on and all the lovingly planted flowers and shrubs were in full bloom. Sophia had brought a couple of her friends and cleaned and polished every inch of everything until Drew was afraid she would wear it out before he had used it.

"Thees lovely things here. Sophia make them beautiful for you."

And she did. The layers of dust and splatters of paint disappeared. The windows were cleaned to a sparkle. The kitchen was almost surgically clean, and Drew was almost afraid to make himself a pot of coffee in case he made a mark on the worktops. Max came with him to choose the furniture and furnishings, which were mostly dove grey and cinnamon with dark grey carpets. It was masculine without being dull. Drew loved the place and was completely at peace there. The first time he had felt that for an awfully long time.

Sophia had turned up after he moved in with a very noisy and yowling cat in a basket.

"Hello, Blue old son," Drew said, opening the top of the basket. "Welcome to your new home."

Blue rubbed around his legs and promptly disappeared out the backdoor to explore. Sophia had gone back out to her car. She reappeared carrying another basket. "Thees Blue new friend," she said, opening the basket and taking out a small ginger and white tabby wearing a pink sparkly collar with a tinkling bell. The cat stared at Drew and emitted a small meow. "She name is Lady."

Drew smiled and took her from Sophia. "Hello, Lady. How do you do."

This brought forth another small meow and also brought Blue in from the garden, who sat down at Drew's feet, staring upwards towards the young cat. Drew put Lady down on the floor and watched with a broad smile as Blue proceeded to lick Lady's head.

"New house, new baby," Sophia said, bustling off towards the utility room.

Not sure that really meant a cat, thought Drew, watching the little cat cautiously exploring the kitchen floor.

Blue's padded cat bed was placed in the lounge in the corner at the side of the patio doors, and he shared it quite amicably with Lady.

Today though, the cats were in the garden being fussed over by Drew's guests. The meat was sizzling away and was poked, once in a while, by John, Adam, and Sophia's Alfie. He felt, as the host, that he should be doing it, but not being any sort of cook, had decided to leave it to the rest of the guys. At least he would have someone else to blame if it was all reduced to burnt offerings. Instead, he busied himself making sure everyone's drinks were topped up.

The ladies were in the kitchen making salads, jacket potatoes, garlic bread, and every other kind of food that people like to eat at barbeques. Drew pinched an olive in passing and was swiped at by

Max.

"Hey, you. Wait your turn."

"I'm starving. If I drink anymore on an empty stomach, I shall be flat on my back before the food's cooked."

"Then don't drink anymore," was the tart return.

"Spoilsport."

Drew went out into the garden with another handful of beers. John was having a go at the meat and it was looking good. The smell was making Drew's mouth water.

"Here you are, John lad, get your chops around this." Drew handed John one beer and the others to Alfie and Adam.

"It's OK, Drew, we'll get our own," said Polly, heading towards the kitchen with Cassie.

"Sorry, Poll, only got two hands."

"You men can never multitask anyway."

"That's not what you said this morning, you minx," came from John.

"You wish," Polly said over her shoulder as she disappeared into the kitchen.

Drew sat down and looked around him. Surrounded by his wonderful friends and living in this beautiful house, he couldn't have been more content. He stretched his legs out and looked over towards Adam and John. It was only now that he noticed how thin John looked. He had always been a robust-looking man with a muscular build, but now he looked somehow stooped and grey. Drew sat up straight and looked again. He had been so busy with the house and various fundraising functions that he hadn't seen John and Polly for a long time. They had arrived earlier that day and were going to stay the night. In the bustle of unpacking the car and the grand tour of the house, Drew had only now actually looked at John and didn't like what he saw. He didn't like it one bit. He was ill. That was obvious. Drew sobered up so fast it was almost as if he hadn't had a drink at all. He wanted to speak to Polly, but this wasn't the time. He would just have to wait until later. He found his eyes constantly turning to look at John. As if sensing his eyes, John turned. He looked straight at Drew, and the smile from one of Adam's jokes died on his face and from his eyes. Drew suddenly felt sick. It was as if, by this reaction, John had acknowledged Drew's suspicions.

The day wound on and everyone seemed to enjoy themselves immensely. As the sun went down, the fire was stoked up and they all sat around it talking, laughing, and relaxing. No one was inclined to go inside until the fire died and the chill in the air made the ladies shiver.

Sophia and Alfie made their goodbyes. Sophia was not really used to drinking and, after a couple of glasses of wine, had become quite talkative with her accent becoming more pronounced as the day wore on. Alfie looked at her indulgently and translated when necessary. Her face glowed in the firelight, and she looked truly beautiful.

Adam and Cassie were not far behind, as Adam had to open the office in the morning. Cassie kissed Drew warmly and thanked him for everything. When she went to take her leave of the others, Adam came and shook his hand before turning his back to the others. "Drew, John is—"

"I know," said Drew, cutting him short.

"Thank God. I thought I was the only one who noticed. What do you—"

Drew cut him short again. "Don't know, old son, but I mean to find out."

"Phone me, will you."

"Course. When I know."

After they had left with much waving and shouting, Max and

Polly started clearing up and loading the dishwasher. Drew took the opportunity to steer John into the lounge and onto the comfortable sofa. He poured them both a whiskey and sat down on the chair facing him. They both sipped their drinks in silence for a few moments, and then both spoke at once. They both smiled, and John put up a hand towards Drew, stopping whatever he was going to say.

"Drew, mate, this is difficult. I've never liked being ill and always shrugged it off and got on with things. Farms don't run themselves, and nobody pays me if I don't work, but this time...." John leant forward and dropped his head to look at his hands clasped around the glass.

"What is it," Drew said, his throat closing up again.

There was a silence, and then John drew in a deep breath. "Pancreatic cancer."

Drew went cold. He could feel the blood draining from his face. He knew about this type of cancer and knew also that it was always fatal. One of the partners in the company he worked for some years ago had been diagnosed and died, all within a year. He had been cheerful right up to the end when the pain became too much. John had been a friend for over twenty-five years; he and Polly had been a lifeline for Drew's family all that time. It was inconceivable that this wonderful man who loved life so much could be struck down with this awful disease. His eyes filled with tears and he started sobbing.

"Don't, Drew. Please don't. Tears won't help. Polly and I have already tried them."

Drew couldn't stop, though. He punched the arm of the chair, got up, and walked over to the French windows. He took a tissue out of his pocket and scrubbed at his eyes. John came and stood alongside him. Both of them looked out into the illuminated garden, where the bright flowers glowed under the lights.

In the doorway of the lounge stood Polly, looking at them silently, and Max just behind her, looking bewildered. Polly went and sat in the chair that Drew had recently vacated and looked at the backs of the two men. "So he told you then," she said to Drew's back.

John answered her, "He had pretty much guessed."

Max walked over to the two men, gazed up into Drew's face, and then over towards John, who said boldly, "I've got cancer."

Max gasped and put her hand over her mouth. Everyone was silent until she asked John, "How long have you known?"

"Not long," was the terse reply.

Polly stood up. "I'm going to make some coffee. I think we could all use some, I know I could. Can you show me where everything is, Max?"

Polly knew that the men needed some more time. She used her time in the kitchen to explain everything to Max and to give her a chance to have a few tears. She gave Max some kitchen roll and put her arm around her shoulders. "I am trying not to upset John anymore. He started losing weight and feeling generally unwell a while back; he was finally forced to see about it. When he was diagnosed, both of us spent days crying and then raging, and then crying again. Then we had to tell our boys, and it was more of the same. We have now got to the stage when we feel almost cried out and angered out. We now just want to get all the treatment we can and hope for the best. The prognosis is not good, but we will try anyway. The treatment itself is pretty rough, and John is in two minds about having it. He says if it can't prolong his life, what's the point in destroying the bit he has got left."

Max looked at this small, neat woman in her smart navy linen trousers and a white t-shirt with a pink patterned pashmina around her shoulders and marvelled at her calmness. It was almost as if she was comforting Max when it should have been the other way around. She said this to Polly and got the reply, "I cry almost every day, but I was determined that this was not going to be one of them. The days to make memories are going to get fewer, so I want to have lots of good memories to savour later. That's why I took so many photos today. For memories."

Max felt her eyes welling up again and busied herself with the cups for the coffee. By the time they went back into the lounge she had herself under control.

John had said much the same thing to Drew, and the four of them spent the evening just quietly talking. John had hospital appointments in the coming weeks, but once they had touched briefly on them and made Polly promise to keep in touch, the topic was pushed onto the back burner. They talked about Ben, their eldest son, who was working on the farm and had moved into Luke's cottage. Jessica was never likely to be using it again, and Luke was concerned it would fall into disrepair or be vandalised, so a fair rent was agreed on, and Ben and his girlfriend moved in. His girlfriend was a lovely girl and helped Polly with work around the farm in addition to her teaching job at the local primary school.

Their middle son Steve was also working the farm with his brother and had moved into the main house. Jack, the youngest son, was finishing soon at university and would also move back. This had always been the plan, but it was supposed to give John and Polly some time together and some holiday time. The farm would be passed over to all three sons when John retired. It seemed now that circumstances had changed all that. John and Polly had planned a cruise after Ben learnt the ropes of the farm business. That had now become impossible, making Polly sad that they couldn't have this precious time together. So they agreed they would do everything they could to make each day enjoyable. On that note, they all went off to bed.

Drew lay for a long time thinking back over the years that he had known John, and once again, the tears ran from his eyes. He cried silently for a long time. He would have to tell Jessica. He had promised Polly he would do it, but it was something he was dreading. Polly and John were her longest and dearest friends. Drew's tears started again; Max lay beside him, still and silent, feeling his pain.

CHAPTER 3

Jessica checked the internet to find out how long it would take her to get to Luke. It was going to take about seven hours, so she decided to do it in two stages. She would do most of the mileage on the first day, stay overnight somewhere and continue for the shorter journey on the second day.

She went back to the internet and booked a room about 90 miles from her destination. Her Jeep would be good for the journey as the roof came off and would be nice along the beach roads she planned to use. She packed quickly with mostly light clothes and a couple of soft sweaters. She threw in a light coat just in case.

The next morning, she showered and washed her short streaky hair. She applied some heavy factor sun cream and some light makeup and donned a pair of caramel-coloured shorts, a white vest, and tan, soft leather sandals. She threw her bags in the back, locked up, set the alarms, and took Gertie next door to her "Uncle Fabio," who she loved, and his old Labrador Lupo, who she loved even more. She told him she would be away for a few days and got a hug and a packed lunch from his round little wife. She was on the road by 9 am. The sun was warm, but the air was a bit keen so she was glad of the short, white cardigan she had dragged out at the last minute. Her printed map was on the seat beside her, anchored down by her handbag. Luke had taken the satnav, and she would have to rely on the old-fashioned system after forgetting to install a new and upgraded system.

She bowled along nicely for the next three hours, but a call of nature caused her to stop, so she took the opportunity to have some lunch. She ordered a Spanish omelette, which was a fancy name for potato in eggs cooked in a pan. However, it was quite delicious. She finished with ice cream and coffee and was on her way again in an hour. By this time, the sun was high in the sky and warm so she put a hat on and took off her cardigan. The roads were busy around the beach areas and quiet on the open roads, so she made good progress. She made one wrong turn, which added 20 minutes to her time, but other than that, the map was doing pretty well.

As she drove along, she thought deeply about her relationship with Luke. They had been together for quite a few years now. In the beginning, Luke was fine about her career, but as her fame and fortune grew beyond all expectations, he started to have a problem accepting her wealth. He worked more and more as if to prove he could also earn big. If she asked him to forget about the money, they had plenty, and they could spend some time together and maybe travel a bit, he would get moody and change the subject. If she tried to get him to tell her what was bothering him, he would take Gertie and go for long walks without her. She never brought the subject up again when he came back, which just pushed everything under the carpet and made things worse. She was sure it was the money. He had a macho thing about it. *Why did women not have a problem about being with a wealthy man but men had a problem about accepting money from a woman regardless of how much they loved each other? I suppose it's the age-old "man the hunter" reason. Anyway, they could talk about it over the next day or so.*

She hoped his partner would let him have some time off. She had not met Luke's partner yet. They always seemed to work so far away and put in long hours, so she just put up with it and waited for Luke to come home. She had heard a lot about this Spaniard who was Luke's hero, though. He was a self-made man who had learnt carpentry skills from his father and went on to become a jack of all trades in the village he lived in. This was not enough. He wanted to learn properly, so he went to live in the city with his aunt to attend college. He took courses on bricklaying, roofing, plumbing, tiling, and anything needed to be a housebuilder. Electric was the only thing he didn't do. Apparently, the course was too long, and he was in a hurry.

He borrowed money from his father and uncle and bought a piece of land. The land was on a hill with a fantastic view of a lush valley with a river running through it. The only snag was that there was no road, and all the materials would have to come across a bumpy field, so he dug trenches for the pipes and wires and then built a road. He hired the people he knew from college and the village, and they built beautiful houses. The houses sold for large amounts of money because of the quality and the wonderful location, and that was the start of his successful business. Most of the men who worked for him then still worked for him. He treated them very well, with generous paid holidays, financial help with buying their homes, and time off if they needed it. He knew all their families and children, and they would go through fire for him. Jessica was looking forward to meeting this paragon. *I'll bet he's a total asshole with delusions of grandeur,* she thought with a smile.

The rest of the day's journey went well, and she pulled into the hotel car park tired, hungry, and in need of a shower. She enjoyed a long shower, changed into white linen trousers and a soft sleeveless tunic, and went down into the dining room. She was starving and polished off a large meal of seafood paella and an ice cream dessert. She sat at the bar for a while enjoying a brandy and looking around her. She hadn't been to this hotel before and had only seen its photos on the internet when she booked. She was quite surprised at its size. Her room was equipped with a huge bed, a sofa, a desk, and a large shower cubicle. The bar and dining room were also a good size, so the few people present were very scattered.

Her Spanish was quite passable (even though she didn't get much practice), so she struck up a conversation with the barman, first apologising if she made a language gaff. She asked him about the hotel and when it was built, as it looked fairly new. It was actually around five years old and the centre of the building was an old Spanish house. Extensions were built onto it, but the outside brickwork and roof were kept as close to the original house as possible. The inside of the house had been completely gutted and then brought up to date. Many of the salvageable bits and pieces, like old Spanish tiles and carved wood panels, had been incorporated into the hotel. The bar itself was built with old wall panels.

Jessica got down from the stool and looked at the front of the bar. The carving in the wood was magnificent. Vines and grapes twined around flowers and carved goat's heads; it was dark and burnished with age. She exclaimed to the barman that she thought the carving was wasted at the front of the bar and should be on a wall where everyone could admire it. The barman laughed and said that the guy who built the hotel said that if you spent lots of money at the bar, you should have something nice to look at when you finally fell over. Jessica laughed and ordered another brandy, enjoying the company and reluctant to go to her room yet.

"Who built this lovely hotel? He must have been Spanish to keep so much of the history of the house. Most builders throw everything away without a second thought."

"I did," said a deep voice over Jessica's right shoulder.

She spun around on the stool, her hand on her chest and nearly fell off. A large brown hand steadied her and she stood up. The barman had a wide grin on his face and she turned to look at the man who had startled her. He was a head taller than her, burly, with black hair cut very short with a hint of a wave and a few grey flecks. His mouth and eyes smiled at her and his white shirt enhanced the deepness of his tan. Later in her room she would marvel at how she managed to take all this in within seconds.

The brown hand extended in her direction. "I am Antonio," he said as she took his hand. "Nio to my friends."

She felt a jolt as his hand enclosed hers.

"Please allow me to buy you a drink as an apology for your fright," he said in English.

His voice was deep with a fairly pronounced accent. He sat on the stool next to her and the barman put a misty cold glass of beer in front of him. The fact that it was done without him ordering it told Jessica that he must be a regular.

"So you like my hotel then?"

"YOUR hotel," Jessica said, turning on the stool to look at him.

"Yes."

"YOUR hotel?" Jessica said again as if confirming.

His smile widened. "My hotel."

"Wow," she said. "I thought you were just the builder."

"Yes," he answered, his smile crinkling his eyes.

"You are a man of few words," she said smilingly. "I feel like this is an interrogation."

"Not at all. You asked and I answered. I bought the old house years ago and didn't know what to do with it because it seemed like it couldn't be anything else but what it was. It was very large and would have cost far too much to restore it as a home. But it was too small to be split into flats. So eventually some of the local people suggested a hotel with a nice restaurant so they could eat out with their friends and family. So here it is."

"And I am very pleased," she said.

They talked for a while and then moved over to a table and more comfortable chairs as the bar filled up. By the time Jessica finally decided she was tired and needed to sleep, they had talked about many things. A lot about the hotel, and Spain in general. Antonio told a lot of amusing tales about the local community, many of whom he had known for years. He was brought up nearby but had moved away with his work, bought some land, built a house, married, had a son and daughter, divorced, and threw himself into his work to pass the time.

His life seemed to mirror Jessica's. She was almost mesmerised listening to him talk, his voice reminding her of brown velvet. He had a very powerful presence. A force about him that was almost tangible. He would be a good person to have on your side, but she reckoned he would make a formidable enemy. As for herself, apart from her name and the barest of details, she told him almost nothing about her life. If she had, she would have had to tell him about Marty and she wasn't ready to share those details with a stranger. If he thought this strange he did not remark on it. The only question he asked was where she was heading for the next day. She just told him she was visiting a friend. She did not elaborate and he did not press for any further details. It was almost as if he knew that she had given him all the personal information he was going to get.

They had drunk a pot of coffee, but even that didn't stop Jessica's eyes from wanting to close. Antonio saw this and stood up.

"I am keeping you up when you are tired. It is too late for me to travel home tonight, so I shall stay in the hotel. I have a room here. Maybe I shall see you at breakfast tomorrow. Goodnight, Jessica, and thank you for your wonderful company."

Jessica also stood up and extended her hand to him. He took her hand and kissed it. His lips were smooth and warm and she could still feel the kiss as she fell into bed.

She slept soundly in the big, comfortable bed. After her morning shower, she took some care over her appearance before packing her few bits back in her case and heading down for breakfast. She went into the dining room and quickly looked around. She felt a hollow, empty feeling when she saw that it was nearly deserted and the person she was searching for was not there. She dawdled over her coffee in the hope that he would appear late, but as the waiters started to clear all the tables ready for lunch, she knew that he was gone. She wasn't sure if she really was happy or sad. He had somehow drawn her into his life with his powerful personality, and she felt that she might have wanted more of it. Her underlying loneliness was welcoming company.

That way lies potential big trouble, she thought. But her mouth curved into a smile as she thought of him. *Oh, yes. Big trouble. Anyway, I reckon he's younger than me, so he won't be looking for any old birds.*

She checked out, wheeled her case out into the bright sunshine, and continued on her way.

CHAPTER 4

Drew spent the day after the barbeque with John and Polly. The lump in his throat refused to go down. After breakfast, the sun came out and it turned into another glorious day. They all sat on the patio and talked about all manner of things except the one thing—the elephant in the room. Max prepared a lovely lunch and chilled a couple of bottles of Prosecco.

During the course of the lunch, John sat back in his chair and asked, "OK, old mate. Can I put you down as an executor of my will?"

Drew stopped chewing his mouth full of food and just looked at John. He finally managed to swallow. Cleared his throat and squeaked out, "Yes," feeling the tears sliding down his face again.

"That's good," replied John, ignoring the tears, "'cause I already gave the lawyers your name."

Drew got up and walked away down to the end of the garden under the archway with the climbing clematis and to the bottom fence. He sensed a presence behind him and turned to see Polly lighting up one of her few cigarettes. They stood there in silence and looked out over the fields.

Finally, Polly spoke, "John has accepted that there is nothing else to be done and he has to face the inevitable. You must do the same like the family has had to do. The only thing remaining now is to make his time left as wonderful as possible. He is so fed up with everyone's pity; it's making him bad-tempered. You know what he was like. If the children were ill, he didn't handle it very well, and if he was ill, you could never keep him in bed. He was brought up by a family of farmers who couldn't afford to be sick. His mother looked after three of her own children and two of her brother's when his wife died. She sent the children to school however they felt because she just didn't have time to see to them with all the other stuff she had to do. Our children, and even you and I, have been brought up differently. Softer and more pampered. But John always looks at illness as a sign of weakness, so this is all very hard for him. Please, Drew, can you deal with your grief in private and present a smiling face to John? I know it will be hard, but that's what I want. If you can't do this, then you will have to stay away."

This was a long speech from Polly, who used to keep all her conversations short. She never had time for people whom she said "Ran off at the mouth."

Drew smiled. "Still a bossy chops, I see."

Polly smiled back. This was the kid's nickname for her. When they had holiday days out, she was always in charge and was nicknamed "bossy chops."

"Yeah, you could say that. But seriously, we all want to do as much as we can in the time left. I need your help to organise trips and visits to places. Things we have never done before. The boys are needed on the farm and I'm scared I won't be able to manage on my own. As you may have noticed, I'm not very big."

"No, really," said Drew. "And all this time, I thought you were standing in a hole."

Polly's elbow dug him painfully in the ribs. "You know, after a bad start of about 40 years or so, you are turning into rather a nice man. I shall have to thank Max."

After that day, Drew's semi-peaceful life turned into frantic activity. He organised as many things as he thought John could manage. They picked a lovely day to go sea fishing. Drew felt a bit seasick all day, but John had a great day. He caught enough for all the family to have a wonderful fish supper washed down by some grand local cider. John's face was brown and glowing and his smile, while telling his boys about the fight to land the biggest fish, brought the lump back to Drew's throat.

Polly saw this, caught his eye and slightly shook her head at him. To cover up, he walked across the kitchen and opened the back door for Charlie. To his surprise, the cat actually went out. "Bloody hell," he said, peering out the open door. "The bloody cat's gone straight out."

They all laughed. Ben said, "He goes out the same time every night. He'll be back in a minute. It's the fastest pee you'll ever see."

For the first time in weeks, John had a good night's rest. A couple of days later, they all went to the theatre. Lady Clara managed to get first-night tickets for the *Bristol Old Vic*, so they all got dressed up, although it was a bit upsetting for John as he had lost so much weight that nothing fitted him. He finally smiled when he realised a very old suit fitted him for the first time in about 15 years. Drew hired a stretch limo for the occasion. They all went into hysterics when the limo pulled up to the front door and they realised he wasn't going to get out of the driveway without some serious toing and froing. After about a 33-point turn, they were finally on their way.

It was a very grand occasion and Lady Clara was there to greet them all with glasses of champagne. She was a patron of the theatre and seemed to know everyone. It made Polly's day when she was introduced to a couple of film and TV stars, and it made John's day when he was invited backstage to meet the cast. On the way home, John slept. Polly kissed Drew's cheek, squeezed his hand, and rested her head on his shoulder. That was thanks enough for Drew.

John's treatment was really taking its toll. His face looked gaunt and his clothes hung off his really thin frame. Polly couldn't stand it and went out and bought him some new things. Once he was dressed in new jeans and sweaters that actually fit him, he looked better. The sweaters had to be a bit thicker than usual as he was feeling the cold, which helped to make him look a bit fatter.

He had grown a bit of a beard, disguising his thin face a little and Polly got in the habit of stroking the soft hair. This brought out some of the old John when he said if she wanted to stroke something, he would find something more interesting and definitely more worthy, and the usual slap from Polly, albeit a gentle one.

There was a country fair over the weekend with a tractor-pulling competition, which John loved. The weather was dry but overcast so Drew got seats in the stands and kept John wrapped up warm with a couple of tartan wool blankets. Steve and Ben had taken the day off and kept everyone supplied with hot coffee, hot chocolate, and a variety of foods. The tractor-pulling competition was something Drew had never seen, so John talked him through the rules and finer points. Despite the growing chill, John was determined to stay to applaud the winner. Polly was concerned about him, but he brushed aside her concerns and told her to stop fussing. However, she was right. John took a turn for the worst and had to be hospitalised.

Drew blamed himself until all the family had a go at him, Max included, and told him that these last few weeks had been wonderful for John, and they couldn't thank Drew enough. It still didn't completely eliminate his guilt feeling.

Drew had been trying to get hold of Jessica for days, but her house phone just switched to answerphone, which must have had at least a dozen messages from him on it by now, and her mobile just made strange noises. Desperate, he managed to get hold of Stacey and told her about John. She had known John for years, too. Apart from the leisure complex connection, she was a local girl who had gone to school with the boys. She had spent many hours around the farm and enjoyed meals in the big kitchen with the family. She was devastated at the news and said she would do everything she could to get in touch with Jessica.

Stacey didn't know where Jessica was. She had phoned Stacey a few days ago and shared her plan of surprising Luke with a visit. She was fed up with waiting for him to come home. So, she decided she would go and see him for a change. It wasn't a definite arrangement, so Stacey was not sure if she had actually gone. The house phone switched to the machine just as Drew had said, so Stacey tried the mobile. And also, as Drew had said, it was making funny noises. *What the hell is wrong with the damn thing!*

After several other tries, Stacey gave up. She suddenly remembered that Caro had been visiting. Maybe she knew what was going on. She called Caro, who sounded out of breath when she answered. "Sorry, Stacey. Can I phone you back? Toby is stinking the place out, and I'm just in the middle of changing him, or I would be if he would stay still long enough."

Stacey called again and told Caro about John. She broke down into tears and couldn't get a word out. Finally, Stacey asked about Jessica, telling Caro that everyone was desperate to contact her. "And what the hell was wrong with her phone?"

Caro informed her that Toby had put Jessica's phone down the toilet and she had bought a new cheap one until she could contact her provider. Caro had to search for the piece of paper with Jessica's new number on it as she had forgotten to save it.

By the time Stacey got the new number, it was fairly late. She didn't know whether to try to reach Jessica or leave it till the morning. Thinking about it—the news about one of her oldest friends couldn't wait—Stacey tried the new number. The phone rang, but no one answered. She left a brief message, then another one half an hour later, and a third one an hour after that. She finally went to bed, taking her phone with her. After a very restless night, by the morning, there was still no reply. *Where the hell is she?* Now, Stacey was starting to worry.

It was only much later that she found out that Jessica had no signal for much of her journey along the coast road and listened to Stacey's messages many hours later.

CHAPTER 5

Jessica continued her journey along the coast. She stopped at a particularly beautiful spot and ate a cooling ice cream from a small, isolated café. She spoke to the young girl serving and learnt that her father had opened the café after losing his job; her family lived just along the beach. During high tide season, when surfers thronged the beach, the café would get really busy. The rest of the time, only people who liked the secluded beach visited the place. It was quiet and peaceful without all the tourists, who didn't know about it. The café had a few tables under sun shades and catered for simple snacks. A day in the sun on this lovely beach with a toasted sandwich, salad, and a cold drink for lunch seemed like sheer bliss. *Maybe she would come back and do just that one day,* Jessica thought.

She said goodbye to the girl and, a bit reluctantly, continued on her way. The landscape started to change. It was more built up now and Jessica stopped to consult the map. There seemed to be a lot more roads than the map was showing since it was quite old and not updated. *Well, if I get lost, I would have to ask the way and hope that someone knew where this new complex was.* As it happened most of the local people knew about it and could direct her quite easily.

She parked her car and spent a few minutes looking at all the activities. There were workmen swarming about everywhere. Some were high on the scaffolding and many more were at ground level, pushing wheelbarrows and carrying building supplies. She carefully looked around but couldn't see Luke at all. She got out of her car and walked towards the opening in the fencing. A workman hurried over to her. He wasn't pleased that she was walking around the site without a hard hat on. "Health and safety," he kept saying.

He pointed out the site office and told her to go there. She picked her way through the rubble and knocked on the door of the portable cabin. Someone shouted something from inside, but the voice was drowned out by the drill that started up behind her. She presumed it was OK to go in and opened the door. A loud voice shouted in Spanish to shut the door as he couldn't hear on the phone. She quietly closed the door behind her and looked at the broad back of the man pacing up and down, phone clamped to his ear and arms wildly waving. She had seen that black wavy hair before and felt her mouth curve in a smile of surprise and pleasure.

Antonio was still facing away from her. He finished his call, threw his arms in the air, and swore loudly. She laughed, making him turn quickly around. His eyes widened and his mouth opened in surprise before smiling widely at her.

"Jessica, what in the world are you doing here?" he said, pulling a chair out for her. "I'm so sorry we missed each other at breakfast this morning. I had an urgent call to get back here. My partner had to make an unexpected journey up the country. A problem about supplies."

Jessica laughed again. "Is your partner Luke Benson?"

"Yes, it is," again Antonio looked surprised.

"That's the answer to your question about the reason for my being here then. I'm looking for Luke."

"Luke," Antonio said, a frown creasing his brow. "Is he a friend of yours?" Then a look of understanding crossed his face and he smacked his hand on his forehead. "You're Jessie."

"Yes, I'm Jessie. I thought I would surprise him."

"Oh, no," Antonio sunk down into the tatty leather chair in front of the untidy desk.

Jessica sat down in an equally tatty chair opposite. "What do you mean 'oh no?'"

Antonio leant forward, his elbows on his knees. "Luke has gone up country to a quarry that supplies us with much of our stone and bricks. There is no cell phone signal there, so I have to wait until he contacts me. I won't be able to let him know you are here. Why didn't you let him know you were coming and he wouldn't have gone?"

"Well, then it wouldn't have been a surprise," retorted Jessica.

They both sat in silence for a few minutes. Antonio got up and switched on a kettle on the top of a grubby cupboard. "Can I make you a coffee?"

Jessica regarded the dozens of stained cups with distaste. "No, thank you," she said politely.

Antonio eyed all the cups and then switched off the kettle. "I don't blame you," his white teeth gleamed as he gave a wide smile and a bark of a laugh. "Pretty awful, aren't they," he said as he inspected the cups.

Jess returned the smile and stood up. "Well, I had better see if I can find somewhere to stay while I'm waiting."

"Whoa, wait a minute. Everywhere will be full. Early holiday season. Luke stays in a shared house with a few other guys, so you wouldn't want to stay there. There is only one option left."

"And what would that be?" Jessie said, her shoulders slumping.

"You stay at my home," Antonio said, spreading his arms out and smiling again.

A shaft of sunlight came through the dusty window and made his black hair glisten like a raven's wing.

"Oh, no. No. I couldn't do that."

"Why…don't you trust me," Antonio said, his eyes twinkling at her.

"Well…."Jessica blustered, completely wrong-footed.

Antonio burst out laughing. "It's OK, Jessica. I have a housekeeper and her handyman husband who live on the premises. And it so happens that I have a dinner party tonight with three other couples as guests. One couple lives nearby and they go home, but two couples stay over and travel back in the morning.

"So, you see, you will be quite safe. Normally, Luke would also join us. The guests are all people who are involved in the business, although we don't talk business in my home."

Jessica looked at him, still feeling a bit doubtful.

"Come on, Jessica. I will take you to my home now. I can leave all this for today. Come and have a proper coffee and some lunch and we will get to know each other."

Jessica finally smiled and Antonio let out a whoop, making her laugh. "Come, let's go. Is your car outside?"

Jessica nodded.

"OK, follow me then. It will take us about 30 minutes to get there, but it's a nice drive. Wait, let me get your luggage and we will go together in my car. Yours will be quite safe here till tomorrow."

Jessica unloaded all her luggage and some bits and pieces, moved her little jeep into a shady corner, and put the roof up.

Antonio's ride was a big, hefty truck with four seats in the cab and a long, flat back, which was carrying a selection of tools and dusty sacks. Jessica gingerly looked inside, but the seats and floor were surprisingly clean and she climbed in. The efficient air conditioning soon took the hot air out of the truck and the cab was comfortable with well-sprung and soft seats.

The road they were driving on was getting narrower and steeper. They climbed up and up, passing olive groves and a few isolated houses on the way. They turned onto a flat tarred road, which was a lot less bumpy than the previous one. Antonio had told her about the area. He had moved to this region many years ago and when his business became successful, he bought some land and built the home he had always dreamt of. The road they had just turned onto was the start of his land, and many of the olive groves along the road were also his. The olives were a very lucrative business, which was a good safety net if the building company ran into difficulties.

The road started to ascend again and Jessica looked behind her. The views were nothing short of spectacular. There was even a sight of the glistening blue sea in the distance. They rounded a corner that was lined with tall trees and she got her first sight of the house. It was wide and white and simple with a balcony that ran around the whole of the first floor taking advantage of the magnificent views. The windows had shutters of white wood and the roof had deep terracotta-coloured tiles. Climbing plants with flowers in every hue were growing up the walls. There were garages at the side of the house and Antonio pulled into one of them.

He hauled her suitcase out from the back of the cab and she gathered the rest of her bits and followed him. She stopped at the front of the house to look once again at the view and heard the front door open and a torrent of Spanish coming from inside. It was so fast that she only caught some of it. It seemed that Antonio should have let them know he was coming home early and bringing a guest.

The big double-wooden door opened and a small, rather wizened woman of undetermined age was being kissed on the cheek by Antonio. He replied in a rapid Spanish to reassure her that nothing was wrong and that he was bringing Senor Luke's lady to stay as he was away. The old lady's face was wreathed in smiles; she stood on tiptoes to embrace Jessica and bid her to come in.

"Jessica, this is my oldest friend and my housekeeper. Her name is Alisha Magdalena, but everyone calls her Lena. You will meet Pablo, her husband, later. He looks after the property and also keeps an eye on the olive groves and the workers. Some of them he has known for years, so they don't look at him as a boss only a friend."

Jessica moved inside the cool interior of the house. The walls were mainly white, but some of them had beautifully carved rich wood panelling with lovely old carved Spanish chairs in front of them. There were old paintings of Spanish noblemen and flamenco dancers. The carved dark wood curved staircase gleamed against the white walls and pots of flowers sent their scent into the air. The house had a sense of love and peace about it, which seemed to permeate her body.

Antonio led her upstairs and Jessica looked down into the hall from the gallery above. The terracotta tiles on the floor were partially covered with colourful rugs, and these were duplicated in the upstairs hallway.

He opened a heavy carved door and stood aside for her to enter. He walked across the large cool room and threw open the shutters. The room had a rich, deep green carpet and green and gold brocade curtains. The same material covered the wide carved bed and was warm against the white walls. The double doors behind the shutters led out onto a large balcony. Antonio stood by the wrought iron rail and looked out at the valley. Jessica looked around the room and straight away felt at home. She joined Antonio on the balcony and also looked at the view.

"In all the years of living here, I never get tired of looking at this."

They stood there in silence. Antonio placed his arm around Jessica's shoulders and she was surprised at how natural that felt. She didn't move away and stood and felt the warmth and power of this handsome man. Finally, he gave her a squeeze and moved back inside the room.

"I promised you coffee and lunch. I will leave you to freshen up and meet you downstairs when you are ready. Turn left at the bottom of the stairs straight down the corridor to the terrace at the back where coffee will be waiting."

Jessica quickly freshened up in the big marble bathroom and changed out of her grubby clothes into a flowing and soft, long muslin dress in pale blue, which showed off her tanned skin. She gave her hair a good brush and added some silver earrings and sandals. Judging by the admiring look Antonio gave her, she had obviously made a good choice. She felt totally at ease as she settled into the padded cushions of a swinging chair and accepted a fragrant cup of coffee.

CHAPTER 6

rew had been trying to locate Jessica. He had made numerous calls to no avail. He had also phoned Luke and felt like throwing the phone across the room when he got Luke's answerphone as well. Max watched him lose his temper and grabbed him from behind in a big bear hug. She hung on until she felt him relax against her. He turned in the circle of her arms and rested his chin on the top of her head. Her hair was soft and smelt of shampoo. "Oh God, Max, what am I going to do if anything happens to John before I can contact Jessie?"

"Well it's not for want of trying. If Jessica goes off the grid without telling anyone then she's only got herself to blame. John is in the hospital and in good hands. There is nothing we can do except hope."

Drew had promised to go down to the school with Max to meet Kate. They were organising a black tie event at Clara's pile. There would be a couple of popular dancing groups and a chart-topping star who was doing an hour-long concert. This alone was worth the ticket price.

Clara had pulled out all the stops and called in as many favours as she possibly could. The entertainers, for the most part, were giving their services for free. Most of the very expensive raffle prizes were donated, which ensured a good sale of the very expensive tickets.

Drew and Clara had become a formidable duo in organising fundraising events and were now greatly sought after by numerous large companies. The first black and white ball they organised had raised a large enough amount of money to undertake all the maintenance for the school, build an extension, buy computers for the students to learn on, and still leave a bit of a kitty for the future. Photos from the event after all this time were still finding their way into various magazines, and the high-profile guests still talked about it.

Kate had been away on holiday with her father. She seemed to treat him more like a friend. This was not lost on Max, who found that easier to deal with. She was, however, glad that Kate was back. She had missed her daughter a lot. Their bond was very strong. Drew envied this. His own relationship with his daughter was back on an OK basis, but they would never be as close as they were once.

Max dragged out a couple of overnight bags and started to pack a few things for both of them. The idea was to meet with all of Clara's helpers and finalise the last details of the forthcoming bash, sort out some final advertising to sell the last few remaining tickets, and then spend some time with Kate at the school. They had booked into a local pub (where by now they were well known) rather than bothering the housekeeper at the school to organise a room for them.

Drew felt very tense and decided to forgo his usual quick shower for a relaxing bath. He ran it fairly hot and dumped some of the contents of a bottle into the water. Max stuck her head around the door whilst it was running and sniffed the steam. "I hope you know how expensive that bath essence is that you are being so extravagant with. It cost an arm and a leg."

Drew lowered himself into the hot water, sucking in a breath at the heat. "I'll buy you some more."

"Don't bother. I never liked it anyway. I'll give you the name of some that I do."

Max wandered back into the bedroom and idly picked up the evening paper that Drew had thrown on the bed. The headlines screamed up at her. TV STAR AND ADOPTED SISTER JAILED.

She sat on the bed and read the rest, a smile spread across her face.

"The star of a well-known daytime chat show, Michael Swift, was today jailed, along with the woman who for years purported to be his sister. The two of them had a whole assortment of false passports and were being sought by police in three countries for child exploitation, child abuse, and rape. Added to these charges were also ones for brutal beatings after several women came forward. After exhaustive investigations, the police at Interpol have finally pieced together the couple's history.

"They were both adopted by a perverted couple who exploited them until their teens when the two teenagers turned the tables on them and continued to bring them nothing but trouble for the rest of their lives. The couple died in suspicious circumstances, leaving their estate to the children.

"The police had doubts about the deaths but were unable to prove anything. The children were, by then, young adults who sold up the house and all the contents, then disappeared.

"After further investigations, it was discovered that the couple flew first to Thailand and then the Philippines, where they set up brothels for under-aged children. When things got too hot for them in both those countries after rumours of child murders, they returned to the UK.

"They both went through extensive plastic surgery and set up new identities. They got jobs on local radio stations with false CVs and graduated to TV, where they established successful careers.

"The TV company they worked for was horrified at the revelations but then admitted there had been a few complaints from young girls about some physical abuse by Arthur Hale (the star's real name) and had chosen to hush them up because of his popularity. This has brought forth a potential case against the company. The allegations are to be looked into.

"Several women had come forward to give evidence of violent abuse and rape by Hale and the assistance by Cicely Cram (the real name of his 'sister') in setting up meetings promising them TV stardom. Some of the women chose to give their evidence, providing they were not named, but

"The jury was out for less than an hour and declared a guilty verdict for both Hale and Cram. The judge proclaimed his disgust at the dreadful things the evidence had uncovered and sentenced them both to 20 years each, with no possibility of parole.

"There was loud cheering and clapping from the gallery as the couple were led away. Hale showed his super white teeth in a smile as he was taken down. This prompted the judge to remark. 'It is very obvious to the whole court that the accused has absolutely no remorse.'"

Max sat on the toilet seat while reading the whole report to Drew. She fetched them both a glass of wine and they toasted Melanie and hoped she had heard about it. She was on a fashion shoot in the Maldives and was now one of the highest-paid and most well-known models in the world. Drew was proud he had helped to give her the first break of her career, the rest she had done herself with some help from Max and her company. He just wished that Marty could have been here to see it. Despite her beauty and wealth, and although she had been seen around with some male escorts, there was still nobody special in her life. Maybe now, with the closure of her past horrendous ordeal, she could move on to a happy life with someone who loved her. They both hoped so as they clinked glasses.

Drew relaxed down into the water and smiled until he thought about John and the fact he still hadn't heard from Jessica. *Not like her to be unreachable. She could be with Luke, but he was also unreachable. Where the hell were they?*

He stood up, water cascading from his body, and reached for the towel. His relaxed mood had evaporated. He marched back into the bedroom, dripping water everywhere, and reached for his phone. Once again, he tried Jessica and Luke, and then Stacey, who still hadn't got any news for him. He sat down heavily on the bed until Max shouted at him. He got up, leaving a wet patch on the cover. She snatched it off before the rest of the bed got wet.

"For Christ sake, Drew. Go and get dry, and we'll give Polly a call. She should be able to let us know about John and maybe she's heard from Jess. It's a slim chance, but you never know."

Polly's voice sounded weary as she updated Drew on John. The oncologist had seen him and laid out all the options. John asked the doctor if any of the treatments would prolong his life and pushed hard until he got an answer. When the answer was "probably not" and that the treatments would be debilitating, John decided he wanted to spend his last weeks with his family without being sick and sleeping all day. The oncologist had a meeting with Polly to discuss pain-relieving medication to make John as comfortable as possible in the time he had left.

At this point, Polly's voice broke and Drew felt like his heart was breaking with it. He explained about the difficulty getting hold of Jessica and said the he and Max would call in on their way back tomorrow. Polly informed him that John would be home by then and would be pleased to see him. With that, Drew put the phone down with a huge lump in his throat and tears in his eyes.

CHAPTER 7

Jessica spent a relaxing afternoon talking to Antonio and enjoying a light lunch. He had been married and had a son and a daughter who had now grown up. His son was at medical school in London, and he was very proud of him even though he hadn't followed his father in his business. His daughter was a skilled horse rider and was in Vienna, helping to run a stable training Spanish lipizzano show horses. He had offered to set her up a riding school, but she loved the challenge of training the beautiful white horses to do amazing dances and wanted to continue for the moment. He missed them both very much but was very pleased that they were both doing so well.

Jessica was very conscious of the powerful charisma emanating from this man. Her eyes were constantly drawn to him even when he was silent. She knew now why Luke had such feelings for him and admired how skilled he was at whatever he did. Luke had always said that Nio would never ask anyone to do anything that he was not prepared to do, and all the workmen, no matter how skilled they were, knew he could do it equally as good as them, if not better.

Antonio poured them another glass of the excellent white wine that was in the cooler. "Just this one and then I must prepare for my guests." He observed the fleeting look of panic on Jessica's face and added, "You will like them."

"I'm sure I will," Jessica said. "Are they all Spanish?"

"Peter, who married my sister, comes from Scotland and is my lawyer. He speaks Spanish with a rather strange accent. Roberto is my oldest friend. We grew up together in a small village and worked for my father together. He knows as much about building as I do, so I paid for him to learn to be an architect. That way, we can work together without treading on each other's toes. I come up with the ideas, and he yells at me and tells me it's impossible, then he goes ahead and draws up the plans for it anyway."

Jessica laughed. "Do you always get your own way?"

"Sometimes. Usually. Nearly always."

Jessica laughed again. "What about the rest of the guests?"

"Roberto's wife is Swedish, gorgeous and very talented. She paints the most wonderful Spanish-inspired illustrations. Prints of the originals are on the walls of many of the hotels in Spain, in magazines, and on walls and in art galleries. Most of the ones you have been admiring on my walls are hers. They are the originals, though."

"Of course they are," said Jessica, smiling.

Antonio also smiled. "Sorry, I didn't mean to boast."

"Of course, you didn't," Jessica said with a look under her eyelashes.

Antonio playfully prodded her. "OK, point taken."

"The guests," Jessica reminded.

"Ah, yes. The third couple also works for me as well as being my friends. "

"Do you have any friends who don't work for you?" Jessica said quietly.

"I have you," he replied, also quietly.

Jessica's eyes locked onto his, and for an endless moment, she was drawn into the brown velvet of his eyes as she let the shock waves run through her before finally looking away. Antonio felt it, too, and stood up, turning his back to her. He stood like that, looking out into the garden for several moments before turning back towards her. His obvious erection was on her eye level and couldn't be ignored. She stared at it before lifting her eyes to meet his. He made no attempt to conceal it, and at that moment, something between them was born.

"We should get ready," he said, holding out his hand to her.

She pushed herself upright on the arms of the chair, rejecting his hand. She didn't trust herself to touch him. She walked ahead of him, feeling heat on her back and neck that had nothing to do with the dying rays of the sun. The ghost of Luke walked between them.

The dinner was more than excellent. Delicious cold spiced soup. Then beautiful grilled fish followed by the main course of steaks, so tender they could be cut with a fork. Abundant bowls of salad and a variety of vegetables were placed around the table. The dessert was a chocolate dream. Soft sponge with a hot melted chocolate centre. All together, it was a meal that would easily grace any fine dining restaurant.

The conversation was conducted almost completely in English which Jessica was glad of. Her Spanish was passable but not brilliant, especially given the speed of most lively talking around a Spanish table.

The guests sat comfortably, nursing glasses of fine port. Roberto's wife, Inga, was, as Antonio had said, gorgeous. Tall willowy figure, intense blue eyes, and a mop of white blonde hair. Jessica might have been jealous of her if she hadn't liked her so much. Inga had a tinkling laugh and a wide, friendly smile. She obviously adored her husband, and Jessica was surprised when she learnt they had been married for 11 years and had three children. They looked as if they were newlyweds, and she told them so. They both laughed and said that everyone said the same. Roberto was built the same way as Antonio. They could have been brothers.

Inga leant in towards her husband and kissed his cheek. "Look at him," she said, "he's soooo sexy. He's more addictive than drugs and far longer lasting."

Roberto put his arm around his wife. "I've got a job to last very long at all with this gorgeous wife around."

Antonio looked fondly at this handsome couple and his eyes rested briefly on Jessica as if he was sensing her reaction. The look was seen by Peter's eagle eyes and he got a jab of misgiving. He liked Luke and could sense something intangible was happening between Antonio and Jessica that could spell trouble. Antonio relied on Luke a lot in his business and their friendship had grown over the years of working together. A rift between them caused by Jessica could mean disaster. He shook off the feeling. Too early to dwell on that. Probably means nothing. All the same, he had never seen Antonio look so softly at any woman for a long time.

The other couple were very young and a bit shy. They were introduced as Antonio's cousin and his wife. Later in the evening, she found out from them that they had been brought up in the same village as Antonio but had lost both sets of their parents within six months of each other. They had been taken under Antonio's care, put through school, fell in love, and married. He had made sure they had a newly built house to move into, and they worshipped him. As they talked, Jessica felt a lump in her throat at the unstinting generosity of this man who took two orphans who were not family and made them his cousins.

Everyone slowly moved into the lounge whilst two young girls who were helping in the kitchen cleared the dining table. The chairs and couches placed around the lounge were deep, soft, and comfortable. Jessica was surprised to see Roberto fetching an elaborately carved wooden chair with a high back and setting it in front of the carved wall panels. A carved wood and green velvet-covered footstool was placed in front of it.

"Oh, no, Roberto," Antonio said, shaking his head.

"Oh, yes, Antonio," replied Roberto.

"Yes, yes, yes," chorused everyone else.

What is going on, Jessica thought. *Are we going to play games?*

Roberto opened one of the carved panels on the wall to reveal a cupboard. From within the cupboard, he brought out a beautifully decorated Spanish guitar and a wooden rest. He placed the guitar on the rest and then came and sat down beside his wife. Lena and Pablo came quietly into the back of the room as if they were expecting this. They settled comfortably at the back of the room in two big carved chairs, the same as the one placed for Antonio.

Antonio sat in the chair with his foot in its tan loafer resting on the stool. He ran his fingers over the strings and tightened a couple of pegs. Then he played. The hairs on the back of Jessica's neck stood up. Spanish flamenco music flowed through the room, and Lena and his cousin's wife, Theresa, clapped sharply to the rhythm.

The other guests sat and were enthralled by the sheer power of the music. One after another, the rhythm changed. At one point, the two Spanish ladies used castanets and sang to the music; the sound was magical. It was better than any flamenco show Jessica had ever seen, and she was spellbound. Eventually, Antonio stopped and put his tongue out as if he was gasping. Lena brought him a glass of wine and a glass of water. He drank the water thirstily and sipped the wine. All the guests stood and helped themselves to wine and handfuls of nuts and grapes. When everyone had settled down again, Antonio resumed his seat.

Now, the mood changed. The guitar played soft, lilting melodies. The music was wistful and romantic and the couples moved closer together. Jessica was reminded of an old song *While My Guitar Gently Weeps*. This guitar was weeping. She looked at Antonio's face. His eyes were downcast and his body was hunched over the instrument, his fingers rippling over the strings, completely wrapped up in the music. She had to take a deep breath. She felt as if she had been holding her breath for a long time. Just as she inhaled, his eyes raised up and met hers. Again, she felt the jolt. The look was seen for the second time by Peter, and again he got an uneasy feeling.

Finally, Antonio's foot came off the stool and he stood up. Nobody moved at first. Still spellbound by the music. Then they all started applauding. Jessica also stood up, but her legs felt wobbly. *The wine,* she said to herself.

Lena came in with coffee, and afterwards the cousins wished everyone goodnight. They fiercely hugged Antonio and then Lena and left. They were followed by Roberto and a sleepy Inga. Peter and his wife, Antonio's sister Consuela, were staying and started to make their way towards the stairs. Jessica also started to walk behind them until Antonio's hand on her arm stopped her.

"Stay and have a nightcap with me," he said quietly.

She hesitated.

"You don't have an early start tomorrow."

"Well," she still hesitated.

Then he said the one thing that decided her. It hit her like a cold shower. "Luke won't be back till about lunchtime."

She felt her back straighten. "It's been a wonderful day and a magical evening, but it's late and I'm tired."

Antonio's face fell. He immediately realised his mistake in mentioning Luke's name. He raised up her arm and softly kissed her hand. If anyone else had done that, it would have made her uncomfortable, but at this moment, it was entirely right, and she could still feel his lips when she entered her room.

Further down the hallway, Peter breathed a sigh of relief.

CHAPTER 8

Drew and Max spent an exhausting day with Clara. She seemed to have boundless energy for all the phone calls and endless lists she kept referring to. Who knew that these events took so much organising? Drew thought that all the arrangements had already been done and it was just a matter of showing up in his tux. No such luck.

The few tickets left were up for sale on the internet, but six of them were offered to some radio stations to use as prizes in some competitions. Clara had devised a clever competition. She had obtained jingles from various TV adverts and some film-themed music. The listeners had to guess which product or which film they came from. As soon as they got a wrong answer, they were eliminated. The one that guessed the most answers won a pair of tickets. The competition would be run over a week and the winners would have a free makeover (given free by a local beauty salon in exchange for some free advertising), a hired tuxedo for the men, and dresses for the ladies (supplied free from a local hire shop, again for the prestigious advertising) and a hired limo to pick them up. These arrangements alone took dozens of phone calls, with Clara's plummy voice working overtime on the charm.

There were flowers to organise, then chairs and tables, glasses, the three bars, and car parking. If everything went to plan, and with minimum outlay to subscribers, the charity was in line to make a great deal of money for the variety of worthy causes that were set to benefit.

Eventually, everything seemed to be done. The few things left to deal with were left in Clara's capable hands. Drew and Max walked wearily to their car. As they had promised to call in, they headed towards John and Polly's home. Not really feeling up to it, but knowing they had to if they wanted to sleep later.

John was at home tucked up in a comfy chair in front of the TV. Polly had a curry cooking for all of them. As soon as Drew smelt it, he realised that apart from a few snacks, he and Max hadn't eaten anything all day. Trust Polly to cook for everyone. The eternal earth mother. They spent a while talking to John, who seemed bright but painfully thin. Polly brought in TV tables, and they all ate in the lounge rather than moving John into the kitchen.

"This reminds me of holiday times when we ate in here and all the kids took over the kitchen table."

Polly laughed and said with her mouth full, "It was easier to get the spilt food off the kitchen floor than the carpet in here."

They sat and ate the wonderful spicy curry and fluffy rice, followed by cheesecake. John ate very little, but Polly hadn't piled his plate high like she had done for years while he was working the farm.

After the meal, John's eyes started closing, and so they made the excuse of packing up the dishes to have a word with Polly in the kitchen. She opened the back door and stepped outside to light a cigarette. Drew dumped the dishes on the worktop and Max started loading them in the dishwasher while Drew followed Polly outside. They stood silently together, leaning on the wall. She crushed her cigarette and her head dropped onto his shoulder. Wordlessly, he put his arms around her and her tears shook her whole body, coming up from deep inside her. Drew held her and let her tears flow, knowing that she needed the release and couldn't do it in front of John or the boys. Max stuck her head out the door, saw what was happening, and went back inside to put some coffee on.

Finally, Polly's tears stopped and she stepped back, wiping her eyes. "I keep trying to imagine my life without him, and I can't. I had visions of us growing old together. Travelling. Seeing something of the world before we were too old, knowing the boys were running the farm. Now, the dreams are all gone. My life has always centred around John, so what will my centre be when he's gone? The boys don't need me anymore. I can't stay in this house. It's too big and has too many memories. I love him so much. I'm going to be like half a pair of scissors without him. What a waste of a wonderful man."

She paced backwards and forwards, wringing the tissues in her hands and running her hands through her hair until it stuck up all over her head. Drew had never seen Polly like this—ever. She had always been the voice of reason. The calm in the midst of the storm. For once in his life, he didn't have an answer. Max stood in the doorway with two cups of coffee, which she wordlessly handed to them and then went back inside.

"Where are the boys tonight?" Drew said, his voice sounding rough from the lump in it that Polly's tears had created.

"They are down at Ben's cottage. You know, the one Jess lived in. By the way, have you located her yet?"

"Left dozens of messages, but no reply yet. Will try her again later."

Polly started pacing again and lit another cigarette. She started crying again and he took a step forward. Polly put up her hand to stop him. "It's OK, Drew. I can't seem to stop crying every time John can't see me. I am just longing to see Jessica. I really need someone who isn't family, if that makes sense. John's mum cries all the time and the boys can't bear to see their dad like this. I need a friend to lean on."

"I am doing my best to locate her, but her phone is faulty or something. Stacey is on the case, so she'll track her down. You'll just have to lean on me in the meantime."

Polly squeezed his arm and gave him a watery smile. He went back inside. The kitchen was all pristine and the dishwasher was humming away. Polly came in behind him. "My God, the fairies have been in and cleaned up all the mess. Thanks, Max."

She put her arms around Max and gave her a hug.

"John's asleep, so I stayed out here. I didn't want to wake him."

"It's OK. It's the medication. I'll leave him for the time being. Don't worry. I'll give him your goodbyes."

Drew and Max drove home in silence, deep in their own thoughts. As soon as they got home, Max went straight to the bedroom. Soon afterwards, she called out to Drew. He was feeding the two cats, who rubbed around his legs and bleated for food as if they had been starved for days.

"You two are getting far too fat. Sophia feeds you too much. Go out and catch a mouse."

Lady looked up at him; her big eyes seemed horrified at the thought before she resumed an unladylike scoffing.

Drew went along the hall to the bedroom to find Max freshly showered and dressed in a beautiful cream lace nightgown with thigh-high splits and with her hair gleaming like burnished copper. She walked across the floor and, without a word, pulled his sweater over his head and kissed him deeply, her tongue in his mouth and her breasts rubbing against his bare chest. Still kissing him, she undid his belt, then his waistband, and then bent down and removed his shoes and socks before undoing his zip and pulling down his trousers. His erection sprang out to meet her, restrained somewhat by his underpants. He started to say something, but she put her finger against his lips. She led him to the bed and pushed him down before pulling off his underpants. His penis stood away from his body, thick and proud, and Max sucked in her breath. She lay alongside him and continued kissing him deeply.

He went to raise up but she pushed him down. He relaxed then and let her do whatever she wanted. Her hands were all over him, stroking and scratching. She rubbed oil on her hands and stroked his penis until he thought it would burst and started to groan and thrust upwards. At that point, she took her hands away, bringing forth another groan. She stripped off her nightdress and again oiled her hands. She then proceeded to rub her hands all over her body while he watched her. His hand strayed to his penis, but she slapped it away. She continued to rub her hands all over her body, including all the intimate places, until finally, she knelt astride him, the tip of his penis just touching her. He tried to thrust upward, but she lifted her body up and prevented it. She leaned over and kissed him again deeply, her hair brushing his face and her breasts touching his chest. He was totally out of it by then, on another planet. Unaware of anything but the feel of her.

Slowly she started to impale herself upon him. He tried again to thrust upwards, but again, she pulled away. She kept teasing him until she knew he was almost at the point of no return. Then she took him fully inside her and stopped. He moaned but stayed still until, by the feel of him inside her, she reached almost the point of climax. Then she started moving up and down on his shaft, getting faster as she reached her peak, taking him along with her. Her shout was followed almost immediately by his, and the spasms felt by both of them arched their backs and shook their bodies, leaving them breathless and trembling.

Max slid off Drew's body and he turned on his side and cradled her in his arms. They stayed that way until their breathing returned to normal, and their bodies started to get cold. He hadn't realised how tense he'd been, and now in the afterglow of their lovemaking, he felt tears trickle down his face. He thought about John and how much he loved Polly and how the close intimacy they had shared would now be gone forever. He rolled over and pulled the duvet over them. They didn't talk, and just as Drew was drifting off into sleep, he remembered he hadn't rung Jessica. There was no way he could get up now. He would get up early.

They were still wrapped in each other's arms in the morning.

CHAPTER 9

Jessica had walked up the long staircase to her room feeling as if she was being dragged there, pulling against a string that was in Antonio's hand. The temptation to spend another few minutes with him over a nightcap was overwhelming. It was only the mention of Luke that had burst the bubble. *What was wrong with her, for goodness sake?* The only excuse she had was that she hadn't slept with Luke for many weeks and was starting to need release. No, that wasn't it. If she felt that way, it didn't take much to start her juices flowing, but they hadn't. She just craved his company. Maybe she was lonely. She dismissed that idea, too. She spent long periods on her own and now she'd had a wonderful evening among some lovely people. She didn't feel lonely at this moment. *Don't know,* she said aloud.

She opened the shutters and walked out onto the balcony. She hadn't turned on the lights, so she stood there quietly in the dark, smelling the beautiful fragrance of the flowers and looking up at the blue velvet sky with its twinkling stars. She became aware of some movement below her on the patio. She heard people talking in Spanish and recognised Antonio's voice. She craned her head over the parapet to see who he was talking to. She couldn't really see, but it sounded like Lena. She didn't mean to listen, but when she heard her name in rapid Spanish, she listened a bit harder. The voices were speaking quietly and quickly, and she could only catch a few words. Among them were her name several times and Luke's name. From some of the other words she caught the general drift of the conversation.

Lena was saying, "You must put her out of your mind; she

belongs to someone else."

There was a silence.

Antonio said that no person "owned" another.

Lena snorted, then said that he knew what she meant. "She is Luke's woman, and he is your friend."

"I know, I know. Do you think I don't remember?"

"Nio, I see your face when you look at her. Even your music tonight was different. You must break any ties before you do much harm to everyone, including yourself."

The two of them strolled further into the garden and Jessica could hear no more. She watched them, the strong man and the small woman with her arm tucked through his. She went back inside and thought about what she had heard; she knew it was right. She must stay well away from this man. He was far too dangerous.

She went to bed but couldn't sleep. Brown eyes and guitar music running through her dreams. She decided to go outside for a walk in the cool air. She went out onto the balcony and listened to make sure there was no one still in the garden. She wrapped her robe around her and stole softly downstairs to the small door at the back of the house.

The night air was soft on her face and the dark garden was fragrant. The sound of insects chirruped and buzzed, and the lush grass was cool on her feet. She walked down the garden towards a bench that was under an arch of thick vines and sat down. Her mind started to dwell on the feelings that Antonio had stirred up in her. She hadn't felt anything like this since her first days with Luke a long time ago, and years before that, with Drew. *It was just the excitement of a new man who found her attractive,* she told herself. *For God sake, Jessie girl. What rubbish,* she almost said out loud.

Men came on to her all the time and she brushed them all off with a laugh. This was different. She knew it and he knew it.

Almost as if she had willed him there, she heard a soft step behind her and knew it was him. His hands caressed her shoulders and his mouth came down to kiss the back of her neck. His breath was warm on her skin and she shuddered. Thinking she was cold, he knelt down behind her and wrapped his arms around her, warming her with his body. They stayed like this for many minutes, leaning into each other and sharing their body warmth.

He stood up and she almost cried out at the loss of him until he sat beside her on the bench. Her facing one way and him the other, and wrapped her again in his arms. Her head rested on his shoulder and his lips were on her hair. They stayed like this for a long time, both almost afraid to move in case they broke the spell. His lips finally found hers as she turned her face towards him. The kiss was deep and long. It held no passion, but something passed between them that was more profound. A promise, a longing, a wish for the future, a beginning. Their lips clung and caressed, unwilling to part but knowing they had to. Jessica sighed and moved her head. Her hand came up and smoothed his face and she stood up. Antonio's arms went around her waist and he rested his head against her belly.

"We can't," Jessica said, her voice husky.

"I know," Antonio said, letting her go.

The reason was not spoken of, but it didn't have to be.

In the morning, she showered and dressed in blue shorts and a pleated white top. She slowly walked down the stairs, wondering if everyone was up before her. She heard voices and walked towards them. Breakfast had been laid on the terrace and Peter and Consuela were sitting there chatting over coffee. She glanced quickly around before they saw her, but there was no sign of Antonio. She felt disappointment wash over her before she smiled as the two at the table turned around.

"Good morning," they both said cheerfully. "Did you sleep well?"

She went out onto the balcony. "Wonderfully, thank you,"

Jessica lied as she sat down.

She poured herself coffee from the pot on the table and looked up as Lena stood beside her. "I cook eggs. I will bring."

"No, really," Jessica started to say, but Lena just flapped her hand and continued towards the kitchen.

"Are you meeting Luke later today?" Peter said, leaning back and crossing his legs as he lit a cigarette.

"Well, I hope so, although I have no idea what time he will be back."

"It depends on how long it takes him to haggle out a good price. The company he is visiting is notorious for holding out for the best price. Sometimes, it can be a quick agreement, and sometimes, the manager can drive you mad. They say it depends on what mood his mistress was in the night before."

Both the women laughed.

Lena came back to the table with a dish of beautifully cooked scrambled eggs. She also brought large slices of tomatoes, which had been fried with herbs, fresh crusty bread, and tangy Saville marmalade. It wasn't until Jessica had the food in front of her that she realised how hungry she was.

Peter and Consuela had already eaten, so before she started eating, they bid her a warm goodbye with hugs from both of them.

"Give Luke our regards when you see him," Peter said. "He is such a great bloke. We are so sorry we missed him."

"I'll tell him when I see him."

Peter had seen Jessica flick her eyes quickly around a couple of times and knew she wanted to ask where Antonio was. He had made up his mind not to tell her. He knew he was being childish but he didn't want to give any assistance to her in case that would encourage the feeling between her and Antonio. He thought it was very obvious.

At least, to him, it was.

As they were walking away, Consuela turned back to Jessica. "Oh, sorry. Nearly forgot. Nio will be back about 10 o'clock to take you back to the site. You can wait there for Luke or take your car, go to the beach, and meet him when he gets back."

Jessica enjoyed her breakfast. As soon as she finished, as if she had been watching, Lena came out and sat down at the table opposite her. She poured a cup of coffee and nodded in acknowledgement at Jessica's thanks for the lovely breakfast.

"I have read your books," she said, sipping the black coffee.

"Which ones?" Jessica asked.

"All," was the reply.

"And did you enjoy them?"

"Yes," was another brief reply.

"That's good," Jessica said.

There was silence whilst Lena sipped her coffee, and Jessica was about to get up from the table when Lena spoke again. "You write a book after your child die."

"Yes, I did."

"I cry when I read. Very powerful book. You feel better after you write?"

Jessica sat in silence, thinking. *Had she felt better?* The pain was still there, just below her ribs. It had never gone, but the book had been a kind of therapy that helped her cope with the raw grief that her son's death had brought. "Maybe a bit. It diverted my mind for a time."

"All your books good, but that one my favourite. I read just after my brother die. It helped me too. I could not cry and keep it all inside. Book help me to cry for him."

"I'm glad it helped you," Jessica went to rise.

She didn't want this conversation. It would upset her and start her thinking about Marty.

"You are very successful lady with your own money. Is that why Luke works so much? Does he want as much money as you have? He should be with you, enjoying your life and family."

"I know," Jessica settled back in her chair and poured another coffee. "I keep telling him we don't need any more money. We have enough to go travelling. Spend some time together. That's why I'm here, to try to persuade him to take some time off."

Jessica thought about what the old lady had said. She had realised at once what had been at the back of Jessica's mind for a while. She never seemed to have any time with Luke now. When she was writing, she wanted to be on her own so Luke could spend as much time away as he wanted. But once the book hit the shelves, apart from some book signings, which Luke could have gone to with her and never did, her time was her own. She couldn't remember the last time they had spent more than a few days together. Many of the book signings were in exotic or exciting locations and that would have been a good excuse for them to spend some quality time together, but Luke could never be persuaded. In the end, she just didn't bother asking anymore. It did cross her mind he had someone else, but with all the hours he was working, and the fact that, for convenience, he was sharing a house with three other workers, she dismissed the idea. So that just left one reason. He just didn't want to be with her.

She looked at the old lady whose dark eyes were searching her face. "I will have to see. I won't know which way it will go until I see Luke whenever he gets here."

She finished her coffee and went up to her room. She packed her few things together. The sun was looking a bit hazy with some clouds building, so she changed into loose beige linen trousers and a cream vest top, brushed her short hair until it shone, added a pair of small chunky gold hoop earrings, and half dozen matching bangles, and carried her bag downstairs. She left it by the big carved front door and went through the house out into the garden.

The fragrance of the many flowers hung in the air. She walked across the grass towards the pool glistening in the early morning sun, her eyes straying to the bench under the vines and stopping her for a moment while she remembered. There was an elegant summerhouse down in the far corner, which she had seen from the house. She walked towards it and was surprised at how large it was up close. There was a veranda all the way around with lots of wicker furniture. She sat down on a big padded sofa and looked around at the beautiful pool area and garden.

After a few minutes, she was curious to see inside and tried the door. It opened easily and she stepped inside, not really knowing what to expect. There were windows all around, but the room was fairly dark due to the heavy blinds shutting out the sun. The back wall seemed to be covered in photo frames. Jessica couldn't see who they were so she pulled a blind up slightly to let in some light. There were dozens of pictures of a girl and a boy in various poses and at various ages. These were obviously Antonio's children. They were both dark-haired and beautiful; his daughter had a figure most models long for. There were also quite a few that featured a stunning, slender woman in tight riding breeches and with a mane of dark hair that rivalled any of the horses, her wide smile showing her perfect white teeth.

On one side of the wall were lots of framed photos of beautiful women, all autographed to Antonio and all with a selection of personal messages to him. The women were an assortment of blondes, brunettes and redheads with long, short, curly, and straight hair. In other words, he had no preference, it seemed, when it came to women.

Jessica let the blind back down and walked out, closing the door behind her. She walked slowly around the pool. *Was this summerhouse a place where he brought his women to seduce?* Hot sun, cool water, virtually no clothes, ideal situation. After all, she had been in the same situation with Luke and it was a hot scene for them.

Jessica didn't know why the thought upset her. She walked slowly back across the lawn and saw Antonio's Range Rover coming up the drive. His smile when he saw her would have warmed her if she hadn't still been mulling over the photo harem, so subsequently, her greeting was rather cool, bringing a slight frown of puzzlement to Antonio's forehead. He loaded her bag into the boot and after she had said her goodbyes to Lena, they headed back down the hill in a bit of an uneasy silence.

After a few minutes of travelling, Jessica's phone started to bleep.

"Ah, you finally have a phone signal," Antonio said.

Jessica looked at her phone and let out a gasp.

"What's wrong," Antonio said, looking sideways at her.

"I've got dozens of messages. Something must be wrong."

She started to scroll down through the messages and then started to listen to her voicemail. Antonio watched her out of the corner of his eye and saw her face get paler and paler as she listened to the messages. Feeling very concerned, he pulled over to the side of the road and was even more concerned when he saw tears running down her face. "Jessica, whatever is wrong," and he took her in his arms.

She pushed his arms away and sobbed out the news that she had to go home immediately as the husband of her oldest friend was dying. She sat up straight and started hysterically, trying to think of a way to get a flight, pick up her car, where was the nearest airport, did she have enough clothes, did she have her passport, what about Gertie?

"Who is Gertie?" said Antonio, puzzled. "Your daughter?"

"No, the dog. It's supposed to be with a neighbour for just a few days."

"Oh," said Antonio, not really understanding.

Jessica started crying again. "Oh God. They say John is really ill. I don't think I'm going to get there in time to even say goodbye."

Antonio turned her to face him. "Jessie, stop crying and listen to me. Look at me, Jessie, and listen."

At his forceful words, Jessica stopped crying, sniffed a few times, and looked at him.

"Will you let me sort things out for you? I have my own plane and I am a qualified pilot with years of experience. I will file a flight plan from the small local airport where my plane stays.

"I will get one of the men to take your car up to the house and put it in the garage. You will phone your friends in England to meet you with clothes and anything else you might need as soon as I know when the landing time is. If you haven't got your passport, I will send a couple of lads to your house with your keys and they will meet us at the airport, which is about halfway to your house anyway."

"Luke?" Jessica sniffed.

"If he's back, he will go with us. If he's not, he can take the first available flight, or I will fly him when I get back."

Jessica sat back in her seat. She looked at him. "Thank you so much," was all she got out before she started to cry again.

Antonio started the car and continued back down the road as Jessica dialled Stacey's number. After getting most of the information about the situation to date, she phoned Drew and heard about all the trips they had organised for John before he got too ill and the care that he was having.

"Jess, John hasn't got long. The sooner you get here, the better. Polly is coping, but she really needs you to be with her. She's starting to fall apart."

Jessica explained about the flight and asked Drew if he could pick her up as soon as she knew the airport and time. Also, what was the weather like there? Could Stacey get some clothes together for her?

By the time they arrived at the site, most of the plans were in place. From being hysterical with the sheer impossibility of it all to having everything organised in almost the blink of an eye, it felt like a weight had lifted from Jessica's shoulders. She would never be able to thank Antonio enough, but she would try to find a way somehow.

Luke still wasn't back and they were still unable to reach him. Jessica was not feeling very happy about it, but there wasn't anything she could do. *Damn, Luke,* she thought, *never around when you need him. Once upon a time, he always wanted to be with her. Now, it seems he never wanted to be with her.* She really felt vicious towards him. *We have got to sort this situation out sooner rather than later. Either we are a couple and in a relationship, or we are not.* Maybe the closeness she was feeling with Antonio has brought to light the distance that always seemed present with Luke. He used to be her rock, someone she could always rely on. What had changed that? Now, he was never around, and this couldn't go on. Even his phone calls were getting more and more scarce, and his visits even more so.

Jessica suddenly got the empty feeling back again. They had loved each other for so long and so completely what would she do without him? *Well, she seemed to be learning to be without him lately,* she thought, her lips tightening and her eyes filling with sudden tears.

Her dark thoughts were interrupted by two young men asking for her house keys and the whereabouts of her passport. Also, they needed some instructions to give to her neighbour about Gertie and possibly some money for her keep. She sorted the details out, with Antonio translating the bits they didn't understand. They drove away in a nearly new Range Rover, which would ensure a fast ride to her house and back to the airport.

Antonio was walking around with the phone up to his ear. He

told her the plane had been re-fuelled and he was waiting for flight times, etc. The flight would land at Bournemouth Airport which was the nearest one.

Jessica looked exhausted even though it was still only late morning, so he sent one of his workmen for some coffee from the local bistro. The cups in the cabin were still rather unsavoury, and it looked as if she needed a boost. Her phone rang just as she sat down wearily on a hard, plastic office chair. It was Stacey asking about flight times. Both she and Drew would be at the airport to meet Jessica. She asked Stacey for the latest news on John.

Stacey told her that, at the moment, John was at home, but the doctors thought it should only be for a while as a hospice would be better for him. The care there would be round the clock and although Polly and their sons were doing their best, it was getting too much now, and they were exhausted. The pain medication was not taking the edge off anymore, and the other night, they found John lying on the bathroom floor, unable to get up and crying. They managed to get him back to bed, but in the process, Polly had hurt her back. This was almost the last straw, and they all realised they couldn't give him the nursing he required anymore. Plans were now being put in place to move him. Stacey thought that Jessica should just be in time to see him at home.

While Stacey was talking, Jessica felt her eyes brimming again, and this time, she let the tears flow down her face. Antonio watched her from across the room, and as soon as her call ended, he knelt on the floor at the side of her chair and wrapped his arms around her. She sobbed into his shoulder for a long time. He waved a workman away from the doorway and gave him a signal to close the door.

Jessica's sobs slowly stopped and she became aware of the hard muscle under her cheek and the tangy scent of aftershave. She moved her head and met his brown eyes as she sat up straight, feeling a bit foolish. She sniffed and Antonio handed her a handkerchief. She wiped her eyes and nose and balled the hanky up in her hand. To her surprise, Antonio held her face between his hands and kissed her eyelids, then her nose, and finally her mouth. She wanted to move away from him, but the pull was too great. She gazed deep into his eyes and then she kissed him. The kiss was deep and probing and she felt herself being drawn into him.

Again, his arms went around her, and her head dropped onto his shoulder. They stayed like that for long moments. Silent and close. During those moments, something unbreakable was born between them, and no matter what the future brought, their fate was sealed.

CHAPTER 10

Caro and Ashley looked around their warehouse at the rails of garments on plastic-covered hangers. The clothing line they had started with Jessica's blessing and ideas was finally taking off. It had taken them some time to get the look right. Jessica did not want any way-out fashion and outrageous styles like a lot of the other fashion houses. Her range had to be soft, stylish, and wearable. She wanted the material to feel good against the skin, nothing rough or stiff and scratchy. The fit had to be loose and flowing to flatter even the figures that were not stick thin or very young.

The range designed for the summer season featured flowing dresses and skirts, loose soft trousers, and mix-and-match tunic tops like the ones Jessica herself favoured. These could be topped with lined, long-length jackets or soft wool jerseys. The range came in all sizes and, most importantly, was affordable. Samples had been taken around to many of the well-known chain stores that ordered just a few pieces at first until they saw how quickly they flew off the rails, and then the reorders came thick and fast.

The winter range, with its pastel-coloured draped coats and jackets in soft wool, took off like a rocket, followed by a range of tailored trousers with matching swing-back coats and shirts with a superb fit that flattered all sizes.

Caro had consulted her mother about most of the styles and sent her pages of sketches. As time went on, she started to know which pieces would be agreed and which would be rejected. Therefore, she made most of the decisions herself, just contacting her mother in case of doubt about a style.

The new winter outfits were moving slightly away from the usual pastel shades to include a complete black, grey, and white range. This was totally different from the "JESSICA" trademark look and was moving into unknown territory. Caro was sure it was going to take off, but after the hard slog of getting the brand known, she didn't want to blow it now.

Drew once again had come up trumps. He had enlisted the help of his old friend Clara, who had, in turn, enlisted the help of some famous stars to model the clothes for a magazine photoshoot and, hopefully, a fashion show in one of the big London stores. Caro was over the moon and was waiting for Clara to come and pick up the clothes and let her know what sizes were required. There was going to be a cross-selection of ages and sizes, which made a complete change from the usual stick-thin models. Some of the stars were in their 20s and slim, some were in their 50s and not so slim, all of which would help to show the versatility of the range.

Caro couldn't wait. She knew her mother was on her way over, but with Uncle John so ill, there was no chance she would be involved in any of this. She had left everything up to her daughter and son-in-law for a long time now and trusted them with the day-to-day running of the business. She simply didn't have the time to dedicate herself to anything other than her books and the film spin-offs. Ashley was a huge help in pushing the publicity. He seemed to know everyone in the media and milked them shamelessly. So, the business seemed all set to have a good year.

They couldn't persuade Jessica's Spanish dressmaker to come over but found a young couple and their parents who had started up a dressmaking and alteration business. Their work was superb. The samples they'd made had got them their first orders, and now they handled all the manufacturing. So far, they were coping, but if the orders increased as they hoped, they would have to expand, buying new machines and hiring some extra staff.

Clara turned up and, in her lovely plummy voice, enthused over the whole range of clothes. She tried on quite a few and looked stunning in all of them. She was hoping to model some of the pieces, especially a long black sheath dress with a bodice embroidered with white flowers. The dress fitted her like a glove, and the matching short embroidered jacket could also be teamed with casual black jeans or smart tailored trousers. She fell completely in love with a black faux fur jacket with a white quilted satin lining and a white jacket with a black and white striped quilted lining. She put in an order for them even before asking the price. "Sod it," she said, twirling around in front of a big full-length mirror. "I'm going to treat myself even if I have to sell a family heirloom."

She went through the rails and picked out individual items that she thought would suit many of the various celebrities and quite a few that she wanted made up in various sizes. This, she explained, would show how versatile the range was by dressing everyone the same despite their age or size.

The afternoon flew by and they all decamped to the nearest wine bar to relax. The photoshoot would be set up as soon as everyone had free time. This was easier said than done as all the celebrities had full schedules, but a provisional date had been set for three weeks' time. Anyone who couldn't make it on the day would have to make alternate arrangements with the photographer.

Drew was acting as PR and was busy organising the fashion show. Most of the stars would not be appearing as the security arrangements and insurance would be an expensive nightmare. Instead, he had co-opted Melanie to organise an array of gorgeous models (most of them colleagues and friends) to strut their stuff. All in all, everything was moving along nicely.

While in the wine bar, Caro called the nanny to find out if everything was OK at home and if she could bathe Toby as Caro might be a bit late. The nanny said Drew was there and was already bathing Toby.

"Strange," said Caro aloud.

"What is," said Ashley.

"Dad's at home with Toby."

"I expect he's waiting for Jessica's flight time," said Clara. "Your house is nearest the airport."

"But Mum's coming into Bournemouth airport," said Caro, standing up and gathering her handbag and briefcase. "I'd better go and see what's up."

Drew was sitting on the sofa with a clean and sweet-smelling Toby, reading him a story about Bob the builder. At the moment, that seemed to be Toby's favourite. He listened intently to all the drama that his grandad was putting into the building crisis that was happening between the pages whilst munching on a biscuit. Caro watched them fondly from the doorway. This handsome father of hers had changed into a doting grandad (who Toby called Gramfy) and Toby adored him.

Toby saw her and raced into her arms, and then his father's, jumping up and down, and then running back to Drew and climbing back on the sofa. "Gramfy is worried about Bob. He's not going to get the playground finished. His machines are broken."

The story was brought to a dramatic close by Gramfy, with both of them whooping and cheering when the playground was finished. Toby was then put to bed by his dad, enabling Caro to talk to Drew.

"I thought Mum was coming in at Bournemouth."

"She is. I expect she's already here, but Luke got a late cancellation and is coming in at Gatwick."

"I don't understand. Why is he not on the private plane with Mum?"

Drew explained what had happened, that Luke was away and got there after they had left, only to have to pack in a hurry and get the first flight he could.

They all had a comfortable hour chatting over toasted sandwiches, salad, and ice cream before Drew left for the airport. He was not entirely easy about having to be in Luke's company for the long journey to the West Country. What would they talk about? His affairs. Jessica's affair with Luke. John's illness. Then what. It would be dark for the whole journey, so, no discussions about the scenery either.

The flight was on time and Luke was one of the first through the gate as he only had hand luggage. The two men shook hands and made their way out to the car. Luke thanked Drew for picking him up and shoved his bag in the boot. They were both tall men, but Luke looked as if he was literally squeezing his body into the seat of the big Mercedes. Even with the seat racked right back, he filled all the available space.

Christ, thought Drew, fastening his seat belt, *forgot he was such a big bugger.*

The journey had already got off to an uncomfortable start. However, much to Drew's surprise, after the initial silence whilst he weaved his way out of the airport and onto the motorway, the two men struck up a conversation about a variety of things, including the building trade, the unemployment for young people, the fashion line of Jessica's, Toby, John, and Drew's refurbished house. Before they knew it, they were turning into the driveway of John and Polly's farmhouse. They just sat quietly for a few minutes, knowing they had to go in but putting it off. Luke turned in his seat to look at Drew. "What am I going to see, Drew? Will I be able to bear it? John's been a friend for many years."

"You have to bear it for Polly's sake. Whatever you have imagined, it will be worse. John's in a lot of pain and is coping as best he can, but his days are numbered. They are moving him into the hospice soon. He doesn't really want to leave the house, but he knows the strain he's putting the family under, so he's agreed."

Suddenly, they were bathed in light as the front door was flung open and Polly stood in the doorway. Both men got out and hugged her in turn before moving into the warm and homely kitchen.

"Jessica's here. She's up with John and I'm giving her a bit of time. She's been away for quite a while and they've got some catching up to do. I only allow one visitor at a time, so you two will have to wait your turn."

She moved over to the coffee machine and busied herself, filling it with coffee and water. This gave Luke a chance to look at her. He hadn't seen her for quite a long time, and the change in her was not good. She looked gaunt and grey, and her hair looked lank and dull. The toll on her from John's illness was very marked and she really didn't look well at all. As she turned, both men gave her a wide grin, almost as if they both had been thinking the same thing.

She sat down at the big old table and started to ask them questions about their lives. Most of the questions were aimed at Luke, as she had been seeing Drew regularly, but she didn't seem to be taking in any of the answers. Her mind was elsewhere.

They heard Jessica's step on the stairs and Luke stood up. He was across the room in a couple of strides and wrapped Jessica in a big bear hug as soon as she came through the door.

"Why don't you two go into the sitting room? You've got some catching up to do. Drew can go up and keep John company. I'll bring you all coffee when it's made. I'm going out for a ciggie."

Jessica clung to Luke, feeling almost too sad to cry. Luke had forgotten how much he loved her until this moment. They had not spent enough time together for the last couple of years and he wanted to make up for that. Even at this sad time, he could feel his body rising to meet her and moved slightly away, not wanting the needs of his body to intrude on her grief.

Jessica felt the desire in Luke and even though she understood him moving away, she welcomed the desire. She felt she had been starved of affection for so long she was withering inside. This was not the place for desire, but soon.

Luke finally went up to John and stayed for a long time until his old friend slept. He didn't tell them what they had talked about. John had left a list of instructions for Luke to carry out after he was gone, and Luke promised they would be done without anyone knowing.

Polly's boys were staying at the house in case they were needed in the night. Drew was also staying in the box room as it was late and too far from home. Luke and Jessica would stay in the old cottage where it had all started for them. Ben had arrived to pick them up and take them to the cottage. Jessica had a feeling of homecoming and Luke had quite a lump in his throat seeing the old place again. His labour of love all those years ago was now changed a bit but still looking good.

They sat in the warm, cosy room for a while, lost in their own thoughts, then almost as one, they stood up and walked into each other's arms. Their bodies were on fire almost immediately. Jessica could feel the juices flowing copiously from her, and Luke's erection was straining the cloth of his jeans. In a matter of minutes, they were upstairs and tearing at each other's clothes. Finally, free of them, they fell on the bed, frantic for their bodies to be joined.

Luke's erection was huge and almost painful, but Jessica took him inside her with ease. They moved together slowly and deeply, but because of the height of their passion, neither could last for long and both cried out together as their climaxes tore through them. Their breathing was ragged and hoarse and it was many minutes until they were able to speak.

"I love you, Jess," Luke said, kissing her bruised mouth.

He was horrified when she started crying and wrapped her in his arms until he realised it was just a release of the tension she had been holding in since she got the news about John.

They stayed wrapped closely together, but after a short while, the desire for each other started again and they made long, slow love till the early hours.

CHAPTER 11

John never did make it to the hospice. He died in the dawn as the sun coloured and warmed the room, closely surrounded by his loving family.

Jessica and Luke had just finished a delicious breakfast of eggs, bacon, and toast, reminding Jessica that she hadn't eaten since the airport in Spain when Polly phoned with the news. She sounded strangely over-calm, as if drugged. Jessica leapt up the stairs to get dressed as she was still in her dressing gown. Luke, who was dressed, started to wash the dishes, thinking that he had better clear the decks as he didn't know when they would be back.

When they got around to Polly's, the doctor was there. He was a lovely man who had lived in the area all his life and had gone to school with John. He had brought all three sons into the world and was now sitting at the big kitchen table, hunched over a cup of coffee and looking visibly upset. Jessica went straight to Polly as if to embrace her but was stopped by her raised hand.

"Don't, Jess. I'm OK. I'm trying to hold it together. I feel as if I have cried buckets of tears and now I don't want to cry. John's pain has now gone and he's at peace. I can't cry about that. God knows I didn't want to ever be without him, but you wouldn't keep an animal alive with that much pain, so I'm glad he finally let go. He held on for so long, and he got to see all his beloved friends and family to say his goodbyes. That was the final wish he had, so, thank you all for being here. Now I'm going outside for a smoke. You can join me if you like, Jess."

They walked down to the end of the garden. Jessica had a lump in her throat that she couldn't swallow and really wanted to cry. She managed to keep the tears at bay, at least for the moment.

Polly grounded out her cigarette and turned to face Jessica. "Would you think I was really heartless when I told you I'm glad he's gone? I don't think I could bear watching him in so much pain anymore. I felt so totally helpless. Towards the end, I couldn't even hold him to give him comfort."

"Oh, Polly. I know how much you loved John, and so did he. Those happy years you had were what kept him alive for so long. He told me this. He didn't want to leave you ever, but he knew he had to. As soon as you were surrounded by your friends and family, he knew you were safe."

The two stood looking out over the fields when they were startled by a sad, mournful howling as loud as a pack of wolves. Everyone came out of the back door when they heard it and stood in a group and listened to Chad howl his grief for his master. This was the final straw for Jessica and the tears poured down her face. The howling finally stopped and Polly went to look for Chad, feeling she needed to comfort him. Jessica went with her, but they never found him. They looked everywhere, but he was nowhere. Two days later, Ben came back in with the tractor and found him in the barn. He was dead and lying on John's old tweed coat. They buried him in the woods with the graves of the other long-gone family pets, wrapped gently in the coat.

Over the next few days, family members, friends, and business colleagues were contacted; everyone wanted to pay their respects. Every available seat in the small church was full. John wanted to be cremated, and his wicker coffin was threaded through with flowers of every colour and variety. Many people stood to read poems or give a short speech, and the donations for the local hospice filled the wooden collection bowl.

The wake was at the local pub where John had spent many happy hours. After a few pints, the local people came out with stories about his antics that had them all in stitches. It was a release of tension for Polly and the boys, and they felt it was a fitting send-off for him.

His ashes would be interred in the woods behind the house where Marty's ashes were, and a tree planted. There would be a small family service for this when the time came.

The will had been read, but the family knew its contents anyway. The farm was left to the three boys with the option that if one of them wanted to go, the others could buy his share. The farmhouse was split half to Polly and half between the boys. This division applied if it was sold also. All moneys and savings were to go to Polly.

Everyone finally drifted off. Polly's boys had work to do on the farm before the end of the day, so there were just the four of them around the kitchen table. They sat around the table with glasses in their hands. No one wanted coffee, so they stuck to the spirits.

"To John," Drew said, raising his glass. "And may he give all the angels the run around and not ask what they're wearing under their dresses."

They all laughed and raised their glasses.

"Now," Luke said seriously, "I had a long chat with John last week, and he gave me some instructions to carry out for him."

Polly frowned. "Did he? And what the devil are they?"

"I've got them written down so I wouldn't forget." Luke took a well-creased piece of paper from his pocket. "Firstly, John requested that after all this is over, Polly is to go over to Spain with Jessie for as long as the two of them want to be together. There is a savings book in joint names that Polly knows nothing about. This should be enough money for her stay."

"The sneaky bugger," Polly said, smiling.

"It was saved for a cruise whenever the chance for that ever occurred."

"Huh," Polly said, "That was never going to happen."

"Anyway," Luke said, looking at Jessica. "Is that ok with you?"

"Don't I have a say in it?" Polly said.

"No, not really," Jessie replied. "If that's what John wanted, that's what you'll do."

"Better have a look at my passport then. Not sure if it's still valid."

"Right then. Next on the list. John's father left him a Rolex watch. John thought it was worth a bit. He never wore it on the farm, he got a cheap one. The boys have all got their own, so he took it to the local jewellers and had it engraved for Drew."

"Whaa," spluttered Drew.

"He said you were like wine, easier to stomach when you matured."

Everyone laughed, and Polly patted Drew on the back.

"I don't know what to say. Did you know about this, Poll."

"Who do you think took it to the jewellers? Pick it up tomorrow."

"Next on the list. Jessica."

"Oh crikey," Jessica said, topping her glass up with sherry.

"John said he didn't think you knew that Caro came to see him with Ashley and Toby. Toby got restless so Ashley and Polly took him out for a walk. While they were gone, John had a long chat with Caro and she told him all about this new fashion business she had started in her mother's name. John thought that after he was gone, Polly needed to be involved in something other than just the bits she does for the holiday complex, which is only in the summer anyway. So he has instructed his lawyer to make money available to buy into the business in Polly's name, hopefully to be a partner if Jess allows it. He ran it by Caro and swore her to secrecy, and she is all for it."

Both Polly and Jessica sat with their mouths open and stared at Luke.

"That bugger is still running my life after he's gone."

"Oh, Polly, I think it's a great idea. Look at you. Since you lost weight, you're a real stylish woman. Just the sort to be on our team. Please say yes."

Polly also topped up her glass. "OK then. If you think I could do it."

"You'll be great. We'll hash out the details in sunny Spain over a few glasses of wine."

"What about you, Luke? You've known him longer than all of us."

"I'll take care of that," Polly said, standing up. "I didn't know about the other stuff, but John also gave me some instructions."

She went to a drawer in the kitchen and took out some papers. She sorted through the papers and took out three or four sheets. "You've been involved with the leisure complex from the beginning. John and I hold quite a few shares in it. This brings us a small income and gives us a say in how it's run. John knew that I wouldn't want to be involved any more than I already am, so he split his shares between the boys and you. The main company owns 51% of the shares, and John and I hold 20% each, with the remainder held by a couple of local companies. John's wishes were that 10% went to the boys, who will get the rest when I die, and the other 10% to you. He said that he didn't think you would stay in Spain forever and should have some incentive to come back to the West Country where you belong."

Only a few times in his life had Luke cried, but he put his head in his hands and wept. Everyone was shocked at this big man hunched over with his shoulders shaking. They all leapt to their feet, including Drew, and clustered around him a bit confused as to what to do. Jessica knelt beside him and put her arms around him. Finally, he straightened up, looking sheepish and feeling foolish. But no one seemed to think it was unusual. After all, if you can't cry on a funeral day, when can you cry?

"I don't know what to say," Luke said gruffly and blew his nose loudly on a handful of tissues Polly handed him.

"John thought the world of you and what you had made of yourself. This was his way of saying thank you for all the help you've given him over the years."

They all finally went their separate ways, feeling wrung out and exhausted. Glad this sad occasion was finally over.

CHAPTER 12

The premier of the film from Jessica's book took place two weeks later. She had refused to go in deference to Polly, who was still deeply grieving. It was only on Polly's insistence that she changed her mind. Polly, Caro, and Ashley jointly persuaded her to go, that without her book there would have been no film, and that it was important that she was there. So, she turned up at the glittering occasion in a long, black halter-necked dress with long sparkly earrings and shoes, with Drew resplendent in a tux by her side. She failed to get Luke to go with her (as she knew would happen), but he was in the audience and met them afterwards for a slap-up dinner at the Dorchester Hotel.

The lovely girl who starred alongside Tyler as the female lead was superb. Her name was Jilly Smith, and she was spotted in the chorus line of a West End show. She was primarily a dancer, but she had been to acting school and was enchantingly lovely. Her shiny dark hair was cut into a bob and framed an elfin face with almond shaped and expressive eyes. After the film test, everyone was blown away. Both Jilly and Tyler had a presence on screen that shone out, and it proved to be explosive partnering from the first minute of the film. It was a low budget film, but the critics raved about it, and there was many a wet tissue hidden away at the end. It would never break any first-night box office records, but it spent many weeks in the top five films and made Jessica and the producers a shed load of money even more when it went to DVD.

Jessica, Luke, and Polly flew to Spain three weeks later. Luke wanted to go back earlier, but Jessica objected very forcefully. It was the nearest to a raging row they had ever had, and so Luke gave in and stayed. There were papers to sign and Polly's passport to sort out. Drew took on most of the donkey work regarding all the paperwork, etc. After speaking to Antonio to let him know what was going on, Luke informed everyone that Antonio was flying over to pick them up. He thought it was odd for Antonio to leave the work to his men when the finalising date was so close.

Polly was quite excited to be travelling on a private jet, and, in her heart, so was Jessica, but for a very different reason. All through this awful time, and all through her reunion with Luke and the passion they had shared, ran a thread of thought about Antonio. It seemed to be always there, and she couldn't block it out completely. He had a place in her brain that she could not shut out, so she learnt to live with it. The earlier journey to England, with just the two of them sitting in close proximity, made her uncomfortable at first, but watching him handle the plane and his expertise, giving them a faultless flight and landing, put her at ease. They talked about nothing much, but his warm gaze and constant eye contact didn't need words. Although she wanted to get to Polly and John, she was almost sad when the flight ended. He escorted her through the terminal to meet Stacey, who was there to drive her. Stacey's eyes lingered on Antonio a bit too long, and Jessica felt a crazy bolt of jealousy run through her. He said goodbye and walked off to the other side of the airport. Jessica's eyes followed him, and she turned to see Stacey watching her.

"What?" Jessie said crossly.

"Nothing," said Stacey, a smile curving her mouth.

Seeing Antonio again after nearly a month, she felt the almost familiar jolt. Luke greeted him warmly and gave him a bear hug. As Luke was not into much emotional stuff, Jessica found this surprising. Polly was greeted warmly with a handshake and then a hug. She looked at him long and hard whilst he was busy with their suitcases. *So, this is Antonio,* she thought. Jessie had talked a lot about him, and so had Luke. Polly was prepared to dislike him. He seemed to be a kind of paragon of virtue, according to them. However, by the end of the flight she had joined them in their views of him. He was friendly, courteous, and utterly charming. His eyes were alert and intelligent and he treated the airport staff with politeness and smiles.

They boarded and took off without any delays, the whole thing appearing effortless. Luke sat beside Antonio, and they conversed intently about business. Polly and Jessica relaxed in the comfortable seats at the back and looked at the white clouds below them. For the most part, they were silent, each deep in their thoughts. Jessica almost jumped when Polly suddenly spoke quietly. "I think Luke has got some competition."

"What?" Jessie said, turning in her seat.

"I saw Antonio's eyes when he looked at you."

"I don't know what you mean," Jessie said stiffly glancing towards Luke.

"It's OK; they can't hear us over the noise of the engines."

"What are you talking about?" Jessica could feel her face going pink.

"You know very well Jessie girl. That man has eyes that positively glow when they look at you. He is doing everything in his power to stay as far away from you as possible. That, in my book, is a dead giveaway. I might be very sad and grief-stricken, but I'm not blind."

By now, Jessica's face was positively burning. "OK, yes, I do find him very attractive. We have spent a bit of time together, but nothing has happened, and it won't. He is Luke's friend and partner. I couldn't do anything to spoil that."

"You say nothing happened…."

"No, it hasn't," Jessica said forcefully.

Polly held up her hand. "Whoh, what I was going to say was,

nothing may have happened physically, but something has certainly happened. I just can't put my finger on what it is yet."

Jessica stayed quiet and continued looking out of the window. She knew in her heart that Polly was right, although she was very reluctant to admit it. If Polly had spotted the attraction, she would just have to hope that Luke did not.

At the airport, two of Antonio's guys were waiting for them. One had driven Antonio's Range Rover and the other drove a works van.

"I have arranged for you all to spend a couple of days with me if that's OK," Antonio said as he loaded the suitcases into the back of the Rover. "That will give you ladies some time to relax and give Luke some time with Jess until you return to your own home. It's a long drive and you can go whenever you are ready."

"Did you arrange this?" Jessica hissed at Luke at the first opportunity.

Luke looked startled. "I thought you would be pleased to have a couple of days with me before you go back."

"Yes, of course I am," Jessica said, forcing the tension in her shoulders to go down. "I'm a bit stressed, that's all. I just wanted to get home."

"Course you do," Luke said, putting his arm around her shoulders and squeezing her to him.

Polly looked avidly out of the window at the passing landscape. They stopped off at a café on the beach for something to eat and drink and then continued onwards up towards Antonio's vineyards. They stopped at the side of the road to show Polly the breathtaking views. They all stood outside and looked. With the sunshine warm on their heads. Polly gave a huge sigh. "This is just what I need after these last awful months."

Jessica hugged her friend, and they continued up the long driveway to the heavily carved front door. Polly's eyes darted from side to side in amazement. They were greeted by Lena, who gave Antonio a warm welcome in rapid-flowing Spanish and then extended her welcome to Luke and Jessica. They introduced Polly, and she was, in turn, welcomed by the elderly lady, who had been fully briefed by Antonio regarding Polly's visit to Spain.

They left their suitcases in the hall and were taken up to their rooms by Antonio.

"If you want to freshen up please take your time. I will wait for you out on the patio with some refreshments."

Jessica and Luke were in the same room that she had slept in before. She went straight to the bathroom for a quick shower and Luke went down for their bags. When she came out of the bathroom wrapped in a big soft towel, Luke was searching his suitcase for a change of clothes. He immediately took her into his arms.

"God, Jess, it's so great to have you to myself at last. I know it's been traumatic over the last month, but I've really missed being together with you. Staying in separate places has been a real strain."

He started to nuzzle her neck but took a step backwards when she said sharply, "I should think you must be used to being in separate places. A separate place is what you've been in for a hell of a long time now. If you missed being with me, why do you have to stay away so much."

"Please, Jess. Don't start this again. Can't we just enjoy our time together now?"

"So, for two days, we enjoy ourselves, and for the next four weeks, I won't see you."

"Where do you get this four weeks from?" Luke was beginning to get cross.

"Do you think I'm deaf and stupid? I know that's how much time is left before the complex is completed. I heard you talking to Nio about it."

"Then you know how important it is for me to be there."

"No, I don't. Antonio was a successful businessman long before you came on the scene. I'm sure he can handle things while you take some time off occasionally."

"You'll be busy with Polly anyway."

"Yes, I will, but probably not for a month. What's going to be your excuse when she's gone?"

"Oh, for God sake. There's no reasoning with you. I'm going to shower."

Jessica quickly dressed in a short blue sundress and knocked on Polly's door. "Come to escort you down in case you get lost."

Jessica's smile was very strained. She obviously was unaware that her balcony doors were wide open and Polly in the next room had heard every word.

Antonio was waiting on the patio beside a table full of bowls of tapas snacks and a very large jug of cold sangria. He entertained them royally with humorous stories of the building trade, Spanish life, his children, and many other things. The photos in the pool house that Jessica had been curious about were all the girls who worked with his daughter in training the magnificent horses that enchanted everyone who saw them. The glamorous older woman turned out to be the leading trainer of the female team.

Well. Mystery solved, thought Jessica with a secret smile.

Luke finally made an appearance. His jaw was clenched, which gave him a ferocious look. It was not lost on the host, and it took several glasses of sangria before the usual friendly face reappeared.

Antonio, who was heading back from the garages after starting up Jessica's jeep, was in the garden below their room, had also heard the raised voices and was disturbed by them. He didn't want to lose Luke. But he didn't know the reason: Luke's involvement in the business or the fact that he wouldn't see Jessica again.

Anyway, he would make their time here so good that it would sort everything out. *You hope,* he thought with a wry smile.

CHAPTER 13

Drew felt exhausted after the funeral. He had spent a lot of time with John and had watched him deteriorate day by day into a shadow of the man he once was. Now, he desperately needed to put that image behind him and do something joyful. The film premiere had been a welcome distraction for a couple of days, but underneath, he was still feeling empty. He was so pleased to get back to his home. He hadn't spent too much time there lately and missed his own space.

He sat relaxing on the deep, comfortable sofa with a cat on either side of him. Blue was purring, but little Lady purred louder. She hadn't grown much, so she was obviously always going to be a small cat. He looked down fondly at her and wondered how such a loud sound could come out of such a small body.

Sophia was bustling about in the kitchen. Drew had kept in touch with her as he was going to be away from the house rather a lot. She had taken the cats to her house for a few days and had brought them back today. She had run around the house with the vacuum and duster and was now wiping down the kitchen. Drew couldn't see a speck of dust anywhere, but it seemed that Sophia did, even though no one had been living there very much lately.

"Dust come down from air every day. Don't have to be people to make dust," she said, vacuuming around his legs.

Suddenly, she switched off the machine and sat in the opposite armchair. This was unusual as Sophia only ever sat at the kitchen table.

"OK, flower. What's wrong?" Drew said, knowing immediately that something was off.

Sophia sat on the edge of the chair, her hands clasped in her lap. "My daughter; she run away with this music man and left granddaughter behind."

Drew just nodded, knowing there was more but waited for Sophia to tell it in her own time.

"Granddaughter now with me but have long journey to take her to school."

"So, you want to leave me," Drew said, his heart sinking to his knees.

"No, not want to but will have to change hours, days, something. School got after-hours care, but very expensive."

Drew smiled. "Is that all? I thought it was something really bad."

"Meester Drew, it very bad."

Sophia's eyes filled with tears. Drew knelt at the side of her chair. "I will pay for the after-hours care. Tell the school to send me the bill, and you come to me whatever days suit you. In the holidays, you can bring her here with you. She can watch TV or play in the garden."

Sophia's howls scared the cats and they both hotfooted it out through the open French doors. Whilst Drew was looking for a tissue box, Clara passed the cats in the doorway.

"Golly, what's wrong with your lady."

"Hello to you, too," said Drew, looking flustered.

He never could handle women's tears. He never knew whether to embrace and risk opening the floodgates or keep a safe distance and hope they blew away. Clara got the full story and went off to make some tea. *The English medicine,* thought Drew, handing out bundles of tissues. Finally, Sophia left amid lots of "Thank you's" and "Bless you's" and sniffles.

Clara poured another cup of tea and launched into some details of the next venture to raise money. The last one had been a roaring success and, with the entry fee and the auction, had brought in a sizable amount of money even after the expenses had all been paid. Before Clara went off on a long diatribe, Drew cut her short. "Clara, my darling. I don't know where you get all your energy. I feel totally drained, so before I start anything else, I need a holiday. I don't know where yet, but I'll work on it."

"That's fine," Clara said, nodding. "The death of your friend must have hit you hard. I can understand you might want to recharge your batteries."

They sat quietly, sipping their tea.

"What about Italy?" Clara said

"What about Italy," Drew said, puzzled.

"Would you like to holiday there?"

"Don't know. Why, what have you got in mind? Are you going to take me?"

"No. Of course not. But I've got a friend with a villa in Italy. It's near Lake Como. Got its own pool in a secluded location and is fully equipped and comes with a car and cleaning service. I've holidayed there myself and it's wonderful. I know it's empty cause she just came back. She only lets it out to people she knows. I can vouch for you if you like."

Suddenly, Drew liked the idea very much. "I will have a word with Max. I know she's very busy, but she should be able to get some time off."

Unfortunately, from Max, it was a resounding no. "Drew, I'm up to my eyes. I've taken quite a lot of time off lately. What with spending some time with John and fundraising with Kate and the school, I now have to catch up with my work. I might be able to get away for a long weekend, but no longer than that."

Drew went ahead and arranged it with Clara anyway. Max would get there when she could. He meanwhile would have some relaxing time catching up with all the bestsellers and topping up his tan. He never used to like his own company very much, but now he was really looking forward to not having to please anyone but himself. Something that, in the past, he was highly qualified for.

The trip was soon organised. Sophia was again babysitting the cats. The flight proved to be a bit difficult. Even though it wasn't the main holiday time, people were still booking their holidays. Obviously cheaper during term time for those without children. Drew finally managed to get a very early flight. It meant getting up at the crack of dawn, which was probably why it was available.

He got a bus from the airport. Clara had given him all the info. She said the bus was far cheaper than an airport taxi and far more interesting. She was right. Drew enjoyed the trip and even the heat was welcomed after leaving a very wet Britain. It was a ten-minute walk to the villa, unfortunately uphill, and dragging his suitcase, but the elevated location had a cool breeze and a wonderful view. The key had been left in a wall safe, and he had the combination.

The villa was everything that Clara had said. Cool, with minimum clutter, a fully functioning kitchen, and a well-stocked fridge and wine rack, as he had requested. Steps at the side of the house lead to a roof terrace with comfortable loungers and umbrellas. The same furniture was repeated around the sizable pool. *Yes,* thought Drew, *I'm going to enjoy this.* He would have liked Max to be there with him, but he had that to look forward to later.

He stripped down to his swimming shorts, selected a book from the pile he'd brought, and settled down in the late afternoon sun. He read a bit, then dozed a bit until the sun reached the horizon in a blaze of red and orange.

After a shower, he couldn't be bothered to cook for himself, so he found the car keys on a hook in the kitchen and opened the garage to find a small white Fiat car. He had to rack the seat back as far as it would go to allow room for his long legs. Once he had done all the adjustments, the car was fairly comfortable and hummed along the road quite nicely. He looked around at the views and found some eating places along a strip of road leading down to a harbour. He parked and wandered along, looking at the menus displayed outside. At one restaurant, he was pleased to see that the menu was printed in English beneath the Italian. He settled for a traditional Italian pizza with salad and a beer and sat down at an outside table.

He sat relaxed and watched the passers-by. Lots of young boys and girls with long, tanned limbs and tousled sun-bleached hair were busy docking a large sailing boat. Their white teeth gleamed as they exchanged banter and smiles, and Drew suddenly felt the passing of the years. *Was he ever carefree and easy in his own skin like these young things?* He didn't think so. His mother was a hard and joyless woman who kept a tight rein on him and succeeded in squeezing out every happy thing in his early life. He couldn't wait to leave home and rarely visited his mother unless it was Christmas or her birthday. Even on these occasions, there was no joy in anything he gave her. At the end, he gave up trying to please her. It took him many years after her death to realise that these early days had formed his temperament. He was irritated when things didn't go his way, just like his mother, and would distance himself from everyone like a sulky child. Just like his father before him, he sought love everywhere in the form of affairs, not realising, until he met Jessica, that these were all empty relationships. But even when he had everything, a wife who loved him, children, and a successful business, it still wasn't enough to quell the deep-seated need in him. He had done a lot of soul searching since Marty's death and Jessica's leaving and had finally come to terms with who he was whilst he was down at the school with Kate and Max and after talking to John. They had shown him that people didn't care if he was handsome or rich or if he had charm or sex appeal. At the school, he was just Drew, who played with them and made them laugh with his attempts at signing.

He watched the boat crew tie everything up and jump off the boat. They strolled elegantly down the road towards the next restaurant, where they pushed the tables together and grabbed the menus. His food arrived and he ate, all the time watching the tanned youngsters with a kind of deep yearning inside.

He drove home and slept soundly, only waking when the bright morning sun lit up the room.

CHAPTER 14

Polly settled into Jessica's home and started to relax. Her shoulder seemed to have been up around her ears for weeks, and the tension had been making her back ache. It was good to finally not have to worry about anything.

Luke had stayed for a couple of days but was like a cat on hot bricks. In the end, Jessica told him that she wanted to spend some time with Polly before writing again, so he should clear off. The relief on his face hit Jessica like a pain in her stomach. *He can't wait to leave me,* she thought, watching him hastily pack.

Her goodbye to him was brief and brusque and was not lost on Polly, who walked away into the kitchen. Luke made more fuss saying goodbye to Gertie than he did to Jessica. The dog was old now and spent most of her time warming her bones in the sun. She whimpered sadly, seeing Luke preparing to drive away, so he took pity on her and took her with him. She sat tall on the front seat and looked as if she was smiling. He looked at her fondly and ruffled the hair on her head. He looked into the rearview mirror. Jessica always waved from the terrace until he was out of sight, but not today. The terrace was empty. Jessica didn't know that he was in a hurry to get back because he wanted to speed up the final stages of the handover to the owners of the complex so he could plan some travelling for them. Anywhere she wanted to go. Seeing the deep regret of Polly that her time with John was so cruelly cut short when they planned to finally spend time together brought home to Luke how unpredictable life could be. He wanted to be with Jessica and get back to how they used to be. They seemed to be drifting apart and he missed the loving and happy way they used to be. Jessica was his life and he was getting really scared he would lose her.

Jessica went slowly into the kitchen, poured two glasses of red wine, and took them out onto the terrace. She sat in one of the padded cane chairs and propped her feet up on the balcony, sipping her wine, a faraway look on her face. Polly joined her, carrying a loaded plate of crusty bread with cheese and apples. The two friends sat quietly, enjoying the snack and the wine. The sun was low on the horizon and still had warmth against their skin.

"What's up with you two, Jess?" Polly said, leaning back in the chair and looking at Jessica over the rim of her sunglasses. "You were so happy and in love. Now, there is a coldness between you that I never thought I would ever see. What on earth has happened?"

Jessica pushed her sunglasses onto the top of her head and sipped her wine. "Frankly, Pol, the answer is I don't know. Luke just seems to be so wrapped up in work he hasn't got time for me. I don't know if it's because he chooses work to be on his own, or because he just wants to keep earning more and more money. That way, he won't have to accept anything from me. When I'm working, I don't mind being on my own, but when I'm not, I get really lonely. I think of all the things we could do together. We are not getting any younger, and there will come a time when I won't want to go gadding about all over the place, but now I feel ready to visit some new places."

Polly crunched the last of her apple before asking a question that raised Jessica's eyebrows. "Has Antonio got anything to do with this restless feeling you've got?"

"Why the hell would you think that?"

"I said before, Jess, that I feel something is going on between you and him. I don't mean physically, but it's something I can't quite put my finger on. It's like an electric vibration in the air."

"Oh, for goodness sake, Pol. You make it sound like a twopenny novel from Victorian times; I've only just met the guy."

"That means nothing. You don't have to know someone for long to feel a connection. With Luke so distant, someone paying you attention is like an aphrodisiac."

"So, you think it might be because I'm lacking attention."

"So, you admit there is something," said Polly, lighting a cigarette.

"I'm not admitting anything."

"You just did."

Jessica was beginning to feel uncomfortable with the direction of this conversation. Polly was not wrong with her observations, but Jessica was finding it difficult to agree with her out of a sense of loyalty to Luke. It would seem like she was being slightly unfaithful if she admitted feelings for another man.

Polly uncannily read her thoughts. "Don't think you are being disloyal to Luke because you like his friend."

"That's just it. He is his friend, and yes, we do feel a connection even though we have not voiced it, and never will as long as Luke is his friend and business partner."

"Then don't you think you should make your feelings clear to Antonio. Tell him that you want him to stay away and that you love Luke and don't need anyone else."

Jess nodded. "Yes, that's what I will do the next time I see him."

Even as she spoke, she felt something inside her tightened with pain. She knew Polly was right. This should be nipped in the bud before it all got out of hand, though it was going to be really difficult.

The subject of Antonio was pushed under the table, and the two friends spent days lying in the sun, splashing in the sea, and eating good food either at some wonderful restaurant or lazily on the terrace at home.

The weeks turned into nearly a month, and Polly knew she would have to go home soon. Stacey was pushing Jessica to start the new book, which had been postponed for quite some time now and was causing concern with the publishers.

Ashley had been in touch with Polly over the start date for her job. He wanted to go through some of the relevant details, so she was completely familiar with the business. He also wanted her to see a potential studio apartment he had found. He said it needed some work done, but it had the potential to be a great place. It was in a good area and fairly near the warehouse, so she wouldn't have to travel far.

Polly could feel emerging from her black mood and was now beginning to look forward to doing something. She had worked hard all her life, and this leisure time was great and just what she needed, but she could hear John's voice in her head saying, "Come on, my girl. Enough of this lying around before you get too used to it."

A tanned and relaxed Polly got a flight back the following week. Before that, Jessica booked them a spa day and they enjoyed various massages and treatments, including manicure and pedicure, followed by a visit to the hairdresser for some overdue trimming. Jessica had been clubbing hers back in a stupidly small ponytail that looked more like a tuft sticking out the back of her head. She was glad to have the short pixie cut back again. The sun had bleached her highlights so she left the colour as it was. Polly had her dark hair trimmed into a short bob and had a chestnut tint, which shone like a penny and matched the colour of her eyes.

When she arrived at the airport all her sons were there to meet her and were overjoyed that the downcast and sad mother that had left was not the one that came home. They all missed their father a lot and were very worried their mum was never going to bounce back from his death. They talked around the big kitchen table over a lovely meal, and Polly told them that she had accepted their father's death at the beginning when the doctors had explained there was little hope. At the end, when he was in so much pain, she prayed for his release and later felt guilty for doing so. That was before he had begged her to end it for him. Then her guilt disappeared, as she knew that was what he wanted. She couldn't have done what he asked, despite her deep love for him, until someone up there had answered her prayers.

Polly spent a few days with her boys and then visited the holiday site. When she was satisfied that everything was running smoothly, she packed up everything she needed and stored away the rest before heading off to Caro's house and her new life.

CHAPTER 15

Drew enjoyed a week of his own company. This was the first time ever. He always wanted to be in the middle of everything, from parties and dinners to BBQs and even board meetings. He had to be the centre of attention. His voice had to be the one they listened to, and he rarely ever heard anyone else. The whole week he had spent exploring the beautiful area around him and eves-dropping on other English people's conversations. He got a good insight into their lives and families just by listening. While sitting down in various places, at a restaurant, by the waterside, or on the beach, an assortment of people talked to him, especially when they heard him speaking English. For once, he gave out very little information about himself but encouraged them to talk about their lives instead. He found himself fascinated by the variety of stories they shared.

He met two elderly ladies whose husbands had been friends and also worked together; their husbands had died in the same year. With families going their own way and feeling very lonely, the two decided to holiday together. Twenty years later, they were still doing it. Their husbands had left them well provided for. After selling their houses, they moved into small adjoining flats and enjoyed their retirement. They had been all over the world. Some really exotic and unusual places and had a wealth of stories to tell. Drew took them both to dinner, and over several jugs of wine, the tales got more risqué, and he found himself roaring with laughter at these lovely ladies. His friends would never believe he had such a wonderful time with two 70-year-olds.

He also had a long conversation over numerous cups of coffee with a guy called Travis and his partner Percy, who insisted on being called Perry because he hated his real name and Perry was a lively and fizzy drink that suited him better. Drew, who had never had any dealings or friendships with gay couples, warmed to these two from the start. They obviously adored one another and even finished each other's sentences. They had met at a gay pride parade 15 years ago and, after talking, realised their birthdays were on the exact same date but two years apart. They thought that was an omen and had been together ever since. Their families had finally come around to accepting them, although it had taken a long time.

Travis came from a wealthy family who were in business and very religious. He was expected to take over the family business. When he finally came out, he was disowned. His family, with the exception of his younger brother, had never met Perry and probably never would. They spoke to Travis from time to time but didn't want any other contact.

Perry's family was the complete opposite. His parents loved their son to bits and had known he was gay since he was at school. They welcomed his partner with open arms. As long as he made their beloved son happy, they were happy too.

Drew enjoyed their witty banter. It seemed they didn't have a care in the world. He ran into them several times over the next few days, and they sat and enjoyed coffee in the sun. Only on the last day, as they were saying goodbye to him, they asked him to wish them luck.

"What for?" Drew asked, puzzled.

"I'm giving my darling one of my kidneys on Friday," Perry said, clutching Travis's hand.

Drew's mouth dropped open, and he immediately jumped to his feet to hug them both. He felt his eyes welling up and swallowed several times to clear the lump in his throat. "I wish you two lovely people all the luck in the world," he said, and he really meant it.

He then went on to talk to an Italian chap who spoke excellent English; he was a chef in a hotel. Food was his passion, and he wrote down several easy recipes for Drew to cook to surprise Max when she finally arrived.

Two girls in the local barbers chatted to him whilst the senior one cut his hair. He didn't have time before he left home to go to his usual one. He sat very nervously in the chair while the girl and her assistant spoke to him in broken English whilst he tried to explain what he wanted. Another chap spoke good English and translated for him. All in all, she made a pretty good job of it. A bit shorter than usual, but it suited him.

The next people to interest him was a middle-aged couple who joined him at his table in a busy restaurant. They looked vaguely familiar, although he didn't know why. They had a pleasant meal, talking about the weather and various places of interest they recommended for him to visit. They moved outside to the terrace, and Drew ordered a bottle of cold white wine. During the second glass, a woman came over to their table, said an "excuse me," and asked for their autograph. Drew perked up, and when the woman left, he asked them if they were famous and why didn't he recognise them. They looked at each other for a long moment before looking back at him. Drew had never been an avid TV watcher, so anyone in the regular shows would not have been familiar to him. In fact, apart from a few TV and film stars, he probably knew very few. He found out that the couple had been in a long-running series for many years, which he obviously hadn't watched. He probably half recognised the faces from a magazine or newspaper.

He racked his brain for any further info. But got nothing. He didn't want to cross-question them, but they started telling him their story anyway. They had played neighbours on the show and were good friends. Quite a long time later, in their private life, it turned into much more and they started an affair. They kept it secret for a long time, a long, stressful time. They wanted to be together but knew if the producers of the show found out, they would be fired on a moral rule. Eventually, a newspaper got hold of the story and it all really hit the fan. Gwen (the lady) was immediately divorced by her husband. They both got written out of the show, but Jeff's wife refused to divorce him, and over 5 years later was still refusing. Due to the press constantly pestering them, they moved out of the UK and lived secluded and privately up on a hillside. They had moved a couple of times to avoid the press but had now got tired of running and stayed put. They liked the area, the local people didn't bother them, and apart from an occasional fan, they weren't pestered. As Jeff remarked, it was old news and yesterday's wrapping paper.

When Drew got back to the villa, he phoned Jessica. "Got a great idea for your next book, Jess. Short stories about people's lives."

Polly was still with Jess but would be returning in the next week to sort out the flat that Ashley had found. As there was no chance of spending time or going anywhere with Luke, at least until the whole building thing was finalised, whenever that was, Jessica listened to Drew's ideas and found herself getting interested in the concept. She had been giving the next book a lot of thought and had not come to any decision regarding the plot, so this idea of his fitted the bill nicely.

Within hours of waving Polly off at the airport, Jessica was sitting at her computer doing a rough synopsis of the stories she would use. She had taken some of Drew's ideas and added a few of her own and had the next book planned out.

<h1 style="text-align:center">CHAPTER 16</h1>

Polly stood in the middle of the loft that Ashley had brought her to see. She looked at the cobwebs hanging in curtains from the ceiling, the dusty wooden floor covered in blobs of paint, and the raw brick walls. The room was huge and had been used as a stockroom for a decorating company, hence the paint. Ashley had roughly drawn up a plan for the renovation, and the two of them rested the paper on a dusty windowsill and tried to visualise how this massive space was going to be transformed into a liveable space. Polly was picking up on Ashley's excitement and enthusiasm and looked around, trying to imagine what it would look like when divided into rooms and the walls clean and plastered.

Ashley's plans had two bedrooms down at the far end. The main bedroom would have an en-suite and both would have wall-to-wall and floor-to-ceiling cupboards. There would also be a large separate bathroom with a shower. At the other end would be a fully fitted kitchen overlooking the high street at the front of the building, with a utility room alongside. The middle and main part of the room would be the living room, with a dining area to one side. There were several windows looking over the high street and some looking out over the car park at the back. When it was all cleaned up, it would be light and airy and after some new double-glazed windows were fitted, it would be a lot quieter.

The longer Polly stood and looked at it, the more she could see what it would look like. She couldn't wait to get started. All the main services were already there, so as soon as she approved the plans, Ashley had a team of builders waiting to start. In her mind, Polly knew what the colour scheme was going to be, so she would spend the next few weeks shopping for her new home. In the meantime, she would stay with Caro, who would accompany her to work each day. Polly had a lot to learn about the business and was sure she could do a good job. All in all, she was looking forward to her life going on in a completely different way. The only thing was, she so wanted to tell John all about it. So she did. She lay in her bed at night and told him about her day from start to finish until falling asleep. She wasn't sure he could hear her, but she hoped he did.

She had a long phone conversation with Luke after he found out she was back home. Jessica hadn't bothered to let him know as she had promised, and he had found out from Stacey. He wanted to know how everything was running at the leisure centre. Now that he had shares in the place, he had a renewed interest in what was happening there. Polly had been in touch with Alan and had all the up-to-date news, which she passed along to Luke. They then discussed at length her plans for her flat. Luke just wished he was there to do the work but trusted Ashley's crew would do a good job.

They then turned the conversation to Jessica, as Polly knew he would. He seemed to want to talk, unusual for Luke, so she let him. He was feeling very guilty about leaving Jessica for long periods. He admitted being restless when she was writing but acknowledged that he could have occupied himself a bit nearer home so he could still have been there when she had a break. He had plans for them as soon as this job was finished, which was probably in a few weeks. He wanted them to pack some bags and book a world cruise. Something that would encompass lots of different places and take them away for a month or more so they could be together to mend their relationship.

While Polly thought this was a good idea, she knew for a fact that Jessica had started the new book and would not want to stop writing yet. This looked like it may cause trouble, but she didn't mention it. That was between the two of them to sort out. She told Luke she was glad that he was going to spend more time with Jessica as she constantly missed him.

There was a pause, and Luke cleared his throat before saying, "If I don't watch out, I will lose her to Nio."

Polly felt as if the wind had been knocked out of her chest. "Whatever do you mean?" she said, her voice sounding a bit high.

"You must have seen the way he looks at her. And she very carefully keeps well away from him."

"Well then. Surely, that proves that she's not interested."

"They were very friendly in the beginning, but after John's death they seem to get closer and then further apart. Come on, Poll, that is a classic sign that they are trying not to admit there is an attraction. I've been there. You fancy someone like mad but know it's not possible, so you try to ignore them in front of their partners in case they suspect something."

"I'm sure you are wrong. Jessie loves you."

"Yes, I know, but she's lonely and craves company, and Nio was there when she needed him. He proved that with the flights laid on for her at a moment's notice."

Polly cleared her throat. "Are you going to get annoyed if I speak my mind?"

"Oh, for Pete's sake, Polly. When did you ever beat around the bush? I'm not going to lose my rag when someone tells me the truth."

"OK. Why is it necessary for you to work so much? Jess has loads of money. Enough for the two of you to have a good life, and you are not short of a bob or two. You have enough to pay your share so you wouldn't feel like you were a kept man, so why are you so driven to be away from Jess all the time? You both spent long enough getting together and now you seem to be hell-bent on staying apart. I don't understand. It's no good feeling scared of losing her when you can't be bothered to care for her. She was very brave, walking away from a comfortable life and a husband who treated her badly and starting a new life from nothing, and she knows she can stand on her own two feet without help from you or anyone else. All she wants from you is your love. She doesn't need you to supply her with a home or money or anything material, she's already got all that. So, if you can't be with her to love her and care for her, she will be vulnerable."

Luke sucked in a deep breath. In his heart, he knew that everything Polly said was true. He had neglected Jessica and was going to change all that. He just hoped it wouldn't be too late. He was winding up the last of the things he had to do and would be on his way back to Jessica soon. He told all this to her, and they said goodbye, with him feeling a lot easier in his mind. Not so Polly. She had this tightness in the pit of her stomach that the feelings Jessica had for Antonio were not going to go away in a hurry. She just hoped that Luke could mend fences and that it wasn't too late. If they had drifted away too far from each other, there would be no going back, and that would be a shame.

Anyway, she had lots to occupy her in the coming months, so Jessica's problems were having to go on the back burner.

CHAPTER 17

Antonio prowled restlessly from room to room. His peaceful life had now been upset. Luke was due back soon. Antonio knew he wanted to hear everything about Jessica but also knew it would make Luke heartsore. The thought of his friend, who had been his right hand for so long, and Jessica together, making love was killing him. He had known about her ever since his partnership with Luke had begun, but she was just a shadow in the background. The guys on the site had always ribbed Luke whenever he got back from his home visits. They would make rude gestures and ask if it was worn up to a point yet. Antonio clenched as he couldn't stand to hear anyone be crude about her.

Lena watched from a distance and stayed silent. She knew why he was like this and also knew there was nothing anyone could do. She was worried that it would all end badly.

His car was waiting outside, and he knew that he had to be on-site when Luke turned up. There were things to be discussed about the final few weeks before the complex was handed over to the owners. There had been quite a few cases of looting from completed properties lately, and Antonio wanted the site watched every night until it wasn't their responsibility anymore. The looters had stripped some of the new houses of all their bathroom fittings, electrical fittings, and, in a couple of cases, the whole kitchen. It could cost a fortune to replace everything again, and Antonio was going to make bloody sure it wasn't going to happen to them so close to the finish. He drove off down the long hill, taking in the sight of his olive trees along the way. There were workers in and around the trees, making sure that this year's harvest would be a good one. He stopped at the side of the road to greet a couple of the workers, asking about their families and the state of the olives, all the time knowing at the back of his mind that he was delaying the meeting with Luke.

He finally pulled into the site, noticing that the security fencing was still up. He asked one of the paving crew if they had seen the lorries to remove the fence around, but they all shook their heads. Just then, Luke came out of the site office with a broad smile on his face. They greeted each other warmly before Antonio asked about Jessica.

"Can we go into the office, grab a coffee, and have a chat?" Luke said.

This was a bit of a surprise for Antonio as Luke was a hard worker who didn't spend too much time drinking and talking when there was work to be done.

"Sure," Antonio said, ruffling the bristly topknot on Gertie's head.

Luke made them both a coffee in the cleanest of the mugs before sitting down in the office chair. Antonio sat in the swivel desk chair while Gertie flopped down in the doorway and waited for Luke to speak. Luke cleared his throat and took a sip of coffee, almost as if he didn't know where to start. "I have been rethinking my life lately. Since John died, it's brought home to me how short life is and that this is not a rehearsal. We can't go back and do it all again. This is it. I am not getting any younger, and I've come to realise that I spent a long time waiting to be together with Jess and I seemed to have spent an even longer time being away from her. Our relationship is strained at the moment and that's my fault. She has been asking for at least a couple of years now to spend some time travelling; seeing all the places we have only read about; being close and happy like we used to be. I have always made work an excuse not to do this. Fuck knows why. Now I want to do this. I love her. She has been my life for a long time, and I can't lose her. I want to try to finish this job as soon as possible so I can be with her. On the drive here this morning, I wanted to turn around and go back to her. If it wasn't for Polly being there, I would have."

As Luke talked, Antonio could feel his stomach muscles tightening, and his coffee threatened to come up. He could not put into words what he felt for Jessica. He had no right to feel anything, but he did. This was happening for the first time after a long time. He had never been short of female company, but many of them saw the house, the plane, and the money and thought they were onto a good thing. He never had time for any of that. With Jessica, she wasn't after anything. She had her own life and her own wealth. She was beautiful and entertaining, and all these things he found new and refreshing. Like Luke, he wanted to be with her. Now, there was no chance and no hope.

"Anyway," Luke continued, "Polly will be going in a couple of weeks. As soon as she goes, I want to be finished here so I can get started with my plans, if that's OK with you."

"Course it is," Antonio said, standing up and turning away to prevent Luke from seeing the tears in his eyes. "When you're ready to go, let me know. The job is nearly finished, so you don't have to be here till the bitter end."

His voice sounded croaky even to himself, and Luke looked sideways at him until he coughed and cleared his throat. "Right, let's get to it," he said briskly, going out the door, not being able to bear any more talking about Jessica. "What's happening about this fence?"

"I decided to leave it up for extra security with all these looters around. They did a new block of flats earlier this week, so the men told me. It won't take long to take it down later on."

***

Jessie started on her new book and closed herself off from the world. She thought of letting Luke know about Polly's return but forgot. She didn't think he would be interested anyway. *He'll be too wrapped up in work to care,* she thought. If she had heard the things Luke had said, she might have been less hurt and upset. It was lovely having Polly there, but the sour feeling from her last conversations with Luke niggled at the back of her mind and stopped her from fully enjoying herself. She thought she was doing a fair job of covering it up, but Polly had seen a lot of that over the years with Drew and all his nonsense, so she saw right through the brave face.

Anyway, Polly was back home now and starting a new phase of her life, so Jessica absorbed herself in the new book, and pushed thoughts of Luke to the back of her mind. Stacey turned up the following day to discuss the upcoming book. She was a bit doubtful about the short story aspect. It was not a concept that seemed to suit Jessica's style of writing. All her previous books had a start, an enthralling story, and a good ending. Short stories had to pack all that into a very small frame. Most authors never wrote short stories and the ones who did never had much success with them. Stacey talked over her misgivings with Jessica and then said she would hold off on any advance publicity until she had read the first draft.

Stacey had spoken to Luke the day before. She was very surprised at the call. She hardly ever spoke on the phone to him. They had long conversations when they met in person; after all, they had known each other since they were teenagers and were brought up in the same area, but on the phone, well, big surprise. He wanted to let her know that he was going to take Jessica away for a while. He wanted them to travel and needed to know what places, if any, Jessica would be interested in so he could start making plans. Stacey said she would try to push her into a conversation about it and let him know. He had sworn her to secrecy as he wanted it to be a surprise, but she felt she had to point out that Jessica had started on another book and that the publishers were pushing as it had been some time since the last one.

"Damn the book," Luke said forcefully. "I'm sure they can hold off for a few weeks after all the money Jess has made for them in the past. At the moment, her health and happiness are far more important. Also, so is mine, Stacey."

Stacey was close to Jessica and had known about the strained atmosphere, so she was pleased that Luke was going to try and rectify it and said she would help in any way she could. Luke put the phone down and started leafing through a pile of holiday brochures he had picked up in the town.

The night watchman was not able to make it tonight, and since the company had not been able to get anyone else at short notice, Luke elected to stay on very late until one of the other workmen could go home, get some sleep, and then come in for the rest of the night. Luke could then go and also get some sleep. Antonio had a meeting with some potential new investors in the evening and was not able to help out, but he was grateful to Luke and told him to come in any time he wanted the following day as he would be there to oversee everything. The handover of the properties was coming up very soon, and apart from a few last snags, everything was finished. To pass the time, Luke intended to hunt through the brochures to see if there was anywhere that he fancied going.

The workmen all drifted away, chattering and smoking, and everything was finally quiet. A few cars went by in the street, but they tapered off as the evening wore on. Gertie lay sprawled across the scruffy piece of carpet and snored. Luke leant back in the chair, his long legs stretched in front of him and his head resting on the back of the chair. A small desk lamp shone on the discarded pile of brochures, some of them showing exotic places. Luke sat quietly and daydreamed. He thought about the cottage he had renovated with love and care and decided that would be his future work. Renovating old properties, but only when Jessica was writing. Something he could use his skills on and would give him pleasure, and something he could stop and start whenever he wanted.

He was suddenly startled out of his revelry when Gertie stood up and started to growl deep in her throat.

"What is it, girl?" Luke said quietly, standing up and reaching for the torch.

He switched off the desk light and slowly opened the door whilst holding onto Gertie's collar. A white van was parked just inside the security fencing and he saw three men dressed in dark clothing. Two were outside the front doors of two units, trying to break in, and a third was opening the back doors of the van. He shouted, switched on his torch and aimed the beam at them, and then he let Gertie go. She went bounding towards the van, barking and bristling and looking terrifying. The two men by the doors started to run towards the van and the third man reached into the back of the van.

Luke saw the muzzle flash and saw Gertie hurled backwards with force. He stopped short and shone the torch beam downwards. Gertie was screaming and whimpering.

"You bastards. You fucking bastards. You shot my dog. You bastards."

Luke started running towards the van and two more shots rang out. The first one hit his shoulder. He staggered but kept going forward. The second one was at a closer range and pierced his heart. Luke went down like a felled tree. The van screeched out of the gate and into the night. Jessica's face swam before him. She was laughing up at him, her hair sun-bleached and her face tanned and glowing. He smiled back at her as his life's blood ebbed away.

Another trail of blood stretched yards along the ground as Gertie dragged herself towards her loving master. She died with her great bristly head resting on his outstretched arm.

Luke's relief watchman found them at 2 am and, with tears streaming down his face, phoned Antonio.

CHAPTER 18

The police were crawling all over the place, but nobody had a clue what happened. Luke's body had been taken away after the coroner and the forensic team had finished. Antonio made sure that Gertie was taken by the local vet until plans had been set in place for her body. He knew he couldn't tell Jessica over the phone and didn't want the police to break the news to her, so, eventually, he decided to go himself. He wasn't sure it was the best thing to do, but there was no one else near enough to do it. He would phone Drew as soon as he had told her and, if necessary, would fly over to get him.

It was quite a long journey to Jessica's house, so he went home and packed a bag. If she didn't want him there, he would find a hotel until she had someone with her, and he could leave her in safe hands. Stacey would be the ideal person, but he didn't have her phone number.

It was early evening before Antonio got to the gates of Jessica's house. He rang the bell and waited, it seemed like, for a long time. Eventually, a tinny voice on the gate intercom asked who it was.

"Jess, it's Nio."

There was no reply. He looked up and saw her standing on the first-floor terrace. He waved, and she disappeared into the house. He heard the security lock click and the gates opened. He parked his car and got out, immediately realising that his legs were shaking. He had rehearsed what he was going to say throughout the journey, but now that she was standing in the doorway in front of him with a broad smile on her face, all the pre-planned words emptied from his mind.

Jessica looked at the strained unsmiling face that hadn't returned her greeting and knew something was very wrong, as the smile died on her face. Her hand went to her mouth as she stood aside to let him in. Antonio said nothing but just wrapped her in his arms. She knew then that it was Luke. Her body sagged and he half carried her up the stairs to the lounge.

Jessie's face was drained of blood. She sank down on the sofa. "Tell me, Nio. Has he had an accident?"

Again, he reached for her, but she pushed him away. "For Christ sake, Nio. How bad is it?"

"I don't know how to break it gently, Jess, but Luke was shot and killed early this morning."

"Noooooooo!" The wail that Jessica emitted was like an animal. She jumped to her feet and started pacing back and forth. "This can't be right. Are you sure it was Luke?"

"Of course, I'm sure, Jess. We don't know who is responsible yet. The police are working on it, but we think he interrupted some looters."

He went on to explain what Luke was doing there and all the other information he had. By then the tears were pouring down Jessica's face, also down Antonio's. They clung together, standing in the middle of the room and let their grief wash over them. Their bodies shuddered and shook for a long time with the force of it.

Eventually, Antonio persuaded Jessica to take a sleeping tablet and go and lie down. It was very late, but he knew he had to make some phone calls to her family. She gave him her book of numbers before she fell into an exhausted sleep. The first one he phoned was Drew and then Stacey. He knew they would know what to do. He told Drew that if there were any problems with flights, etc., he would arrange it, but he didn't want to leave Jessica on her own. He also told Drew that he would arrange things on this side as he was familiar with the procedures of the country. Drew only knew Antonio from conversations with Luke and Jessica but found him invaluable at this time and told him of his gratitude.

After ending the call, he wondered what Drew would say if he had told him he would do anything for Jessica. Just to be near her, even at this awful time, made him feel whole again. He loved Luke like a brother, and they had got very close over the years, but he knew in his heart that Luke would expect him to be there for her. Luke had hinted that he thought Antonio had a soft spot for her, but he had laughed and punched Luke playfully on the arm.

"You're seeing things, my friend. The heats gone to your head," and he had walked away before Luke could see that he had hit a nerve.

Things moved quickly. Drew and Caro arrived, and Antonio left. Caro was pregnant, and the flight hadn't been very good for her as she was suffering from air sickness. Polly would be there the following day. Jessica had room for the girls, but Drew would book a hotel.

Two days later, they were all picked up by Antonio, who took them to his home. He had arranged Luke's cremation and for the service to go with it. He had contacted all the friends and colleagues that Luke had known and arranged for the service to be in Spanish and English so everyone could understand. He explained all these arrangements to everyone over a beautiful meal in the garden of his home. Nothing had been overlooked and all the expenses had been taken care of. The service was to be in a lovely Spanish church in the local town where so many people knew Luke. Everyone would then be driven by a fleet of cars back to his home for the wake. All the food would be laid on by him and the ashes would be picked up the next day to be flown back to the UK with Jessica for a memorial service for all his English friends.

Polly had already met Antonio and liked him, and now he pulled both Drew and Caro under his spell. Nothing ruffled him and all the arrangements went smoothly and effortlessly. Drew was very impressed by him and the two of them got into long discussions about who knows what. His hospitality was faultless and Jessica, for the first time since she got the news, was finally relaxing a bit, although still looking pale and drawn.

On the day, it seemed like the whole town was out showing their respects. Flowers were placed on the coffin by everyone who could reach it, and the small church was full, with the doors open for the people standing outside. To say that they were all amazed at the crowd was an understatement. Jessica never knew about his popularity and he had never told her. So much she hadn't known about him after all.

The wake lasted for a long time, with food and drink flowing and people she didn't know paying their respects to her. With pressure from all who knew him, Antonio was almost forced to play for them. He protested strongly, but Roberto and Peter, who were both there, said that Luke loved his music and that he must play.

Once again, Jessica was lost in the wonderful music. Caro was transfixed, as was Drew, as they were all drawn under its spell. It would be something they would never forget.

CHAPTER 19

The memorial service in Luke's home town was every bit as fitting as the previous one. The church again was full, and there were many readings from friends. Some poems and some just memories of him. His ashes were interred in the wood with Marty and John and a tree planted with a plaque underneath like the other two.

Jessica returned to Spain a week later. She wanted to be on her own to grieve like she had before and found it difficult with people around her. She would get back to her writing. A TV company was already interested in making a series from her short stories as soon as they were finished.

She cried for hours when she got home. She felt as if she had been bottling the tears up, and when the dam finally broke, she couldn't stop. She looked at the photos that were stored on her laptop and recalled all the happy occasions. The early days when Luke still had his beard; Gertie charging about in the sea and almost drowning them both; Luke sitting in the garden of the cottage in his boxers, drinking a glass of wine. They had just made love and had wandered downstairs in their underwear because it was such a hot, clammy evening, and they sat outside to cool off.

She started smiling as she remembered. They had only been outside a short while when the sky went inky black, and it rained. The two of them stripped off what little clothes they had on and danced around the garden in the rain. Luke plonked her down on the grass and made love to her again, their bodies slick with rain, before running inside to jump in the shower, as by then, they were both cold.

The memory made her cry again as did the next photos of Luke in a tux at a Rotary Club Xmas dinner. He looked like a film star and towered above her looking totally different than usual. She wore a shimmering silver/grey sheath that clung to her. When she was dressed, as soon as he saw her, he had to make love to her. She protested strongly as her hair and makeup were all ready to go. So, he made her kneel at the side of the bed, flipped up her dress, pulled down her panties, and knelt behind her. The quickie was very satisfactory, and they went out glowing. Halfway through the evening, she whispered to Luke that, in the rush, she had cleaned herself quickly but forgot to put her panties back on. That was like a red flag to a bull. Luke found it impossible to concentrate on anything anyone said and was almost rude in his indecent haste to get home. She chuckled at the memory of the passionate night she had waiting.

The shots of Luke in bathing shorts climbing out of the pool, water glistening on his brown skin, and his hair slicked down stopped her for several minutes. She gazed closely at it, drinking in the image. How beautiful he was, and what a waste of a life for thieves to take just to steal someone else's property. She cried again for a long time, and then she was cried out and Luke would soon go on to become a lovely memory.

Antonio constantly phoned her and they got to know each other well over hours of conversation about their previous life and the people in it.

Eight months later, he came to her. He stayed for a day to talk to her. She was still unsure.

The long conversations continued by phone and emails.

Four months later, he took her to his home. She never returned to her house.

EPILOGUE

BREAKING NEWS

The death of the well-known author Jessica Cameron occurred suddenly last night. It has been reported that the death was from a heart attack. The author just last month had celebrated her 89th birthday with a lavish party for 100 people at the Dorchester Hotel in London. At the time, she had been in good spirits and surrounded by family, friends, and many of the world's famous film stars.

Returning to her home in Spain, she had retired to her room after an evening with friends, and her death was discovered later that day.

Ms Cameron spent her 20s and 30s as a wife and mother. She started her writing career after the breakup of her marriage to Andrew Cameron and soon became a renowned author with many bestsellers to her credit.

She became known internationally after the publication of her book *An Obsession to Die For*. The book was written after the tragic death of her son and was widely acclaimed. The book stayed on the bestseller list for many months and made it to the top spot again after the release of the film, which followed. The book was written while the author was in seclusion in England's West Country and she herself was instrumental in making the lead actors in the film into international stars. The unknown actors were picked for the film for their likeness to the picture Ms Cameron carried in her mind of the main characters. The film prompted a spin-off television series, which ran for over two years.

Ms Cameron had a long relationship with Luke Benson, an English businessman. Although they never married, and Mr Benson never travelled with her on most of her many foreign trips, Ms Cameron always referred to him as "the lovely rock that I come home to." The relationship ended after 7 years with the death of Luke Benson. He was murdered at the building complex he was involved with. It is believed that he tried to apprehend some looters who shot him and his faithful dog.

This followed just a matter of months after the death of one of her oldest friends. Ms Cameron went into a period of deep depression and went into seclusion after the deaths. During this time, she wrote her blockbuster, bestseller book of short stories, *All About Love*, which was made into a television series.

The seclusion ended with the published revelations of her passionate affair with Antonio Cantelli. Mr Cantelli was a wealthy and charismatic property tycoon who possessed film star good looks. Ms Cameron had known him for some time before they became close. After their marriage, the world's press followed them wherever they went. Despite a slight age difference, the media intrusion, and the early disapproval of family and friends, the couple stayed devoted to each other for 27 years until Antonio's death 6 years ago in a car crash whilst on his way to join his wife at their holiday home.

Antonio's passion for Jessica never waned, and people who knew them spoke about their relationship being complete in itself and that they needed no one else except each other and their family. One close friend said "They were both fantastic people, and they threw some wonderful parties, but you always got the feeling that they did it because it was expected of them. They were never far from each other, and there was always this feeling of an aura around them that excluded everyone else. Even if they were on opposite sides of the room, they were always totally aware of each other. It was uncanny.

I don't really think they needed anyone else in the whole world. Everyone expected the bubble to burst one day, and it would all end in tears, but it never did. It truly was 'an obsession to die for.'"

Antonio was driving to meet Jessica in Italy when his car was in collision with a truck on a winding mountain pass in Switzerland. His car went over the edge and tumbled hundreds of feet before bursting into flames. On being told of his death, Ms Cameron went immediately into seclusion in their home high in the hills of Spain and was rarely seen again in public for the next four years. Whilst in seclusion, Ms Cameron wrote several books of short stories loosely based on her life with Antonio (usually known by the shortened "Nio" by most of his friends and family) with most stories eventually finding their way into films or TV.

Her former husband, Andrew Cameron, died several years before her after a long battle with cancer. He had continued to be her mentor and friend throughout the years, and after their son's death had given up his business interests and went to live in the country. He worked tirelessly raising funds for a variety of charities, including local schools for impaired children. His handsome face and charismatic manner extracted money from people and companies worldwide. He continued a long relationship with Maxine Duffield, the wealthy co-owner of one of London's biggest advertising agencies, but the relationship finally ended because of conflicting business interests and long periods spent apart. Andrew went on to marry Countess Anna Sobrovny, a renowned beauty and a woman whose many well-publicised and indiscreet affairs all over the world caused him to divorce her after only five years of marriage. He remained unmarried until his death, and although rumours of him fathering an illegitimate child were never proved, in his will, a large sum of money was left to the son of a previous barmaid. Everything else was split between a well-known patron of the arts, Lady Clara Ffoulks-Ward, for the distribution to various charities specified and to his grandsons Toby and Morgan Mead.

Jessica Cameron-Cantelli was truly a great lady who brought pleasure to millions through her books and films, and she will be sadly missed by all her fans. Her business empire will now pass to her daughter and son-in-law, Caroline and Ashley Mead, who have been company administrators of Ms Cameron-Cantelli's business interests for many years.

Her body will be buried next to her beloved husband in the Spanish hills above their olive groves. A small family memorial will be held in the West Country, and a tree will be planted alongside those of her son's, her ex-husband's, Luke's, and her close friend's, in the woods of the beautiful Martyn Memorial Gardens overlooking the sea.

ABOUT THE AUTHOR

They say everyone has at least one book in them and it has taken me a few years to complete mine.

I am a mature lady living in Somerset. I was born and brought up here but left to live in Hertfordshire and then in South Africa. Only to come full circle back again years later.

I have two grown-up sons and two grandchildren (all loved dearly), and my partner of more than twenty years who is my "better half."

I trained many years ago as a window dresser and also worked in the tax office before going into advertising in newspapers and on local radio. I've always been an avid reader and always felt that I could write, so I finally did it.

Hope you enjoy the read as much as I enjoyed writing it.